Other titles by João Gilberto Noll available
from Two Lines Press

Harmada

Lord

Atlantic Hotel

Quiet Creature on the Corner

HUGS
AND
CUDDLES

JOÃO GILBERTO NOLL

HUGS AND CUDDLES

TRANSLATED FROM
BRAZILIAN PORTUGUESE BY
EDGAR GARBELOTTO

TWO LINES
PRESS

Originally published as *Acenos e afagos*
© 2008 by João Gilberto Noll
Translation © 2022 by Edgar Garbelotto

Two Lines Press
582 Market Street, Suite 700, San Francisco, CA 94104
www.twolinespress.com

ISBN: 978-1-949641-38-7
Ebook ISBN: 978-1-949641-39-4

Cover design by Rafael Nobre
Typeset by Sloane | Samuel

Library of Congress Cataloging-in-Publication Data:
Names: Noll, João Gilberto, author. | Garbelotto, Edgar, translator
Title: Hugs and cuddles / João Gilberto Noll ; translated by Edgar
Garbelotto.
Other titles: Acenos e afagos. English
Description: San Francisco, CA : Two Lines Press, 2022.
Summary: "A narrator's journey to discover his true self and the outer-
most reaches of sexual and artistic expression."-- Provided by publisher.
Identifiers: LCCN 2022002082 (print) | LCCN 2022002083 (ebook)
ISBN 9781949641387 (paperback) | ISBN 9781949641394 (ebook)
Subjects: LCSH: Brazil--Fiction. | LCGFT: Novels.
Classification: LCC PQ9698.24.O44 A6413 2022 (print) | LCC
PQ9698.24.O44
(ebook) | DDC 869.3/42--dc23/eng/20220124
LC record available at https://lccn.loc.gov/2022002082
LC ebook record available at https://lccn.loc.gov/2022002083

1 3 5 7 9 10 8 6 4 2

We were fighting on the cold floor in the hallway. A sharp drilling sound was coming from the dentist's office. And the two of us, fighting on the ground, would sometimes roll down the stairs, all the way to the lobby. We were kids, working surreptitiously so our true intentions could remain unnoticed. Suddenly, our two bodies stopped and lay there, waiting. Waiting for what? Neither of us knew for sure. The improbability of an open invitation produced a burning struggle. The boy, my classmate, was locking me in his arms that very moment. His body felt so strong on top of me that I had to surrender. How was the surrendering person supposed to feel? And what were the consequences of those feelings? I told him about another classmate, for whom the promise of reddish pubes was starting to show. Pubes? I ignorantly pronounced it "pubis." The hairs appeared first at the groin. Or a little farther down, almost on the sack. My friend had never heard of that curly plumage partially covering up the sex. In my limited comprehension, those entangled threads should be the crowning of a person's sexual awakening, even if the crowning was of something that I did not yet understand. What could possibly come after the blooming of that small mane still seemed so far in the distance, and in the meantime nothing could match the novelty of our budding genitalia. We both believed that the body's excitement would be ripe with the arrival of pubic hairs. The adult lust would then be launched. We lived, suffering in anticipation for the day of that blessed eruption. The capillary areola around the sovereign genitalia would emerge not only for the function of protecting paradise—excitement would come precisely from the manipulation of that bush, usually darker than a person's hair. For some, the hairs represented the zenith of a fuck. For others, touching them at the beginning was inspiration for what would follow during an encounter. Once one passed through the dense pubes, one reached the pubic center, from which the most lucid points of physical delight radiated. It was thus necessary to know how to handle the pubic hair so we could take advantage of its power over the flesh. And the two of us there on the floor of the hallway were cursing in our silent and endless struggle. Then the boy made a gesture as if strangling me, and I sneaked my hand between our bodies and grabbed his hard dick. That was enough for him to move his weight off my slim body. Free from that tight embrace, we sighed in discreet moans. The afflicting noise of the drill wouldn't stop. The possibility of being caught by the dentist made the foggy feeling I had even more dramatic. A feeling somewhere between gratification and its immediate denial. To escape the dilemma, we fought, we kept fighting, we kept rolling on the floor. We pulled down our shorts and stood on our knees, back to back. Perhaps that position could help us to camouflage a little from any curious eyes in the building. That was how we projected our pistols, to forbid those sensations we wouldn't be able to reconcile for the rest of our lives. We would never again feel so horny so unexpectedly. Although I was not able to ejaculate because of my immature organism, a sunken delight remained in me from that afternoon onward. A delight that I would never be able to reproduce. Today's oblique grinding should not impact us in our classes tomorrow. Our dicks were ahead of our maturity; they were growing like people do, but they were still not half as big as a full-grown cock. As for ejaculation, for the time being, it could be neglected in favor of the pubic hair's unstoppable, catalyzing force. We didn't know yet the appearance of the fluid that would accompany us for the rest of our lives. We knew that sex should be between a man and a woman and that from a struggle in the sheets children were born, children who would then run around like us. Our bellicose embrace was an event that could only be experienced because it strayed from the main story of our lives. With time, the wind would sweep it into the trash. We were wild kids reinventing ourselves at every sign of puberty. My father had given me a book about sexuality, whose author, João Mohana, pontificated like the priest he actually was. I never jerked off so much as I did while reading that manual. Several pages were smeared by the jets of my new great discovery at the time—yes, semen. The fact that we were there with our hard-ons could not have been foreseen, but it was happening, and neither of us knew whether it was nonsense or an initiation to ecstasy. We compared our penises: mine with a still-reluctant tip eager to get out of the foreskin's nest, and my friend showed off his proud tip in shades of pink and purple, entirely free from the foreskin. We were afraid the dentist would open his door at any moment and catch us in our arduous carnal impasse. The danger was a tempting ingredient for a new burst of eroticism in that erogenous dissipation of childhood we were experiencing. Everything ached, for there was no pleasure that existed as itself, only pleasure that leaked into some other painful experience from our lives, flowing like a poison. We seemed to be ready to fight again. At that point I already knew animosity would be fueled by our attraction. And my friend knew, too, or was he an idiot? As much as I had taken in his body, perhaps he still didn't realize that our tumid embrace was in fact pleasure, and we would never tire of repeating it from that moment onward. Addiction. We could not forgive ourselves for the intensity we were feeling for each other. The chiaroscuro in the hallway was an accomplice to what we wanted to both explore and suppress. The permissiveness evoked by the penumbra, however, was not enough to put an end to our general argument. We were rubbing each other so much that our bodies became bruised and scratched here and there. Certain parts of my body were even bleeding. We looked like reptiles, winding around each other, lying on our sides, now face-to-face. Where the body of one receded, the body of the other advanced. Suddenly, distressed, trembling, the boy brought his ass close to my mouth. His ass gave off a taunting scent of intimacy. I couldn't reject that intimacy, and it was there that I traveled, intoxicated, to the most secret part of him, without asking or offering anything, without thinking. I tried to quiet my fascination with his ass. That's when my urge to become one with him overpowered me. I moved in close to his ass and licked it. He shuddered. The place he meant to hide because of hygiene was a secret treasure, an opium for the seeker of pleasure. That forbidden taste came to my mouth, exciting me more and more to the point where I entered a trance. I would rather have had my face there, against that boy's ass, than in the notebooks of my daily homework. We swore we would not tell anyone about that afternoon. Never. We would bury it inside of us, each day a little more, until we were adults, and when the image of the fight on the cold ground would be so crumbled we'd never be able to fully reconnect the pieces. We would become a tomb in which to bury the toy we had created of each other's bodies. I ran into the street, leaving the boy and the scent of his insides behind. The boy used to say he'd be an engineer when he grew up. I wouldn't say anything. Years later, when I was a teenager, I leaned against a lamppost to smoke a cigarette at the end of a long day of my life as a masseur. I had to work, my father was going through serious difficulties. The memory of the boy who had offered me his most secret territory came back to me. It happened because I caught a glimpse of a nearly invisible image during the last massage of the day. It was summer; the breeze coming from a noisy fan brought me some relief, and I touched the new client's body, taking it into my hands. The body was a man's, and that man, I don't know why, reintroduced me to the theatrical fight in the dark hall of so many years before. Yes, his features were impressive. In fact, they reminded me of the boy's... I asked myself if his skin was the same as my friend's, the friend who'd wanted to be an engineer. The body in my hands reminded me of the intestine prose of that dark corridor, the corridor that echoed the rustling noise of the dentist's drill. Poetry was coming from the chewed silence my massage client dictated to me... He suddenly excused himself, took the gum out of his mouth, asked for an ashtray in which to deposit it, and from then on, he reminded me even more of the dark nest of my boyhood. Everything could be immersed in his silence, everything, even a disguised identity. Everything could be immersed in his silence, yes, even the disturbance my hands were causing on his skin. A confession wanted to come out of us both, but it didn't have the force to pass from our mouths, so it faded out of reach. I bent over him and his body said: Here's where it hurts. Where? I asked and he put my hand on the back of his neck, turning to me with supplicating eyes. A little bit of me evanesced in its tiredness. I went to have a cigarette at the corner bar. My mother came into the bar to take me to my cousin Cida's wake. Cida had fallen victim to a mysterious illness that was striking everyone. She was dressed in white in the coffin. I looked at her a little, as everyone does when arriving at a wake. Her mother had painted her nails with pink enamel… we try to draw out the autonomy that once existed in the deceased's physiognomy and expressions from the now-yellow skin. The mother of the dead was my father's older sister. I looked at my aunt. She seemed to quietly proclaim that a force came from her, the mother of the dead, the mother of each of us, the mother of all, and her dead daughter would not take away her maternal passion, the sleepless nights she spent in a vigil to the agonizing. She didn't cry. My now-dead cousin smiled at me from the door of the playhouse at the far end of the yard. She was not even eleven years old and already wore lots of her mother's makeup. My cousin's transparent gown showed her small tits. My excitement on the eve of puberty imagined them hard. She always took me to the playhouse at the back of the yard. At the time, I only thought about fucking, even though I hadn't stuck my hard dick in any holes yet. Too young, I still couldn't ejaculate. At most, only a washy lubricant came out of my eager dick. At that time, I already suspected that I would be hungry for sex as an adult. I sat on the floor of the playhouse as my little cousin, standing, raised her skirt, took off her panties, and then I ran my finger along that spot of delight. I put my finger in a little bit more. She moaned, fidgeted, and doused my hard finger with her early vaginal fluids. I was there with my little turgid cock, though still unable to release semen and fertilize. We were in the most complete darkness. I stood up and put her hand on my dick in bloom. Raul was a little friend of mine and I preferred his cock over mine, for he was circumcised—he showed it off at the steel urinal at school, as if the cutting of his foreskin had already imprinted him with an adult, full-grown, superior mark. The tip of his dick seemed like the tip of a weapon about to fire an electrifying projectile at those deserving of its vigor. In the meantime, my little friend and I continued in the dark hallway where the dentist drill ruffled. When our secret sessions in the playhouse ended, I'd go to the backyard and try to satisfy my carnal yearnings. The golden sun, wanting to begin the final hour of its decline, encouraged me in an intransitive way, for at that moment I had no solar mission to retain or propagate. The color in the air fully inspired me, no object was needed. All I know is that the liaison in the chiaroscuro of the hallway years before, when my friend and I had touched each other to learn how to extract the best from our bodies…all I know is that I never forgot that encounter. Interestingly, he had seemed quite convinced of his future: he would be an engineer. Re-inhabiting those burning hours after touching my little cousin in the pitch-black of the playhouse, I'd begin to fear losing the bodies that had embraced me in my adventures in the darkness. I farted. And I ran away ashamed. I had the impression that I had woken up after a long sleep. I had grown up and was a man in love with a body I had never sheltered in my arms. Now, the skin was that of a fellow from the seminary who didn't give a damn about me. Or did he? He was leaving the seminary to study medicine. Listen to the sound of my knuckles knocking on the door of his room. He opens it; it's night already. I ask him if I can come in to talk for a bit. He gives me the space to pass. I sit on a chair with the backrest and seat made of straw, just like the one in Van Gogh's room. As I sat down, I felt an immense desire for the young seminarian, very young like me and very olive-skinned, who knew how to use the most beautiful words in the Portuguese language. When he spoke, like now, I felt my mouth salivate to the point that a little of the warm, frothy liquid overflowed from the corners of my lips like I was in the midst of a convulsion. This time the seminarian told me of his childhood in Tapes. Of the country life with the sheep, of romantic walks in the fields in winter. He was the son of a farmer. He confessed that he preferred to do his homework among the sheep. He used to play the flute among the animals, sometimes with a thick woolen cloak to protect him from the Minuano wind. As he told me all this, I was admiring his half-exposed chest through the flap of his pajamas. He kept talking and I could feel my cock swelling underneath everything, everything. He kept talking and I retreated into the night's hidden place between me and myself: darkness the only matter surrounding my repressed lust. But before going to my room, I dared to touch him on the shoulder. I laid my hand on him, but as I retreated, a slight squeeze was all I could do, unable to fulfill my desires. I went to my room feeling my quiet heartbeat: no matter what I decided to do with my life, that machine inside would not fail me until my time was up. I was thinking about that, in that icy hallway, and arrived at my room in the seminary not believing in God anymore. My body's engine would expire only when it had to. Maybe late in the afternoon, before dinner. Maybe I'd last until the next morning, maybe until the noon sun. And I was an atheist anyway. I was no longer part of a cosmic plan designed by a despot. But for the time being, nobody should know about this, at least not in the seminary. I wanted to stay for a while longer. From then on, I'd open my mouth with disgust to receive the communion. I'd chew the little anemic crumb, crunch out all my non-bodily beliefs. I'd lock myself in the bathroom if the communion wafer bled. I'd spit the blood from my hemorrhage in the toilet. Clotted blood even. However, my stay in the seminary was guaranteed. I had needed to run away from my father's constant financial struggles. When I closed my bedroom door, the light went off. I drank a glass of water in the dark. And then I smiled. I pulled that smile out of my guts, dedicating it to the extinction from which my life would thrive and flourish. My mother was asleep next to me in the double bed, where one day my father had inserted—passionately, I hope—the seed that made me. I told my mother I was afraid my nightmare would become my biography. In the nightmare, I was running naked from headlights that chased me, like in the movie *Pixote*, which I would watch only a few days later. My mother brought my head to her chest. I was already grown. On the street, there was always a man wearing sunglasses. I couldn't bear the fact that his eyes followed me behind those silvery, frosted lenses. I didn't exactly know how to explain the feeling that something disagreed with me. Somehow I knew that whenever I was in public, there was someone there who didn't want to see me living free. The problem was that my consciousness was damaged by the abuses of this thinking. My thoughts overloaded my consciousness, infesting it with all-powerful vultures. I wanted to be God, that was clear, but I suspected that pursuing such a divine career would require a greater theological imagination. For example, I needed to get out of the seminary, and the closet, and dedicate myself to robbery, crime, carnal offenses, and vice, and never look back. The devil was sweet. I'd like to become a woman and incorporate that poisonous character. Because my idea of the demonic art of love asked for a female component. What I really needed was to build a family, retrace my father's steps. That day, I committed to recovering my health and stopping my suffering. And I decided to tell someone about it. I went to my friend to ask for help: the engineer, now a grown man, for whom I felt an enormous fondness. He was one of the few people for whom I didn't nurture a sentiment of perpetual anger. We were about the same age. On a sunny Sunday afternoon, we went to a beach called Belém Novo on the Guaíba river. After stripping down to our shorts, I understood why I wanted him by my side for the rest of my life and beyond. Walking and whistling back to his office, I rambled about the mundane routines that oppressed my chest every day. I had stopped showing up for my duties. Each shift demanded specific tasks, so much more from me than I had. My trash was accumulating. I'd shake my head until my mind got clouded, and all I could say was: I don't know, I don't know. In that vacuum, I sat across his very tall desk. A dark, chipped piece of furniture. Yes, we were in his office. And he, once again, looked gloriously beautiful. Why are you here? he asked. I shared my struggles with him, and he invited me to go out and explore new paths. He slapped me on the back of my neck, and I almost wanted to start a fight with him, until we hurt each other and knocked ourselves down. Then, we'd cure each other, amen… He was much more pragmatic than anyone else from our generation, so I felt hopeful about his abilities. We went to the movies. As the movie progressed, we looked at each other in the dark, and each one saw in the other, I'm sure, the substance that was missing in ourselves. Just that? Yes, nothing more than that. Out in the halls of the shopping mall, I stared at a black security guard and I asked him, distressed, trembling, if he wanted to be my bodyguard. Starting that afternoon, I wanted to write another story. It'd be better if it started with a bluff. I told the security guard that I was an entrepreneur in the construction field. That the construction business was going through a prosperous phase. That I would need his services from eight in the morning to eight in the evening. I already had another man on duty for the night shift. The muscular man thought about an answer, raising one of his eyebrows as if a sign of malice. I noticed that my engineer friend had left, giving me room to exercise my unquiet desires. The security man seemed receptive, but, whenever possible, he'd feint and return to the safe rock he stood on. I smelled his breath, raspberry-like. I imagined his courage in uncovering bad intentions in men. It was only then that I realized I had organically moved from the movie to my own self as if there were no break between the spectacle and my brute life. I had gone from the movie theater to the halls of the shopping center without noticing any frontier between the two poles. Sure, if I hadn't asked him that question (do you want to be my bodyguard?) and hadn't fixed my eyes on the green tones of his sunglasses, he might have already taken me to a dark room from which no one left unscathed. Something needed to be left inside in that room, someone's honor maybe, someone's virginity perhaps. My engineer friend must have detected my talent for conversation with the kinds of men who are always ready for action in busy places. With the force of my disturbance in the face of such presences, I'd distill for them the impulse to fabricate a narrative. Who were "they"? They were characters talking on their walkie-talkies, I don't know with whom exactly, but certainly with someone who, watching through cameras, dictated which way they should go, whom to approach, whom to blame, whom to punish. Not infrequently, the device would silence those incomprehensible messages that piled on each other, and the walkie-talkies would emit noises that clawed under our sensitive skins and pierced our ears, already hurt by so much contraction. Very close to the handsome black man—though he was a bit stocky for my taste—I felt that I could love him until he dropped dead. Perhaps, for him, having an orgasm was just a matter of embracing someone and nothing else, no penetration. Maybe, for him, having an orgasm was only an accident that happened to be simultaneous with the phallus vomiting. And then, realizing the pubes are wet, he's freed from the task. When I pulled away from him and smiled, he seemed interested in the game that could be played between us. We talked about meeting up later that afternoon. Where, where? I asked myself, already on the way home. Any old corner is good for those unsustainable rendezvous. After we came all over each other, we wouldn't have anything left to share. If it were up to me, however, I'd like to fuck all the men in the world and half a dozen women, but at that time of personal crisis, the truth was that I was feeling kind of impotent. Some might argue: What would you do with the security guard if he needed your hard cock? That's when I paused, stalling at the corner. True, the security man would ignore my cock. I don't know, you never know, you never know…but, then, would he fuck me? And was my ass any good for such an incursion? I crossed the street feeling that I needed my engineer friend more than ever. And I went to see him in his greasy office. I sat down across his chipped desk, and he told me: I'm going to meet up with a friend on a ship in the harbor; want to come with me? A ship in the Guaíba? I asked. A ship, he answered, hurrying toward the docks with me trailing behind him, begging: calm down, calm down, man! As we ran, I experienced the encounter with the security guard in advance, a meeting that I would miss that evening because I was following the story of my engineer friend, for whom my heart could not quiet. There I went again, dragged by his overpowering

magnetism. With the security guard, I acted as if I
was in an abandoned theater that had never even
been finished, and never would be. In the first act, I
undress in front of the stocky man. He has a cough-
ing fit. I wait. I sit, unwrapping my whole body. The
security guard strips. The image of unwrapping fits
him perfectly, too. I lie down on the hard floor.
Little shards on the floor prick my back and butt.
He moves over me and has an orgasm. I appreciated that his quick ejaculation caused him to get off
me so swiftly. I never saw the security guard again,
neither in reality nor imagination. But what a surprise when I saw the crest of a German submarine
in the Guaíba! It seemed a little beaten down; it
had surely endured many battles. But what did I
know about submarines? Nothing. I stopped at the
dock with my mouth open. My engineer friend, by
my side, introduced me to that life-size toy. I
wanted to grow up to be fit for an adventure. But
then I remembered that I was already an adult, and
had been for a few years. Ever since I was a teenager, my engineer friend had always provided me
with my first compliments, despite his usual reti-
cence. The truth is that we were both grownups
now. And we were there, side by side at the nearly
ghost harbor in the city of Porto Alegre. At the
dock, the hull of a German submarine. It whistled

gravelly, powerfully. And from within its dark carcass, through a little horizontal door, the head of a
bearded, graying man appeared. My engineer friend
told me the guy was German, born and raised in
the same region as my ancestors, and I would soon
understand who he was. I never knew this, but the
engineer seemed to speak German. The imposing
sea creature came closer, and a bearded German
invited us inside. We barely crossed through the
horizontal door, when we were urged to slide down
a smooth iron pole. I remembered some Metro musicals where dancers slid down golden poles. Was
this the initial protocol to formally invite us to visit
the vessel's belly? Employees of this aquatic mystery asked us to sign the register book. They told us
the book would be returned to the headquarters of
an NGO in Berlin. They might get in touch with
us. They might? Get in touch? A promising gesture,
although I didn't feel I belonged among these
evasive endeavors. The man delivering the initial
information spoke in Portuguese, he was a Brazilian
guy from Diamantina and worked on the submarine as a cook. As long as my invitation included
the engineer, I would accept it, even if it turned out
disadvantageous for me personally. We now had
another pole running between our half-bent legs,
and at the end of the slide we found ourselves in a

bronze-colored space, beyond austere. A horrifying space, to be honest. I swallowed my spit and asked my engineer friend what would become of us in these maritime bowels, since I could not engage in any conversation with the mostly German-speaking crowd. Huh? But so far, they've only spoken English, he answered, half-annoyed at my bewilderment. In fact, he was right. This old friend took my hand and led me into a candlelit chamber. The receptionist and another German guy entered the room, pulling an enormous trundle bed covered with ragged sheets, as if someone or many someones had just used it. It was like a hospital bed, but much bigger. As it passed by me, I sensed a profusion of smells, but in the midst of them all, I could smell a very particular one—something pungent and dry as a male. The bronze bedframe had unimaginative, disillusioned etchings. When the bed passed beneath my nostrils, what I most truly sensed was a fetid smell. I wondered what they were doing in Porto Alegre. The engineer said we were going to take a ride in the submarine up to where the Guaíba met the sea. A ride in the submarine? But how? Staying inside was like being home at night with no windows and several burned-out lamps. What if they never let us go, I silently sighed. It wouldn't be so bad, but I'd rather not go. The engineer seemed completely comfortable with the underwater excursion. They would take me out to the sea and from there God knows where. That massive underwater chamber, sealed from the outside world, already smelled of secretions divorced from their libidinal labors. Soulless, sour, indigestible secretions. If the vessel could provide me with pleasures that were banned on dry land, if I could delve into new libertine delights, then I'd be content. Then they could take me on that wave, and I would never return. After all, what did I gain by staying in Porto Alegre, always hungry while pretending to be satiated? It was then that I reiterated to myself—for the umpteenth time—that my engineer friend was a very interesting man. He had rough features, like nearly all men. An animalistic promise came from his unrefined features. I looked at the German captain and his helper and I understood the party was about to start. I was not much interested in the Germans. They looked like defeated officers without any options left, forced to retire before their time, living off the proceeds of some NGO. I looked at my engineer friend, and I was suddenly delighted. Yes, for the millionth time. He was my long-time friend from way back, when you could still walk on Rua da Praia at dawn and sit on a bench in the Alfândega Square. He had accompanied me on those nocturnal pilgrimages, searching for something that could still not be spoken. At that time, he had looked asexual; but four, five years later, he started dating a girl who lived in the Floresta neighborhood, and with whom he went to Sunday matinées at the Orfeu, Presidente, Eldorado, Ipiranga. I used to meet them for the matinées at the Colombo, another movie theater in Floresta, where they showed Metro musicals. He never got married. And I never learned of any other woman traveling over his dark, almost hairless skin. At that time, my nighttime circle of friends liked to praise the presumed delights of my engineer friend. He's closeted, they'd say. We used to spend our evenings at the Torpedo Bar, owned by an Italian we all knew. The bar was located on Alfândega Square, a reasonably innocent area at the time. We considered ourselves to be what was then called "discreet." I always liked that word, because it gave the idea of secret idylls—accessible only for the initiated—experienced underneath certain dawns. "Discreet" also referred to those who, in daylight, were seen as full-time macho men, some even married, above any suspicion. But in the underground hours, there they were, tasting what they so anxiously longed for. Everyone there was "discreet," lovers and experts of their own bodies. And when we pronounced that word, we tasted audacity, bravery, and the opening of a universe full of agile subtleties, of mischievous filigrees, where we could experiment with erotic trends. There was a future in those circles. We all learned the art of cunning, so we could not only be accepted but also become the object of desire for the ineffable brotherhood. Anyway, now we're staring at each other with some wisdom, without hurry or excuses, beleaguered in the German submarine, this Second World War's steel junk. I suddenly confronted my engineer friend as if saying: Our hour has come at last. Slowly, my body began to feel erogenous from head to toe; and his, too, I thought. Our cocks experienced a sui generis pulsation. A moment when you feel the phenomenon happening in the other's groin, and the other feels it happening in yours, without anyone having to lower their eyes to check the genital areas. This tepid dilatation is transparent on your face, your eyes, your lips. Your whole body turns into seduction, and you want to die if the act won't be realized. The central point of this lust firms itself, gradually, in darkness behind the zipper. You own your lust, it's yours. Now, keep going, let it flourish. We had already lived the prelude of this act together many times before. But we had always aborted it. And our underwear, always wet.

Sometimes, we perspired so much that we followed the trajectory of the drops of sweat falling from each other's earlobes—earrings in a furtive flight from their own capacity to adorn. We gasped; we wanted to die of excitement. But nothing. The shift is over. The two characters distance themselves from each other, even though they are tempted to check each other's groins. Frustrated, the language of bodies is silenced and they become impervious again to anything that is not sober and succinct. Did anybody set our choreography in motion? Every little thing burned in me, everything grew sensitive to the external, inaugural touch. I raised my hand to touch the body of my friend. It was right there, ready for me to feel the fire of his skin. A skin I had been forced to stay away from all those years. With my hand in the air—while he observed it—with my hand like that, I heard the captain shout out in his scary German something that, to my surprise, the engineer understood. Maybe my friend was a Germanist, hiding this secret from me for decades for no reason. Now, I could see that his knowledge of Germanic affairs had some usefulness. Maybe I was about to learn the art of this knowing myself. He and the German man seemed to cultivate a friendship immersed in itself, hidden from the outside world, and now they were about to consummate it in the deep, deep waters at last. There was no officiant, but they would declare themselves husband and wife. Which was which? A simple ceremony, a bit rough even. The German captain discussed topics that were immediately translated by my friend. I couldn't follow the German's speech through my friend's translation because I was suffering from crushing jealousy. After all these years, I had finally realized that I was truly, brutally in love with this engineer friend. And now that we were about to manifest the magic spell that had been timidly burning inside us, he comes to show me his German lover. My engineer friend, a light olive-skinned mestizo, pulled me by the hand and we fully entered the chamber, where five or six guys were already standing and, apparently, waiting for us to initiate some kind of rite. I then heard a noise typical of those old movie projectors. And sitting next to the engineer—falling deadly in love with him again after decades of carrying this passion inside me in its larvae state—sitting down I saw they were projecting a movie about certain militias, ambiguously Nazi. These militias set fire to everything Jewish: banks, books, theaters. After the job was done, they would hide in holes: under bridges, humid alleys with no exits, sewers inhabited by rats or men with unspeakable desires, and hotels reserved for lacerating orgies. They ventured into the night, always with the objective of exploring each other's bodies. Always wearing hats with the swastika on the front. On the screen, monumental cocks came out of pants dirty with blood, vomit, and cum, of course. Skinny teenagers sucking the cock of the colonel in his gala uniform. This military man, when not being serviced by the young men, gallantly inspected the incendiary activities. I looked at my friend's magnificent profile and whispered to him my doubts about the meaning of what was happening in the German submarine. Was this a fictional movie or a documentary of today's Germany? It's today, right? He touched my leg as if to say: not now. Feeling weak, I thought of where we could go that night, in case the night was still ours. At that moment, I could have been in the company of the security guard in some nice little hotel on the Duque de Caxias street. What amazing games we could have been playing in bed or in the shower. I realized I was a prisoner. And being a prisoner underwater was to suffer exponential claustrophobia. I asked the guy behind me where the bathroom was. He didn't get it, obviously. I gestured I was going to unzip my pants and take my cock out for a piss. He smiled and looked at my pelvis with an understanding air, knowing the party was about to get better. Then I asked my engineer friend if he knew where the bathroom was. He said something to his partner and pointed to a door nearby. On one side of the mirror, there hung a picture of a young man, blond and naked. Below the picture, a piece of paper glued to the wall had several signatures, mostly German names. As if they were evaluating the young man's undisputable beauty. He indeed had appeal for someone like me, going through a sexual drought as I was. It was a picture in profile. The side of an admirable butt. His cock, huge, semi-hard. The semi-hardness gave the young man a mysterious air. Looking at the picture, I felt like someone who had just fucked then surprised his young partner by taking a piss before getting ready for another casual encounter. I took a peek at the trashcan with a German flag covered in blood inside. The yellow, a good match to the sanguine red. When I left the bathroom, where I had done nothing—maybe because of my tension—I noticed that the crew had been partying while I was gone. They had taken advantage of my absence, which I thought had been brief. But, apparently, it hadn't. Regardless of the duration of my disappearance in the bathroom, the fact was that, in that interim, the crew and guests had entered their hands into the caves of each other's bodies and placed their mouths on exuberant chops of flesh. The air smelled like a horse stable. My engineer friend was naked like everyone else, and their tired cocks were dripping semen that had already been spilled. I noticed that my friend had a tattoo on his circumcised foreskin, and that tattoo disturbed me: a tiny bee. It seemed that for some time now he had been part of this maritime club from which he was now trying to exclude me. This brotherhood, whose objective was to experiment with the vortex of libido, was trying to sneakingly avoid me. Me, a friend of the studly Brazilian guest. Did they suspect I was a spy? I wish I was. How did my engineer friend manage to hide this part of his life from me? He, almost brown, had surrendered himself to the white skin of the North. I had chills just thinking that, after being in this place, we wouldn't be able to realize the silent promises we had cultivated for years. He had a tattooed cock and would give it exclusively to the secret gang of Germans. Were they an NGO for the debauched? The bee was a very intriguing peculiarity. Now it turned into a big bee as my friend offered his almost full erection to the cult again. His foreskin was a shade darker than his face and his arms. I never thought I'd be so in love with this dark man. His pubic hair was as thick as the mane of a black lion. I could lose myself in his pubes as if in a dense forest. I just had to throw myself into a blind flight with only one thing in mind: explore his delights. But, because I didn't want to lose his friendship, I started writing nervous lines of his ingratitude over the absence of his skin. But, where was the submarine heading? What new waters would take it to a new destination? I had a German last name, but the gang on the ship wanted nothing to do with my Germanic roots. After all, my ancestors arrived in Brazil after fleeing misery and hunger back home. Today's German citizens are ashamed of the deviant and bastard descendants like me. They prefer to forget people such as myself and focus instead on the mixed race of this infamous El Dorado. And the submarine kept going and going, and I was afraid they'd turn me into a captive. Someone capable of providing sexual services, but of the third category—the lowest. So badly paid that I'd have to feed myself with the generosity of the guests. They surely saw me as one of the last remnants of the Germanic diaspora. And besides, I also had Portuguese and Native Brazilian blood. I was only partially descended from the illusion of the blond North. Moreover, I never succeeded in Brazil. I had just a few belongings. So, sadly, I started thinking about what I could do for the rest of the trip. That is, if I still had any leverage to choose, at least at the private level. I sat on the floor. I sat like a rescued dog would, with a family on the porch. Not only sat, I lay down. Feeling terribly cold, I curled into a ball and tried to fall asleep. Just when I was about to declare my anxieties to my friend, everything seemed to fall apart and there was nothing left for me to do besides accept this captive love affair as pure frustration. I confess, I cried a bit right there, all curled up on the floor. However, I was already envisioning that I'd go to the battle the next day with or without the engineer—if there'd even be a next day after being in that vessel of orgies reserved for the lucky few. My friend didn't look me in the eye anymore. Surely, he'd continue behaving like that the next day; maybe in the next harbor he'd ask the crew to throw me to the sea with my hands and feet tied. I already felt buried in a whale's guts, having only one thing in my mind: set my shame to a rhythm, since I wouldn't be able to reach a clear destination. Everything felt better with some rhythm. If they fed me, it'd be alright. If they didn't, I wouldn't care. I'd go back to my sleepy reality and act out my own nightmares, create my true horror movies. My sadness over my friend's lack of affection had left me resentful and exhausted. If we were to assemble for some sort of human activity, my body would shrink to hide itself. I tried to imagine what kinds of sea creatures would be able to envelop the shell of this giant metal heap. I'd feel embraced. When we arrived at our destination, if a destination existed, I wouldn't tell anybody about my isolated excursion. I told the engineer about my broad plan for my next phase after our aquatic adventure: in exchange for my doglike loyalty, they would offer me a job, so I'd stay busy inside this vessel. Maybe some kind of slave work. Surely, in exchange for two meals a day, if that. The next morning, they'd name my position. Before beginning, I'd offer silence to the ocean's mysteries. Mysteries prefer not to be named. Their strength comes from the exhaustion of the lexicon. That's why they're mysteries; they hide themselves on the other side of expression. There, the channels of the Self would be obstructed from any unhealthy curiosity. The submarine's secrets had such strength that they started vanishing with the depth of their guardian. The fact is that I was woken by a sunbeam, but I couldn't guess what time it was. What I noticed was the worn-out iron creature had finally anchored in the harbor. I decided to leave for the city's anonymity. Without even bothering to look for my friend. But then I saw he was right there, mounted on the carcass, furtively staring at the sky. I walked toward him and offered him my extended hand in an uncompromised salutation, nothing more than that. He grabbed my hand, said he'd continue his trip. I hoped he'd look me in the eye again. In vain. My friend said he'd keep going and reach the farthest seas. That he had nothing better to do. That he simply needed to improvise his actions now. I'm done with all the planning! he repeated several times. I found that very strange. On dry land, he was someone who methodically calculated all his moves. And he always liked to point out that that was his most exalted quality, if he in fact had any. Now here he was, completely submissive to masculine whims of maritime dimensions. I kept noticing how the hours still waited, with serenity and prudence, for the engineer to occupy them again. Or was it none of that? Yes, everything could be wrong. Would I start playing the role of the eternal resenter who could not conquer the love of a gentleman? In the past, I didn't even have to notify him if I wanted to see him. I'd knock on the door of his torn hideaway, and he was always there, ready to meet me. Despite being parsimonious with his demonstrations of affection, he was always there for me. Even when he was busy with clients. In those instances, he'd ask me to sit on a chair in the corner. But I never waited too long. Once, he said goodbye to a client and came over to me asking

what we'd do that afternoon. I couldn't keep my
eyes off his red tie with yellow dots. If the tie was
suffocating me, I could only imagine how it felt on
him. So I got up, got closer to him, and loosened
the knot. He stepped back a little; I advanced a little. I should have done what I wanted to do most at
that moment: get a little closer and kiss his lips. He
kept his tie loosened for the rest of the day. We
went for a beer in a bar where the television blasted
our eardrums. Now, for this meek farewell on the
top of the submarine, I wished I could get closer
and give him a hug, then a cuddle, the prelude of a
touch a bit more sensual, or almost. A gesture, at
last, of affability between two bodies, right at the
moment I was leaving the scene. Without resent-
ments. Run my hand on his arm, caress it for a bit,
and then leave. But not even that was I able to do.
And I turned to the docks and saw that I was in the
harbor of the city of Rio Grande, where I had once
been as a child. I rented a car to drive back to Porto
Alegre. I thought about spending a few days on a
piece of land I'd inherited from my father, a small
farm near Jaguarão from which I tried to extract my
family's livelihood. But nature could not comfort
me in that instant; not even the goat I used to fuck
with my humiliated cock, leaning against the back
of a ravine. She was avoiding me now. Whenever I

called her, she'd turn away, grazing on her shrubs. I'd had two difficult rejections in such a short period: the engineer and the goat. I enjoyed fucking the creature, going deep into her darkness and coming out with my pelvis drenched by her fluids. In truth, she was not just some object for my sexual discharge. I felt an enormous affection for the animal. Whenever I went to the farm on my own, I'd lay her down in my bed and embrace her. I used to kiss her eyes, her hips—she'd loosen up. The animal's shape adjusted perfectly to my shape. There was no need for a more human cuddle. In the zoological realm, with neither a bed with sheets nor fancy rugs, affection still hurt, but in a benign way. I could tell she adored me, too. Whenever I approached her, she'd present her rear to me, ready and willing to receive me and celebrate our bond. To keep her love for me, I'd be willing to turn into an animal myself; I'd renounce my human features in exchange for her solicitude toward my sexual desire. As usual, I was possessed by an insatiable desire. One day, I went after her and found her near the creek. Then it sunk in: the goat was pregnant. Night was falling. So, I stopped at the first hotel I saw down the road. At the front desk, there was a man wearing a gaucho costume and drinking *chimarrão*. He offered me the *erva-mate*. I politely thanked him and declined. He called his wife, who came over, promptly. Take this gentleman to a room, said the man in the gaucho costume. The woman went up the stairs in silence. She stopped in front of one of the largest doors. I wanted to say something that would justify my travels from one point to another within the state. Should I tell her I was on vacation? But who vacationed without luggage? She left the room's door half opened and gave me the regular spiel for a guest who had just arrived: remote control, buttons on the radio, the shower. I sat on the double bed trying out the mattress. She sat down, too, as if distracted by anything that wasn't the usual ABC's of the room. Suddenly, she realized she had nothing else to explain. And we looked at each other. To compensate for the loss of my engineer friend and the goat, I could have sex with this woman right in this bed. Let the man in the gaucho costume drink his tea downstairs. We just needed to lock the door. If I fucked her right here, I'd have to close my eyes and imagine another body receiving my flesh. The woman's body wouldn't be enough for me; I needed another—in my imagination, of course, forming a pact of steadfast lust with me. With her alone, I wouldn't be able to maintain the rhythm of a normal fuck, I'd soon go soft. While she had her orgasm, I would suddenly

find myself dead on the beach. There was something about the fake gaucho's wife that annihilated
my fragile horniness; perhaps it was the smell of
the food she was preparing downstairs. Perhaps my
horniness would only stay while the atmosphere of
uncertainty about another hot encounter remained.
At any moment, her husband could knock on the
door and shout her name. For my own safety, a
third body would need to show up between us—a
body of ultimate attractiveness; yes, an imaginary
body, which I would engage with in a voracious
scene. With the voracity lent from that third skin
(absent, I repeat), I could heat the proprietress up
with my libido. I bet it wouldn't take much for her
to catch fire. To prevent her from noticing the mis-
match between real and fictional bodies, I'd lay her
down with her legs spread. She wouldn't be able to
ascertain the origins of my excitement. It didn't
matter how complete the appearing figure really
was. The image was ready to jump into the scene as
if it had been waiting backstage. It had a life independent from the imagination of the one who had
summoned it. As much autonomy as the mental
figure had won, the undeniable source of this delirium in the shape of voluptuousness was a lacuna in
my own soul. The hotel owner should strictly respond to what I wanted from her: receiving my

genitalia's shaded hunger. A reception that could result in good performances from both of us. This woman may have cultivated another imaginary dimension inside herself as well, another carnal spectrum. Who would be the fourth character in that hotel bed? Who was the woman invoking? Thus, the act of fucking consisted of a ritual with several guests. Even more than four. During that very same erotic connection, my chosen imaginary body could be replaced with another and another and so on. But, in the end, no alliance materialized between the hotel owner and I. Not even a caress. Much less cuddles… A nod…perhaps? And so I stayed on the balcony by myself for a while, looking at a duck circumnavigating a small pond with a fountain in the center. Early the next morning, I was back on the road, listening to *chorinhos* on the radio. All was perfect, no time for sorrow. Just kidding; I was very sad that I could not count on my engineer friend any longer. It still hurt me a lot because it meant my separation from a sexual exponent that had never been mine nor ever would. Through all those years, I listened to him and he to me, without us having to invoke any other friendship. We had never touched each other as lovers, true. But it was as if we were both saving ourselves for the day in which our bed would become the lushest garden. This had been my mistake: waiting and waiting for the day that would make the wait worthwhile. I kept telling myself about the noble quality of that passion, without making it sound too maudlin. Porto Alegre, without my engineer friend, would be the southernmost tip of tedium. To whom would I sing "*Quem acha vive se perdendo*" by Noel Rosa? To whom would I dedicate my jerk-off sessions after I got home from a Bohemian encounter with him? Those post-encounter masturbation sessions got me through the days; they almost made it seem like I had a satisfactory sex life, since I relied on the precipitating presence of my chaste lover. Even if that vicious platonic friendship frustrated me many times, masturbation absolved me of my deprivation. I bet he also jerked off after our nocturnal encounters. Our chastity gifted us with a friendly atmosphere, without any major attrition. Attrition is so common with couples in their little accidents of the sexual sphere. The touch of one still needed to be felt by the touch of the other. Once that happened—and only then—we wouldn't be able to continue being just friends anymore. And there was no other alternative. Still, it's unlikely we'd ever treat each other as lovers in our day-to-day. There was always the ardent expectation of a physical encounter, even if continuously frustrated. And this somewhat painful yearning didn't corrode the hope for lightness and freshness, sagacity and humor, so typical of young lovers. Without copulation—or even an initial touch—passion thrives by preserving its pulsating potential. We live with the promise that this sexual yearning might one day be realized. It's like the majestic absence of an advent. Or of any passion invoked before the bodily appetizer is tasted. One night, a long time ago, the engineer walked me home. It was raining, but only he had brought an umbrella. Before going into the house, I watched his steps for a moment. He walked in the rain so slowly. The wet asphalt mirrored the lights from the posts. Like in a crime movie set in San Francisco. I think the engineer was whistling a Chilean song at that moment. When I undressed in the bedroom, my cock had a life of its own, as if free from my body; it looked like a vessel stretched to its max, alive, kicking. Hard as I've ever seen it; fervent droplets of lube came out of it. Some nights, we'd go to a sauna, but we'd never let our towels slip down our waists. Our sexes felt strangled, as if wanting more air. Until the day came when he departed for good on the German submarine. And he even made a point of bringing me to his fucking crazy send-off. It was only because of the oceanic orgy that I learned he had a bee tattooed on his foreskin. What did it mean? A pact with honey? Would he promote diabetes in harbors across the planet? Where would his next port be? I was listening to a piano piece by Satie on the radio when I parked my car in downtown Porto Alegre. I crossed my fingers between my legs and listened to the music. It was so diaphanous that I felt like a mortal, marked by an elegance and on the verge of death, tense, with nothing to hold on to. Crossing the Alfândega Square, I noticed a small crowd forming a line. I got closer and asked why. It was for people to donate their meek jewelry and their little money to a grand cause, the Brazilian cause. For the Republic, they added. A mass response was expected. The country's renegades would feel obligated to withdraw to the nation's most inaccessible center, where each person would become part of the arduous purpose of the collective. How so? I asked myself. But I also wanted to contribute. I felt the front pocket of my pants. I pulled my wallet out and rifled through my money. I grabbed three bills and joined the line. A colossal silence underscored the hour's earnestness. Even traffic seemed congealed—no honking, no cursing, nothing. I was arriving late, as usual, to public nature. Where was I that I hadn't seen the ads for the campaign? I remembered the German submarine and its bunch of hedonists, with all the time in the world to throw away the body's crisis instinct. I asked myself how long my engineer friend could endure the guts of the ocean. Or would he break through the monster's corroded shell only to die of exhaustion, infected with various STDs? Perhaps in my very chaste arms. I arrived in front of a woman collecting people's livelihoods and noticed that the amount I was going to donate was too little. Was I becoming as uncharitable as Porto Alegre? I opened two buttons on my shirt and took off my chest the chain my mother had given me many years before. I passed it into the woman's hand and felt like I had fulfilled my duty, even though I hadn't learned the exact cause of the campaign. And was there any cause? The piece of jewelry, of reasonable value, had the maternal bosom meticulously embossed on it. The child at one breast. Distant symbols from a campaign for breastfeeding from two decades before. The chain could represent some kind of down payment, preferably earnest, no matter if the genesis of the cause was exalted or not. Because of this detachment, I'd be able to go through life with efficacy and purpose, at last. My wife was in the living room wearing only a bra and panties as if she had been waiting for me. From the shower, I told her I had spent the night drinking and sleeping at my engineer friend's house. I couldn't remember how many nights I had been out. Groggy as I was, I hadn't remembered to call her, I said. In the bathroom, I noticed blood on my cock. What had happened? I could only conclude that I had not in fact passed unscathed through the submarine gang. Someone had taken advantage of my body while I was asleep—perhaps they had given me anesthetics, sedatives, morphine, so they could dominate me. However, they must have done something else, too, so my cock could keep its erection. Maybe they worshiped necrophilia. They appreciated motionless bodies, like mine might have been. My prick was washed and clean now, and it didn't seem to have any wounds on the glans or foreskin. It seems the blood might have come from the submarine's innermost place. And then I suddenly remembered that, during my moments of sleep on the ship, I indeed felt like warm shoulders moved repeatedly over my groin—which responded to the stimulation like a naïve little puppy. Maybe I hadn't had a choice. Maybe the choice of physical damage was part of the menu, like a sophisticated type of orgy. However, a transparent memory from the nights I had spent underwater occurred to me. Yes. I had felt my cock strangled, and right after that, its release. I could see the fury of my semen firing against a German sheet. My cock had responded very well, while the rest of my body remained lost, with only sparse islands of lucidity. The sheet had a mysterious purple monogram sewn by an unsteady thread. This piece of bedding seemed to be part of the captain's trousseau. I asked myself if the captain had been my partner during that prurient adventure. After all, who had used me, somebody from the German squad or one of the few visitors? What if it had been the engineer? Perhaps he had taken advantage of my blackout, deciding we had to do what we should have done so many years before? That'd have been fine, I'd say excellent even, magnificent, even if he had chosen to shut off my consciousness. I was feeling as if my recently recovered memory had been scraped from the deepest, deepest depth, where I recognized with some difficulty the submarine's evanescent presence. But the ass I fucked—yes, now I remember—was for sure the white ass of a German. Did I pass out because I was given some clandestine substance? Was that substance some kind of experiment from a big European laboratory? Such a powerful lab could finance adventures and testing in the oceans' depths. To find out what exactly? Of course, it could be a medication to heal a consumer's anal tissues in a matter of hours. That's why they fucked so much in there. The day before, in the deep ocean, I had craved—with terrible fervor, but certainly too late—physical contact with the engineer. Maybe we had even consummated: one's chest against the other's, a hug, a kiss wet with saliva, the inaugural orgasm. My wife might not have been near the bathroom at that moment. I could no longer hear her sweet voice singing French songs from the 15th and 16th centuries, primarily the ones by Josquin des Prez, of whom she was fond. Her distinctive soprano had the power to inspire me. One time, Clara caught me kissing a cowboy in the middle of the eucalyptus trees on our modest farm. Guys like that farmhand didn't talk to me, nor did I talk to them. Our bodies did the talking. Clara pretended she didn't see us. Libidinous acts like that—with anonymous company, or someone who was not part of my immediate circle—kept my desire alive and fresh, but they also made me very nervous. There was always the fear that the partner could use our session of erotic revelry for blackmail. (After all, I had a teenage son, and I didn't want him to find out about me before it was time.) Fucking a stranger at night in a deserted alley, or in the bathroom of a movie theater, was the most immediate intensity that life provided me. I left these compulsive contacts ready for another round. When the anonymous figure calling to my cock abruptly emerged from the shadows, I'd have a premature orgasm just imagining what was about to happen. Most of the time, in the instant our bodies engaged each other, I'd already be shooting my cum, wetting our clothes—if we weren't naked. When I boldly opened a stranger's shirt, I'd unleash a constellation of caresses. The hand on the shirt buttons is no lesser of a gesture than the hand on the Bible. They both touch on a fetish—be it the button or the Good Word—and begin the work of feeding our infinite hunger. When, however, I find myself in a joyful spirit in the company of someone for whom I nurture a solid, already born affection, I need to close my eyes as I feel the first contractions at the base of my cock getting ready to shoot. I need to close my eyes to let the diaphanous, imaginary flesh descend over me—the one that will save me from the reality of my daily bed. Perhaps a fresh body will come today in my fantasy? Perhaps it is about to appear? The approaching face is still wishy-washy, indistinguishable. Before I can even decipher the contours of this visitor, I go ahead and place the apparition under my retina. This way, I protect the image, I keep it all to myself. There is no harm in trying to incubate the image behind my eyelids. Here inside, the image evolves, and it grants me its singular and obscene enchantment. That's when I comprehend, without noticing, that I ejaculated from only the apparition of the elusive image. My orgasm took place in the viscera of that evanescent flesh, but still produced the usual sticky cum, the same metallic smell of semen, once again lacking the legitimacy to perpetuate the species: simply cum, already wasting away, remote and laid to rest. This half-lit image vanishes, never to come back. Was it of anyone in particular? It was, in principle. However, at the end, a second image began covering the first; and then a third one, and maybe a fourth one would have entered if I had taken longer to cum. But, to whom belonged the first body that ended up vanishing? First, to someone breathless. However, I have another body here on my side of the bed. This one, yes, is made of flesh, bones, and blood. And of cum, too. And shit. And from his mouth issues a post-fuck lyricism, but he pronounces it with dandruff on his beard. My wife never mentioned the subject of my rapture with the farmhand among the eucalyptus trees. She seemed to appreciate in me what she didn't have in her erotic character: an unstoppable attraction to physical outbursts, including experiences in public spaces, with the fear of being caught. She forced me, in this way, to rush toward a series of low-quality, promiscuous sexual encounters, without any facts or appreciation. Since my episode with the cowboy among the trees, my wife had been singing more. When she sang, the sensible world temporarily disappeared. Her voice grew with so much thirst, so much art, that the sound seemed to come from an abstract source, immaterial, absent, and not from her throat, damaged from two packs of cigarettes a day. We hadn't had sex in more than five years. She seemed to be fine with that. I surely was. At least, she didn't seem to feel like a victim of a faggot husband's disinterest. She never pressured me to fire the farmhand. He's still there, always tempting me. But, faggot or not, the implicit compromise of having to fuck someone long term—or at least as long as the relationship lasts—such marital megaplans had always made me suspicious—though I myself had fallen into one, being by her side. Maybe she had her own flings, why not? Honestly, she was attractive, came from money, though without the convenience of any major financial inflows lately. We slept in separate beds, but in the same room. Sleeping in the same bedroom represented the construction of a solid family picture for our teenage son. I'm exiting a movie theater with my boy now. We go to the food court. He's ordered something huge, typical of his age. What he hurriedly sticks in his mouth could feed an army. I tell him to wait while I go take a piss. I go into the bathroom and see a crowd waiting for their turn to shit or piss. I push the door of a stall. A guy inside calls me in. I can't think of anything, much less that my son is waiting for me and could come into the bathroom at any time. All I can think of is that the barely delineated shadow in the stall may be one of my imaginary figures, materialized in skin, smells, the vigor of blood, the real tumescence, his cavity masterfully lubed with lotion. For any one of these reasons, let me go and never come back. This time, I wouldn't have to close my eyes to see the unreal man within me. This time, he would be tangible in that stall. And I would indulge myself in him, looking into his eyes from the start until the conclusive moment. Now, yes, I could clear my mind of lascivious images, and finally reach out to the compacted carnal mass without the regular interruptions of jumping from one imaginary partner to another. Oh, the banal inconsistencies of my virtual erotic trip. The first lustful touch would have to come from this seducer's burning presence in such a random scene. Yes, a fleeting contact, without the mediation of anything or anyone. Without the mediation of language even. There would be nothing to think about in the presence of the sudden and unrelenting figure in the fetid cubicle's gloom. The strong smell of piss and feces in this bathroom had already excited me from the get go. It was in places like this that I first initiated my adult life. They always made me want to go sniffing around in a frenzy. I closed the door and all I could do was kiss the body that had been waiting for me. While I kissed him, I realized I hadn't even had time to look at the face whose tongue explored my mouth with such audacity. In the struggle, we knocked each other's teeth. We opened our pants; to speed up our filthy act, we started jerking off our own cocks. Three, four shots of cum gushed out, and slowly dripped from our pants. Who came, me or him? Both? No one, perhaps? I left the stall without taking the time to see the face of who, in principle, wasted his cum on me. I wash my hands, wipe the sperm stain on my pants with water, leave the bathroom, and sit in front of my son again. Let's go? I ask. Let's go, he answers. In the car, he tells me he's sleeping at his friend's tonight. Can you take me there? I stop in front of the boy's house. At the gate, my son claps his hands. A dog barks with fury. A door opens. It's a man about my age. We seem to recognize each other at the same time. We used to be friends when we were young. Friends or lovers? We smile while he holds the dog's leash, who has calmed down, and my son enters the nest of his friendship. I get out of the car. He lets the dog go and comes to the sidewalk. In school, we were two animals, two dogs who only thought of fucking and fucking and nothing else, until we went to bed to sleep and soon woke up to reenact our fight. Now, on the sidewalk, we looked at each other, displaying our grown bellies. Now, all could come back. But no, no, I had to preserve the passion for my engineer friend until he returned to Porto Alegre. Who were those Germans who took him away? He, the most stingy in demonstrations of affection to any friend—he was the only one who never got married. At least, before his departure on the submarine. But, I, there, in front of the boy's dad, seemed to be entering an insane delirium. Before this man, still handsome and luminous. A badly dressed woman came up and begged us to help our country. I searched in my pockets. Again? I protested in silence. But anyway, the campaign to assault people's savings for the sake of various causes opened me to the possibility of, at least, getting closer to the father of my son's friend. We. Why don't we start living together with both our families under the same roof? At first, we'd be just two buddies, hanging out maybe once a week. Then, we'd travel, I know we would. On a whim, we both made the same gesture:

we took our wedding rings off our fingers. We deposited the tiny golden-plated circumferences inside a box the woman was carrying. Although my engineer friend was constantly on my mind, I was always willing to notice some amorous, even if fragile, signal from a third party. That man and I, standing on the sidewalk, were about the same age; we showed discreet wrinkles, but that wouldn't be any impediment. We could leave our sons some money for the movies. And they'd go, like good buddies, while the man on the sidewalk and I would run away on the weekends and go camping in São José dos Ausentes. We were both without the blessed rings on our left hands. And that would signal our emancipation from the family—a family that we had created ourselves. I couldn't think of any better way to escape from Porto Alegre boredom. And our wives? At that point, they'd already be by their new lovers' sides. Everything would work out. And our sons? They wouldn't even care about our story. That's when he said the situation in Brazil is getting worse. And we both smiled at his awkward comment. In fact, our shared past, suddenly revived on the sidewalk, should not include any subject that brought attention to the truth of what was happening, or that our opinions of each other had already formed. We looked at our fingers, no longer with those golden handcuffs. I thought about giving him a caress. A cuddle, perhaps. Maybe not yet. Maybe just a nod, almost inconspicuous. I didn't dare caress him. We exchanged numbers and talked about getting together sometime. On my way home, I stopped at a red light. A handicapped man came up, asking me to collaborate with the republican cause. Each person employed a new approach to begging. I rolled up my window, just how I liked to be sometimes: mean. No, no appealing discourse could affect me, I had only my own comfort in mind, nothing more. And I had already given my jewelry away earlier to help avoid the Latin American catastrophe. Now more? When I got home, my wife noticed right away I was not wearing my ring. I told her I went for a swim at the Grêmio Náutico União club in the Moinhos de Vento neighborhood after I dropped the kid at his friend's. The ring came off my finger, spiraled down through the green water, and fell into the drain. She immediately removed her ring. Which also came off easily. I needed to be alone. It had been a lot for a single day. Two men renouncing their wedding rings…who knows if the gesture wouldn't end up giving us access to a more interesting common destiny. I had always put myself in between love and sex. Usually, sex won. Now, I was idealizing a love affair between two mature men, more or less settled in life, neither of whom had the sleazy ways of my engineer friend. Maybe I wanted to have some control of my blinding, disorienting lust. I can't fuck all the men in the world. But I wish I could. On my halting way, I followed a homoerotic version of Domingos de Oliveira's ultimate desire to have all the women in the world. It was a pity having to repress my libido for there were so many men I could still have a good time with. Now, I would work my magic with the father of my son's friend. Strange, I felt jealous of the physical proximity between my son and this man. Would they be talking now or what? I was feeling jealous of this guy demonstrating his verbal ability in front of my boy. My boy, always so shy, was now having a cheery heart-to-heart with his friend's father. This man certainly exaggerated his friendliness in front of boys who were looking to have some fun, nothing more than that. I was starting to like this man in his forties who had kept the light of his twenties intact inside him. Was he a sportsman? Did he play tennis, golf, or what? I already felt my body, from head to toe, going into an erogenous frenzy. My wife was lying down, wearing a very old négligée, which she kept wrapped in tissue paper inside a box. Sometimes, I'd open the box and smell its lightly

scented contents. It reminded me of Carol Baker
from the movie with the same name, a cinematic
evocation of the synthesis of women's clothing. The
giant poster showed the actress laying on her side in
a type of baby's crib, sucking a finger. My wife knew
that I was into the idea of revealing, to the inexpe-
rienced partner, the triumph of animal audacity.
Maybe she was now interested in re-awakening her
pubescent self for me. With her disheveled hair,
she'd use our bed as a Garden of Eden for delights
that had been abandoned, but were suddenly revived. I took my clothes off and laid by her side in
her bed. She was watching TV. I started getting
hard. It felt like I was about to touch my engineer
friend, or, in my new version, the father of my son's
friend. Yes, it was better to close my eyes and try to
imagine the man I'd talked to on the sidewalk,
overlooking his garden. The return of my engineer
friend to Porto Alegre was improbable. I'm sure
people were fighting over him in the German submarine. That brown man amid the Germanic hunger. Even if I had an intense affair with either
one—the engineer or the man on the sidewalk—
there'd be one night, I guessed, when I'd need to
close my eyes if I was fucking one or the other. You
use the body of one to cum on the body of another.
Nobody's immune to love's misfortunes. Burnout

would come, of course, as an inevitable consequence of a tight romance, one size smaller than it should be, one person confined within the other. With my eyes closed, I would think of a body that I, likely, was still unaware of—be it from this real world or strictly from my imagination. Or a mixture of the two possibilities. I thought about caressing my wife's skin, right there, next to my skin. A cuddle. Or just a hug then. No? I touched, with my trembling hand, one of her breasts under the neckline. She turned to me. And I kissed her on the lips. We were not surprised. It seemed we were about to go back to the same rhythm of fucking from our early years. I put my cock in her with tenderness—very different from the manner I was used to. Humping my wife in bed, I felt ready to renounce all the other temptations of libido once and for all. We could even make a new baby; perhaps the girl we both dreamed of in our moments of candid connection. I was a good father, it was true, and I'd transfer my sexual energy to the job of maintaining a family—always looking forward to the birth of our little girl. With the girl's arrival, I would come home and tend to my children's demands—help them with homework or go to my boy's school to smooth out any misunderstandings with a teacher. Later in the evening: the kids in their bedrooms, the girl already asleep, the boy stuck on his computer, my wife and I in our double bed, me getting closer to her, lying on top of her, getting into the rhythm, digging into the wet depths between her thighs. She had some kind of wall inside her that wouldn't let me get through. A long time ago, her breasts poured milk. I wanted to taste what my son did when he suckled on that breast. But I only got close before I backed away. Yes, maybe this time we'd beget another child—which we weren't counting on and maybe didn't even want to have—a child that would help compose a picture of a family with a good foundation, so we could save my business at the problematic farm. I was fucking my wife with brio, and she called me "stud" at each stroke, like I was a horse. I didn't know what excited me more: the titanic parallel between me and a stud, or the pure and simple entrance of a powerful animal into our dirty new liaison. Certainly, my wife and I would share the stallion's erotic figure, stimulated by a frank spirit of fraternity, on the verge of incestuous. With my family expanded, it was likely I'd sell my dilapidated little farm and open a business in Porto Alegre. By then, I would have forgotten my engineer friend and the father of my son's friend. Perhaps, I'd already be immune to the daily temptations of other men. Perhaps, in the erotic domain,

I would only desire my wife, as I was doing now, diving deeper and deeper into her flesh like one digs after a treasure that has finally begun to glow, without being too blinding: it's just a glow. Her orgasm met mine; they suddenly clashed against each other and vanished in a matter of seconds, leaving us exhausted, loose again. The bodies I renounced would no longer weigh on me. I'd close my eyes above the body of my female partner and imagine I was fucking the body of the whole universe. I was made for this libidinous epic. I'd copulate with all my male partners through one body only, and only once—and eventually, with some female partners and some animals too. I'd even copulate with an old lady from whom I'd once tried to run away. She used to live in the apartment next door when I was still single. She knocked on my door saying she was having a crisis stemming from her low blood pressure. I took her to her apartment and put her in bed, so I could call an ambulance. I sat by her side and told her everything would be alright. Gasping, she pulled me by the sleeves and asked me to hold her. When I did, I saw that her octogenarian breasts were still whole, still deserving of a man like me suckling on them, on that plentiful white flesh. It took me a while to find her nipples, so low that they were almost to her navel. It didn't matter, there was an enormous field for me to explore. I sucked on those breasts. I brought my hand to her endless pussy, which had dispatched eight children in its lifetime. The folds of her labia were dry, but still feverish. "Dry" is the label for the destiny of the elderly. Suddenly, I panicked that the old lady could have a stroke or something. She could die from all the excitement. And if that happened, I'd have problems with the law, even if I had helped to shorten her suffering. Down on my knees, I still had time to open my pants, and I jerked off on that old, semi-naked woman. My cum shots hit her in the mouth, and she licked my cum, and licked it... and then she passed out. I brought her a glass of water, which I slowly poured over her almost fune-real face. She opened her eyes, and I told her she needed to rest. It was good, I said. She licked her lips again. And smiled. I was moved by that smile and kissed it. Then, I slowly started backing away until I closed the door and went into my apartment, where an Organ Concerto by Haydn was playing. I sat down to concentrate. To train my attention. Until the moment my pubes started itching from the remnants of semen, which turned it into a late celebration of sexual desire—perhaps a mortal one, I don't know. I got up, undressed, and got in the shower. In the middle of washing, through a crack in the window, I watched my neighbor as usual. He was only wearing a speedo, washing a shirt. I had the impression he was aware of my gaze. Suddenly, he looked around as if confirming that some pervert was watching him through one of the city's cracks and gaps. Interestingly, he didn't look at the spot from where I was admiring him. From that point on, I started fearing for my health. Perhaps, my physical condition was on the verge of collapse, like my old lady neighbor's. But what an ass I was admiring through the window! When was this insanity going to stop? Wasn't it enough for me to just watch from a distance, without the slightest chance of getting close to the guy to praise him for the caliber of his ass? In the face of my hunger, enormously frustrated like so many others, I cried a bit in the shower. Still, I knew that the only receptacle of that cosmic energy would be her, my wife, mother of my child and the others still to come, if they came. On the weekends, we could go to our small, troublesome farm, and in contact with nature, in the open sky, I'd find the strength to improve our production of eggs and vegetables. Which wouldn't be easy, since I have never been a practical man. To act in ways that could bring direct and immediate benefits demanded too much of my attention. And my attention had been failing me, to the point where I didn't know how to tackle some activities. At night, I'd take medication for my hypertension as I went into our bedroom. Properly medicated, I'd lie down and ask my wife to come join me in bed, and she'd follow me, knowing that I was already excited, ready to embrace her and insert my chastened cock into her peaceful and sensible vagina. The next day, my widowed father-in-law was coming to visit us. He would give me the best advice about being the helmsman of this boat. I cried out for a love without a name, since it was still out of my reach; when, at last, I poured all my cum into this astute woman, who swallowed my sap between her legs, smeary from the both of us. It was so difficult to free myself from those plans for love, like the one with my wife, plans that went beyond my moral pedigree. I felt too forgetful to pursue the roster of my lovers. I got up, went to the sink in the bathroom, and washed my dick. I always washed my cock in bathroom sinks after fucking. Like a child after doing something wrong; a little trick I did after gushing potion from my middle-aged body. I went back to bed, my wife wanted more. She wanted to hug me; then, she wanted to nurse my cock, which was clean and beautiful again. Her blowjob was noisy because of her voracious mouth. Then she changed position, broadcasting her desire to be fucked in the ass. I got more and more excited as my greedy schlong entered her asshole, and I started to feel that the woman I was fucking was precisely the same one for whom I was dedicating my most energetic thoughts at that moment, if you could call the vortex which she was diving into with me and from which I treated myself to what I would consider the zenith of my life so far "thoughts," at all. She was no longer a woman at the point of satiating me, she wasn't anybody anymore, she was nothing. I spilled my semen inside her glorious ass. She swooned, withering at last, lying down and giving in to sleep. When I awoke, I got up like I had an early appointment somewhere. I went to get the paper at the door. There goes this man who is me now, going into the bathroom: I accept him a bit more each day, this man, sitting on the toilet early every morning. By the time I finished reading the paper, I had shit enough for the whole day. That morning, I read some disturbing news. A German submarine had sunk off the coast of Angola. It got stuck in the remains of another shipwreck. That insolent invention with its worn-out iron was indeed a piece of German junk from the Second World War. It was inhabited by some kind of disorienting international force, always moving around the sea, without fixing itself in any port. In summer, they gave themselves a one-month break at the harbor of Hamburg. Nowadays, not even that. They claimed they came to confuse, like Christ. The crew was mostly Germans. What united them was an aristocratic taste for sodomy. Some observers thought it was possible the ship-wreck was planned by the German intelligence ser-vice. Suspects of the maritime depravity started re-ceiving hard treatment not only from the police but also from the citizens of cities like Berlin and Hamburg. Many gays traveled to various European cities, or to New York, Toronto, or San Francisco, with the hopes of finding asylum. Suspicion and hostility had now infiltrated the Army, clergy, and universities. Bombs were exploding in nightclubs that promoted homoerotic attractions. The only Brazilian in the submarine was a man from Bahia, also the only survivor. Speculations mounted every day that the vessel had wrecked as the result of a terrorist attack orchestrated by the German gov-ernment. Where was my *baiano*? How was he? The cadavers had been transported to their European country, because the authorities demanded forensic analysis of the victims' anal orifices so they could measure the extent of the damages. There have been speculations about the morbid eroticism of the German state. There was strong evidence that sodomy was widely practiced in the vessel via ostensible, and even dramatic, configurations among dozens of participants. Sexual intimacy between two people was now a hesitant, palliative experience. We were about to enter the orgiastic age. When harbored, the crew opened the submarine to the local male population. It was necessary to investigate just how far those sadomasochistic practices went. They found asses entirely lacerated. Cocks bruised by so much confrontation with their partners. I searched the internet for any news about the episode. Generally, one news story mirrored the next which mirrored another and so on, until one came along that was different from the rest, a story that turned the news inside out, perhaps trying to exclude any sacredness from the facts. The news agency that produced the story lived off contradiction. It sought to extract the truth from its despotic, omnivorous, massive aura. In this counternews there was not a single note about the baiano. It was good, in my opinion, that this fraction of negative news didn't reveal anything about the baiano. The silence from this outlet meant that, after the shipwreck, he didn't hesitate and instead chose to run from the headlines straight to becoming a Lutheran missionary refugee in the backlands of Angola, establishing himself on the banks of a muddy river where fearful hippopotamuses and alligators bathed in the water. In the missionary tribe, he held a child in his arms and felt the feverish skin of that small anonymous being. The boy wheezed heavily. And the engineer ran after a doctor to ask for help. I gave up trying to learn more about this man, at least from the time when he joined the submarine gang to today. I read something on a website that was new to me: one African diver, upon bringing the drowned bodies to the surface, got an involuntary erection when he saw the cadaver of a young gymnast from Bonn. A reporter took a picture of this African diver at the moment his groin displayed a visible bulge as he stood by the alabaster skin of the deceased. When I saw the picture, I teared up over another unrequited love. This diver lived in Hamburg; he was on vacation in Angola, visiting his family. He was immediately fired from the job he'd had at a café in Germany. Later, I read the news that the Angolan diver and the beautiful young German had had an affair. As if the readers didn't already know. What was surprising to me was to learn that the reposed state of a lover could provoke an erection in the body of the one who's left alive. All over Germany, those suspected of practicing sodomy encountered severe backlash. And my engineer friend, where was he now? Had he been deported or had he not even been able to re-enter Germany after his stay in Angola? And did that stay really happen? Was he dating an Angolan, so he could get over the death of his German lover? Had the engineer experienced the miracle of saving himself from drowning? The Germans were infuriated by African migrants. They were stealing their jobs and recreational areas. Children of African parents were occupying seats on amusement park rides. I didn't understand anything anymore. I decided against trying to guess the engineer's destiny any further. Let him be with his petty mysteries. Right when I could foresee things rekindling with my wife, that news arrived! My engineer friend could reappear in Porto Alegre at any moment. And I, as usual, would be waiting for him, no matter the fate of our love story. Yes, because people on the internet began speculating that the engineer was not the one in the submarine during the accident. But then who was the baiano who, according to the news, was able to escape the shipwreck? Some kind of premature dementia began manifesting itself in me. Like so many other people, I ignored the credibility of sources. The problem was that, for me, fidelity or not didn't make any difference anymore. The fiction of things ensnared me to the point where I was unable to untangle myself from it. And what was left of so-called reality would find an ineffable refugee in the consulate of all nations. I look at my love for what he is: a Brazilian stud staying at a beach on the Angolan coast, surely, so he could rest from an excessive period of ardent insomnia. He took a plane and got off in Berlin for his colleagues' funerals. I would learn later that he regretted this trip to Germany. He was forced to answer in an interrogation. He had his anus searched. They stuck a rod in his ass, a rod with a light on the tip. They wanted to scan the poor man's rectum. It hurt more on the way out than on the way in. All good things must come to an end, goes the saying. In the operation, when they pulled the rod out of his ass, the engineer twitched in pain. He struggled to get up from the hospital bed. I'm not sick, he whispered to his pillow. The engineer never found out why they had to plunge a scope into his viscera. Maybe they were preparing for a party inside him. Lying on his stomach, the engineer put his head under his arms, so he couldn't see what was going on. His ass had never gotten fucked. With his anus in good condition, he was dismissed from the interrogation room, as long as he swore to never get close to diabolic circles like that again. And just so you know, they said: you'll be followed. Yes, his stay in the submarine had been attenuated by a single fact: he'd fucked but was not fucked. The officers felt a bit of admiration for this adventurous fucker. Some smiled, others laughed out loud. It didn't matter if his cock came out of the act covered in shit. It mattered, yes, that he was the master of the orgy; namely, that he butt-fucked the whole squad and was always ready to go all over again. So, it seems he indeed fucked the entire submarine. The debauched sailors had commented amid their laughs that his schlong was like an explosive that had torn the ship up left and right. They rolled around on the floor, laughing. After months of this equine rhythm, the engineer realized that his body had become so light it could be carried by the wind. He had to drag himself from A to B, leaning against the walls. His legs became sticklike. Eventually, he was saved from this brutal weakness. He was helped by the Gay Society of the Seas, which, at that point, had settled in London in a more secretive manner but with a more combative profile. Desperate, certain gay factions from Germany started practicing terrorist acts—death was everywhere. If the engineer came looking for me during this dramatic phase, I'd leave everything behind to follow him, even with him being sick as he was, practically without any physical autonomy. I'd be his nurse, his only companion. I'd leave some possessions to my son and wife. He could have me whatever way he wanted, as a man, or a woman, or both at the same time. I'd leave some money to my family and walk out with only my clothes to restart my life wherever it pleased him. Of course, preferably in Bahia, maybe in his hometown. I'd leave my minor possessions, like the house in Cidreira, to him, this baiano whom I would free from the slavery of the body. In exchange, he would not reject my servitude. I didn't see the point of continuing to speculate if the engineer had survived, now resting on the Angolan coast, or if his body had the luck to not follow the logic of shipwrecks. Every piece of news I read was contradictory. One day, I'll write a story for my teenage son. I'll tell him not to feel ashamed of his father's attitude. I'll tell him about these melodramatic things that are part of anyone's life. It's necessary to reiterate the norms of sentimentality each step of the way. It's necessary, after I'm dead, to reinterpret the role of a father—unfortunately, still using pre-formed words. My son has grown so much, he looks like a man. My wife got pregnant again. She lost the child. She almost passed away with the eight-month-old fetus. And I can't avoid feeling some kind of relief, though I also wanted to have the child. I used to put my hand on her belly and feel the infant kicking. But I also feared the engineer could arrive at any moment, while I'd be involved with a new child. I take my teenage son to the swimming pool at the União in Quintino, where he trains. We enter the club, he disappears—certainly he went to the locker room. Since he's grown up, I've never seen him naked. These guys train all styles of swimming. I take a seat on the bleachers and don't want to be seen by anyone. I want to be a man hidden in the shadow of the marquee, while the sun intensifies its dizzying light—it's almost noon. Lately, I haven't done anything for anyone or myself. I'm just a shadow. My son swims butterfly. No, I've never seen him naked. He swims butterfly with his beautiful physique, made of real athletic tissue. At night, I'll go knock on his bedroom and ask him to tell me what he's been reading. In the meantime, he swims butterfly with that torso from the movies. When he goes back to the locker room, I go after him. He dries off, naked. I look at his nakedness and I think: I am responsible for that. He's a man, and I have to take my eyes off his body and talk to him with the voice of a father. However, he's so beautiful that I can't even believe it. Disguising, I bring my gaze to his torso, follow his stomach, down to his circumcised penis, and now I bring my eyes to his muscular legs, to his feet with toes creased by the pool water. I travel back up his body, keep going up, until I hear his voice say Dad!? It seems he asked me something I chose not to understand. He is simply him. And I love him like I've never, probably, been able to love anyone. Dad!? he repeats. I say, yes, I'm your dad. He's dressed already, wet hair combed back. He never really learned how to dry himself. Clumsy guy. I thought of touching him, more than a touch, an undaunted cuddle though always restrained. Or maybe just a hug… but that was no longer possible. I should have done that in his childhood. It seems I had predicted correctly: we would grow apart, with great care. And there'd come a time when we wouldn't even greet each other, if we met at a social event or something like that. Why? I don't know, and not even he would have the ability to figure it out. That young man was there, in front of me, all dressed now. Maybe he already hated me for some reason I didn't know. Maybe the reason was the imminent threat that I would become the son and he the father. I would die from this love. In a matter of days. They were two men in a locker room, one in each corner, one of them was the father, the other the son. They were two men who could have created the greatest projects together. But no, they chose to grow apart. They were two men who seemed to inhabit the same loneliness, and yet were moving away from each other, since they could foresee great turmoil if both converged on the same point. Nevertheless, he was still there, in front of me, in União's locker room, and I could give him a last kiss. It would be a father's last embrace of his ungrateful son. I kissed him on his lips, yes, and I left the club and walked to a house where rent boys simulated massages in the twilight. I was back to being that dispersed man again, not the guy focusing on his wife anymore. The boy I would meet at the massage place would look like more than an individual, because they were all the same, each one possessing the same secret gift. His traces would move with jilted fluidity. I would live with the same refusal. Just to provoke him. What is certain, in the meantime, is that I was moving away from my son and toward a bathhouse with massage services so I could do what I needed most: to touch and be touched. I went into the dark room. Indeed, absolute darkness. You couldn't see anything at all. You were touched and could reciprocate the touch or not. Lottery. Gasps seemed to multiply with each encounter. Sultry moans and whisperings. An Inferno of rumored delights cut short. The body that wanted to play with me had a calm demeanor; once in a while it would just tell me come, come, and I'd ask myself where the hell does this guy want to take me? Isn't he satisfied with kissing, our close breaths, masturbating each other, my finger wrecking his ass? Where else do I need to go? Our random pairing alone could embody an obscene graciousness all by itself. It'd be like redeeming the bad luck of finding ourselves in that place, in the middle of such scorching fetidness, which even made the partygoers faint in the middle of everything, creating a great commotion around us. Moreover, everyone should leave that darkness with the dangerous sensation that they fucked without a name. I left the dark room with a towel around my waist and stretched out on one of the lounge chairs. I thought of looking for a salacious masseur, so I could, before him, close my eyes and receive a third body of arid constitution, born from either direct experience or the imagination, or from a mix between the two. I asked the gods that the images produced in my brain dominate my interior field. On the surface, I keep on fucking, but my attention is turned inward, where an erotic ideation makes me run my mouth over his entire body. In the inebriating rhythm of these thoughts, I'm shocked to see a young man who has just arrived. It is my son—he's only eighteen years old! He hasn't seen me yet. I think about leaving the bathhouse through the French exit. But would I spend the rest of my life trying to hide from him? It's then I see that he's undressing by the metal lockers. He is with the son of my friend, the one who followed me in the improper gesture of giving away my wedding ring. I am lying naked on the lounge chair, and I'll stay here. Let them see me and let me see them. Let the world contain the three of us in the same space and time. My son looks like his mother. His friend doesn't know who I am, and he looks at me, yes, and he has a semi-erection. My son's friend looks like his father. What does he see in me? Some atavistic suggestion of his father's youthful past? I am a common man, one who doesn't shoot at close range and is capable of alleviating another's burden. A man who leaves no trace. And maybe my very ineptitude in standing out is the reason why my son's boyfriend has an erection when he sees me. I, a common man like so many, will not bring you paradise or sorrows. I am the anonymous man, the one who can disappear without leaving any memory behind. That's why my son's boyfriend is carried away with an instant erection, and so am I, I'm not going to deny it, I can't control myself. My son is the one who knows how to keep a poker face. I wake to a man wrapped in a towel trying to tell me something. He asks me for some money to help the South American cause. Another with the same obsession. And this obsession has reached a continental dimension. Even at this bathhouse we're not saved from the ritual begging. Everyone is asking on behalf of not only their nation but now the neighboring countries too. Who has created this circuit of pleading that keeps spreading? Who's benefiting from it? And moreover, doesn't everyone else lose? Have they predicted there might be some disagreeing with the bleeding plea for the cause? It seems they haven't. I ask the man to follow me. I go to my locker and grab my wallet. I give him a generous bill so he'll let me sleep at last. He thanks me, all tearful. I knock on the masseur's door. He comes out. I see there's a big-bellied man lying inside the room. The fat man seems impatient with the momentary interruption of his professional services. The masseur tells me I'm next. The customer leaves the room with an angry look on his face. As if he had been passed over because of my insidious request. He wanted more, of course, but didn't dare to ask. I go in. The masseur changes the sheets where I'll lie down. He asks me to lie on my stomach first. I obey, fall asleep. When I wake up in that semi-dark chamber, I tell myself I'll be chaste outside my marriage from now on. I need to get money from my locker to pay for the massage. The professional looks at me sideways, with a half-smile. I know his expression wants to tell me something beyond the massage itself. I'll need more money then. This game is going to cost me a fortune. He locks the door. There goes my intention of investing my whole sexual appetite into my marital bed. I remove the towel from my waist. I had no intention of moving forward with this transaction, but the man in white enlists me, and I'm in no condition to refuse. He undresses. And we start our battle upon the massage table. The table makes a horrible noise, it starts breaking apart. We move to a bare mattress by the wall. He murmurs words that are absolutely out of place for such contact. He calls me "love," "sweetheart." And what's worse: I believe in the sentiment of the words coming out of this guy's mouth. Maybe he had been observing me for a while. After all, I'm a frequent guest in the bathhouse. This guy I'm making love with, on a mattress with no sheets, would abandon everything to follow me. And I would abandon my family. This guy and I would make a visceral pair. Not even old age could tear us apart. I get up, wrap the towel around me, and get the money to pay for his added service. I'm generous with my tip. Then, I go home. I knock on my son's bedroom door. He opens it. I tell him that business on the farm is getting better and I'm thinking of buying him a car. He should take some driving lessons, get a license. After all, he just turned eighteen. I thought he was going to get mad at me. But he seemed happy with the promise of a car. Where would he go behind the wheel? Who would he take with him? I don't need to touch him to show him my affection. I just need to give him a car, much easier. The last time I cuddled him, he was on his mother's lap. He cried out, and I'm not sure he understood my gesture. He kept crying, and I stepped out to smoke a cigarette. When I came back, the house rested in crystalline silence. As if I lived alone. I sat on a chair in the living room. I waited for the next familial episode. My wife is lying in bed, her back against the wall. She watches television. She just accepts me for who I am. She follows me through all my seasons. Phases in which I avoid sex with complete determination. Not phases, more like years. Then, there are seasons, like now, when I want to fuck every day. Clara knows I'm approaching her to suggest we have a compact version of an orgy, just the two of us. She liked it when I suggested this to her for the first time, a few days ago, in the car, going to the movies to rewatch *Barry Lyndon*. Bingo: she turns off the TV and starts undressing. I pull my clothes off, scratching myself in the process. I put my finger between her wet, tepid lips. I'm burning; I think this will be our best fuck in years. I mount her, knowing the right moment to penetrate. But my cock won't get hard. It's the first time I feel impotent and my cock gives no hope of returning to life that day or the next, or even in the near future. Going soft is a common bump in the road for any great lover, even the most athletic ones. That night, however, I felt something in the air that made me believe shit was serious, that I needed to see a doctor if I ever wanted to have a full erection instead of this pathetic penis, shrunken with shame. I got off my wife and went to the bathroom. Certainly I wouldn't be able to fall asleep, all bothered with my impotence. I needed to go out, back to the bathhouse, find that masseur again, ask for a massage, and get fucked in the ass so I'd have a plan B if my cock decided to go permanently soft. Yes, because if I presented him with my back, he wouldn't see my frontal disability. If I ended up impotent for the rest of my life, I'd get used to getting fucked, yeah, I'd start liking that action, maybe I'd get addicted to it. I'd have anal orgasms, that's it. Addiction. Yes, addiction, a dictatorial need to surrender every time desire was aroused in me—and it had been happening more frequently recently. Now and forever would become one, simultaneously part of a carnal and metaphysical current. Between the experiences of now and forever, there'd be periodic drains to transport the residue of the present into the dead chimera of tomorrow. Honestly, I don't know why this insane trafficking between here and there needs to exist. With luck maybe one could sketch an image, even if confused, of the eternity between one experience and another. Then the two lovers wouldn't have to abandon their embrace. Even if they parted. Tonight, my pecker has shrunk disastrously without any remedy in sight. I have stopped distilling libido. I have stopped taking advantage of the generous pus flowing from the wound. I've begun to feel hungry without a chance to satiate. My soul complains, but I no longer have the flesh to translate its suffering. My wife goes back to watching TV. I leave the bathroom, still naked, and ask her to listen to me. She brings her eyes to meet mine and waits. I lower my head. It's a summer night. The struggle of trying to fuck without success has left me drenched in sweat. The night watchman's whistle reminds me that I must do something about my overall sloppiness. I look at my wife. She's asleep. I get dressed to go out. I step carefully; the house is asleep. I close the door, *pianissimo*. The moon is an invitation, I don't know to what exactly. I'm in front of the bathhouse. It's all dark, closed. I remember the masseur's name: Bernardo. I call to him. First, in a low voice. Then louder, each time. I seem to be someone standing in a somber desolation, asking to enter the first catacomb available so a brother can renew me. Dogs start barking because of all my shouting. I hear the key in the door. It's him, Bernardo, who shows up. I say I came to pick him up for a drink, have some wine. He's only wearing shorts. His physique belongs to the ideal proportions of the world. True Greek art, though already a bit in decay. His bellybutton stands proudly atop a trail of hairs that spreads into a thicket of pubes down below. He says he's going to put on a shirt and be right back. I take account of him slowly, trying not to think of my recent erectile dysfunction. There, alone, waiting for the masseur so we could hit the town, I thought I was on the verge of losing what little I had accumulated so far. Almost nothing, to be honest. Compared to my closest classmates from school, I was the only one who hadn't multiplied my family's assets. My meek inheritance had been enough so far. Better, they kept me grounded. My material world existed in a morose state, unhealthy even, but with no major disasters. I felt, yes, satisfied with the strictly symbolic values of my assets, just as I felt about the ties I had with my wife and son. Hard to believe, but today I was part of a family, something I couldn't imagine in my youth. What did I possess that I could convert into cash? An apathetic little farm, trickling a reluctant monthly profit. I'll repeat to exhaustion: the family, barely supported by the sad farm, also has a house in Porto Alegre. In a neighborhood with laconic inhabitants living off furtive crimes typical of their class. Bernardo came back. He was wearing a white t-shirt and yellow shorts. Vatican colors. I thought I could offer him this piece of information later in the evening, and if he laughed, I could steal a kiss from him, lick his tongue with mine. But where in Porto Alegre could we allow ourselves such an audacity? Where in the city could you do these things besides semi-clandestine enclosures or in the sewer, pure and simple? I was living at my limit. So much so that I wanted to become the masseur, always prepared for the moment the flesh was asked to decide. I tried to laugh so he wouldn't need to console me. I tried to be a man, give him three pats on his back, steal a quick kiss on his face, like a macho who allows himself some liberties, going with the flow of being hammered, though the booze was still to come. But I was afraid of going soft again. Though I knew that failing with another man was not so paralyzing, since, in such a case, one can just proffer his butt and let the other one fuck him, as painful as that can be. In the end, after struggling to extract pleasure from my internal misery, I'd turn over and lie on my stomach, my lover's semen nested in the deepest abyss of my ass. After a while, I'd fall asleep. I'd fall asleep remembering the tip of his glans pressing its way into the darkness of my guts with a rare determination. And the explosion of sperm inside me, I would also remember that. Next time, the impotent would be better off opting for reliable fellatio, simply falling to his knees with his mouth open to the offered cock. But again, for now, I try to laugh so Bernardo won't suffer the temptation to console me. I'm in the middle of the sidewalk, smiling, and Bernardo returns my smile, amplifying it. It's then he says we could go inside the building; there's nobody in there. This guy, who was getting ready to travel through the night with me, was now asking me to enter the deserted bathhouse. What did he notice in me that made him decide? Did he realize we could amp up our game in the ambiance of the sauna? I go in, and I follow him along the dark hall. He asks me to hold his hand, he'll guide us. His hand is smooth, perfect for massages. Bernardo refuses to turn on the lights and explains it's better this way. It won't raise any suspicions for the bathhouse owner. Besides, if we fuck in the dark, in a world without shapes, it'll be easier for me to evoke the ghost of a third man—his body is oblivious to the darkness in here. Before he arrives, without warning, I notice an agitation in the darkness, imprecise figures, reminiscent of the earlier enactments, dozens and dozens of bodies lulled by a eucalyptus aroma. This aroma suggests one is in a place where the beautiful, healthy, athletic, and restorative are worshiped, miles and miles away from the population's messy dramas. Then the skin of the third man emerges, exuberant though rarefied, offering its nakedness to the mirage's proprietor, this guy here, who plans to leave all this arduous debauchery behind one day. But, meanwhile, the image's proprietor takes himself inside the deserted sauna to play a role in this blind battle without winners or losers. We kissed each other with anxiety, sometimes making the noise of lips missing the intended target or roughly retreating from the other's lips. A jelly-like feeling, perhaps. I was an authentic image-maker of erotic larvae. Bernardo could use the rich repertoire of images from his massage customers; I did not possess such a private reserve of so many men—in truth, I only had my engineer friend, and he was safe now, no longer a castaway. The eternal postponing of our carnal contact supposed a promise of the most breathtaking quality. While this suffering lasted, we'd be rehearsing our craziest choreography. By delaying the party, we bolstered the power for our bed's eventual Eden. After all, we had already decanted that sentiment from our shared abstention. Our chances were immense. I—who had never made love to him, who hadn't experienced the bliss of his pores—had an endless field of fantasies to explore on his body. Maybe I would find the sum of all my absences in my engineer friend. I promised myself, on the day we finally became available to each other's nakedness, I'd manifest a special touch on the bee tattoo on his foreskin—I'd teach that insect to make honey. I'd find myself on his skin like an austere sultan. But not yet, not today. Today, I still belonged to Bernardo. We were devouring each other in the sauna's shadows, each exercising his own abstract contortionism. Our bodies crashed against each other in the most unlikely positions, and I'd leave that place covered in bruises and with a cigarette burn on my dickhead. I felt no pain from the ember on my skin; I didn't notice any lit cigarette. I didn't sense an ambush. I started jerking off so Bernardo and I could come together, or at least close. We both went at it, with the same intensity, in search of that expanded minute—something that, once grasped between our figures, only provoked more lust in such hungry turmoil. I imagined my engineer friend naked, and I wanted him even more as I saw him beating my cock off, his face so close to it, to receive my creamy ropes on his face. Bernardo stopped; he had shot his load, it hit me. In Bernardo's company, I brought the memory of my engineer friend to life, but from that moment on, his image no longer existed in the dark cosmos of the sauna's eclipse. That severe darkness seemed more sensual than any visit from a full-color erotic ghost. The blackness could shelter lovers from the deprivation of sight. The darkness negated everything I needed to see. All that was left for me to do was to stick my hand inside a tantric body and gradually intoxicate myself with my soul's dispersions. There was nothing and nowhere I could fix my gaze besides the deepest dark of darkness... I wanted to present myself to the shadows with total availability. There was now a sharp concentration of skin, as if nothing else existed. Everything I needed was here, a few feet away from me in the dark. Bernardo brought his nose to my hand, which had just jerked off my dick. I didn't think my dick smelled bad. I thought he was just performing a regular inspection between tricks. How many acts broken by intermission? Anyway, he wanted to know if the thing down there still had a male scent. A scent of emphatic muskiness, which some colognes try to intensify by adding tones of the wilderness or something like that. Bernardo couldn't see what was happening to me; I didn't need to examine my intimate parts *post-coitus*, a moment almost always inglorious. The truth is that I left this encounter the same way I had come in, shrunken, after some timid suggestions of tumescence. And if I came? Well, I ejaculated. A lot of people come into this world thanks to a semi-hard dick. The cum erupts, even if indisposed, to award the timid health. One sticks his penis into a wet obscurity and feels obligated to launch his milky gift into the depths of hell. But today, the ghost of my friend in a faraway land hadn't shown up to help me. I was unable to replace Bernardo's body with the engineer's image. I couldn't run to his embrace. I'd make all the promises in the world to have the engineer back in Porto Alegre again. He was a sad man, and I had a sincere appreciation for sad men. I'd give him a kiss. And a touch that'd turn into a cuddle, and a cuddle that'd turn into abandonment. Abandonment and a feeling of satiety. Satiety and then a renewed involvement. Bernardo took me to the door and out into the torrid night. He stood there, in front of the bathhouse. He was the one who seemed satiated. He spoke with clarity, without his usual speed. He didn't babble. He was satiated while I felt bad, in a state of scarcity, wanting to try another man, hoping that *he* would know how to instill the vigor that had recently run from me. We shook hands and said goodbye. Bernardo's satiation didn't sit well with me. When he wanted, I receded. Now that I wanted, he cooled down. If there existed a perfectly synchronized embrace between lovers, by way of Aphrodite's tricks, I could get over trifling concerns such as bad breath and things like that. Hours earlier, during our first fuck, Bernardo had called me my love, my sweetheart. Why had he abandoned this vocabulary in such a short time? If those words had really meant something, I could've asked him to let me reign a little more over the realm of his desires, let me be the man to restore his erotic ambition. Anyway, I couldn't go back home, I thought, walking fast down the street. I needed to go somewhere in the city that I still couldn't identify, and as soon as possible. Walking down José Bonifácio street, I saw a rent boy hanging around Redenção Park. I approached him and asked how much it was. He gave me his price, which I thought was reasonable. I invited him to go to a bar first, right there on João Pessoa street, and he agreed. I said I'd pay him later. The boy said that was how things worked, anyway. We had many, many beers. Sometimes, he'd go behind the counter, showing some familiarity with the bar owner. And he'd come back with things in his hands. Things he'd pour into my glass. He'd say it was just to add some flavor. I knew that was not it; that it was a sedative or something—I had read articles about these rent boys who dropped mysterious pills into their client's drinks so they could more easily steal their wallets when they passed out. I saw all that coming, but I had no strength to avoid such a disaster. Let the boy exercise his own nighttime rites, let him steal whatever he wanted from me. I was offering everything, letting myself become enraptured by what was unfolding. It came to me that, before I lost control of the situation, I should reach out to the boy's body and excite him. Before he could steal everything from me, I needed to approach that body now stretched in bed—it might have been a bed in a cheap hotel typical of those types of encounters, I don't know, I don't remember where I was—but I approached him and started undressing him, slowly, trailing my tongue across him, from head to toe and back. When his arousal came, obeying his age's dynamo, I'd deal with my own body, whack my cock and overflow white champagne over the whore's freckled skin. It'd be a wank not to the pale young man in flesh and bone, but to the maddening idea I had of him during our spectacular drinking binge. My cock would grow in length and width, and I'd join our two pricks, frottaged into a single phallus, like I was doing in this moment—if only I could still find some enjoyment with my head being so nebulous, and without being in any condition to discern a full impression, let alone achieve any conclusion. What I know is that the boy stood up and I fell from the bed, grabbing his legs. What did that begging position mean? Maybe a biblical scene. Wrapped in a sheet, I looked like a leper begging for a miracle. Or an individual already paralyzed, spending his time crawling at the feet of luminous young men. I was in no condition to distinguish a set choreography from a living picture like this. But while I was thinking about that, out of nowhere came a kick in my stomach, and I shut up. Now I was a slave. I had no chance or voice. I was sure the boy would end me right there. He kicked me in the chest. From what I could see, a splash of blood gushed out of my arm and hit me right in the eye. If it were a movie, blood would spray on the camera. There, lying on the ground, without feeling any pain, lying there, hazy, hazy, I touched my groin. I had recovered a stable erection. For good? My erection was steady, without the need for manual stimulation, steady and firm. In the past, during fuck sessions with random partners, I had found myself in hairy situations, but I've always been lucky in not injuring my cock. I brought my hand to my groin, and I noticed my dick throbbed, offering the forthcoming orgasm to the night. I felt my semen was about to spurt, overwhelming me with fantastic abundance. I was about to cum, the thing was going to explode, yes, but in that moment, I received another kick, this time in my groin. Again, I didn't really feel any pain; what I know is that, upon being kicked, I finally came, so intensely it seemed an act of dying. Then I passed out. When I woke up, I didn't understand what was happening. I couldn't even identify the surroundings where my body lay. Hushed voices all around me. Suddenly, they brought a stretcher to the side of the bed and carried me away. Later on, they opened my pajama shirt, spread something gooey on my chest, and affixed some instruments to listen to my heart. On the screen, images of the king-muscle looked like a planet surrounded by gigantic clouds. Along the borders, a legitimate sky formed a storm—black and purple. The noise my heart produced in the equipment was bombastic, frightening. Its rhythm reminded me of heavy metal percussion. Before that day, I'd never imagined I carried the potential for such a magnitude of sound in my chest. In that moment, I had no doubt I was nothing more than a

machine, and everything depended on this con-
traption's whim. That didn't make me sad. On the
contrary, it increased my appreciation for the body's
insular construction. I surrendered to medical ex-
ams, waiting for the moment, hopefully imminent,
that I'd be discharged. I simply had no autonomy in
the circumstance. And that bothered me more than
the concussions I had suffered. I could hear children shouting outside my window. That sound hurt
me. Unable to be among children playing made me
feel as if I was banned from human joy. If I found
the strength to get up and leave, I'd be stopped in
the hospital halls. Later, they stuck me in my room
again, closed the curtains, and turned off the lights.
I fell asleep. When I opened my eyes, my wife and
son were by my side, bent over me. There was a
strong smell of flowers. Was it my funeral? What
was this remnant of consciousness that evoked me
and my family, was it a virtue or, on the contrary,
did it just want to instigate my vain denouement?
My son and wife's expressions now formed a gaze
as if I were indeed a corpse—they frowned over the
faltering vessel of flesh that still retained and represented me. I told my son my body hurt so much.
Bruises, he reminded me. I asked him to bring me
a mirror so I could see the damage. I was bothered
by the possibility I wouldn't find the same face I'd

had before. But what did my former face look like?
He brought me a mirror. What's hell is that I really
didn't remember how my physiognomy looked before. Plus, my sight had declined tremendously. A
stubborn cloud covered my eyes. Disfigured and
dominated by forgetfulness, I yearned for sleep.
Only my wife and son grounded me a little. And if
I managed to reconstruct a remote passage back to
what I had been…would that bring a new tone to
my composition? I opened my pajama top. I
checked the contusions on my chest and the ones
down my belly and groin. The only thing my brains
kept intact was the freckled body of that whore, exploding with a unique anger. My wife and son stood
by me, but I couldn't tell if they had access to the
police report, constructed before I was dramatically
brought to the hospital. I forced my memory beyond, before the rent boy, but the act of recall also
hurt me. Remembering was asking too much from
my ruins. The vacuum of consciousness turned out
to be colossal. I was floating on the hospital bed as
if being lifted by small ocean waves, and my wife
and son were gone. Was my atavistic vision a kind
of unexpected euphoria that marked the final moments before the end? Before the final moment, a
certain impulse arises, and the prognosis improves
to the point where there's some hope for recovery;

until, hours later, out of the blue, comes the fall. Amid these considerations, an image began to inspire me: two men fucking in the dark. Were there still erotic zones to explore in them or myself? So somber was the scene of these two men that their figures could not be discerned—their presence was only felt through the sounds of their moans and contact. With titanic effort, I brought my hand to my cock and balls. My prick was once again big and swollen after its momentary prostration, just like the last time I had seen it in that state. Where was that, again? Had I been alone or with someone? I could reassemble my memory via the reconstruction of each physical environment corresponding to my fornication. I always had the habit of registering the weather conditions during every dirty encounter I had in a personal notebook. What was the weather when I fucked my wife for the first time? It rained hard, and we arrived soaking wet at a motel. Before going to our room, we crossed an internal courtyard that reminded us of the motel in *Psycho*. Was it hot or cold? Mid-season. Spring, if I'm not mistaken, rosewoods were blooming in Porto Alegre. It seemed efficient to relive all the nuances and carnal paths I've experienced via this method— surely my most unforgettable moments. Today, I may have about forty notebooks. I'm very sensitive to the weather and its changes from sun to rain, from warm to cold. I never found conversations about weather, temperature, or seasons boring. Now in the hospital, for example, it is cold, and the light is intensely white. I, who've had so many random lovers, in cold and warm weather, needed to remember them so I could get through my inertia and loneliness. The two men moaned in the dark. My wife and son remained intact in the core of my memory, but even they couldn't give me anything more than merely being my wife and my son. Tomorrow, when the staff decide to open the curtains and I can bathe myself in light, I'll ask them to bring me a pencil and paper. I'll write the messages. It'd be a shame to miss the opportunity, though I don't believe I'll have much left to say by tomorrow. But, in case words come to me now, regardless of their meek or non-existent content, they'll transmit their inherent enchantment. Words' natural enchantments would come from this deficient fountain here: me. In the meantime, this is it: the insistent image of two men fucking in pitch-dark, broadcasting fragments of dirty talk, moans and groans, the glories of pleasure seekers. I felt gunk in my hand, thick and syrupy like melted sugar. I had ejaculated. Maybe my sleeping son had his own wet dream at that exact instant. He was going through a phase of nocturnal emissions. During sleep, his crotch displayed this uncontrollable, huge bulge. And what about me, was it really an ejaculation I had? The truth is that sex took over my life. If I died now, I'd have a respectable ledger of small and distinct thrills to show for—all because of sex. I was constantly reborn with every outburst of libido. As much as I'd get disappointed by one partner or another, and as much as I needed to escape from someone's presence after I came, I knew how to touch another body; it was as if I'd touched a live wire and died, then was born again from the same electric shock. First, I followed a path from arousal toward erection; then, from culmination to exhaustion. After that, I'd also embark on some sort of path to insomnia. To escape the sensation of being an idyllic impostor, I could perhaps turn to the wall and count to ten—this was part of an agreement I had with an angel friend of mine, so I could fall asleep fast with the promise of a dreamless sleep. After all, these considerations alleviated my daily condition. Which was a lot already. Again, I smell the two men copulating in total darkness. I hear a commotion, typical of those who have an orgasm and catch their breath between one dirty cock and another, one delirious mouth and another, one bodily capsule and another. Everything else felt cold to me. I felt cold, and ideas occurred to me as drafts only—I made peace with them on my pillow and fell asleep with them. On those days, words presented the same meaning to me as teddy bears to children. Without them, I'd feel like the most fragile being among mortals. When I tried to collect the words and hide them in my pajama pockets, I noticed they had already dissolved. The only signs of life came from the unrelenting rhythm of the two bodies ardently grabbing each other in the shadows. The lovers of darkness play a game where they attach their bodies, and together they rise in a crescendo before overflowing; then they retreat only to start all over again. Suddenly, silence returned. It's then I felt a hand over mine. I woke up. The curtains were shut and filtered the day's brightness. There was a strange, ochre-colored penumbra. Now I could hear the nurses speaking and laughing in the hall. Only then was I able to discern who had touched my hand. Simply, my engineer friend. I recognized him like I had my wife and my son. He had returned to Porto Alegre. Had he kept his office with the chipped desk? He'd saved himself and was back in town. Or was he a specter created in my thoughts? So, had he sought shelter and protection from the entity of libidinal resistance in Berlin? It must have been an NGO with one post on dry land

and another one under water. If I could speak, I'd
ask him if the German submarine was still at the
bottom of the sea. Or if it had been pulled out of
the water and its parts sent to some nautical museum in Germany. Did they pile up the castaways'
belongings, their rings, chains, and watches that
still worked fine even after being submerged? I
quibbled in gray areas so I didn't have to face my
engineer friend in all his titanic splendor. I feared I
couldn't handle it. That I'd die. At the same time,
on another plane, I was recovering the memory of
everything, hyperstimulated as I began to see my
love again. All this might sound maudlin for someone who hasn't faced death yet. But when you go
through such an infinite weakness, you start amplifying the wonder you felt in your glory days for
the one who had seduced you beyond your wildest
dreams. I did remember, yes, that I had a history,
even if it was, often or almost always, unruly. I was
again a man among men. My engineer friend represented a bit of that male nobility—somewhat
confusing, truth be told; even more so for him,
who was a virgin to my body and had to confront
my never-ending appetite. Now, here he was, with
his hand resting over mine, making me revisit my
past from the beginning. I remember leaving my
childhood behind, full of desire, craving to be

among bodies that most of the time had the same anatomy as me. I looked at him and shivered. I couldn't accept the idea that, for the rest of my life, there'd be no space to embrace the peerless figure of this blessed dark man. He seemed indeed to be arriving from afar, with his mind still fixated on lands he had just recently bidden farewell to, though I'm not sure if with sadness or relief. His head was shaved. He looked like an apparition, standing by the bedside of his withering friend. I, who still couldn't believe he'd broken his supposed chastity and surrendered himself to the crew of a German submarine—a country with such a sad past. The bee tattooed on his foreskin was a sign from a time when nobody had enjoyed that dick yet. It was a sign that the invader would be stung if he dared to trespass. His skin looked darker now, he had the air of an Arab. Angola's sun? Then, he asked me something. I thought of answering, but there was a colossal weight on my chest, right at the base of my larynx. He asked me if I wanted to stay at his place for a while. He could take care of me. I asked myself if it was right to feel so much desire and desolation at the same time. I was still unwell. And, once again, a man was giving me a chance. This time he was inviting me to stay at his house for a while, right when I was in no condition to leave the hospital alive. Everything arrived late for me. If I had any strength left, I'd get up and try to kiss him. Maybe he wanted the same. He could embrace me and kiss what was left of my hair; and I'd kiss his neck and lick his ear, my tongue crawling through its exotic maze. In my pajamas, I would wave goodbye when he left for the office. On his chipped desk, the engineer would dive into the calculations of a new project. Winter would be so melancholy when he left for his calculations early in the mornings. He'd forget me every day a bit more with each project. That's when I woke up. I as laying on a bed covered with white sheets in the middle of a salon. The salon was empty. A vigil in a chapel? A crematorium? Had the mourners taken a coffee break? All was manifested in white. There was just one other person in the room besides me. He was sitting on a bench, leaning against the white wall. I realized he was my engineer friend. He got up and came to me. We can go now, he said, helping me get up. I didn't feel any pain or discomfort. Nor weakness. The first thing I asked myself was if I had been transferred to a minor version of paradise. He and I, isolated on a white island. And more. I was fully dressed, wearing my old shoes. Shoes? Another reason to suspect I was dead. And on my soles, surprising remnants of the earth—weird, because I was such an urban creature. What was my engineer friend doing here with me? I had no idea, whatever the hypothesis was: me, dead or alive. If I was dead, was my body going through a final delirium in which the engineer was the protagonist? I felt severely cold. I didn't give in to the inertia that was descending on me. My heart beat with a vigorous rhythm. I faithfully kept up with this vigor so as not to expose myself to the worst. I didn't even need to follow the seconds on the clock to confirm the mechanical pace of my heartbeat. My friend offered me his hand, and we climbed out of a sort of ravine whose sides were not so high. Was I leaving a trench? A pit of pipelines? A tomb? I had a headache now. My engineer friend walked ahead, guiding me, informing me: We're going to take a Bandeirante plane; we don't have the luxury of counting on a submarine amid all this. I noticed he regretted saying that. Where are we going? I asked. To Cuiabá first, then we'll see. Why Cuiabá? I asked. We heard a child crying, holding out a piggy bank, asking for help for the Brazilian cause. Right at that moment, I realized I might be someone slowly saying farewell to death. Because I had started to remember. And my engineer friend was back to help feed my memory. With him, life had returned. Life and its functions. My engineer friend would be my new master from then on. I'd never really had one. Suddenly, I trembled at the thought of my luck. I remembered he had a bee tattooed on his foreskin. It was his cock's watchdog. In fact, when I saw the bee for the first time, he might have been living in intervals between fucks, considering he had the men in the submarine available to him at any time. With me, he always played hard-to-get, always kept me on the back burner. Sure, he performed the role of the dear friend, or even boyfriend sometimes, but he sublimated it all in the name of comradery. In the end, our friendship was always reduced to some harmless repertoire. The engineer might have seen me as just an incestuous threat to be continuously rejected to preserve our distant common past, predecessor to our flesh's servility. Let one rekindle a certain sultriness in the other, straight from what we used to be, from our childhood to adolescence, listening to the ice-cream man standing by his truck and playing his jingle to attract children. We'd approach the ice-cream man with so much desire, but with no money to buy anything. We were happy just looking at the cold mist coming from the freezer when the man opened the lid. Maybe the engineer insisted on seeing me through that prism. In those warm old days, we felt alleviated from the pressures of school and chores just by glimpsing the refrigerated compaction of that small well, just by admiring the colors inside. Will I continue receiving only angelic kindness from him, without committing to our physical components? Why was the German crew more deserving of his favors? I now followed the engineer with the intent of stopping if I couldn't get at least closer to his body heat, and, I don't know, lightly touch his shoulder, then envelop him in a cuddle even if it turned out to only be a brief embrace to make him feel my imprisoned desire. We got out of a taxi in front of the old airport in Porto Alegre, practically inactive. We went straight to the runway, where the small Bandeirante waited for us. The engineer got on the plane first. Then, he came out to tell me I could board, too. The pilot looked hunky wearing his sunglasses. Maybe he was a former pilot of the Brazilian Air Force and now worked on commercial flights. Crew cut. The Bandeirante took off with just a few people on board. Everybody looked shrunken in their seats; they were feeling either cold or abandoned, I'm not sure. Besides his classic sunglasses, the pilot also wore a red jacket made of shiny fabric, something from the 50s. An air of James Dean in *Rebel Without a Cause*. In Cuiabá, a scorching heat greeted us. We took a taxi to the house that'd be ours, way beyond the city's suburbs, in the bush the driver told us, bush that got thicker and thicker as we advanced. We arrived at a brick house, still showing the plaster. Inside, the walls were not painted either. I opened the kitchen door. On the table: pans, silverware, plates, two oranges. At that moment, the engineer stepped aside and stood at the window in the main room. He contemplated his new yard. Perhaps he envisioned exercising his talent for gardening. He had his elbows on the windowsill. His butt and thighs stuck out prominently on account of how low he had to bend over the sill. Something was becoming clear to me: he would be my man. And he had set up the kitchen and all its paraphernalia just for me. So, I would take care of the kitchen and prepare good meals for the couple. And I would have to clean and do laundry, too. Something was telling me that if I organized my days according to this mysterious plan, I'd be rewarded with the engineer's body every night. It was the only way I could have everything I'd always wanted. This man would be mine, at last. I just had to be the wife he dreamed of. Yes, this man had indeed been the stud in the submarine. He fucked everyone and left that experience even more discreet than when he came to it. His travel companions had all died because of the catastrophic crack in the submarine's shell. The newspapers described it as a terrorist act. But the engineer, oh, my engineer, was able to escape the disaster and spend time on a beach in Angola. He had lived off fishing on the African coast. He couldn't go back to Germany, because he knew well that the hunt for sodomites continued all over the country. Did my engineer define himself as a sodomite, too? I suppose he liked fucking ass, for sure. Doesn't the word sodomite apply only to someone who likes to *be* fucked in the ass? What mattered was that he was alive. And that made me smile. I was telling all these things to the crowd of idiots tormenting my head with their voices. But they didn't give a fuck about my confessions. I didn't believe all that talk about his retention in Germany after surviving the shipwreck. I couldn't remember the other versions of the story. Did they exist? Well, I gave in; I started accepting all versions, so I didn't have to believe in any. My engineer friend had come back to Brazil to have me by his side. I, the translator of the woman I'll never be. I go into the kitchen and wonder how I'm going to make this happen. I have never cooked before. Now, however, it'll be a different story: the trophy for my domestic skills would be the man I had always been in love with. And we would both play parts in the production of this story. I needed to do well. If indeed my culinary gifts would reward me with his physical presence, then I could already see myself frying eggs, stirring them with shrimp, trying a bit of it from the pan, adding a bit more salt, black pepper, rosemary, basil. I went to tell him that I'd managed to cook something with the little I had found and that the meal was almost ready. He continued standing in the same position, his thighs and butt turned to me as if he wanted to tease me. I wondered if that's how life would be from now on: a world made only of apotheosis. Wouldn't cooking, cleaning, and laundry be my great pleasure if I could deserve my thousand-and-one-nights with him? Yes, I'd have no routine anymore. The laborious execution of the hours would simply be my form of payment for those lustful nights. And every night, I would learn what I never knew before. There was a dress, along with an apron and a towel, hanging from an improvised clothesline near the woods in the backyard. They seemed to have been waiting for me. The animal noises in the forest intrigued me. There was danger, but also a call… On the table with dirty plates, I asked him if he had any news about my wife and son. After all, I had been unconscious for such a long time… At least, that was what the engineer told me. That my grave had been violated. My corpse, kidnapped. Everybody thought you were dead, my man told me with a somber frown. Only I know I wasn't, I said. And you, I hope, I added. I hope you're looking at a man who never died. The police believe the violators wanted your cadaver to sell it to some kind of continental cause. There it is again, the so-called cause, assaulting us on the streets for our money, and now after our own corpses. Why did they choose my body? I felt a chill. A satanic organization would continue to follow my every step even after my official death. And by doing that, were they confirming my resurrection? Yes, they wanted me alive in this story, even if, in the end, my death was to be included in the script. Did they want an individual with a post-mortem resume? Well, they found him. Who would follow me through the forests of Western Brazil? I might have been the catalyst of a big mortuary confusion. I didn't know if I found myself dead or alive anymore. The continental charity brigade seemed unapproachable from every angle. Everything happened in total autonomy. There wasn't any structural center that controlled the embezzlement of the collected funds. Justice washed its hands. I'd say it was a stupid plan, if that wasn't exactly the way the head of the gang had found to disguise himself. Meanwhile, the two of us talked under the starry night sky on the outskirts of the outskirts of Cuiabá.

The engineer kept talking. One hour after your burial, I broke into your tomb, a fairly easy task since the tomb wasn't yet covered by cement or marble. You resurrected me! I roared, as if I was an evangelical having a spiritual conversion at church. And I felt a sense of ridiculousness for being in front of a man who has literally done the impossible. An idea came to me: the goal of resuscitating me was only that I eventually participate in the fabulous and final sacrifice. Namely, it was a super-generous gesture from the engineer that'd also force me to watch the cosmic spectacle of infinite destruction. Would this monumental threat be the source of all evil? Would I be saved from the apocalypse if I joined the engineer on this final day? Would we then wander in the arms of chimaeras? The engineer goes on: When I was a boy, we had a maid named Tina. One day, her father gave me a shovel as a gift. Tina's father was a gravedigger. I used that shovel—which I always carried with me no matter my destination—yes, it was with that shovel that I dug you out of the land of corpses. I opened the lid of your coffin and said, Come! Evangelical rhetoric to evoke the ceremony that the moment required. Your coffin smelled like the white roses inside. They still looked lush. But extraordinarily, they would die before you—who now look so alive and shiny again. The moon bathed the cemetery with its buttery light. I abducted your corpse. You took long breaths without moving your diaphragm. I could tell you were back among the living by the way you coughed. Just the slight discomfort of a mild cold. I put my lips against yours and blew air into you, and still more air. I noticed your skin coming back to life. I laid your defenseless body on my car's backseat. I had no doubt. I knew you had been buried alive. I touched your tepid skin and tried to guess your circulation's health. I felt I was the father of life every time I reminded myself that only I could really reach you. During the short time you were buried, you had enough air inside the space of your coffin. You were rescued from under the ground less than an hour after your burial, so you were still alive when I reached you. My clothes were covered with dirt. The conviction that you were still alive grew inside me during your memorial service. Don't forget that my family had a maid when I was a child, Tina, whose father was a gravedigger. He always returned to this subject, conveying to me that he was quite knowledgeable in the art of gravedigging. He instructed me, with a certain authority, on the affairs of cadaveric residencies. When I finished removing the earth from your tomb, I saw a cockroach on top of your coffin. I crushed it with my shoe; then, I opened the lid. And there you were, the same as usual, with a calm expression on your face, bathed in moonlight. I bent over your body, stuck my mouth to yours, and brought your breath back. When I was a boy, I went to the cemetery in the afternoons to watch Tina's father prepare the graves for new cadavers. Usually, the coffin with a fresh corpse was laid in the same communal grave with the rest of the family's bones, which were now reduced to almost nothing. One afternoon, Tina's father took me to see an open grave. All the way down, I saw a tiny, modest white coffin. A dead child. Tina's father got down into the hole and opened the coffin. I noticed, agonizingly, that it was a perfectly intact skeleton of a child, around five years old, I'd say. It's my son, the old man said. Well, I'm not sure if he still is, he continued. Can the pitiful contents of this box be someone's child? I wondered if the gravedigger applied some special treatment to keep those bones in such good condition. A consequence of his ill-fated fatherhood. Like any other, as a matter of fact. Perhaps, he'd added some homemade concoction to the mortal remains. With such preparations, the dead were deceived with the paint of permanence. Trembling, Tina's old man picked up a tibia bone. The gesture seemed to indicate a ceremony through which, with some severe type of love, he could say goodbye to his son, at last. I wondered if there was a way he could direct the love he felt for his son to me. This could be his moment to change the direction and destiny of his greatest affection. Yes, because, for now, he was saying farewell to his son's mortality. Later, in a faraway future, the farewell would happen in the realm of souls. Because, from that point on, the child would initiate his forceful insertion into eternity. Removing a piece of the skeleton was a masterful operation that deserved a bravo! He was indeed an audacious gravedigger. He handed me the bone so I could examine it. It's my son's, the old man repeated. Through that bone, the father introduced me to the whole of his son, to his body and antics—as he liked to call them. It was around that time that I began to think of becoming a gravedigger. I thought the profession could give me the opportunity to follow the eulogy of a son, a lover, friends, or even a historical figure. It'd be highly didactic, pedagogic even. I was most interested in what came after the fateful day. My curiosity was geared more in that direction than the years prior to a burial. And I was not interested in the afterlife either. I wanted to keep following the gradual dissolution of human matter, its fission into dust. That was indeed the gala history of humanity. As for the subject of the afterlife, I'd have nothing to add. Everybody knows that the examination of our carnal closure is inevitably brief, even laconic, if not inexistent. Studying mortuary degradation is a way of repairing the ignorance of these imperial centuries. All we know is that once a fellow expels his last sigh, we lose contact with him forever. That's why I wanted to be a gravedigger. The dead live longer than the living. They have an astonishingly superior duration. They start their perpetual season inside a closed casket—as far as hair, teeth, and bones are concerned. And their skeletons carry on for decades. It's admirable, the assisting gaze of a gravedigger on these skeletons coming out of their childhood, only to be dumped onto the hard clay. The dead children can rest with comfort, free from the fears of the unknown and the celestial beatitudes. Tina's father used to tell the story of a gravedigger married to a dead woman. He'd bring gifts to his beloved skeleton every Saturday. The passion had flourished as the woman was beginning her decay, when she had her open casket by her graveside, as was the norm for burials at the time. This gravedigger behaved like a feverish lover even when the woman's bones reached the stage of falling apart. He used to tell Tina's father that he would love the

dead woman until his last breath on earth. Her disintegration would last longer than a whole life; it'd
be a true eternity. This endless disintegration had
more stamina than the lifespan of the widower. At
the same time, he could not really be seen as a widower while any corporeal trace of his lover remained. His widowhood per se would be a long
time in coming. Until the groom noticed not a single grain of dust remained from her beloved body.
Only at that moment would our romantic allow
himself to drift away, his thoughts focused on her,
on that image now diffused into everything, already
free of the delusional composition of matter. Then,
yes, he would return to his loneliness. The gravedigger, the colleague of Tina's father, used to say that,
upon arriving at this place, he could kiss the air, the
marble, and everything else, because he'd be kissing
his beloved at her highest point of diffusion.
Perhaps, he could even dilute himself into this rarefaction with a magic trick? How would that be—
the two of them continuing to love each other in
the absolute dispersion of self? The fact is that the
dead woman was alive again in all things. Listen, I
finally stopped him to ask: is there a way I can be
buried next to my engineer friend's remains in the
future or vice-versa? He then opened his arms as if
he were going to hug me. What about my little

farm, what about my inheritances? I asked him, fearing I could lose track of my whole life until this point in our conversation. Do you still have any inheritance to receive? the engineer asked me, showing surprise. From whom, if your father and mother have been dead for such a long time? I blushed. After my time in the hospital and in the grave, sometimes I felt like a baby waiting for the secretive conspiracy that would finally distinguish me from the others. Being resurrected was already such a distinction. I was Lazarus, but nobody should know that. The life that was screaming out of me had started from the point of resurrection. Therefore, I didn't owe anything to anyone who had passed by me before I had died. The engineer came to me in the well of my tomb as an apparition, and he did what God had never done for me. In fact, the engineer had become God, from my point of view as a loyal, vulnerable man. Life before my death didn't count anymore. I had recovered my memory, and that made me an adult again. Sometimes, I suspected I was in a hurry to get back into the tomb. But really? In those days, death for me meant feeding on darkness. Thus, I had eaten that meal already, only in a hurried way. Forget about death; you've now come to this house in the middle of a vast heap of red earth to remake yourself. Here, everything

will do you good. What else do you want? And you?
I asked. Me? After the shipwreck, I gave up. I spent
some time fishing on the coast of Angola and ended
up here. Was that the authorized version of his biography? I wondered. I yanked you out of death
even though everyone else saw you as a corpse. The
secret of banishing darkness from a body that's apparently inert but still has blood circulating—this
secret was passed down to me from Tina's father.
He asked me not to reveal this secret to anyone.
Now, you're grateful to me and will continue to be
so for the rest of your time on Earth. Do I owe him
this much? I wondered. I was still trying, though
sluggishly, to understand the transition between my
death and where I found myself now, on the outskirts of Cuiabá. Coincidently, this transition, this
bridge, was the kind of job that required the super-
vision of an engineer. Here's the man, I thought.
Was it good or bad to live under the same roof with
someone who had doubled my life? Would I be
spoiled or enslaved? I looked at the engineer out of
the corner of my eye. I could never imagine that
one day I'd have a partner, maybe even a life-long
partner, a man who presented me with this unprecedented circumstance. He had revived me. Was
there any room left for miracles? What was at stake
for him in all this? Would he continue to work as

an engineer in the middle of nowhere? Night had
fallen. Soon, I would learn the dimensions of our
nocturne partnership. There were two bedrooms.
The first one had a queen bed. The other seemed to
be reserved as his office—a desk, some books on a
raw wooden shelf. I served dinner—not really dinner, but a type of evening breakfast that is common
in southern Brazil: bread, cold cuts, coffee with
milk, and crumb cake. The provisions were kept inside a kitchen cabinet—had they been left by a
southern gaucho? We seemed satisfied with our
meal, so I went to the main bedroom to change the
pillowcases and run my hand across the sheet to
smooth it out, whether that was needed or not—
things that a mother does for a son before he goes
to bed. These were gestures I did for the engineer
but also for myself, even though there were no
guarantees I'd be included in the mattress's promises. There I was, in that house without paint, turning on the light on the nightstand, ready to tend to
the engineer's wishes atop green sheets. There I was,
choosing to forget about the meek financial results
of my little farm. I also had to forget my son, my
wife, and everything else. I had died for that reality,
yes. I was condemned to live in Mato Grosso from
now on. By the engineer's side. That was the best
part of the story. I had been cured of death by his

arts. And if I were obliged to live, forcibly and eternally, in exchange for this man's love—even if we didn't engage in any sexual contact—I'd live perfectly fine, without a stray thought. Simply the smell of his thick sweat would be enough for my empty routine. My son would probably take over the ragged family business; my wife would marry a much younger man than me; my son would play football with his father-in-law. But here I was, ready to serve as the engineer's wife, if that was what destiny was asking from me. The engineer stood by the bedroom door. The house lay in semi-darkness. I was sitting on the queen bed. Would he like it if I took the first step or no? I said that the day had been exhausting. But I didn't care, because I always liked cleaning and cooking. Lying like that seemed to be what people expected from a body consecrated to womanhood. Was there anybody else out there besides him and me? I didn't see anyone on that first day, except the janitor who brought us the keys. The engineer and I stared at each other, waiting for what should happen next. It was always like this with me, and I believe with him, too: life improvised on its own, hour by hour, day by day, and frequently pulled the rug from under us. Recently, the engineer and I had regressed: me, dying; he, leaving the German orgies behind. We had both exited a long pause. Our lives needed to have full tanks once again so we could dedicate ourselves to corporeal comfort. We needed an armchair, a better table, and a swing for our child. Child? Yes, a child, why not? The semi-arid landscape around us provided the perfect environment for raising a child. The engineer took measured steps toward me, then sat by my side. I was nervous. I had spent my whole life wanting him and now the time had come. I figured that if I didn't have the courage to touch that desired body…if I didn't, at least, lightly caress it with the same weight of a butterfly on the petal of nothing…if I didn't take the initiative that night, at last, our desire for each other would petrify forever. I'd have to leave our home even if I didn't have a place to go. I doubted he had anywhere to go, either. He probably had left everything behind so he could travel. Did he have any material possessions left? Crumbs of some ghostly past? Again, for me, there was nothing. I needed to act, yes, and now. I closed my eyes and landed my hand, as if distractedly, on the engineer's Greco thigh. Then I opened my eyes, my heart racing, and moved closer to him. I kissed one of his eyes, hoping he would close both of them and let me act without feeling ashamed. Indeed, he locked his eyelids. I brought my mouth to his lips. Our tongues touched each other. I couldn't believe the man whose path I'd tirelessly followed for years was moving toward an idyll with the author of these caresses. I took my clothes off. I unbuttoned his shirt. He got up, opened his pants. I noticed he needed a helping hand to get excited. I ran my mouth over his chest and went down to his abs, where a trail of hairs gradually spread until it reached the tuft of his pubes. When I reached it, I saw his cock was still soft. Disappointment. I wondered what the problem was, especially considering he had spent so much time fucking the entire crew of the German submarine. That whole time I had thought that this man, mainly African, but with some Native blood in his genes, had been fucking everyone as a male rite of passage to achieve the verve of the universal semen. But oh no, on the contrary, he had been fucked by dozens of Germans. And now he was impotent. The crew's goal had been to establish contact with the guts of the world by way of a tropical man. The engineer was the protagonist of a sacrifice at sea. And now it seemed he didn't have his office job anymore. I saw that the bee was still on his foreskin, but very tiny now, for obvious reasons. We were lying down; I motioned him to turn his body over. He did turn, and I sat on my knees to admire his back. I spread his butt cheeks. German cocks of

all shapes and colors had passed through that orifice. I slowly inserted my index finger. The finger
went in and out—foreplay lovers do to warm up
with a mini-coitus. He moaned, insolently. At first,
I didn't understand if he moaned out of pain or
pleasure. I dug my finger a little deeper and his
moan sounded like a reminiscence of golden hells. I
feared I'd have shit on my finger when I pulled it
out. But that didn't happen—glory, hallelujah.
Then, I concluded, that was it: he had indeed been
fucked by everyone in the ship, who knows how
many times, and I needed to make sure my prick
stayed hard permanently from now on, so I could
penetrate the one I blindly loved. On my mark
then, and with the help of my spit, I entered that
orifice coveted by the submarine population. This
time he deserved a good old Brazilian cock, which
he begged me to dig deeper into his entrails. The
guy couldn't get enough of it, though he never got
an erection himself. I came. He turned over and
kneeled before me, kissing my groin and pubes. He
licked the remains of my milky spurt as someone
thanking an emperor for his godsend. I was the emperor of fucking, yes, and I was giving him the head
of my cock to be consecrated by friction through
the caves of his body. The engineer slurped the last
drops off my genitalia. And suddenly, he seemed

drunk. Or at least, inebriated. He spun, dizzy, around the bedroom. I thought that was a good sign. My body's production intoxicated him. Let our next contact confirm this spectacular realization. Our first fuck had been fucking amazing! He sat on the bed and slowly let his back fall to the mattress. I moved on top of him and said: Today, our story begins. Begins? he asked. Soon, I was lulled by his sleep. A rooster crowed. What time was it? I asked myself. The luminosity of a new day came through the Venetian blinds. I went to the bathroom to pee. My cock now had a special mission: to fuck the man who seemed to want me as a wife. I went back and watched him for a while. I caressed him. I'd be in charge of preparing meals, washing, and ironing his clothes. If that was the way it had to be, so be it, period. What kind of work would the engineer do to support us? There was still milk and bread from the day before. Cheese, too. The rooster crowed again. I opened the kitchen door. It gave way to an enormous dirt yard. Two chickens pecked at the ground, oblivious to the world. I had never strangled one to eat. Maybe I would need to now. Beyond the fence, a horse attached to a cart waited for its owner. A dog came up and curled at my feet. I would have animals around me—not so bad for someone who must embody the everyday loneliness of a woman. And I'd be Saint Francis of Assisi, too, with my transcendental little creatures. I heard the engineer getting up. He yawned loudly and farted a few times. I warmed up some milk and brought bread and cheese to the table. We would digest them along with yesterday's decision. And for the rest of my days, I would live in the ecstasy of this female abstraction, which was starting to take over. Could I wish for more? This would be the best place for us to be forgotten. Wasn't that a reason to become a couple? To do without everyone else, no? I heard his noises in the bathroom. He spat, farted more, and now his feces made a big fuss, falling into the toilet water. It sounded like children jumping headfirst into a gentle lake. All of that inspired me to imagine our union in the near term. Everything coming from him would be fine, even his shit. When I washed his clothes, I'd be forced to see what I shouldn't. Stains from his dirty ass, for example. Let's agree I'm not the most qualified person to judge people's hygiene, especially when it comes to the orifice of my dreams. The noises from the bathroom were a reminder that his insides were renewed every morning. When those noises reached my ears, they weren't just noises anymore, but the insinuation of a vague promise for later in the evening. He came out of the bathroom smelling like aftershave and came in my direction to kiss me. Lavender scent. I was sitting at the table for breakfast. He bent over me and kissed me. Long enough so I could smell him. And while I did—exaggerating the sound of my sniffs—he stuck his tongue in my mouth, digging deep, almost to my throat. Then he pulled it back, brushing the tip of his tongue on mine. The next moment, his tongue invited mine to explore his mouth. Then, suddenly, he said he was in a hurry and sat down. He said he had a full day. But where? I asked. At work, he said, gazing at the open kitchen door. He stood and pulled a piece of cloth, which seemed to be stained with grease, from his pocket. He pushed it back inside his pants and pulled out some money. For today's expenses, he said, giving me the bills and covering my hand with his. I followed him to the porch, asking myself if this was what I really wanted: to be a wife-cum-prisoner of domestic chores. I looked at that man whom I now called "my husband" and, once more, knew that I'd chain myself to time passing around the clock for him, yes. But, sometimes, the routine hours provoked the worst nightmares in me. Vague guilt made me walk aimlessly around the house, and I couldn't get settled. Who was I, after all? A man who needed to function as a wife inside the house. But a horny stud at night, fucking the shit

out of the engineer. I went to the bedroom to re-
fresh the previous night in my mind. An extremely
feminine robe de chambre lay on the bed—Japanese
motif, geishas serving tea. Next to it, a short note: I
bought this robe in Tokyo when I was traveling on
the submarine for whoever would turn out to be
my girlfriend. Girlfriend, how come? Was I the
girlfriend? This lady here who would fuck him till
the end of time? I started questioning if he had lied
when he said he was my resurrector. Just so I'd have
to thank him forever. So I could be his wife, in
absolute self-denial. It was his wish, I know.
Someone owned my life now: him. And I owed
him my life. The guy's impotence seemed almost
rebellious. Perhaps his dysfunction was not even
real, but part of a plan where I'd support him by
managing the infamous domestic economy.
Obviously, I would need to support him in other
areas, too. The engineer had a wife who could insert a damn good cock inside him every night. That
woman was me. I had to get used to my new situation. Me, who until so recently thought myself to
be dead, was now living in this house exclusively for
my husband, as so many other women do. And I
had always considered myself quite a masculine
man. Interested in working out. Muscles abound,
hairy legs. Why did I have to fall in love with this

man forever? I tried on the Japanese robe and stood in front of the bathroom mirror. I was already another person. I opened the medicine cabinet and saw makeup. I went to work trying to transform myself into an ideal woman. It seemed I was pretty good with cosmetics. In ten, fifteen minutes, I had a face no suitor could complain about. Still, I couldn't really see myself completely as a woman— even though I didn't show any of those gruesome skin impurities you see in most men. I heard hands clapping. I went to the porch. It was a young native woman holding a baby in her arms. She had come by to ask me if I needed anything. A local resident introducing herself. We should be friends: a wife always likes to talk to her fellow female neighbors. I asked her if she wanted to come in for a bit. As she stepped inside the house, I checked myself from head to toe, inspecting my femininity. I really didn't see a woman in me. Perhaps with time, I would. It all depended on the engineer. After all, I was journeying into womanhood for him. Without him, I'd go back to being a man again. Thus, it all depended on how our shared plan would unfold. A plan neither of us ever mentioned. A plan which throbbed in silence. If my day-to-day reality turned out to be deeply lonely, I'd have to react and revise my role as the wife. I'd reclaim the independence that the external world provided. I'd re-engage with public spaces, especially the streets, where "nobody belonged to anybody," as the song went. Upon returning to masculinity, I'd have to lock myself at home, hiding from the toxic curiosity of the locals. For them, I'd be a circus freak. The woman who turned into a man. I'd be the poster child of a transexual transitioning back into virility, like the prodigal son returning home. Many would buy the image of me as the bearded woman. This time, however, the woman was not only stricken with a beard but converted into an absolute man from head to toe. And it didn't matter if I went crazy because of this transmutation in reverse—a transmutation that would turn me back into the man I'd once been. As long as I had the engineer by my side, why not? Even if I kept this incomplete feminine shape unchanged—in case I didn't fully transition and remained in a hybrid stage on the journey from man to woman—even under those conditions, I would never have total access to the local women. Maybe I could even expose my masculine attributes intentionally—though I don't know what I would do with them out there in Mato Grosso. My virility—still manifesting itself under my clothes—wouldn't be able to bloom naturally. I had drifted away from the male function, which had given me a wife and a son. I had begotten. That meant everything for my sexual biography. How would the engineer receive my disobedient macho figure—in case this figure really came through and reattached itself to me? How would we represent our union to the rural population of the Brazilian West? For the time being, I still lived as an expat of my masculine role. I started believing that this role was already lost. The role of father and husband, for example. Who could help me to recover those functions? In case a turn of events with the engineer came about, I could not go back to my old domain in Porto Alegre. If I did, I'd end up dethroning my own image from the past. The throne seemed vacant, yes, but I should not sit on it. Let it stay vacant or let another masculine dynasty usurp it, snatching his new wife and son-in-law to support his formidable plans. So, I was not the same person anymore. I was in a mid-point between being the father and husband, and the female lover of the engineer. How could I go back to a wife who had possibly married another man after my death? Who would be in charge of the little farm? My son? I doubted it. He was part of the self-entitled youth that procrastinated entering into the workforce. Most likely, the new husband would assume the territory's principality, finally making it a source of true profits. I felt I had the right to be a coward—at least when it came to the facts of my familial experience. If my wife's new husband decided to take care of the farm and extract comfort for my kin from its soil, why not? After all, wasn't I dead? Before the deep voice of my farm's new boss, I would bow my head like a good, faint-hearted man. My neighbor had sat down to breastfeed her child. When she pulled a breast out of her blouse, I had to back away. That full breast, with its darker brown nipple and areola, took me right back to my widow's breast. My neighbor's breasts rekindled in me a tender nostalgia for sleep. It happened to her child at that exact moment. The baby girl nursed asleep; she could not distinguish between oral activity and a submerged state. I got closer to the baby. She suckled the milk with mastery. All was one. No division between her and her mother. The child could not feel my presence. Or how much of an intruder existed in me. However, I was being nosy, so I moved away from them and sat back, asking my neighbor where I could find a local market. The young woman gave directions to me. Then she pushed her breast back into the blouse, and I recoiled again. I shouldn't bother her with my oblique desire. I approached the child again. I played with her. She was too tiny to react to my *da-da-da-da*. Did my engineer leave any children behind in one of the harbors of the world? One night, he told me that Viagra never worked to raise his prick from the shadows. But he didn't care about it too much. He had learned how to have an anal orgasm. He was content with that. Not just content. His sexual life had in fact improved so much. The night he told me all this, he got down on his knees before me. I was serving our evening breakfast. He opened my zipper and took out my cock. In a matter of seconds, my pubic hair was covered with breadcrumbs; the engineer didn't care, he got up and pulled his pants down. At this point, I was naked and ready to receive that ass presented to me. He was in a doggy-style position, demanding that I be the man he wanted me to be, someone who'd tear his ass apart and inflict on him the most supreme pleasure, because that tight little hole was not only made to shit, no, it deserved some thick meat, hard and rough, ripping through his blissful anal canal. Back to my neighbor... There I was, all friendly with her and the baby. I asked her to pass me the child for a little bit. On my lap, the baby slept, deeply satiated. Then I walked the young woman out to the gate, which was in a fence that surrounded the residence to protect us. Every morning, as I tidied the house, I touched things as if they were objects for a future museum that would exhibit the routine habits of common people. Because I was taking on womanhood in my day-to-day life, I'd get like that, attentive to every detail of the hours. As long as we lived in that house, the exact portion of warmth and detachment I expected didn't cease to come. The engineer was about to come home. When he did, I asked him what his job was. He said it was a secret, even to the employees' families. The bosses recommended their employees take cold showers or have sex when the temptation to tell the truth to their wives grew unbearable. As a last resort, a gun to his own chest would do the trick. The samurai gunshot. I asked him if, while having sex with me, he was running away from the temptation to tell me about those volatile networks, mysterious services, and omniscient terrors. He kept contact with those secretive domains and I should remain silent in my corner, not questioning anything. I should be available for his sexual prowess, which was extinguished on the frontside of his trunk, but fiery and alive in the abyssal cavern of his behind. I wondered if his current job had some connection to the submarine fraternity. Both occupations were secret. Both were kept from me. From the submarine, I had been jettisoned. Today, my man's actions did not sit well with my justified curiosity. Which was not even that big, honestly. As long as he brought money home—enough to support our lifestyle, plus some extra for my vanities, such as my cosmetics—I would never leave him. I would stay in that hideaway far from civilization to justify the mildly comfortable union I had with the engineer—always dolled up for when my love arrived in the late afternoon, opening the gate with its natural, sad lyricism. In this place, sometimes, I could be more of a woman than most other women. Or, suddenly, I could wake up feeling more like a man than I had ever felt before. One night, this woman was awakened by a strange light coming from the main room. I got up and tiptoed so as not to wake the snoring engineer. The room was bathed with a bright yellow light. I opened the door to the front yard and saw a man atop a ladder, finishing up affixing a streetlamp to a post from which the strong illumination was coming. He looked at me; I shyly saluted him. He responded with a smile, high on the ladder as if to mark his place in the clouds. I stepped closer and asked him the reason for such a strong light in an area with so little foot traffic. He answered that it was an order from above. It might be an authority connected to my husband's work, I thought. The network made its presence visible in different situations on many continents. Omnipresent mafia. Who was now taking care of the plans that drowned with the German submarine? The guy came down the ladder and asked how long we had been living there. Did he know of the engineer's existence? Only then did I realize we had been living in that place for quite a while already, even though it felt like an indeterminate amount of time, considering the lack of big events within my daily routine. Nevertheless, living without conflict was all I'd ever wanted since my early years. Not that I was wasting my time contemplating the malady of boredom, no, nothing like that. Having the engineer every night added an adventurous color to my daily life. What are we going to invent in bed later? I'd ask myself as I swept the house and washed the clothes. And I'd sit down for a bit, taking a break from my chores, feeling like a jubilant wife. However, I did live interchangeable hours, which always felt the same, which always kept me free of any major downtime or pressure, so just like that: pen to paper—I started writing some verses, an endless summer. Other than that, I had to restrain my fire in the long mornings and afternoons. From the kitchen door, I admired his worn-out underwear hanging from an improvised clothesline. Earlier, I had felt so lonely washing it. Before soaking it in the bucket, I felt an urge to smell it. I brought it to my nose and I remembered the wonders accessed beneath that underwear. I leaned my crotch, with a certain casual air, against objects lying around the house. These contacts turned me on; they made me flinch, sigh, and then lie down, drool on my pillow, fall asleep, and then wake up searching for him…until I'd look at the clock and realize it was time for him to come home. In a matter of minutes. In these moments, residues of his physicality would occupy my thoughts. And then I'd think about getting ready for my man's arrival. I'd stay in front of the mirror until I got tired. There was nothing else to do. Everything seemed providential for my undisturbed soliloquy. But, in this situation, the lady named "death"—as my experience as a housewife progressed with every step I took—had the tact to stay as far from me as possible, thus increasing the potential for bliss. I was constructing the hope of immortality in the basement of my body. In the meantime, the idea that I could last forever didn't bother me at all. I welcomed it like a breath of fresh air. These questions arose in my mornings and afternoons and would take me over. I knew I was immune to any mortal blow, as long as I accepted my new domestic mission. A woman alone at home is an Olympian in the face of small annoyances—throwing them in the garbage, where they belong. For someone who already experienced death, six feet under the earth for the span of an hour, more or less, life today presented itself in small discreet beckonings. At least that was how it used to be during the visits of a certain blond young lady. She used to come over and have tea with me in the afternoons. Always cold and silent. Her skin resembled mine. Fair, with freckles. I hid this woman from everyone. She had always visited me, since my childhood. A sophisticated lady, an adult even since back then. During those visits, I'd bring my index finger to my hair and, with a sigh, spiral it into a curl. I always thought this woman wanted to see me as her gendered accomplice. I didn't tell her anything about my change. But I'm sure she noticed it. We hugged each other for a long time in our farewell. She held me tightly against her breasts and only then did I consider the possibility she was a lesbian. I wanted to celebrate that revelation with a kiss on her mouth. But I felt confused and instead receded. I woke up rubbing my eyes; my tears clouded them. I generally had dry eyes, and I always carried eyedrops in my pocket. This time, tears poured out of me. I went to the bathroom, still crying, and washed my face. It was so difficult being lonely during the day. Even more so because my man always arrived late. I was not used to being a wife with only one focus. It didn't matter; I was choosing to continue with this single focus. But, it was difficult, yes, so difficult. In the entire Cuiabá region, only he provided the affirmation I needed. Few had experienced what I had, being resurrected and snatched by their future lover, who had also happened to be my angelical boyfriend during my adolescence. And I'm not even talking about my childhood when everything painfully started. He and I were constructing a true saga. This story had no solution. Telling it was all we could do. The engineer had expunged the death from inside me. Pure luck that Tina's father, the gravedigger, had shared his professional knowledge with my friend when he was a boy. It was my luck, too, crossing paths with a connoisseur of the cadaveric arts and frequent gravesite visitor. And, by extension, connoisseur of the dust in which I'll forcibly have to live, hopefully much further down the road now, maybe even at the end of a long period. I'll be forever grateful to the engineer. Grateful, too, for the authentic devoted wife I'll have to be, following my husband with obedience. The only thing that was stronger than my daily ruminations was our nightly sex, which continued refining itself. It truly fulfilled the core of my necessities. Whenever I exited the realm of libido, I'd return to the slowness of time, either asleep or awake—time that inspired in me memories from my childhood, with its minuscule and secret traces, shameful traces, though insignificant. In my green years, at bath time, I used to climb naked to the edge of the bathtub and see my reflection in the mirror. I'd cover my sex with my hand so I could imagine myself as a woman. Was I successful? Yes, as long as my hand remained in place—that illusion helped me conceive my sudden conversion. I would listen to the rhythmic sound of crickets, accentuating the regularity of the nocturnal world. When I'd wake up in the middle of the night, I'd already feel absolutely compromised by the pace of my routine. The only time I really relaxed was when I was dead—though I had never been one to do things just for show. The engineer was in charge of transporting me to the battles of life once again. And here I am. The electrician, who just came down from the ladder in front of our house on the outskirts of Cuiabá, was now going through his toolbox. He was certainly expecting that I'd invite him to come in and lie down for a bit. But, I was feeling like I had run away from my husband. I should have been in bed with him, ready to fuck if he wished. I looked behind me as if I could sense him, and, indeed, the engineer was standing at the door waiting for me. I didn't say goodbye to the electrician. I walked by my husband without saying anything, just like a child who comes home knowing she'll be lectured. But there was no lecture. I lay on the bed. He came up after me and lay down, too. Maybe some discreet resentment lingered in the air—a resentment that I wished actually existed so we could fuck to cure the possibly open wound. The ones who didn't know how to cure a heartbreak in bed didn't know how good it felt. The resentment catches fire, it seems uncontrollable. But when the two bodies find each other, the recent threat of dissolution works as pure chemistry for the benefit of ecstasy. For the next few days, I ran over lands, more or less arid, in search of a slaughterhouse where I could buy parts of livestock without a middleman. A mustachioed guy, wearing a leather apron, brought me a good piece of rump steak. He looked like a gaucho, an indigenous man born on the border with Argentina. Dark, very straight hair. I want to prepare it for my husband, he's leaving Monday, I said, oversharing this sacred secret. The guy looked at me with mischievous eyes, and I couldn't tell if he saw me as a man or a woman. In these moments of public confusion, I'd lower my eyes as if looking for something lost on the ground. Part of me liked being seen as a woman, receiving lusty gazes that only a man could give to a woman. But there was a side of my desire that liked being chased by a fellow male. In those cases, I'd urge my cock to get hard; I asked him, yes, he, my prick, and he'd respond. And the other man would look to the left side of my groin—even if in disguised ways—where my pecker had assumed his position to defend himself against any threatening softness. The butcher guy passed me a brand-new piece of meat wrapped in newspaper. He winked at me, and I did too, back at him. I hoped the slaughterhouse didn't have any connection to the engineer's work. Although, in those days, I firmly believed that everything had a center, and that the center of everything was my husband's secret activity. I wished I could flirt with the guy in a leather apron, all dirty with cattle blood. That foolish courtship would create a situation with an easy effect on me: to deceive my tedium with the butcher's sensual appeal. But, I was deeply in love with the engineer and I would do anything for our love to never die. I was a lady with only a few attributes fit for the role. I was walking back home through the fields, feeling all prudish, though I didn't know if I looked like a woman or a man. There was a cat I had started feeding that wouldn't leave my side anymore. Sometimes, while the engineer and I fucked, the feline would get in bed with us, rubbing the side of his face on our bodies—our sweaty, indecent, and lightly wounded bodies. The animal took part in our play; he didn't bother us with insidious meows. Sometimes, he meowed as if screaming and his hair stood on end, perhaps he was having an orgasm, in all his loneliness and arrogance. The cat was waiting for me at the gate. He and I gazed at each other as if there was nothing else in the world. Yes, that was what made up my routine—crumbs like that, like the cat and I staring at each other. My day-to-day life was organized around these scraps of moments, and maybe the thread of a beautiful story was starting to form from these little things—they came to the surface so lightly, with such delicate care. Upon surfacing, my intimacies would flow back to the secret plot where they came from. That buoying movement gave me balance. In other words, the possible, banal faults of my days were supplanted by my carnal fever at night. I felt more like a woman each day. Or not: whenever I felt some craving from the past arise inside me, I would immediately access the man I had been in the golden days of my youth. In certain moments, I felt so much longing I thought only sudden death could help me. Other times, I felt so feminine that, yes, I'd fall in love with the man I'd once been. The two lovers coexisted in me. However, I didn't cultivate any morbid anxieties over times now dead. On the contrary, I clung to my love for that man who had given me another life, perhaps the best I've ever had, a life that produced an ocean of voices inside me destined for one heart only. When I walked around the region, I felt like a coiled woman, just like many others from rural areas. A woman who didn't look at men, trying to make herself invisible to the male gaze, except to her own husband's, of course. Sometimes I felt like breasts were blossoming out of me, and I didn't even have to look to confirm they were there. Such vague, fluid sensations. At the same time, every day I prepared myself for the artistry of penetrating into the deepest abysses of a man's anus. I carried a woman's light sweater over my shoulders, without actually wearing it. This modest outfit helped me compose the woman the engineer didn't even ask me to be. I had found the sweater in the bedroom closet. Certainly an article from another female, a previous resident. A sweater for a region with such scalding weather? It seemed to have been saved, yes, for the new woman in residence. The previous woman might have been a wise one. Because perhaps, by tenacity and impulse, she passed—through the sweater, not in a letter—some meaning in gestation to another woman. A meaning that was restless and rarely illuminated through mere explanations. All this so she could run away from the message's exorbitant weight for a little while. I managed, with great effort, to capture the obscure message from this piece of clothing, which came from somewhere unknown, so hermetically sealed that it hid behind the rough fabric, inside the sleeves, pockets, under the collar. It was the first thing I did: turn the article of clothing away, put its back to me. Was I a woman already? I don't know. I was simply trying to decipher what was naturally shrinking in the coarse weaves of a cheap piece of fabric. Yes, I'm talking about the lost sweater, which I threw on the floor and which shrunk as if it had nothing else to declare. But what good would my supposed comprehension do if I were a lonely wife inhaling the smells of the Brazilian forest in the mornings without being able to touch it? My stories did not thrive. I needed another pair of ears for an audience. What would happen if I opened the curtains on my stories for the engineer? Deep down, I didn't even want to know. I'd stay on the porch in the mornings, lonely, staring into space. Suddenly, I'd realize I had already lost the landscape around me and was now only following the itinerary of my interior action. I took ownership of the sweater, even though it had little use in this climate of eternal summer. I carried it everywhere as a

talisman. I'd sit down and put it on my lap to stoke
the cat's jealousy. Everything confused me, but I
know that this confusion was part of a game I
played so I wouldn't grow too attached to any particular role at home. Because the future hides surprises, you know. If one day the engineer decided he
didn't want me anymore, I'd have to quickly reassess
the male's supremacy inside me. It was, for better or
worse, how I knew it to be for most of my life. I
would then leave for some city in the Northeast. I
would arrive there as a man, convinced of his male
functions. Maybe I'd marry a native woman and
have a child with her. This baby's elder brother was
in Porto Alegre. It was too late now for him to learn
that his dad was still among the living. The boy
took me for dead. He and his mother—both so
pragmatic by nature, the opposite of me—would
have already moved on with their lives with dexterity and readiness. I could not despair, because of my
love for the engineer. Or submit myself to some
gender affirming surgery—even more so because
my penis was essential for our sexual practice, especially in our longer sessions. I feared my life could
derail. I was turning into a woman with the form of
a man. Eventually, I'd become a woman on the surface as well. In the meantime, I was neither one
thing nor the other; all I could manage were the

domestic chores during the day and boring my long dick into the engineer's delicious ass at night. The moan he exhaled when I came deep in his darkness was worth an entire life. Fucking him, I participated in his entrails. Fucking him, I knew more about his insides than he did. Fucking him, every night, I accepted the situation that tied me to this somewhat diffused place outside Cuiabá. By the way, the more time passed, the more the scenery dissipated around me. Only the frontiers of your body don't dissipate, I thought of telling him. There comes a moment like this, where it's all the same to be here or there: everything is the same diffusion. Maybe my sudden indifference to the immediate space around me had to do with the fact that I had spent hours in the darkness of a coffin, taken as a dead man. So the world of senses grew a bit foreign to me. I have no idea if I dreamed while I was buried; I don't think so. I was dry, without saliva, when I came out of the tomb. And dreams have the tendency to hydrate. So, no, I didn't dream. And I saw nothing inside. And what difference did it make if my coffin silk was white or blue? I lived near an immense wasteland on the outskirts of Cuiabá now. In this geographic reality, the engineer provided me food and some small change for little luxuries, though I had nowhere to spend the money. I used to keep those unintentional savings in my shirt pocket. In this pocket, the coins jingled. I'd sit down and shake the shirt's breast, listening to the sound of bronze, and in this way, the hours passed…eventually the engineer arrived. He put some money in my hand before leaving for a work trip. Then, he left in a beaten-down black car; the driver had an oversized head. I waved. The engineer waved back. The guy with the gigantic head smiled. I already missed the engineer. Would I suffer being by myself amid this scenery? I crouched down to observe a plant blooming in the garden, and I asked myself if transitioning to the other sex was really the answer. How could I kill certain male qualities within me, which I had learned with so much effort? Maybe I should reach out to my neighbor? She'd bring her baby for sure. I'd feel like a thankful wife having the baby on my lap again. Why was I experiencing this eruption of joy at the chance of having a child in my arms? I wouldn't have felt this way in my previous life—all foolish about the visit of a newborn. Me? Never. What happened then? Before this life, I had been a father, good or bad, with no patience for affectionate gestures for my son, much less for a neighbor's child. Now, I was a better man. Although I was still confused, somewhere between male and female, I satisfied the engineer's desire every night, keeping my right to fool around in the sunny mornings and afternoons on his days off, too. It'd be so painful to spend this undetermined time without anyone to wait for, or cook for, or wash for. Without anyone to fuck—fuck until the other's anus grew inflamed—without anyone to enjoy my cock's lubrication with me…that's something hard to bear. I went to the bedroom and basked in the engineer's scent. I lay down. The cat got into bed, purring and rubbing his short mane on my shirt. I longed for my wife and son in Porto Alegre. I was lying on my stomach, flexing my hips against the mattress. All was coming to my mind: my son's butt, my wife's wet pussy on those hot nights, and, to top it off, the engineer's ass, hungry for my dick. The cat now rubbed against my thinning hair, always purring and impertinent. My untargeted randiness mixing with the cat's sweetness bothered me to the point where I caught the pussycat by the scruff of his neck and threw him against the wall. The scream he let out was not that of an animal. Through that sound, the image of a classmate from middle school came to my mind. Paulinho screamed with the same timbre, intensity, and meaning. He screamed and died. The cat, too? He ran out of the bedroom, and I felt desolate for starting my new period of loneliness this way. If the engineer had witnessed the scene, he'd be mad at me. Yes, he was my man, inevitably he had a moral standard. And I didn't have two masters. I had to follow my routine to the letter while he was away. I had to feel his temporary absence with my memory in a state of grace. And alert. My brutality against the animal brought to the surface a masculine act par excellence: testosterone fury. I was all biceps, useless for sublime causes. More and more, I needed to commit to the woman growing inside me who permanently subjected herself to the engineer's restraint, because only he could enable my apprenticeship in belonging to the modest pace of everyday life. Why temperance? Well, so I could mature into a time in which—miraculously for the scientific world—I'd be ready to shelter the engineer's progeny in my womb. I got up and went looking for the cat. He was hiding under the kitchen table. I got down to my knees and called to him with tenderness. He didn't need much convincing. He came right back to me, sliding his fur through the strips of my sandals. The house was back in order. The engineer would come back one day and find his home at peace, fresh and clean, with something new on display—a vase, or a painting from the street market, or a rug typical of the region. Then, he would return to the post that never ceased to be his. And I would still be dealing with my eternal erection that ripped his intrepid ass apart. Outside, the young woman, my neighbor, clapped her hands again. I answered. She didn't have the child with her this time. She came up to the porch all smiles, saying her baby had stayed home with her mom. For a few minutes, my thoughts grew heavier. I was thinking about my husband as the promise I had to pay for every night. He is the engineer whom I've been in love with since my adolescence in the southern capital. But I've known him since childhood, I told myself, my head cloudy from so many thoughts. Do you have any rubbing alcohol? she asked. My mother said I need to disinfect my breasts. The baby woke up with little cold sores at the corners of her mouth. I went to the bathroom and saw I had some. I called her. I wanted us to get out of view of curious pass-ersby; I wanted to be cautious. Cida sat on the toilet, and I sat on the edge of the bathtub. I wet a piece of cotton with alcohol and pressed it to her nipples. Cida moaned as the alcohol touched her tiny, natural fissures. I asked all the saints to keep me from getting excited before those swollen tits. Every time she moaned, I felt I was a dry mouth approaching the transparency of a fountain. Why would a woman get excited when she sees another woman's breasts? Besides, I was not just any woman, but this one right here, with her zipper almost splitting apart from the bulge of a cock on fire… right? By the way, my prick had been working a lot. Just when I thought I'd take a sexual vacation while my husband was away, when I thought I would be able to simply go to sleep, there came this young woman, accepting my service of rubbing alcohol on her nipples. Nipples I could suck on because they were being offered—naked, warm, hard as stones—to me. She was lactating, right, but could I be introduced to this lactose diet? I would know how to feed from her breasts regularly. Those generous, unforgettable, appetizing breasts. I trembled in that bathroom; I was crazy horny, but unable to live up to that desire. I pondered: If I got involved with this woman with straight black hair, would I be saying goodbye to my home at the end of the world? I should continue to blindly obey the commandments of my man because the diffuse canons of my routine could only come from him. He was the one who, without knowing it, dictated the rules. I came back from death through the hands of the ex-engineer. And I, having lost the ties to my family and little farm, didn't have a job anymore. He, on the other hand, seemed to occupy his hours to the fullest. However, when he got home, he smiled with his tail between his legs, as if he expected some calm or dull aplomb from me so as not to confuse him. All this was happening while I kept working on my capacity to become a certain type of woman—and I should never get tired of practicing this exercise. I didn't need to think about my new lifestyle anymore. I was on autopilot. The fuel for my subsistence came from him, and it was already secured, but only to the point to which I deserved. I feared he would get tired of everything. Did he have another choice, or was he in the same inescapable situation as me? Those two boobs staring at me, slightly cross-eyed, the nipples on a bifurcated path, but nothing more than a path—those two breasts could be taken only for their nutritional value. And I should respond to that situation via my female nexus; after all, I was a woman waiting for her husband to return from who-knows-where. To go all lesbian on those breasts would not be an advantage to my discreet position as wife to a small hero—or perhaps he was greater than I could even imagine. A hero who surely wouldn't fit into the modesty of my circle—though, during the time I was solely dedicated to him, I barely had any energy and curiosity to cultivate other interests. So, dizzyingly, I kissed one of those nipples available to me. I kissed it with a smile on my face, like a friend who pays homage to the beautiful glow of her friend's baby. My kiss didn't go unnoticed. Cida got chills; her whole body shivered. And I, well, I ejaculated, wasting liters of semen in the dungeon of my underwear. I don't think she noticed the resident in my crotch had vomited its bliss behind the fabric. I led Cida to the door. My pubes were soaking wet. I kissed her on both cheeks. I needed to stop being so horny for her. I should wait for my husband and keep on with him, all the way to the finish line without any more struggles or distractions. In a certain way, this had been an ideal I had always aimed for. In Porto Alegre, when I still lacked access to the engineer's body, my incursions into libido were diverse and extravagant, but the end result was always somewhat curt. Upon bidding farewell to my nighttime partners, I always felt the acute exhaustion of my endeavors. At that time, I didn't have anywhere to store my overflowing semen. Now, every night, I cool off my consciousness a little, making use of the hallucinated pulsion that dies in my sleep, only to rise again the next day in the trembling darkness of my room. In turn, I take care of everyday activities; for example, I venture out of the house after small groceries or for someone to repair the bed's wobbly leg. It didn't cross my mind to dwell on jealousy over the engineer's unknown whereabouts. It was worth it to keep seeking what was necessary to deserve the blessing of a man who came home and placed a wet kiss on my mouth at the end of the day. And then what follows: his pants down, revealing a pathetic dick, but displaying, also, a purple asshole, tight to receive my ready beast— ouch, he exhales, and I say it hurts only in the beginning, that soon enough my cock will hit the right spot of that ass just returned from enigmatic seas. He's burning and burning, and suddenly he's all fire until he calms down again and carries my milk inside him; the milk which once conceived a child; the child who's a man today, and whom I'll never see again. Two months later, the engineer returns from his mysterious absence. He walks into the house with a leg in a cast; he says it was a silly fall. I help him into the house; I sit him in an armchair. He asks me to remove the cast. I don't argue with him, even though I know that could delay the bone's recalcification. I grab a pair of scissors and cut through the cast. In a matter of minutes, I have his dark hairy legs exposed to my desire again (like the rest of his body, of course). I bring in a bucket with water and wash his leg with devotion. I pass a piece of cloth over it. He sighs, kicks back… There's something about his skin that appeals to me so much. I ask him about the history of that broken bone again. He shuts down. I find this silence noble; I don't dare violate it with conclusions. He's my man. And I keep on incarnating his lady. Or his soul. My engineer still limps a little, but he says it's just hesitation about firmly placing his foot on the ground. I serve lunch. Pancakes covered with *doce de leite*. I put strips of cauliflower around them. Sprinkles of parsley on the border of the plate. A recipe from my neighbor. I just refined it. When I see him eating, I don't need anything else. I lose my appetite. Then, I put him in bed. He complains he's tired, things are not going very well. Is it work related? I ask. Yep, he agrees, it's work. I could take this chance and ask him what he does when he's gone for such a long time. But I don't ask him anything. I can't accomplish anything that's not concerned with the living room, the kitchen, and the bedroom where we share our bodies. In the sheets, we cuddle a bit, we roll around. He gets animated, doesn't look like the beaten-down man who had arrived earlier. We suddenly stop. We fall asleep. In the middle of the night, he wakes up and calls to me. What is it? I ask. It's nothing, I can't fall asleep. Sleeping is a waste of time, he says. I slide my hand up his thigh, I kiss the pores of his chest. I pass my tongue over his nipples and suckle on what seems to be hardened into its pure form, without a clear function. Male nipples forget to grow; they're just aborted archeology. Survivors as erotic taboos, underutilized. I sip on this biological mystery. Something comes out of them, yes, I quench my thirst from them. I inhale him closely. It smells of everything he went looking for on his travels, things which I will never know, nor even want to know. What I smell is an indistinguishable scent of dissimulation so agile that it won't allow me to compose any historical trace, any lineage. Nothing fails to assure me or pushes my buttons. I live on a spiral of tension that makes me dizzy, but it eventually calms me down. His tongue travels across my body; he doesn't seem to know which part he's licking. He engulfs everything in me so blindly. The rooster crows. The dawn breaks in. It's neither day nor night, it's all the same when he's here like this. I get some distance to look at him, naked, already on his stomach. I top him. I'm light, he's on his fours. I ride him, I ask him to keep going and going, always, forever, until he can't. He reaches the furthest point, I get off him, turn him around to face me, I go for his nipples again, which are now swollen, I latch my mouth on them, and I suck them until there's nothing left but another chest—the childish chest of a hairless man, like an arid plateau. Two days later, he leaves again. As always, I wonder for how long. I'm used to it by now. I also leave for the open field, which sears under the sun; I need to buy meat for tomorrow. I run so nobody can look at me for long. I'm a stain that gallops, slipping through the brown grass here and there. I'm standing by the freezer in the slaughterhouse, in front of the man with the leather apron stained with bovine blood. I'd like some rump skirt, I say. He seems pissed off when he brings the meat. I look the same as usual. And here comes another conqueror who wants me now. He says the package is too heavy; he can carry it for me. It is heavy indeed. I give it back to him. We laugh on the way home. He walks into the house, says he wants to put the package of meat in the fridge. He notices everything, says my house is pretty, big, and gets a lot of morning sun. I make coffee, ask him how many spoonfuls of sugar. He doesn't say anything, walks into my bedroom with me, gets undressed, and undresses me. Will he see me as a woman with a dick that I would never turn into a pussy? But I see that the stud is already sucking my cock, playing the role of the hungry bottom. I've got a good dick, I have to admit. When it's hard like this, like a sword, even I wish I could suck on it and give it a kiss on the way out. However, it's just a wish since I can't figure out how to bring my mouth to that phallus, offered as a gift of the species. My lips simply don't reach it. The meatpacker from

Mato Grosso cums with my cock in his mouth. I ask him for a little help, to beat me off. First, he shows the typical lassitude of one who just came. But soon, he decides to pay attention to me, reciprocating my gesture as a way to reward me for my previous performance. You never know, there could be some future encounters. And so he does his job. I scream discreetly. My cum explodes on the guy's ecstatic face. He runs to wash his face in the bathroom. I don't want to see him anymore. After today, I don't want to cross paths with his large body any longer. I'm going to start buying meat in another neighborhood. I'll be waiting for my love to come home with my face all flushed from having walked to a slaughterhouse much farther away—I'll go flying above myself, close to the trees' canopy, I'll go, yes, I'll go without anyone, I'll go in peace. I needed to hide my furtive (or not so furtive) encounters from the world. My master could not learn about these clandestine contacts of mine. Not that he asked me for exclusivity or that I inflicted myself with chastity outside our bedroom. For the time being, I was a woman in a man's body. I felt good this way. If I wanted to conjure this mutual attraction that had existed since our school days—this attraction so fresh and singular each additional day—I would need a certain sobriety. I could not relive my youthful extravaganza; it'd be too much, it would damage me. It was the anus of my traveling man that concentrated my sexual affirmation. Did I deserve such a proverbial fit? And does such merit ennoble the experience? Or does it not matter? The road was in the middle of so much vastness. Peaceful waves carried me further, and I said: Yes, I want this creature I see. So I stopped. It was a wild dog looking at me. But I shut my body down and kept going. The animal growled, showed its teeth. But I had a traveler about to come home. I arrived at a slaughterhouse I'd never been to before. There was nobody there: a ghost town. I called hellooooo, clapped my hands. Cows and bulls were indifferent to my presence, they only knew how to graze. In general, I find cattle boring, they don't show fear or rage, neither interrupts their indifference. Maybe because they are slaughtered every day, they become used to living in a microsystem that's totally alienated from our greed. Thus, they avoid suffering. Grass numbs the herd. A few steps away from me, cattle cars were stopped on the train tracks. A horrible smell came from them. As if a mad machinist had abandoned the train, leaving everything behind to perish. I noticed a lake all the way down, and I ran to it. I wondered if it was Sunday or a holiday, so desolate was the landscape. I took my clothes off and got into the lake. A thick wood board was suspended at the narrowest point between the two shores. It might serve as a bench for people to sit on before going for a swim. On the board, an overused soap bar, probably to wash clothes. I sat on the board and began washing my body, which was overheated from walking underneath the scalding sun. Another man, also naked, showed up on the shore of the lake. He held his clothes. Then he put them over a rock. He asked if he could sit on the board as well. He said he swam there every day. I said of course. We started chatting. He was what's generally called "mentally challenged." An adult on the outside, but a disturbed child inside. Are you married, sir? he asked me. I said: No, I live alone in a shack by the road that goes to Mercês, where I was born. I enjoyed imagining myself in that condition, maybe because the day was ending. Little did he know that I exercised the female craft in almost everything I did, and didn't want another life. My cock was bigger than his. And upon noticing this detail, my mind switched from the wilderness around us to the memory of the engineer, who'd be arriving at any moment, coming out of his mineral silence to make me drool with spit and orgasms again. I turned my attention back to my swimming partner, making small talk

such as how you could find this type of weed everywhere around here. The guy seemed less than human, he could not function outside the remnants of
his childhood. In him, any intention of forming a
full sentence ended up bursting apart like bubbles.
He lowered his head, became small, impregnated
himself a bit more with the lake. He seemed to in-
tegrate with the water in such a way that an observer could not discern him from the landscape.
He became a stain. He moved the syllables in his
mouth as if tasting them, maybe without fully understanding them. He pronounced words his own
way and he'd look at me, seeking recognition. Then,
we were out of topics. In silence, we raised our
hands in the shapes of shells in the air as if we were
asking for help from the skies. Suddenly, an unexpected gesture surged quite melodramatically.
Languorous. However, the gesture soon coagulated
from the lack of meaning. This choreography
seemed to touch the soul of the man. He slapped
his hand on his belly to celebrate. Celebrate what?
Well, not even he knew. But I knew the man had
captivated me. So, I danced those same movements
with him. Only our arms performed it. We tried a
couple more numbers. The man didn't need to say
anything else. He got out of the water before me.
He looked for something in the pocket of his shirt

and brought it to me. I got out of the lake and grabbed the piece of paper. It was some sort of receipt for a contribution to the Brazilian cause. He showed me the receipt, then asked me for a donation. Could this man, with his apparent innocence, give me any clues about the campaign that would make all the difference? Perhaps a somewhat challenged man could give me an explanation beyond logic. It'd be just enough if he could reveal the mystery of these donations through his gestures and animal sounds. I gave him the money. It was my fate already. Even here, far away from the cities, the shady campaign, which hadn't enlisted me, emerged again. I raised my arm as if holding a glass of champagne up high. The man followed my gesture. With my raised hand, I felt the drink's bubbly shadow spilling over my elbow. The man laughed. I laughed even more. Maybe the man couldn't solve the mystery of the majestic contributions. Perhaps there wasn't even any mystery in that sweeping wave of pocketed donations. Perhaps the only real mystery was the population's monumental goodwill in the face of the unrecognizable solicitation for help. Despite all that, this guy, so independent of human speech, could have an effortless enlightenment that would mesmerize an imbecilic listener such as myself. I was a listener addicted to verifying worn-out replicas of things in the mirror of words at the expense of a verb's physical seduction. Every expression the lake man manifested seemed to rise in search of gesture and dance. The lake man watched the horizon's splendors, performing with the grace of a celestial monarch, whom I was getting to know right then and there. Where did this contemplative fountain come from? From someone who received special medical care, which surely was the case for this man? But this special care probably didn't reach all the way here, in the wilderness. And the donations' purpose could not be translated by him or anybody else. All an individual could do was to throw his last dollars in the bottomless pit of this popular mega-fund. And then subtract himself from himself and soar. Of course, to arrive at that point with any honor, the suicidal individual needed to donate for the cause over and over again. Ultimately, everyone who pays that type of white tax will be invited to leave. Whose hands would take over those billions in the continental safe deposit box? The lake man had an expression in his eyes as if they saw magnificent spheres, absolutely oblivious to the nation's bedazzlement. He didn't feel the need to dress like royalty. He was a naked king. I whistled a song; he followed along. "*Serra da Boa-Esperança*" by Lamartine Babo. Why? I have

no idea. Perhaps because the population was entering a parallel world like the one in the song. That
world up in the mountains, "the last darling." How
would this idyllic "good fortune" be the pinnacle of
a whole country? Perhaps this slow peasant would
become part of a future caste. I insinuated I wanted
to cuddle with him, but my gesture fell short. I
counted to five and kissed his hand. It was the first
time I saw his ring. It had a stone the color of ruby.
When I got home, I looked at myself in the mirror.
I noticed my face was starting to lose the hair that
composed my beard. Was I slowly becoming a
woman? I hoped that when destiny finished forming this woman, I wouldn't be senile yet, and thus I
could still recognize her, making her sovereign in
the hospitality of my body. There was nobody at the
slaughterhouse; I came home empty-handed. I'd
have no meat for the next few days. It didn't matter.
I would start cultivating an ascetic life. No meat, no
makeup, no sex outside my marriage. By the time
the engineer finally returned, I would go back and
try to find the ghost slaughterhouse again. Maybe
there'd be somebody there this time. I took my
clothes off, sat on the floor in the lotus position,
and succumbed to the interval between his departure and return. The days I went through in this
interim could not be narrated. I will only occupy

the omitted experience. Between being a man or a woman, I choose both. And nobody shall follow me. I ended up staying in the lotus position for a lifetime. My hair grew a foot longer. I had the novelty of gray at my temples. My face had bid further farewell to my former beard. Someone coughed near me. It was him, I knew it. The man seemed so immolated. A serious wound on his arm. We're moving up North, he said. I could choose to continue in my passive listening and ignore the enigma of my beloved. But not this time. I helped him sit down and said that moving forward, I needed to know where he went every time he traveled. He answered that there's no time to clarify doubts. Do you think I've been running away? he asked. From the police? I suggested. There was anxiety in his voice when he said we needed to hit the road again before he could make any confessions. Like me, he looked older. I hoped that during our next chapter of running away the engineer would have time to explain what was behind the whole mystery. But for now, I just wanted him to answer me: What are you running away from? Running away? he repeated with a poker face. It was the first time I felt a bit of hate for him. And I would hate him even more if it became necessary. If that could free me from the longing I felt during his infinite travels—perhaps

he was expanding his sexual empire? I would detest
going through the hell of being a jealous woman.
The truth is that, between the thin line of hate and
turbulent passion, I would assume the role of the
Roman wolf to her man, ready to keep him safe in
the nest of a home. Men, surely his employees, kept
bringing boxes and boxes into the house, and I
didn't know what was inside them. Are you a drug
dealer? I asked right to his face. Tense silence. What
kind of drugs? I insisted. He was lying on the couch,
holding his wounded limb. All I had was this stupid
love to give him. Maybe an attraction to someone
with an arm hurt like that was inadequate. But I
would run away with him to the end of the world
and beyond. I was almost a woman now; my gyne-
comastia bursting beneath the blouse hurt me. I
would show him those little breast buds before we
departed, and they'd be so hard, not from producing
milk, but because they had just sprouted from my
body's force—pubescent nipples revolutionizing
my anatomy. While men worked around us—re-
minding me of crowds of slaves erecting the
Egyptian pyramids like ants in a colony—while
these tireless men kept coming and going through
the porch door, I woke the engineer and brought
him to bed. We could still hear the men talking,
entire conversations, even with the door closed. I

had my man with me, reaching under my blouse, grabbing my small blooming breasts, testing the consistency of that fruit. I could see the amusement on his face. I took my blouse off and his hungry mouth kept switching between one nipple and the other. I responded by squirming my body. And I believe that some kind of milk did leak—perhaps some byproduct of my already uncontrollable female fire. I went to his ass and dwelled on it. There was no corporeal scent that surpassed its scent. No cologne, no lotion, no baby powder could even come close to it. In a certain way, I was reliving the excitement of my puberty, averse to the commandments of hygiene. The cat meowed, sensing our escape. He would stay behind, in those semi-arid fields on the outskirts of Cuiabá. And the couple would run away north, perhaps even to another country. But before our escape, the engineer had quiet days, sucking on my titties like he was only now discovering a female's succulent gift. I treated the engineer like a real baby. I appreciated his curled body in the embryonic position but, at the same time, on the verge of maturing, because his muscular physique intoxicated me more and more with its familiar force and appetite. As he switched from one tit to the other, I could see him drooling. He was gorging on my body. I lived that moment as some type of ecstasy because, for the first time in my life, I was producing food from my carnal matter. I was a sort of conduit for his ascension through my new morphology. I was a man revealing his inner mother through his own skin. I was all udder. My breasts fed the traveler. In a certain way, he needed me more than I needed him. Who else would I nurse if the engineer failed me now? What would I make of this surplus provision if no one else showed up? My engineer procrastinated, holding us back from our flight with his late-stage breastfeeding in our bedroom. In the middle of my ecstatic offering, I stuck my finger up his ass. It seemed shorter, my finger, merely a detail of the female body. Perhaps I was already putting myself atop the domestic hierarchy for being a woman. If you have been here before, you know what I'm talking about. You can live with a criminal, a murderer, or whatever, but if you're a gifted woman— and moreover, a mother—at home, that man will always be grateful to you. Maybe he would timidly ask me for protection in the next moment, so he could go conquer the world alone, only to never come back. However, I was willing to force my way into his journey as much as I possibly could. Even if I still didn't know the reason for our escape—in my hypothesis it was really an escape. No, I had no

more doubts we were running from the Federal
Police. And that the engineer and the men he com-
manded were part of heavy drug traffic. What were
the substances? I listened to the commotion going
on in the living room. I heard whistles, singing,
barfs, farts, laughter. They might be mercenary sol-
diers, living in a different place every day, serving
multiple flags. If this army of international drug
traffic took flight with us, we'd be shielded by arms
and muscles, saved from imminent death every
time we gazed out of foreign windows. I wanted to
be a decision-maker, the wife who takes advantage
of her husband's position to infiltrate herself as an
independent spy in the top brass. But there I was, in
a role below modest, breastfeeding the man I had
pursued since puberty, since childhood. Where
would we go now? When would we leave? Yes, yes,
the man who might be the prince of drug trafficking in Southern Brazil suckled my breasts and
didn't seem to be in a hurry. His mouth latching on
my nipples gave me the sensation of a liquid coming out of me, which would make me cum and
make him an addict, yes. I felt as if I ejaculated
from my tits. This could be a ritual of farewell to the
house that had sheltered us on the outskirts of
Cuiabá. While the engineer breastfed, I didn't know
what time it was, didn't know for how long we had

been delayed in departing. I could only hear the hustle and bustle of the men in the other room. What the hell were they doing? The house would likely be kept as a warehouse for merchandise. I ran my fingers through his hair and asked him if we weren't late. Only then I realized he was asleep. My tiny tits were silenced, in pain; they burned. They were clearly small, but also seemed festive, for they could already offer their substance. Yellow milk stained the engineer's mouth. I feared I was creating a man who would turn against me later. He still had a lot of time ahead of him. I, on the other hand, was excluded from all the action outside the house and would likely grow old sooner than him. Perhaps, it was time to betray him and run away to follow my own chance and will. But where would I go? Return to Porto Alegre like this—like an unfinished project of a woman, unrecognizable to my wife or son for having been through a serious physical mutation—going back like this didn't seem like a reasonable option. All alone, where else could I go? The fact is that I also fell asleep; my finger transformed into an exemplary midget embedded in the engineer's ass. I had a dream where my man ran away to Paraguay. Alone. I stayed behind, trembling, crying. I wanted to caress his hair, always so sweaty. I wanted to cuddle with him for a minute longer. My chest was tight, I was scared, I waved goodbye so I could exorcise our insane impasse—though we never really learned the reason for our hesitation. Only in bed would he lose that air of living under the shadow of insanity. I desperately cried in the barren field as the helicopter took him away from me. Where would I go now? If I was fully a woman, I'd leave for Bolivia, where I could try prostitution. On the way to La Paz, I'd take a road where many Brazilian women waited for their clients. The road split a little town in two. A place for truck drivers to stop, where women abound. They usually turn their tricks by the roadside, inside the trucks. It's more practical and cheaper than a motel bed, you can just fuck in the back seat. Girls sit on big men's laps, and men wait for them with their erections hanging out their flies. They say an old woman walks from truck to truck knocking on the improvised alcoves. What does she want? She goes around distributing pieces of toilet paper to the participants of the nocturnal programs. They say she used to be a whore, but she's now content to distribute fragments of genuine compassion. When she was young, she was disgusted by the sticky feeling after her services. Everybody needs to do a goodwill, she would say, craning her neck so she wouldn't miss any details of the couples' dirty activities. To satisfy the old woman's curious eyes, some truck drivers would reenact their performances in front of her. She would approach the scene, in total reverence. Who provides her with the paper rolls? She doesn't know. All she knows is that they are religiously waiting for her at the door of her shack every morning. She came from Brazil when she was sixteen. In Bolivia, she was met with men's cordiality—something rare in Brazil, according to her. She had always maintained affable relationships with her colleagues. They say a former lover is the one providing for her daily task. He pays her homage, silently coaxing her into social work for the population's hygiene. They even say that he stamps Jesus hearts, encircled in crowns of thorns as is customary, on the endless rolls of paper. Many hookers have reached orgasm while kissing the Jesuses on the thin, thin paper. There's the story of a whore who, upon receiving the piece of paper, screamed as if from pains of a laceration. Later, she vomited blood. And she had an orgasm without anyone's help. She said she felt the same pains of Christ in the Calvary. She showed her fingers, they also bled. They took her to the hospital, where they gave her many transfusions. She was discharged, became a saint. Maybe she's this old lady going from truck to truck. While the silent project of escaping was slowly planned, my engineer still wanted to explore my body. Now, he put his mouth on my cock. When I felt I was about to cum, I grabbed his head and, with a fast and almost violent maneuver, and lots of spit, yes, I penetrated his extra warm little asshole, so so warm and waiting for his nurse. I was his nurse, the one who plugged the gap in his hole for a day or two, maybe less, maybe more, but he would always come back to me in case of future emergencies. He was so lubricated in his rectum that he was unable to hold back a fart. Did he shit on my cock? Just kidding, I was satisfied with his response to my penetration. I was me, a hybrid between man and woman, but the honor of penetrating him right up into his viscera, ah, that belonged to me. Then we got up and got dressed. I started collecting clothes, cosmetics, toothpaste, our dirty underwear. I felt such a rare intimacy with another body every time I touched his underwear. I'd bring them to my nose and inhale the dense perfume of cum, sweat, and shit, all mixed up. If I could wear his underwear, and he mine, life would be partially resolved. But when the lights go down, the chimera of fusion with another releases a bitter aftertaste in this idea. I left many things behind because I knew we weren't leaving to sightsee but to escape, with a still-unknown destination. I needed to accept the engineer's laconic tone. I needed to accept the secrets related to his risky mission. A helicopter came down on the wasteland in front of the house where, for some time, I had guarded the chief's fort—or rather, our fort. Upon seeing the helicopter, I felt a distinct relief: perhaps this would be an escapade to a world of abundance, with no persecutions. A world where everyone was already forgiven. A world where we didn't need to pay for our sins anymore. My husband and I would start from zero. We'd change our lives. We'd have kids. From the grandiloquence of our escape, it was evident the engineer had reached the highest rank. I'd have a maid, several if possible, once we reached our destination. I'd be waiting for my guy at the end of the day, wearing a surprise dress, a special perfume for the occasion—more sophisticated than the aromas I'd wear at night, incisive, regulated by how much lechery dominated the air. Where will this place be? I asked myself. Will it be in Brazil or abroad? It shouldn't be a long flight. It was a helicopter, after all. The men in the gang bade us farewell. There was a minor among them. He was probably fifteen. Reasonably well-dressed in black. He seemed to be defying me. Why only now was he coming to the surface with all his mystery? He had the face of someone to be feared, who had killed many. Despite his green years, his bravery made me dream of staying behind. Of not leaving. In the helicopter, the engineer and I were the only passengers. With the rotor at full speed, the men's hats flew away, forcing everyone to crouch and step back. They ran after their hats—hats with enigmatic inscriptions embroidered under the front brims. The boy in black was the only one wearing his hat with the brim in the back. He was so sleazy. He looked at me again with irony in his eyes, like in a sort of communion with me. He winked at me, and I, back at him. My desire to stay on the ground reemerged. Then, the boy spat. Perhaps a code to imply sudden contempt. I closed my eyes. Only the images prior to the boy's spit interested me. When I opened my eyes, I surprised the engineer with a half-smile in the face of our departure. I was ready to follow this man. And be proud of his high risk activities. If he succeeded in his business and managed to stay away from the police, I could have everything I'd always wanted, as opposed to the tight budget of my past in Porto Alegre, barely getting by with the proceeds from my problematic farm. Although I didn't know the extent of the engineer's wealth, I could already imagine owning an apartment in Miami, a steakhouse on gringo soil, with no financial constraints whatsoever. I'll beg him to

take us to a rodeo in Texas. To Marilyn's grave in
Los Angeles. I would invite the engineer to touch
the headstone with me. It'll bring us luck, I mused,
feeling all smiley and cocky as I so often demanded
from myself. Perhaps, soon, American medicine
could provide me with what I needed to become a
mother, why not? Being a mother to the engineer's
son would make me forget all about my past in
Porto Alegre for good. That's what I needed. My
wife and son counted on my death. They didn't need
my presence to remember the times of our triad coexistence. Moreover, they might even be thinking
of erasing those long-gone years from their minds.
The more the helicopter rose, the more sure I was of
having made the right decision. What would I be
doing now if I were still the father of an adult in the
far Brazilian South? I'd be torturing myself over everything I hadn't done to make our relationship
work. What I know is that an incredible force came
over me in the helicopter. It didn't matter if I had to
go to the ends of the earth with the engineer. I
would go anyway, even if we both met the final bullet in the end. To die by the same gun with him
would give me the right credentials for eternity. I,
too naive to recognize the mousetrap I was getting
myself into, felt like I was some kind of criminal
virgin. Although I loved the engineer, I was aware

that my life was being corrupted, and, worst of all, that I was losing my intelligence by resigning myself to him more completely than he deserved, without thought for my future, which, of course, was only getting shorter and shorter. From the helicopter, I saw the bleak spread of nature down below. It was obvious that I didn't belong to any family in Porto Alegre or elsewhere. Dead, I was living with a man prone to darkness. Mysterious enough to not grant me access to the details of the siege we were escaping. During the nerve-wracking helicopter ride, he was glued to an article in the paper. I grabbed the paper when he put it aside. The news said: "Two French citizens were arrested with more than 84,000 pills of ecstasy at the Guarulhos International Airport on Wednesday." He asked me to throw the paper away as soon as we got off the helicopter. Where are we getting off? I asked. We're getting there, he said. I looked at the undulating greenery below and I wished I could move closer to him, real close, feel his smell, skin, angst. I could feel the fever through his sweat. A liquid so hot it burned me. That feeling of fusion between us in the middle of the flight seemed, yes, like a succinct sacrament from one man to another, without intervention from either God or the Devil. I grabbed his arm, I felt his dense sweat of anxiety. When we fucked, everything was spasmodic. Now, in the helicopter, he didn't seem to cultivate the slightest inclination toward me. When I lived with my son and wife I was numb to any deep emotions. Now, conversely, I felt quite unsettled with him, avid to earn a meager gaze from him; without sex getting between us, like when he used to say, with a certain astute voice, "I think I'm lucky." Lucky about what? Lucky to know me? A long time ago, in our youth, after reading a few poems of solemn beauty by Ricardo Reis, he stopped and said: "I think I'm lucky." And he looked at me. Who was he addressing with that phrase? I was the only one near him when he proclaimed that. In those moments, he would look a bit opaque, confessing to a sentiment hidden behind his mask, something that didn't feel complete, perhaps because of his condition as an eternally single man, always unattached. I grabbed his hand. I didn't know what to do with it so I gave it back to him. To live for my man was to have less each day. He seemed to enjoy this gradual detachment. Soon, the helicopter would descend into the immensity of the jungle, which was starting to impose itself on the landscape. Between branches and the foliage, I caught the image of two jaguars fucking, expelling monumental roars. Suddenly, a clearing in the forest. It was time to descend. The roars of the feline passion defied our flight. We only landed because they allowed us. The pilot whispered something to the engineer. I noticed a house near the edge of the clearing. Would we live there? I brought our bags into the house, which was really just a shack. There was a bed inside. We bade farewell to the pilot. I remembered the engineer's request to throw away the newspaper report on the 84,000 pills of ecstasy. The request didn't make much sense in the middle of a forest so far from human civilization. Suddenly, I feared we'd end up suffocating each other in that place. It was the first time we'd been so isolated from the world. And right there, in a tropical jungle! Where would we buy provisions, our mosquito repellent? The closest market was 70 kilometers away. By foot, of course. There was no public transportation. No roads. He sat on the bed and said we didn't have any other option. He'd be arrested if he tried to escape to another country. He needed to stay in Brazil and wait for the whole thing to cool down. In an inhospitable place like this. A place the police would have a hard time finding. I sat on the bed, too. Then I lay down on my stomach, elbows on the mattress, and I was surprised to see that he expressed a new aspiration: he seemed to be awakening to a sort of mysticism in himself. Mysticism for my consumption, perhaps. His severe expression seemed to anticipate his domination of the forest. Wordlessly, he stammered his heroic disturbance. He would live in bloody battle with the jungle while continuing to provide amphetamines for the metaphysical recreation of men and women. Whoever wanted the entertainment that cocaine provided could have it, ruthlessly. This beautiful male specimen meditated upon arriving at his new home in the forest's fringes. I could read his meditation. If we found ourselves with no way out, I'd propose a suicide pact in the jungle. Like the early Christians, we'd be devoured by animals such as jaguars, snakes, wild dogs, swarms of bugs, and so many other horrors. There was pride in his silence. I would help him disguise his shady business, though I didn't know the full scope of his smoke and mirrors. He should become the mediator between white-collar and blue-collar crimes. He was made for this job. Because of his looks and the way he dressed, he'd be embraced by both classes. One could imagine my engineer having a glass of expensive wine with an executive but also drinking a beer in a dingy bar in Morro da Cruz. No one from these two extremes would find his presence strange. Maybe that's where my passion for his character came from. Precisely because it was hard to pin him down. I could see him buying some land in the region and raising cattle, living up to his spiritual ancestry of a gaucho. He would be taken as a rancher and entrepreneur in the logging business. Yes, he stood high on a pedestal, and, in our shared loneliness, he would be the one reigning above my mortal demands. Clinging to cleaning and cooking was all that was left for me. Perhaps I'd get some helpers. If he still allowed our intimate life, perhaps I could still attack his empire from behind on the erotic domain. Now, I would penetrate him until he bled. He would never trade this guaranteed (and sometimes explosive) orgasm for a clean, harmless, insipid fuck. If I were to defeat this empire, there was the gloomy threat of my cock losing its verve by being poisoned in the engineer's cavernous hole. I bet he'd eat from my hand if I just half-ass fucked him, inserting just the tip, nothing else. That'd be my method to punish him for the things that had begun to bother me more each day. He would do anything to guarantee the quality of his nightly service in that bedroom, which didn't even look like a bedroom. It looked more like a utility room where I'd practice nursing. After all, being someone's caregiver is to provide them with a bit of physical vigor, a bit of warmth. I got up. From that point on, I would start being difficult. I'd learn how to negotiate with the cock I owned. My penis would have a price tag, even if it was going through a less powerful phase. The engineer would have to pay for it. He could pay me with cuddles if he wanted, no problem. This small commercial transaction would create enormous anxiety within him, I know. He'd be hanging by a thread; plus, there'd be tension between us. To avoid getting bored, I'd have to stop my transition to the female guise. I should reinvent myself again, revert the transition, go back to being a man in full physical force so I could face him as an equal when the first quarrel in the somber jungle came. Evening was falling in the clearing. Soon, we'd be attacked by mosquitoes if we didn't bring out the repellent. The former residents had left a matchbox on the stove. I thought of making a bonfire to retaliate against the insects. I found branches and logs on the ground. The fire turned out higher than I expected. I concluded I'd have to accept the damned reality of living in a jungle. I also concluded that the engineer had succeeded in his role as a traitor. He had never consulted me about the new destination. It had been a trap. He kept secretive about what led us to escape. I felt unhappy watching the flames grow higher and higher. In following this old passion of mine, I found myself in the worst of all worlds, unable to see a way out. I was living the existence of an enslaved woman. There was nothing I could do to change or attenuate the situation. Although the engineer also found himself at the end of the world, he was still the commander-in-chief. If he disappeared in the jungle, his squad would come after him; if I disappeared, it would be the repetition of a dead man vanishing—it would make no difference. The status of formerly dead doesn't confer any wisdom, much less prestige. On the contrary, the belief still remains that the person lost a bit of soul during his death. His soul is damaged. He becomes an incomplete zombie, brandishing the qualities of his temporary amnesia from dawn to dawn, but without someone to provide shelter and rest to his ghost. It would be useless for him to slice his hand with a razor to prove he bled, that he was still alive. Nobody would want to be associated with a man who had already tasted earth. But it was necessary to make things happen; I needed to ensure our self-imposed presence in that jungle did not resemble a prison. We were living in exile, without any chance of reversing the immediate circumstances. Would we resume our long sex sessions? Would the lack of options cause growing animosity on both sides? The fire flickered slowly for the lack of wind, it crackled the kindling I had gathered at its base.

The heat of the night was reaching, perhaps, its zenith…true access to hell. On top of the heat from the fire, the region's temperature alone could melt your brain and fog your vision. The engineer might be lamenting his luck: if he had been caught by the Federal Police, he'd be in a cool cell by now; in Porto Alegre's temperate climate; jailed, yes, but far from the ungratefulness of this land where the temperatures climbed to 44-45 degrees. Here, we didn't have a jailer to guard us 24 hours. The role of a jailer alternated between the two of us, leaning certainly more toward the engineer; though, apparently, he was turning out to be a tyrant oblivious to his function. Night had fallen. But I no longer knew the difference between afternoon, morning, night, and dawn. In fact, this confusion has always existed. Schedules never worked for me. My destiny seemed to be outside such circumstances. I had always been a vacant space for anyone to park in. Until I started kicking the invader out to go looking for other parishes. Now they could call me the goddess of fire. I wouldn't abandon this combustion any time soon— at least not until the engineer called me to fuck. When that moment came, nothing else would matter anymore. I bet the same applied to him. Looking at the flames, I felt like a condemned woman over and over. Time would have to move quickly for us so that we could finally jump, in the blink of an eye, from this period of imprisonment to one of absolution. How many years would pass? If I were arrested too, I wouldn't even have his criminal exploits to boast about. With the trial, his life as a drug dealer would come out of the shadows. After the capture, I wouldn't qualify for a plea deal. And so I chose to ignore everything about his career as a gangster. In fact, closely observing him, I learned that crime is a profession like any other. The only difference is that you get dirty with blood…there's that. I had washed a bloodied shirt of the engineer's one time when he came back from a trip. Of course, as usual, I didn't ask him anything. Since I had never been told by him or anyone else about his activities, I couldn't really accuse him or serve as an accomplice. The police wouldn't be able to extract any elucidating information from me, even under severe torture. Unless I slandered him. No, I wouldn't know how to create a story and dramatize it for the police. I always chose to ignore the truth about this man. Since our youth, this choice had always been an obvious one. Most likely, the engineer had spent several stints behind bars. He was a wanted man. Possibly a fugitive. While we waited to endure (or not) the immense ordeal between the crime in uniform there and the crime in civilian clothes here, we kept living, sharing our little idylls and delights. I was a passive wife, participating in the environment of trafficking without knowing which side my biography suited. Had his initiation into the world of drug trafficking started in the German submarine? Or before? Moreover, I needed to practice some act of delinquency, whether it was dealing with something prohibited, holding myself accountable for a damned transport or burning pieces of evidence. Perhaps he and his gang wanted to preserve my supposed innocence as a potential neutral party to make a deal with the police. Maybe it was time for me to come into the bedroom now and eat his ass, always so red and warm—sometimes even vividly inflamed. The smell coming from it was of mucus constantly reactivated by feces, my dick, and my cum, thus achieving a very illustrative synthesis of human matter. Sometimes his ass looked pink, still tender, fragile, from early morning until late afternoon, raising thoughts about the frequency of his libidinous acts. But, as far as I knew, his butt only went through deployments during the German submarine period. He surely expanded his resume during his stays in the harbors of the world, offering his scarlet jewel to foreign legions. With me, he seemed to get bored between one fuck and the next. Yes, he had resuscitated me before, but he would now die if he could drag me down to the grave with him. On occasions like this, I would get him in the bedroom and fuck him with violence, almost to the point of beating him up. His languid moans joined my vocal thunder in a primitive trance. Shutters closed. When we were finished, I turned on the light. He would express hemorrhagic discomfort from his asshole, but sooner rather than later he'd call me back to bed. The engineer bled. I would also get bloodstained, of course, with his excreted substances. In the bathroom, in front of the mirror, I smelled my hand, smeared with his anal blood, and breathed the scent of the impossible thing we had inherited from childhood—a childhood that slowly withdrew from memory. I could go back to bed now and fuck him, as if I were the big boss in that house in the middle of the jungle. When I penetrated him, he loosened and gripped his sphincter according to his loving rhythm of restraint and release. The orgasm itself comes from restraint, the greedy moment when you swallow your object of pleasure and pretend to imprison it as a treasure. It is then when you, in fact, possess the lover. Release, on the other hand, can be confused with a brief rest, with a momentary withdrawal from the other's fleshly object, with the act of catching your breath for the big blow that will soon unravel as if it might go on forever. Moving forward, if we wanted to save ourselves, we would have to keep to the pace of at least one fuck a day. We would likely be doomed to each other in the future. Maybe what seemed like the same old, same old, was in fact the best of all worlds. Acquiescing to the discreet appeal of our flesh was all we could do. I was drinking water in the kitchen when I heard his whistle. Whose else could it be? Earlier, I had walked around the house, listening to the noise of the crickets. What does their chirping mean? Well, absolutely nothing. I closed my eyes and saw, through the flames, colorless, convulsive particles. It was another face of the fire, its decaying side. This other face was the very inside out that my eyelids were used to covering. It seemed like the admission to a neglected visual field, an exercise of recovering details of an ocular ostracism that happened to be mine. He whistled again, a categorical warning for me to come back. Oh, how I had nurtured a deep, almost perpetual passion for him since the time of our adolescence. If not early childhood. The one who makes passion the center of his life ends up the most vulnerable. Me. And there was him: unchangeable, holding on to his obscure gaze, blood trickling out his ass, staining the mattress. To avoid getting too involved, the unchangeable man only cums at dessert, not with the main entrée. The dessert may even arrive first. He can dispense with everything else. That was the man who whistled to me. That was the man to whom I now had to tend. I was still in front of the fire, going through different eras in my head, recapping scenes and scenarios, being myself in so many situations at the same time. Despite everything, I was available to him when I got to the bedroom door. But then, for the first time, I saw him with a gun. He was in his swim trunks, lying on the bare mattress with its bluish print of finials and macaws. The revolver was lying on a pillow next to him. It was the sign that he could no longer be distracted; he was at the mercy of the siege that was surely coming for him. The engineer would be waiting for the enemy with bullets. Come, he said and took off his trunks. To be a fornicating machine, that's what he expected from me. I'd never learned how to decline this invitation. I wish I could be like him, a hero on retreat. Since I couldn't, of course, a fiercely determined eagerness to penetrate him possessed me: a wish to leave my semen inside him, no matter if it was a sterile field. Inside him is where I wanted to stay, even if in the most ignoble part of his physique, his ass. To fuck the engineer was to fuck something beyond me. That in itself made our union fertile. After all, we had spent decades as virgins to each other. There was always a new detail in his body that added to my delirium. However, we were starting to lose steam. Something spoiled wanted to undermine the dirty lovers' holiness. Still, I bet we'd be in bed soon enough. I'd be at the bedroom door, ready for my expedition into another body. I always left those fuck sessions with the engineer feeling like an animal that had worked hard to earn it. Earn that evasion of self. That immaterial twinkle in the flesh. Later, I would experience the torpor of someone once allured who then retreats, fearing the exposure to abandonment. On these occasions, I would reinvent myself with a certain sentiment one has at the dawn of puberty: the impression of not having a partner, so strong is the isolation of one who chokes in delight then sleeps. Later, as an adult, one surrenders to the illusory impulse to merge with his lover, even if he already foresees the failure of the endeavor. What pulses vehemently beneath a fuck is the insane desire to die in an embrace. If it is necessary to die to accomplish this fusion, then let death take us into its bizarre eternity. That's it, orgasm doesn't necessarily have to do with static procedures in preparation for a sculptural pose. With that naked man in bed, my cock changed shape, not so much in thickness, but definitely in length. It even looked cute, my cock, I swear, and the engineer entertained himself with it like a kid with his favorite candy. Finally, in those moments, he would let his intimacy flourish, timidly, timidly, but hey, at least he was willing to kiss. Just being inside his mouth would almost make me cum, and in fact, many times I came with my tongue inside him. Yes, I wanted to find him in bed now. I took off my underwear and walked toward him. There was a half-opened package lying on the floor. Inside, a white powder, which could only be plaster or cocaine. I couldn't forget I was sleeping with a top executive of a drug trafficking ring. Or maybe not the top, I don't know. A black cat licked the powder and seemed to like it. It licked it with drama, with the intense anxiety of wanting more, licking more quickly. I lay face down on top of the engineer. As I settled in, I felt the mattress get wet with piss. Piss from the prince of cocaine. Yes, the engineer wet the bed. And even that undisguised wetness had an aphrodisiac effect on me. I pointed the barrel of the gun away from me. And I bit his right lobe. He slipped from under me and lay on top of my surprised body. I was on my stomach and felt suffocated. I realized his cock was miraculously pressing hard against my thigh. For a moment I thought to cut off his intention with a brusque, exaggerated movement. With Herculean strength, I was able to turn my body over. I was still underneath him, but we were face to face now. The engineer's cock was so thick and wanted to find a cozy home inside me. I slid my hand between our bodies, looking for some help from my cock. I confess I almost ran to the jungle to hide. I was sprawled under my teenage—maybe childhood—passion without knowing what to do with my poor cock, which was not showing any reaction. From time to time the engineer and I slapped each other to chase the mosquitoes away. It was the first time I was having a penile dysfunction since I had been with him. Had the engineer gone through treatment to cure his impotence? Was it my turn to get treated now, too? What about this coincidence of my cock going invalid just when my love for him caused his phallic restoration? Nothing was inexhaustible, neither erection nor impotence. Who plotted such alternating lascivious expressions between us? Had the gods written the stage direction in advance? I touched my crotch again and found the worst: it seemed I had lost the essential aspects of my genitals. Where my cock and sack used to be, there was now a flooded swampy terrain, a field with no solid ground or protrusion, no traces of what had once made up my most erogenous zone. I stopped resisting him, I relaxed and said softly: Whatever infamy wants. I opened my legs like a woman, crossed my feet around his lower back, and started to study how I felt with his thrusts. The engineer dug deep inside me in search of my always-so-resistant core. Sometimes he didn't even seem to have a cock anymore, so immersed was he in me. As if he were an embryo inside my body. At the same time, I had the feeling I was forming a hymen from a still incipient genital base. A hymen that would only last until the first cock fucked me. And it was his cock! It didn't feel that bad, but it was afflicting to have his cock digging into my deepest, most sensitive point, where the eye cannot reach. It was like being prodded in a wound that has just lost its protective shell. The inflamed friction reaches the edge of pain. What was once pain becomes the edge of pleasure, so unsustainable that it induces you to scream. And I did, I screamed so loud I was ashamed. But, as I achieved this advanced frontier of the female orgasm, I realized the trance was not enough, I wanted more. In that fleshy battle, I was closing one cycle and starting another. Was I the bottom now? Bye-bye to my cock? But I still didn't feel ready to be a full-time female. I didn't want the engineer to get addicted to cumming inside me. I needed to run away from that musty room and never come back—be eaten by a jaguar or bitten by a snake that would then die from my inglorious poison. I could end like that, fine, as long as I regrew the signs of being a man on my surface. I'll carry a piece of paper with my male name written on it so when the Federal Police search for my identity, I'll have it in my pocket. I had left my I.D. at the hospital, or in the grave when I escaped with the engineer. With my information, they would take my body back to Porto Alegre and hand it over to my wife and son. They—who had already buried me permanently—would have to arrange a second burial, barely understanding what was happening. Lying there, crushed by the engineer's body, I thought about my son and felt, with a certain tenderness, that my offspring would have a more serene life than mine. Once, when my wife was traveling, we took a bath together. The tub was big enough for two people. In the beginning, we soaped each other's shoulders and necks for a long time, making so much foam. Gradually, our exposed nakedness was hidden by the dark water. I was first to get out of the tub. I leaned over him, brought my hand to his chin, and shook his head like I did so often when he was a boy. I wanted to caress him, my hand almost went there. The gesture I curtailed got stuck in my head. To this day, it still throbs in my temples… Why didn't I beckon him? Why did I retract my gesture? He got out of the tub, too. Tired of insisting every insinuation was a rehearsal, of involuntarily aborting it, I touched his pubic hair, ran my finger through the bush, and scratched the skin behind it, or maybe I tickled him; I don't know anymore, but I stopped when I saw with my very own eyes that the boy was beginning to like it. His turgid cock came at me like a fresh wound. I was startled not by the size of his dick or his steady erection. What startled me was the red aspect of his glans, which I remembered from his early years as being pale, so pale, like the rest of his body. That redness might translate into a voluptuous character. Then I told him a story he didn't remember: One day when he was a little boy, I took him to the pediatrician for a phimosis surgery. I didn't leave his side by the discreet surgical table. When the intervention was over, I picked him up with extreme caution. He looked at me as if asking for an explanation. I don't remember anything else from that day. But, yes, I thought about that moment as I lay there under the engineer. He had his genitals back in business, while I…well, I'd lost my dick. Not that I already had a vagina per se, but in my pelvic region, the rumble of a certain concavity made itself heard like a nocturnal, subterranean call, though

still uncertain—a cauldron boiling the sauce for my
new focus of delight. I felt I was transitioning again.
I was not just a man unable to embody the role of a
woman anymore. Without the weight of determination, I floated. So I started reflecting on how to
get rid of that animal on top of me. In the meantime, I was trying with everything I had to cum
with my new orgasm, even if delayed. But from
where would I cum? The sooner I came the sooner
I could get away from that stupid endless hideaway.
After all, I was a good citizen, with an absolutely
unblemished life. The engineer weighed helplessly
on me. I brought my hand to my crotch again, and
this inspection confirmed what I'd felt before. I
held a minutely detailed confirmation. Everything
felt watery, undefined, still suffering from its painful partial condition. I needed to stand up to the
engineer's chutzpah and get into a rhythm, focus all
my strength in my pelvis. Whatever the vocation of
my incomplete genitalia, it poured its soup in boiling bubbles. Right there, where I used to flaunt the
proud attribute of a man. Between his body and
mine, my hand wanted to stimulate what was not
yet an established field, rather a liquid soil of permanent experimentation. I couldn't get the image
of my son out of my head. But, finding myself in
this fugitive state, I didn't know what to make of

my young swimmer. The bath we'd taken together was coming back to me now with a precision that made my deepest memories jealous. That's when details expand to reach the magnitude of truth. My son's image formed clearly in my head. His pink skin, sometimes hinting at an ocher tone—perhaps a sign of him entering adulthood. His unshaven. I couldn't believe his lips had been created by me and another person. What had been my percentage in giving those lips such sumptuous shape? I wet my fingers in the new slit of my nascent sex—an organ still without a conclusive north. I was starting to like the manipulation at the construction site between my legs. I started to squirm on the verge of the female genitalia, which I, for the first time, openly maneuvered in an attempt to activate it. From the memory of my son, I started cultivating the image of the ideal young man—one I could have been if it hadn't been for my rush to get to my current state. Now I saw my son in greenish tones, and this could be the sign that he was bowing down to this far distant night in the jungle where mosquitoes chafed on the delicate skin of the urbane. By the bathtub, my boy looked at me, trying to decipher the ambition of my desire. Under the engineer's body, I felt my orgasm rising, even if I didn't know exactly from where it would erupt. My son kissed me deeply but calmly. Our tongues touched discreetly, sometimes traveling to the roofs of our mouths. Gradually, however, this scavenger hunt between our dental arcades reminded us that the right thing to do was to say goodbye to each other. In fact, separation from that point on seemed inevitable in our shared history. But lovers don't say goodbye only once, but frequently, softening the departure. Because you never know if love won't return further down the road, bringing back shame for the thorny past. The one on top of my carcass was not the engineer any longer, but my own son who, at last, was visiting me and moaned and delved into me. I would love it if he could impregnate me. For now, his hard cock wanted to enter me with healthy thrusts. I opened my legs and wrapped them around his waist—yes, like a woman again. His youthful demeanor gave him the impression of a warrior—to my detriment, of course. He was hurting me. I had the feeling his dick couldn't find its footing in my liquid slit, as it kept returning tiredly to the surface, holding inert for a few seconds, catching its breath, deciding what to do next. Where would I get the strength to endure an epic as depraved as this one? My son dominated me in a way I had never been able to dominate him in his childhood. He crushed me with his Adam's apple as

he entered my mouth. A teenager with so little experience, if any at all. His cheap cologne penetrated
my nostrils. Sometimes, his ragged beard scratched
me around the eyes. My pelvis eagerly welcomed
the monumental cock of my own progeny.
Unequaled, I'd say. I was at the center of my consciousness again. My core had rekindled; I saw the
light. I was once again inside myself, that's it. I felt
my son's lips in my blooming vagina. No, it wasn't
his lips. It was his hand. And something else: his
big dick again. He was coming to quench my thirst,
because I was thirsty, yes. He was coming, he was
coming, and he came, flooding me with cum and
piss. I softly expelled the deep roar of that animal I
heard when I first arrived in the jungle. I was underneath the engineer. He was sleeping. I quietly
got out from under him so as not to wake him up.
He snored. I looked at his cock and was startled
that all those centimeters were able to nest in my
sex in its arduous, dilated mutation. Some depth
certainly existed between my legs, but I still didn't
know how to measure it. Trying to look all the way
inside my forming vagina pained me. It was like I
wouldn't be able to come back if I got to the bottom
of myself. That man I called engineer would forever
condemn me to live in his company, in the imprac-
ticable jungle, far from everything, miles and miles

away. He was my jailer. The two of us, confined in the jungle. My old passion for the engineer was starting to empty out in my new and sudden present. I needed to free myself from the obsession that had enslaved me. It depended on me to get away from this place as soon as possible. Before he and I grew sick from hunger and boredom. Although, I risked not finding any signs of civilization in my solitary escape and ending up ravaged by the forest's beasts. He would send a henchman to trace my footprints. The engineer would chain me to a pole and religiously fuck me without spit or lube every night and hit me and kiss me, passing rationed scraps of food to my mouth. But if I escaped, he would never see me again. And if one of the cocaine hitmen found me, I hoped he'd shoot me and finish me off. It's exhausting to feel cornered all the time. So the gunshot would be merciful. Still, I'd rather see myself alone in the jungle and exposed to beasts and insects than have to continually depend on someone out of laziness. But for now, here I am, watching his body on the mattress. Before leaving the bedroom, I turned a little. He snored thunderously. A mid-level authority in drug trafficking, maybe he had never heard that his snoring was absurdly loud from any of his sexual partners. He snored—it could be low glucose—before my trembling person, canceling out any romanticism I still cultivated for him. One step closer to the female matrix, I was ready to desert any chimera of love. I was starting to see him as nothing more than a mediocre drug dealer. This time, I could contemplate him without any delusions of criminal heroisms. His dick maintained a partial erection. I approached and looked at it closely. Between soft and hard, a penis acquires a placid grandeur, an ambiguous beauty. Had his beast finally overcome the erectile problem? I had never observed it so closely before, leisurely, without any distraction, just for sport. What if I provoked it? I could closely approach the tip and receive a full involuntary jet of ejaculation. For the man asleep, the added value to this strange encounter would come precisely from an erection without a defined erotic object. Who inhabited his dream, causing the erection I was admiring? My desire was quiet and incipient according to the new beat of my heart. Speaking of heart, I remembered I had medication for high blood pressure waiting in my pants pocket. There was one more box left. I, a true snake charmer, did not want to wake the cock's owner. The owner of the cock, the one always depriving me of any initiative in that forest kingdom. I preferred to let him sleep so I could wonder. Was his cock bigger than mine? Near his cock's base, the tattooed bee quivered. It must have been a generous influx of blood, stunned by not knowing the source of so much lust. Was it really me? A cat rubbed its fur between my shins. The engineer's cock, perhaps sensing my gaze and nakedness, revealed itself, totally hard. My excitement for a dick seemed insatiable. Sometimes I thought I had already lost interest in that inflatable piece of meat. But when it reappeared, my fascination for this lesser god made me feel submissive and abandoned to its whims again. It had swelled to its max. The cat might be queer too, for he also approached the household phallus to rub his mane and revere its power. The owner of the precious dingaling woke up so as not to leave his lecherous trump card alone with me. Or had our engineer been pretending to sleep so he could spy on my freedom? Upon waking and seeing his stiff sausage, he gave a look of surprise. Or he faked it. Anyway, I was tired of his greedy presence. I already had the best of him without having him. This guy didn't encourage my crystalline interest in him as a whole. He didn't open up with me about his involvement with the drug world or the world outside it. He spoke only of fleeing, fleeing, fleeing. Before, his enigmatic ways used to give me tenderness. Now, in the face of his insane placidity, I had a bomb ready to explode in my soul.

I left the room. I thought I saw my son at the door. I hurried to see him. It was a wild dog instead, showing me its teeth as if it was going to attack me. It ran away when I threw an empty bottle of gin at it. Maybe it was indeed my son who had come through the door. My devotion to my boy's image was so powerful that his specter could have in fact materialized in the forest, miles and miles away from his native land. His living ghost kept me company during my orgasm with the engineer; he participated in it. Soon, I would run away from here and find him in Porto Alegre again. Kiss my offspring. Leave the mark of the lipstick I never wore on his face. Get up to date on that human clay whose seed I hurled from me on an inspired but cold night in June. My wife and I had been staying in a hotel in Serra Gaúcha that night. Guaranteed of the conception, I briefly passed out, I remember. I was flung on the bed, sweating in midwinter. The word became flesh, the evangelical pastor said on TV. I looked at my wife; she had fallen asleep. I turned off the TV. When I got out of my torpor, I saw everything with a white hue. The world had turned albino. I was an astonished man exploring whiteness. My underwear was the only piece of clothing not matching the surroundings: it was blue; it had definitely remained blue. In my intention to beget a child, I had pushed myself to the limit. She was enveloped in white, too, sleeping within her very new pregnancy, amid the pictorial anemia of the environment. So different from the scene in this satanic jungle where the engineer offered his sleep to the hunting. I walked through the clearing, listening to the laments of grim species. From the vegetation, a meager light shone on me like a flashlight. Who was out there? A detective from the police investigation? I dragged my feet slowly, careful not to hit any leaves, twigs, or branches. I avoided making any noise. I stood behind a tree from where I could see the shape of a mysterious stranger. No, in reality, they were two men. One of them had a lantern in his hand. They moaned. I noticed, with a feeling of exhaustion, that one was kneeling, performing fellatio on the one holding the lantern, who looked stronger and more muscular. I was so tired of the eternal hell of libido. I spat, silently. For me and the creatures around me, only fucking redeemed the imposition of this sick story. My hope was reduced to the success of my next ejaculation. And I must say that this ejaculation was rarely accompanied by pleasure. It was more like a relief meant to facilitate sleep. In nothing else did I expect so much from so little. So there I stood, obsessed by the frantic rhythm of the

two savages a few meters from me. When you contemplate two people going at it from the outside,
without getting involved, you could well embark on
a hypnotic reverie. And the hypnosis tends to anes-
thetize the instinct. That's why Catholics so often
have a certain lethargy in their litanies. In the face
of what was developing in front of me, would I
walk away satiated? Those two were close to cumming. The one sucking on the stocky lantern guy
jerked himself off with enthusiasm. Still on his
knees. Who were they anyway? Part of a gang laying siege to our squalid home? Perverts without a
flag? Or, on the contrary, bodyguards of my un-
touchable outlaw? Had they been in the forest before us? They climaxed. Miraculously, I heard the
sound of their semen hitting dry leaves. Then, they
pulled their pants farther down and cleaned themselves with things I could not see. Leaves? A hand-
kerchief? They composed themselves. Then I saw it:
the figure who gave the blowjob to the bodyguard
was my son. My son! And when I was going to call
him to help me avoid the inevitable siege, when I
thought he'd be the blessing I needed to not suc-
cumb to my confinement, when I was about to call
him so he could see me, he ran away, already in the
body of a wild dog, his teeth covered with a dark
stain that could only be blood. Between the spot

where the two had cannibalized each other and his exit through the forest, the boy transformed himself into ferocity shrouded in fur. An animal wanting to disappear into the forest's gloomy consciousness. His shrill howls could be heard from a distance. I couldn't see him, couldn't bear witness to his abnormal canine shape any longer. A shape so gigantic that, at first, it made him look like a hostile mule. The bodyguard howled with his deep voice. The wolf howled back, agreeing. I was now facing the bodyguard. He asked if the boss was sleeping. He probably recognized me from some picture the engineer had taken. Perhaps when I was sleeping. I asked him when he arrived. He said about a week ago. To prepare the ground. The ground? I asked myself. The fridge was empty, there were no bath towels, no cutlery or dishes. To prepare the ground? I swallowed heavily. I was already convinced he was a bodyguard. A very tall man, mixed-race, buzz cut, chest and arms of a bodybuilder—he looked like a bear. He pointed the lantern at me; then he turned it off and coughed. Where's my son? I wanted to ask. But he surely didn't ask the boy who just blew him about his genetic origin. Father! I pronounced, silly, hoping to hear my voice in the exalted manifestation of consanguinity. Was it my son or me walking around with a fever? It was necessary to respect the canine shape the boy had taken. I was not sorry for him. He was a ferocious wolf when he ran into the deep forest. The animal had kept my son's face until the moment he turned toward the forest and vanished. I told the guard I was going to check if things were going well deep in the jungle. I could tell he distrusted my appearance. Perhaps he saw the displaced man in me. Someone who didn't have the strength to take a hit. True, I could be described as weak, as opposed to the wolf-boy, my son, a heroic explorer of the jungle. To the guard, I probably looked like a deserter and informer at the same time. I would, yes, shit my pants if confronted by the Federal Police. He most likely thought he could count on me if I ended up suspected of murder. I, João Imaculado, would indeed report the whole mob of thugs if that allowed me to escape from the company of crime with no punishment. In this environment, I understood that conflicts between gang members happened in tragic colors. In the social class where I came from, the history of families can be kept in the closet. But not where I was now. To begin with, they talked about their radical decisions, such as killing and dying, betraying and being betrayed, burning pieces of evidence, even suicide. And of portentous internal robberies. If the police subjected me to intense torture, I would have a least one name to report. At least one. I would bring this name to the tip of my tongue, ready to deliver it to the inquisitor. His would be the first head to roll. After blowing the whistle on him, the rest would fall. But how, if I didn't know anybody else's name but the engineer's? Was he really the strongest? The engineer was an engineer for real. I had no information on his other activities—neither from his mouth nor anyone else's. And I don't even know if I had what it took to observe things from a distance, or if I was simply a man with a busy inner universe, unable to exchange with the outside world. The engineer should rely on my loyalty to passion. I was the right man to mitigate the hell of escaping. The cops would have to skin me alive to get any information out of me—information I didn't have. If they didn't just kill me, that is. For now, under the distant threat of condemnation, and for reasons I didn't know, I just needed to play along, keep an air of disinterested company. An experienced man, period, who wanted to escape in the next few hours. I asked the bodyguard to warn me of anything suspicious. I was going to go in and rest a little. He said he would go to bed at eight in the morning. Then his next shift would start at noon. If plans didn't change or an unforeseen situation didn't lead us to war. Another bodyguard would arrive the next day. They weren't really bodyguards. They were more like security guards, sometimes acting as sentinels. What's the difference? This one had an accent from Rio de Janeiro. If he needed to, he would signal with a whistle. A signal for the engineer, of course. He was the protagonist. Good night, I whispered to the guard. Good night, he answered in a grave register. As I entered the house, I heard a dialogue of whistles. It could have been the bodyguard communicating with someone deep in the jungle. My son? It was sad being inside the house. There was practically nothing in it. No food. The idea came to me that this deprivation could be how I qualified for emancipation from the female—or even male—condition. Was there a third condition? And as I asked myself, I felt dizzy. The whistling dialogue outside kept going strong. Sometimes there was a certain rhythm to the combination of trills. I went to the bedroom. Of course, the engineer snored loudly. If I was still interested in his body, I could do what I used to do with other lovers. As they slept, I would get very close and find certain stealthy spots or unapproachable scars—unapproachable even to loving eyes like mine. This silent research was like the dessert to a meal already finished. Coffee was still coming: at the end, I'd bring my mouth to the dormant skin and lightly brush it so as not to disturb it, not to awaken it. I started to realize I had already cum enough in my life. I also intuited I no longer had an expressive arsenal of semen to waste on endless flammable nights. In my jerk-off sessions now, I noticed how my sperm was released with less force, it didn't shoot far anymore, it felt watery, without even staining the underwear. Unlike the scandalous gushes of my teenage pollutions. Now, my white gunk scattered a couple of rosettes on my underwear, and at some point they became hard little shells, like mother-of-pearl surfaces with assorted semitones. I turned the barrel of the gun the other way. I would need some training to handle it. I should no longer be a virgin to crime. Instead, I should off someone, perhaps even myself. After all, I was living in an environment on the eve of its destruction. Perhaps in a matter of hours, I would offer my wrists to the police to be handcuffed. Would the two rings linked by a chain leave marks on my skin? What about my soul? With my wrists handcuffed, I would want to recognize what it meant to be nefarious, even if I was not proven guilty, beyond the guilt of passion. In handcuffs, I would feel my childhood crumbling bit by bit, to the point where my early years would irretrievably disappear. I felt the bodyguard's presence behind me. He said I shouldn't play with the gun; things could get out of hand. I turned around and saw he was wearing his own revolver at the waist. He with his, I with mine. I noticed a tiny ring in his ear. With all the fucking going on, I might as well be a sponge of information on ballistics from my sleeping boss/engineer. The bodyguard would give me a shooting test. Then, I'd be apt. At that moment, the engineer jittered, whispering angry syllables. A slurred disturbance, opaque, emitted from a refuge that, perhaps, was at a breaking point. It seems I needed to choose between the two men so I could come out of that place alive. The engineer? Why not the bodyguard? I didn't know the real meaning of it yet, but I know that I started having faith in that choice. Which of the two, huh? At that point, I thought it was best to follow the bodyguard, the engineer already seemed one card short of a full deck. He would be hunted down and crushed. Undoubtedly captured and massacred. Just a matter of time. The two of us, the bodyguard and I, would have better luck breaking through the police barricades. Would we flee abroad? Would there be any hole left in Brazil where we could safely huddle from the police? Would that hole be in the jungle? My soon-to-be fugitive partner, the bodyguard, cultivated a genuinely superior air. I'm not only talking about the unshakable expression inherent to his position. The muscled guy seemed to know quite a lot. He seemingly had no interest in concealing his silent climb through the world of trafficking. From this shift of roles came his unmistakable tension. I softened my eyes when I looked at him and asked if he would teach me how to use the gun. He kept quiet, rehearsed a half-smile, and didn't respond. The heat, almost maddening, felt like a furnace's breath. We slapped our own bodies to fight the insects. I woke every morning covered with red, swollen dots. But I never bothered to wear a shirt to protect myself. The cat rubbed its fur on my heels. Wearing a shirt in this brutal heat would be complete insanity. And I wanted to show off my torso, which was not bad at all. My body lived for another body. The only reason I had not been a prostitute is that I was raised by a pious family. I looked at the bodyguard with dexterity, extracting from him some kind of admiration for me. I wanted to survive, nothing more than that. An intuition flourished inside me. An intuition to save my ass. Should I run away with the engineer or the bodyguard? Alone, perhaps? The intuition was surging, yes, and would come to my rescue when I needed it most, I knew. Damn everything else. Without a second thought, I glanced at the guard's gun. Our hands were free. We didn't know where to put them. The engineer snored. Sweat dripped from our bodies. I told him I was going to lie down. He needed to physically verify that I was indeed looking after the engineer's life. It'd be good if this guy thought I had some influence in the world of drug trafficking. I said good night again. He replied and left. I lay down, careful not to wake the engineer. How could I have loved this man for such a long time? Decades! A nap would do me good now. I wanted to be alert for the dawn. Alert to the jungle's discreet moves. That's when I heard a whistle. I went after the bodyguard. He was still in the same place, at the fringes. He had whistled to show me the moon, which floated immensely in the darkness, deeply bluish, pearled. And we, down here, celebrated the moment, bathed by glacial light. Nobody said anything. He and I panted as if panting was a disease and not a threat. We looked at each other, immersed in that buttered air. We were entering a state of euphoria. He walked away from me a little, turned around, and spat. Was there a message encoded in that spit? The moonlight was so bright that I saw the tattoo of an anchor on his arm. Inside the anchor, the imprint of a vaccine scar. I remembered I'd wanted that same mark on my arm when I was a child. But I was not graced with it. And now I needed to decide my fate; choose between two men to follow. Perhaps both? I didn't want to wait until the last minute to decide. I'd like to have a trump card under my sleeve that would provide me with a solution. Why so much effort to make good on the wisest wish? My forehead throbbed. I feared for myself, a shiver crossed my body. The truth is that the gradual sequence of Monday to Monday hindered my knack for improvisation. And I needed it, improvisation. Tomorrow another bodyguard would arrive, and two guards could make things even tenser. The guard looked bewildered in the moonlight. Me too. And then? An animal began to howl. Another one growled. Voices that seemed to come from a wild dog's mouth, the dog that possessed my son's spirit crossing the jungle. Would that be him? One of the animals' sounds was eerily angry. Was he coming to attack us? His growl grew louder. Insects bit us with more hostility. My white body, shirtless, showing its German ancestry, offered itself to the nervous moment. If I could do something, I would dance. But I didn't know how to dance. The buzzing baffled me. The forest, sleepless, pulsed incessantly, preparing itself for the inconceivable, perhaps. All glittered in the light, so much so that it reminded me of the times I'd taken LSD, a drug I used a lot in my youth, and which I simply called acid. With acid, the whole world pulsed, and sometimes undulated. In this pulsation, any surprise could happen. I'd better be ready for the apocalypse, or a supper among genteel dwarves. I attended a supper like that during an acid trip when I was twenty-one. To nurture such planetary voluptuousness, I would need ambition. An ambition that I could not experience by the engineer's side. But there was still a chance I would seek the body of my boss. I would wait for the Federal Police in bed. Or, before it happened, kill myself with the engineer's gun. We might even look like some sort of Hitler and Eva in their final bunker. Which one was Hitler? And Eva? I heard gunshots. I ran to check. The bodyguard had his gun in his hand, and at his feet, the furious dog lay dead, with several gunshots to its head. I looked at the dead thing and reconfirmed that the beast was really big. It did justice to my son's gawky frame. The guard explained that the wild dog attacked him. He had time to pull the gun and shoot the beast several times. Fatally. Inside the dog's body, in the milky light, I appreciated the image of my son. He looked like me in my teenaged prime, when I served in the Army. When I was slashed on the left side of my face. A fellow troop did it. It was dawn and we were serving sentry in front of the headquarters by Igreja das Dores, at Rua da Praia. The young man said that everything that was his was mine too. I looked at him, astonished. He proposed something like communism in the Jesuit Missions. Then he pulled a pocket knife he was hiding under his uniform and tore my skin apart. I remember that, at first, I thought the scar would suit me well. I still carry that mark of my youth on the left side of my face. The fellow who hurt me lived in Esteio, in greater Porto Alegre. Later we learned he had some history of crime. The newspapers published his previous atrocities. He killed an old landlady from a boarding house he lived at in Floriano Peixoto. Yes, just like in *Crime and Punishment*. I moved slowly, unsure of how to accept his generous proposal that all that was his was mine too. The enthusiastic agreement he expected from me did not come. He wanted me to say the same back to him. All that was his was mine. All that was mine was his. He was right, an assertion like that demanded a passionate reciprocation, an affirmation from me that carried the same weight, the same herculean strength. He even wanted us to swap uniforms, we wore the same size. Why couldn't we just fuck after our shift, in the middle of the night? In one of the bathrooms in the military headquarters, why not? We could have started a hot affair. But no, I didn't reciprocate his fervorous and rare altruism. My jaw dropped. Passion manifested itself in the tiniest details, in variations of tone, in a lock of hair licked on the forehead after a shower, in a postcard shoved in the pocket of the Guaíba river gleaming under a sunset… Details, in the background, without a sender or a receiver. Nobody owned them, because all that was his was mine. And vice versa…deal!—I whispered to his memory, which still lingered inside me. I still preserved him like that ideal sample of the Greek specimen. There were times our innocent flirting would cool off. And he, usually he, would suffer from what appeared to be the imminent breaking of our ties. My colleague in uniform could not accept that everything in life hangs on by a thread. And later, in a bar and sweaty, he would press his leg against mine under the table, nothing more. Maybe sex was what we needed. But the olive green uniform intimidated us. Since our libido could not be realized, out came the knife. And the scar was the soldier's signature on my flesh. On the other hand, I can say I had borne a long-burning passion since my adolescence (or childhood?) for this engineer who now snored in the middle of the jungle. Years went by before we risked caressing one another. Nodding, yes, we did that. Nodding is less committed. It lives at a distance and disintegrates at the slightest blow. The case in the military had been different. My fellow soldier, of Greek descent and handsome, approached me with his immaculate desire. Immaculate but with many incisive touches. The engineer, on the other hand, must have initiated his sex life only when he joined the German submarine. I don't doubt it. In his youth, he always cultivated an air of implausible virginity. He lived a mix of shyness and pride. Among his friends he was reserved, yes. But, at the same time, he possessed a certain arrogance. This sentiment arose mainly at the end of the evening as he headed home, running his eyes over the group as he was leaving, sending us an expression of disdain as we kept our conversations going, especially as we figured out who was going to fuck whom. Not him. He would already be asleep by then, saving his energies for the productive hours of tomorrow. He started drinking from the fountain of libido late in life. That once diligent, handsome man now snores in a bed without sheets, waiting for the militias, which will come sooner rather than later. He's now vulnerable to public abomination, at the height of a maturity he doesn't seem to acknowledge. I was down on my knees by the dead animal at the bodyguard's feet. The moonlight came down on us with more silver now. The dead animal's open eyes seemed to be staring at me.

Could my son resurface from within the beast? Another creature cried in the forest. Or was it my son begging me to pull him out the guts of this exterminated beast? I looked at the guard, almost begging him to assuage my paternal (or perhaps maternal) doubt. I smoothed the thick coat of the wild dog. It was warm. Size of a mule. I remembered seeing huge dogs like that roaming around the Palacio de la Moneda in Santiago de Chile. Did they have some strange public function? Were they to scare transgressors away? And who fed them? One would expect they needed to eat a lot, being so big. However, no passersby could spot them eating. Mystery. For a moment the dead dog of the jungle seemed to revive—a slight shiver, I noticed. I kept running my hand over the animal's back, reminiscing about my son's skin, which got delicate goosebumps when I caressed it like that. The smell from the furry body was brutally invasive, charging my hand in an unbearable way. I felt ridiculous petting a vicious beast. I could have early onset senility, trying to extract my already orphaned son from the dead wolf. But now the murdered animal was worth much more to me than my son, that frequent visitor to swimming pools in Porto Alegre. The jungle resident displayed the same mutilated essence and the same metamorphosis of the person I now was. We

both faced the finality of being eaten by the earth
with no one left to cry for us. No one would humil-
iate us with their tears. Only I could accompany the
mammalian inertia of this wolf. Both the beast and
I could make inevitable midnight associations. His
fellatio on the bodyguard caused the animal to experience the taste of human flesh, yes, through my
son's body—and saved the creature from involuntary self-exposure. He fulfilled his libido a few
hours before being shot dead by his own master.
I—this person now watching the canine monster—
know I won't even attend my own burial. This person I've gotten used to calling "I." Some discrete
hand will take my ashes to the top of a hill in
Jaguarão, or to any other territory that can offer a
modest breeze. And on the top, the officiant will
throw my ashes in all directions. I got up and asked
the bodyguard for the time. As usual, he was closed
off. He looked like he might be Ethiopian. I couldn't
help blinking at his inflated image. He thought for
a moment before half-smiling. I looked at his
crotch and in fact, there, leaning to the left, as with
almost every man, his bulge looked voluminous,
moist, a white stain confirming my son had sucked
his cock. Or was it the animal, now dead, who had
sucked the bodyguard, mistaking his cock for the
ancestral breast of the mother wolf? The mammal

had closed the cycle, he could die now. He had felt some exotic milk inundating his mouth in the end, making the guard turn away to hide his swollen member. What's good never lasts. Had it really been my son, manifesting himself with his living ghost? Had the young man died in the body of an animal? The young man who I watched as a baby behind the nursery glass and who I waved to as if he would be able to wave back? I couldn't let myself be distracted by the signs on the muscled man's bo-hemian crotch. I was finally realizing I had always been a fool at the mercy of inscrutable men like the engineer and the bodyguard. I didn't want to fuck anymore. There was no more fire, just ashes. Occasionally, something crackled in the bonfire. Sleeping embers. The sound of a whistle came. No, it was not coming from the bodyguard, but from the bedroom where the engineer slept. Lying on the bed, he was vomiting. A thick paste on his neck and the mattress. The sour miasmas were already signs of the fury waiting for us in the forest's guts. The circle was closing in on us. I lifted his head so he wouldn't choke. His vomit was solid. Strange, it looked like little sculptures—folk art, say. It caused me pain as well, in my stomach and lungs. Yes, I feared he would drag me down with him. There was, for example, a very picturesque sculpture made from the substance of his vomit. Some type of raft with a fisherman on it casting a net into the ocean. To distract myself a little, I hummed some Caymmi songs. The engineer poured his dreams from his mouth. I cradled his torso and head in my arms as if he were a fallen hero embraced in a Pietà. After all, for a long time—in our youth, or perhaps childhood—he had been my guiding passion. I had believed, day after day, in the silly promise of having him in my arms. Here, now, I didn't feel anything for him anymore. Just a vague protective instinct. Perhaps what was left in me was just a maternal inclination, after all, an instinct to save those in difficult times. I looked at the bodyguard. I feared what was soon to happen. He looked at me intensely, as if searching for immediate complicity. It was still uncertain where he wanted to take me. Amid the constant crises of the drug trafficking world, I was less than a supporting character—I'd go wherever they sent me. I was nobody and that could make me useful in playing different roles in that segment of organized crime. I now hoped more than ever that the bodyguard would take me with him. But, this Ethiopian should not go to Porto Alegre, a city that considered me dead. I was relieved that my thoughts followed a line that ruled out Porto Alegre as a destination and home. It was the only prohibited city for me going forward. I had no other choice but the bodyguard. I had to see in him my pressing fate. I looked at him again and he made that silencing gesture—an upright index finger against his lips. Did the big guy want to infantilize me? Anyway, we were in absolute silence. And how could we fill such a pause? I soon understood: he was inviting me to stage a mournful silence. A mournful silence because the engineer was dead in my arms. The bodyguard sat on the bed. I thought about how it would feel to leave with this man, strong as a bull, a true bear's soul. The man had been responsible for the engineer's integrity until then. He could now be responsible for mine, maybe even for free if I found another way to compensate him. I could pay him with favors. I would show him that I could be a man or a woman, it didn't matter. He'd be a lucky man, with the distribution of cocaine and ecstasy secured. Not to mention marijuana, perhaps even with an international network. I had to seriously start bluffing. It was the first step I thought of upon realizing I was a widow. All bluffing aimed at immediate results. Life in that land's end necessitated the bodyguard believing in his own leadership. I would work for it, with the illusion that I would be the thirsty vassal. The bodyguard would have to believe my performance in the service of trafficking intelligence. After all, I already possessed the female brilliance of crossing the enemy's heart. I was ready to be seen as a businesswoman of addiction. That's right, a businesswoman going on a shopping spree, luring the rich into our evil product. Was the jungle house an outpost? So far I hadn't seen any narcotics storage. If I did, I could approach the packages, open one, and start experimenting with the glory of drugs. The bodyguard would be my pastor. That was what I needed. On the other hand, he would learn that being with me would look good on him. He would take me to meet his contacts. That would broaden my horizons. And that would provide me with the money I hadn't earned since my first death. It would look good for the bodyguard to have the widow of a crime executive like the engineer at his side. His activity in such a profitable business could branch out into espionage. Ultimately, this grandiosity would be my fate too. At least that's what I wanted to believe. We would complement each other. He revealed to me the intrigue and adventure in the transport of coca between Colombia and Brazil. Women detained at the border with drugs hidden in their vaginas. At the Guarulhos airport, men's anuses were searched, where huge amounts of coke would be found. If they managed to get through, they would shit the drug out to supply the million-aire market of London or New York. As I listened to these stories, he looked like a teacher, pumping images of international suspense into my veins, lessons on the rise and fall of souls. He told me what it was like to fall from grace, get chased into a corner and shot at close range in front of a wife and young son. That had been the end of his twin brother, also in the business. According to my best estimates, I was at the exact point of becoming a criminal. For starters, I would follow him around the world, providing valuable information on the prospects and history of a particular country. After all, I had a degree in History, though I'd never practiced teaching. A subterranean voice was ordering me to get away from Brazil. Forever. In fact, the desire to immerse myself in other cultures began to give me the impression of endless opportunities, never of exile. I was sweating from the intoxicating heat emanating from the engineer's body. Before the ultimate cold descended on him, the dead needed to bid farewell to his intestinal eloquence. That dead body burned me. The dead body should long for me until it could finally stop feeling any sensation. I snuggled my head next to the hair I had once combed, just like I had with my father's thick white hair. I told the bodyguard I was saying goodbye to the man I had been in love with for my entire life. Until a few hours before, when I started feeling disenchanted with him. How could we have guessed, during the Platonic times of our youth, that one day we'd be in the middle of the rainforest and I'd be officiating his death? The guard approached us, confessing that the boss could have been poisoned. By whom? I asked. I got no answer. I stared at him firmly, because I could be the next victim. He opened a half-smile and said we should bury the engineer soon. Before the corpse started to decompose. The dead deteriorate quicker in the heat. Along with the engineer, I would be burying a piece of my heart. I was another man now. With a body very close to a woman's. On the verge of embarking on a new chapter by allying myself to the bodyguard. He dictated the next day's events to me: Bury the dead body before the rooster crows. And then move away from the jungle without a destination. Maybe we would find a village by early afternoon. We would test the waters of a human environment. I remembered Che Guevara in Bolivia, his contact with the peasants right before he fell and died. And here, would the natives register our faces only to denounce us later? Would they report me, too, an innocent who didn't even know what he was doing beside a muscled man? We dragged the deceased into the kitchen. To free the bedroom from the mournful air. I opened the kitchen cabinet. I was hungry, but the cabinet was empty. Instead of provisions, a vibrator. A pink plastic cock…to fill whose hole? I chose not to close the cabinet so the dildo could fly out if it wanted to join the suffering hours. I washed in the kitchen sink. When I washed between my legs, a hellish gunk came off on my fingers. It tickled me, and I started to smell the miserable smell of the shapeless substance, a mix of the miasmas of man and woman. I finished washing and went to bed. Was my son still roaming around? At times, I would hear a scream from the forest. It didn't sound like it was coming from an animal, but from someone mortally wounded, who, apparently, refused to surrender. I thought I wouldn't be able to sleep that night. With a son wandering around… His zoomorphic matrix had been shot down by the bodyguard. I was growing more insane each day. Between my outside and inside worlds, a painful rarefaction was gradually emerging. However, I needed to keep myself in this diluted, indefinite, imprecise, mixed center so as not to move permanently into just one direction, outside or inside. The disordered expansion of the inside could metastasize, creating an empire of deformity and madness, pure and simple.

I kept clinging to little things on the outside so as not to drown in my own waters. Sometimes, I approached the outside elements trying to capture a sharpness. Then I looked like a little bird, collecting breadcrumbs with its beak. I was a little bird maybe, but a brute man in my soul. Tasting what the morning light offered. But it's true that the outside world didn't need me. Now, perhaps, I could extract certain brain waves from within and share them with the sun, attempt to formulate other possible worlds with new rhythms and preludes, new sequences and occurrences, new outcomes and entrapments. At noon, the Mato Grosso sun was primed for its convulsions. I had already been stung by the star when I was out in the meadows. It hurt, yes, and it looked golden. Not really, it didn't hurt at all. The lack of dishes, cutlery, and groceries in the jungle house took on diaphanous dimensions. Lack was all around. It had an autonomous existence in itself, with its own invisible dimensions and borders. But, paradoxically, the alternative to the inexistence of things weighed most. Lack of supplies seemed to announce that my destiny from that point on would be bleak. Emptiness shrank back when I touched it with the word. It was typical of emptiness not to get carried away with language. Emptiness only knew how to make itself represented in the kitchen

cabinet: in the multipurpose objects, or more precisely, in the lazy vibrator, hidden in the shadows,
apparently in no hurry to get out of there. By the
way, it was not really there, as it lived in reference to
something else—its double in flesh, veins, and
blood. Any word in the kitchen would sound absolutely flat in face of that hidden nook in the cabinet.
I would kiss any lips available to fight off so much
scarcity. In the encounter of tongues, even without
any larger consequences, we would taste the rice
and beans from meals far past. I see a lizard at the
kitchen door, beside the sink. Its incisive nails deep
in the thick, somewhat parched earth. I closed the
door. A sob came to me. Which could only be experienced by a woman. Which I wasn't yet. But I
would get there someday. Several urgencies came to
mind, but they only knew how to hover fearfully.
Urgencies such as tending to the corpse on the
kitchen floor before it turned into bones; or studying the bodyguard's particularities, so that the muscular figure wearing an earring wouldn't find me
unprepared during the escape—if an escape really
happened; further still, the urgency to carefully observe the naked room (where I had indulged in so
many violent ecstasies), so that no trace of myself
would be left behind. Surely, an eternal smell of
cum, piss, and shit would forever remain. Or was

that smell coming from the corpse? I slowly breathed in the atmosphere. I went into the kitchen and kneeled by the deceased. Distractedly, I put my hand on the engineer's belly. When he was alive, this was the territory of his body I preferred most. From his navel to his sex. I loved traveling through the lean frontier zone to his sin. I reached his penis. I jacked it off. He responded with a soft erection. Hadn't he died then? Yes, he had. But until a certain hour, the dead still react discreetly to the actions of the living. The first time I saw my dead father, I put my hand over his, which then twitched and relaxed, demonstrating his shallow desire to return to the world of the living. I contemplated the engineer's cock with a certain nostalgia. Now that he had finally started providing me with, to say the least, elegant erections, fate had found a way to take him away from me. All the resentment I had built up for the engineer in the past few hours dissipated now. I didn't want him dead. My body responded; it mourned the corpse of my man. I disguised how horny I was by thinking that his remains resembled Christ's. If I could find them in that house, I would bring bed sheets and put them around the deceased as if he were a biblical figure. I was definitely turned on. Screams came from afar. Did they belong to animals or beings familiar with music? Yes, because they were melodious sounds, mixed with the howls of obscure beasts. The bodyguard watched us from his vantage point at the kitchen doorway. He caught my hand on the dead man's semi-hard cock. I needed to convey that I was the engineer's widow—And wasn't I?—so the bodyguard would respect me more—that is, if he weren't his boss's killer. I asked him who he thought was the culprit of the poisoning. Evil forces, he said, jumping to conclusions. I looked at him with intensity. Guards no longer intimidated me as they had in my youth. I now needed to set a scene that broke with the logic of the intimidated. Perhaps the only left thing for me to do was to go looking for natives in the endless jungle. We could also search for a little store to buy beer, lots of beer. Could the bodyguard afford such purchases? Anyway, we wouldn't be able to find any stores within a reasonable distance that would allow us to return the same day. If we managed to come across a store, and if the big guy agreed to pay for seven or eight bottles of beer (my financial life was buried in Porto Alegre, remember?) and if the Federal Police caught us at dawn, after so much beer mixed with cocaine and ecstasy…the besieging forces would not arrest such a cowardly couple, I thought. Maybe they'd find the bodyguard and me in bed. And so they would come

to understand us as husband and wife. Or husband
and husband, it didn't matter. Really? I still couldn't
figure out just how far my female appearance was
able to convey. Who would actually be the husband?
And the wife? I ran to the bathroom, crazy to find
out. Between my legs, I touched, and I touched, and
I touched… And I got excited by the gradual ordering of things, a clitoris had finally sprouted a little
above the flooded area, through which everyone
would fuck me. I started to rub my clitoris up and
down, east and west. I begged for pleasure to come,
quietly, but faster and faster. I put my white t-shirt
over my head, covering my face, thinking I'd do the
same at the time of my capture. I would hide my
features from the photographers from the mainstream Brazilian newspapers and magazines. At
that point, with emphatic and vibrant touches to
the so-called clit, I came. I came with my head
covered. I then uncovered my face and called the
engineer's name. I called him again, and I choked.
Blood came out of my mouth and covered the sink.
I called him again and nothing. It was no use calling him anymore. The loving myth of my entire life
was helpless on the kitchen floor, already decom-
posing. Slowly losing certain lines in his features.
His physical identity was beginning to dissolve.
Nevertheless, I contemplated his face, especially his

mouth. Obscene lips for a dead man. I, a virgin in crime, needed to train for my sacrifice. Because I would eat shit if I had to, I just didn't know the exact degree of my punishment. Blameless. I couldn't be blamed for what I had failed to commit—not out of virtue, but out of an enormous neglect. And so, if needed, I would put the shirt over my face to cover my features. No reader of any newspaper would be able to recognize me. As for my name, people would be confused. How come a woman with a man's name? I had to be cautious, I still had a wife and a son. I wanted to intercept any traces I'd left, though not so much for the shame of my innocent past. There was no turning back on my barren face. On it one could see I was already less than a citizen. What would it be like to judge a woman like me, who lacked the elements that might incriminate or absolve her? But that wasn't the problem. More than anything, I didn't want them to learn of my return from the dead to the world of the living. The news of my arrest shouldn't reach my family in Porto Alegre. Their lives were already upset by the cruelty of the news. I went back to bed as usual. Lately, I spent half the day in bed, thinking about what did and didn't surround me. It was clear to me that the bodyguard wanted to win me over. He came closer and sat on the mattress, by my feet. I suspected he thought I really had some influence in what they call organized crime. So he was here to try me. To offer me his thick muscles, with the intention of gaining information I had acquired during my time with the kingpin. Little did he know I'd never managed to get any valuable information out of the engineer. Did I know anyone else in the drug world besides the engineer and the bodyguard? So many amnesias that make me blush! I now aspired to live chastely. The bodyguard however preferred not to know. He leaned forward and put his hand between my legs. That place—still taking shape, still aiming for a fully formed vagina, a vulva—that place shuddered from his sharp fingers. However, I didn't want sex anymore. I was planning my escape from the flesh to some kind of vagueness, even though this vagueness welcomed the carnal matter of my always changing pelvis. Here was a methodical process, already announcing a promising transmutation. I was studying a choreography that was proto-sensual. I would ride this wave to pass the official test of chastity. Ineffable myths are likely to be invoked when the heart gets lost. I had quite a resume, which qualified me beyond the matters of my pelvis. But I would have to submit myself to maturity, which was a period of amnesiac formation in itself. That's when the first signs of memory's failure happen. But it's also possible to make up for these gaps with some dedication to the developing plot. The journey to the absence of memories begins when someone longs for certain baggage. Upon reaching the destination, the person learns of their loss. And they're told they should go home, as they no longer have documents, money, or disposition. The amnesiac loses the support of the past. I was a man already indifferent to the state of life or death. If needed, I'll vouch for it. When I died in Porto Alegre, I became a provider, since my wife and child inherited some assets—the house and the farm, plus my meager savings. Now I wanted to wash my hands. In my old Porto Alegre days, I would never imagine that I would have to die to experience hunger—I'm talking about this hunger for food, right here in the jungle. My head spins, my belly rumbles. At the start, it hurts. Soon, however, the starving is numbed, sleepless, and has an indefinable presence during his vigil, which isn't guided by God or the Devil. Suddenly, exhaustion gives way to delirium, making the starving want to stay like that. Like on a drug. And then you avoid any sight of food. The poison of malnutrition takes over you, embraces you. The bodyguard and I were already experiencing the vertigo caused by hunger.

One helped the other, with me leading him to bed without the engineer's body near us anymore. The bodyguard put his finger into my swamp, and I was about to give it up for him once and for all. I had already suffered harassment like that in my youth, also with a guard. It felt like I was present today holding a copy of that earlier brute man. Unlucky me, who experiences things before they happen. Unlucky me, unlucky me. And I saw everything inside my body. I, who always had difficulties with biology. My liver was in very bad condition. Swollen, misshapen, indisposed to work. My brain—seen through its labyrinths without an escape, as if in a sadistic game—my brain was quickly losing its memory in rare nebulae formations, even though my rekindled love for the engineer was reposed, in all of its decades, intact in one of the alcoves of my head. But I could not lean on this love anymore, I could no longer rely on the engineer. The sadness over his death was hiding in a corner, in a moving darkness, widening little by little to envelop the scenery. Well, I did have some luck, after all: when the worst settled in, some type of science would come from inside me, out of the blue. On these occasions, someone would knock on the shutters until I said, "I'm coming," and opened the window to the gift of chance. On these occasions, I recovered. And I thanked that semi-retired God. That finger stuck in the perfect spot in my new body configuration was starting to drive me crazy. It really was a different kind of orgasm compared to the one I used to have with the fullness of my cock. A more intimate orgasm, toward my interior, but vivid in a constellation system, nothing linear, unlike the male shot, which moves always forward like a riot squad. In my new configuration, orgasm revealed a strange lament. Penetration is, for the one who penetrates, an act of supremacy. The orgasm of my new genitals encompassed more cyclical gradations than overflowing epilogues. Women sometimes abandon the act in search of a new force with which to start over. It didn't matter, though, that my body, already female, was sometimes snatched from itself to live another woman's fiction, which I was unable to contain. I didn't know what the bodyguard's ultimate objective was when he approached me sexually, just hours after I'd lost my husband. After all, was he the engineer's killer or not? Was I an alibi in his arms in case he needed to play a game for an audience? Audience? Would we have an audience at some point? Would I be the next victim of his murderous kink? I didn't believe, though, that he had brought poison to the engineer's mouth on his own. The bodyguard seemed more like a messenger for some individual or faction of organized crime. The poisoning surely hadn't happened in the last few hours, since the engineer and I hadn't had any food in that time, and we'd barely had any water, which dripped meager and dirty from the tap. I was severely hungry. Besides my hunger, I felt a pleasure I had never felt before with what one could call a new version of the vagina. Unprecedented genitalia had formed between my legs, something close to a vulva, without a doubt, but perhaps still preserving some masculine attributes—it launched itself inward, but it was also eager to have the ability to penetrate. Right, I was miles away from the body I'd been born with. If I wanted to cum now, I would need to forget my previous performances as a male. At that point, I couldn't really call the bodyguard my lover yet. He played with my clit, yes, and I was beginning to realize how much unknown pleasure I could add to my sexual life. When my son had fucked me in the front, my female genitalia was still in its very early days. My slit, now fully formed and deep, had still been very green back in the day. When was that? Oh, things always happened too fast for me. What I went through in a matter of minutes suddenly became a wide field, spanning decades. My son was going through flux, typical of angelic figures, while

I provided him with a mature trance so he could passionately thrive in his swimmer's body. I could say I started becoming a woman that day. And with my own son. He was on top of my body learning how to get dirty. That was what he intended: get dirty with my indigestible substance. The bodyguard picked up the pace masturbating me, and my body responded to the rhythm out to the ends of my hands and feet. My orgasm was being prepared between my legs. I was about to strike, albeit without much hope of fireworks, and I felt that upon reaching the apex of that fuck, half my genital joy would occur inward, in my concave radius, and the other half would launch out toward my partner, whom, at that moment, I no longer wanted. In the meantime, the bodyguard was directing the scene, guiding my hand to his cock, which twitched in quick intervals, about to unleash a stud's thick cream. But his twitches were false alarms. My hand, which had caught his cock ready to go, now couldn't detach itself from that insane and eternally taut piece of meat. At the same time, it was impossible not to realize the emptiness in our gestures. We both seemed like automatons wishing to conclude the scene as fast as possible. The Ethiopian guided my hand to his balls. The two testes were apparently quiet. I groped his scrotum and imagined things being prepared inside that would eventually regurgitate as semen on my face. The truth was, between pleasuring the big guy's obelisk, to which I had returned, and going back to my regime of scarcity, it was a no-brainer: I would stay, yes, fondling that obelisk. Most people and the ghosts around them suffered from violent erotic outbursts. I included myself in that group. And there was no way to avoid this fate. In certain phases of my life, I'd sniffed other people's sperm. The many infusions of seminal shots on my clothes made me into a quiet promoter of these divine secretions. I smelled them with devotion. They say that, before being incorporated into humans, these fluids are formed in other landscapes, some of them in other worlds even, to the point where certain excretions carry remains of cosmic dust. These fluids develop in a free territory, free from the shadow of theology. But a fuck, once concluded, stinks. The relief you feel after ejaculation usually doesn't last long, just long enough to leave a bedroom and see your image in the mirror. In the mirror, you see yourself as you really are: A detached being who urgently needs to connect to another, even if the lover will only last the exact length of a single fuck. He, who had just traveled the distance needed to orgasm, now stared at himself and discovered once again how little life cared for him. I was near the point of screaming. The bodyguard was digging into my so-called vagina, yes, sticking his fingers into my crack again, causing me to hurt, bleed, and scream. I was so wet that I couldn't hold back my piss. I still didn't know how to control that uncommunicative sex, despite it belonging to me. I started laughing, honoring my admission into the world of female pleasure. By the way, I'm already a woman, I repeated to myself over and over, acting like a lunatic in the face of an irresistible novelty. On my side, I was also working toward someone else's pleasure, jacking off that burly man with the enthusiasm and noises typical of wet bodies. Hands slip, impatiently lose direction, but soon resume traveling to familiar territories, then turn back, then turn pale. Hands are sometimes surprised when they prowl through an area in the partner where they have never been before. The bodyguard's sack was wrinkled. Any bump in the road, like the scratch of a stray nail, is not a mistake, since nothing is lost. Whoever goes astray here can burnish their gluttony further ahead. Sometimes he moaned, not necessarily from pleasure, but from pain, due to my poor skills in dealing with his colossal dimensions. I bit him accidentally. A trickle of blood came from his glans, and he screamed. But one only needed to see his expression to understand how much this encounter did him well. We both came at the same time. The white lava of his semen slowly ran down my hand. I was squatting on the bed like a woman in childbirth and I remembered my lovers, one by one, especially those with whom I had shared the task of finding paradise in the caress of our bodies. It looked like I had pissed on the mattress, such was the fountain of my orgasm. I rubbed my hand, dirty with someone else's semen, on the flower-patterned mattress. I cleaned myself. The bodyguard did the same with a piece of toilet paper. He squeezed the tip of his dick and a little bit of cum came out. He fed me, but I wouldn't dare touch him. I just had to be part of his picture, nothing else. His gesture itself could be understood as a milking. The man seemed prudent. His hungry way of fucking told me he practiced hourly erotic exercises. With me, an animal, or another woman in the forest's shadows. Perhaps with the engineer's corpse? I didn't know. Would I get a repeat with this bear before the Federal Police arrived? I asked him to please turn off the light. We both lay down. And we embraced. I wrapped my arms around his monumental torso. When would abstinence from other people's skin finally begin for me? At that point, I just wished I could have some kind of mild asceticism, because I might never be able to keep my vow of chastity. Maybe it was too late to even try. Nothing captivated me more than the foreshadowing of nudity. When I was sixteen, I slept with a prostitute for the first time. First time I had sex with a woman. The building was on Rua Sete de Setembro, downtown Porto Alegre, near Usina do Gasômetro. There was a blackout in the area that night. Two candles burned in the bedroom. I sat on a chair by the bed. The chubby brunette lay down and undressed herself. When I took off my boxers, my unruly cock jumped out. I've never forgotten that image. I carried the memory of my dick, drooling in youthful excess, throughout all the subsequent hookups in my life. I got gonorrhea, of course. It was the price to pay for a destiny that was, at minimum, paternal. Now, I didn't have any other activity to take the place of my flesh's troubled yearning. Unless sex became work for me and didn't induce pleasure anymore. So I would do it to exhaustion. Then, on sabbatical, I would be able to stay away from eroticism's juggernaut. I could turn into a professional in the porn industry. With the advent of AIDS, there was a huge market for bodies made for sex. Actors in this field were dying by the thousands. In my case in particular, the sexual indecision in my pelvis could serve as an extra attraction—although, at the base of my womb I now already carried the female form, blessed with the gift of a clitoris and all. I could consider working in a circus. Maybe that's how I would survive? If I got my shit together, I could travel to Holland and pursue acting, playing obscene roles. I didn't have the slightest hint of fat on my body. I had a friend who had been living in Amsterdam for three years now, doing very well as a sex worker. Was he hot? Look at this photo… I show it to an absent interlocutor. I've carried this photo with me to remind myself that Holland was always a possibility. It could be my chance to once and for all provide for my eternally stubborn subsistence. What interested me most, however, was that my friend in Holland loved to play with his coworkers. And that was that. I needed some cash to make the trip. And if I managed to get it, I would show up at his house and drop my suitcase on the floor. Then give him a kiss and say a few words of sincere love. The bodyguard slept. And when, feeling a crazy need to snoop, I wanted to move and grab his pants—tossed to the side of the bed—he moaned and his cock quickly stretched from east to west. I glanced at his pockets. The pocket with the wallet looked bulky, like something had been between his cock and the money. Even without his body, the outline of his cock remained traced in the fabric. If I went there and pulled the wallet out, I'd be a dead woman by the next day. I tried to feel his breath. Everything at the animal level interested me. Any corporeal scent did me good. Most of the time, I preferred odors that were inhospitable, remote, unknown to me. I disentangled from the hug of the sleeping bear who had just fucked me and went to the kitchen to analyze the corpse. There wasn't much difference between the deceased and the bodyguard. They both gave me their bodies, and I suspected I didn't know how to take full advantage of that fact. What was preventing me? I had been consistent throughout my long history with the engineer. I had lived the whole time waiting to achieve an integrity that was ultimately not part of who I was. Stubbornly, the same aspiration I had now. Dead, the engineer still seemed open to the possibility of dialogue, albeit with his usual reserve. Impossible to believe that the rhetoric about ruling the world would never come out of his mouth again. The dead's mouth, semi-open. The sour smell of vomit which composed small sculptures assured me we weren't joking around here. I sat on a stool to study him a little longer. I found a pencil and wrapping paper lying nearby, so I started to draw the engineer's traces. Drawing came naturally to me. I did a good job with his features. The drawing could help reverse that natural disillusionment that came with death; it could bring back the sublime and profound attraction I had nurtured for him since adolescence. Such a platonic passion in the beginning, and then, later, so physical in its manifestation. Okay, once and for all, since adolescence or childhood? I was in no condition to arrive at an answer, especially now, being a single woman. Single woman or single man? Without the engineer, had I become a woman for good? Or would I return to the male form? I touched between my legs, then I stopped. To whom had I become a female? And how would others see me? Although he was decidedly dead, I wished I could dedicate my time and attention to his body until dawn came. Perhaps even wash him. With reverence. As if we were both biblical figures. I could sing, with my half-decent voice, an aria by Monteverdi in *Orpheus*. I remembered him saying he liked my voice. I remembered him asking for an encore of "The Man I Love." If I could celebrate his memory until dawn, oh, if I could, then I'd be satisfied. I would say goodbye to all our heartaches. And then, yes, I would bury him and recover forever the love that had evaded me the last few hours. In fact, my final contempt for him was the exception that proved my passion had indeed existed. A passion that returned now, in that exact moment, already in a cult with the impossible. I was a man departing as much as the dead are. He just went ahead of me. Watching him, I was, little by little, learning how to extract what libidinal material there was from this melancholic moment. Was I really learning? And who else could I possibly seduce at that hour? Did it make any sense to seduce the corpse? I kissed his mouth. Already very cold and with the appearance of enamel. The contrast between the temperature of the engineer's skin and the room was shocking. Timidly, I ran my tongue between his lips, just to feel that discreetly chipped front tooth again. The result of a fight when he was a child. He'd been seriously beaten, knocked unconscious, left lying on the sidewalk. Who did that to him? The bodyguard appeared naked in the kitchen. He said it was time for us to bury the deceased. I looked through the door, over the forest, and saw that it was true: a meager pink bar on the horizon announced a new day rising. I felt the warmth of goodbye in my genital swamp. Or maybe it was already the heat of menopause arriving for me, earlier than normal. But when my female genitals were not even complete? Can one die before being born? That is, could menopause happen before I reached sexual maturity? The three of us were naked. The bodyguard and I began to move the engineer's body by his arms. The cat joined us, meowing, most certainly hungry. The bodyguard wielded a shovel. On the east bank, between the forest and the clearing, he stopped. I waited for his command. He started digging a hole. I still had a few minutes in which to include the engineer in a ménage-a-trois. Perhaps, stretched out like that, he intended to wait for the sun to come out and tan a bit. A deeper tan, over his existing natural tan, would simply make him superior, worthy of nobility. Subtly, I worshipped his beauty, forever silenced. And he wore his majesty so well. Suddenly, I felt an awkward itch on my crotch. I scratched it with my nails, I looked at it. Was it an STD? No, blood ran down my legs. I was menstruating, was that it? I felt a sudden relief, a weight lifted off my shoulders. I now had a new role. It seemed I could now start to procreate as a woman. The bodyguard didn't notice the bleeding. Maybe my body was just tangibly revealing its opposition to death. As the engineer dried out, I bled profusely. Now that I had my period and everything, now that I could give the engineer a son, he had died and would be devoured by earth. And there I was, alone with the comfort of menstruation. If the engineer could hear me now, he would laugh at what he used to see in me: a reason for disdain. The muscular bodyguard spoke from inside the grave. He said we could get started. We were three naked men in a love triangle, now in the final farewell to one of the vertices. I got down on my knees and put my ear to the corpse's heart. Nothing, really. Then I gave him a last caress. I ran my fingers through his straight hair. It seemed he was only sedated and at any moment would open his eyes and make love to me. If I could, I would resurrect the corpse, giving him back the miracle of resurrection. The bodyguard seemed impatient with my funeral rites. Together, we started pulling on the arms of the deceased. When we reached the edge of the improvised grave, we threw the body down into the hole. The cadaver made a deep, muffled noise when it hit the bottom. The ground shook. I looked all the way down. Self-conscious of the bodyguard's presence, I turned my body a little to disguise a final wave. From my viewpoint, I had the impression the engineer's left arm had dislocated. In the jungle, animals screamed. The bodyguard asked me to help him throw dirt in the hole. I obeyed. Would I have to follow this puzzling man now? By the time we finished the service, the morning had already come, it was completely sunny. The two of us, each on one side of the sealed pit, sized each other up: we would have to face the next few hours with perfect diligence and synchronicity. The bodyguard sported a discreet erection. That trusted alarm was sounding even in the makeshift cemetery. Right at the edge of the engineer's indigent grave. Had those two been lovers? And had the bodyguard had a fling with my son when he used to hang around here? I felt jealous of everyone and no one. In some moments, the images of the engineer and the bodyguard meshed inside of my retinas. Who was one and who was the other? Which one was I escaping with? I started to suspect no one had died; perhaps only me. I vaguely remembered detaching from my body so suddenly I didn't have time to agonize. Precisely at that passage, I had come. With the male sex I'd had at that time. And on and on I went. And I realized it didn't hurt. When I was alive, having the engineer's company was like spending an afternoon in a foreign city, or in his body itself, where I used to have the overwhelming feeling of being back in my childhood: the same neighborhood, the same details on the façade of the building, the same long sigh, the same nothing, the same everything. And, above all, the same light. By the way, is there anything more difficult to evoke than the sensation of an alien air in the place where one currently finds oneself? But, nonetheless, the sensation was still amazingly woven throughout my new reality, with certain shades of clarity. What did this *je-ne-sais-quoi* look like? Would it be possible to name this thing dispersed in time? This thing could be just a delicate sleepwalking figure inserted into the flat, surrounding images. I lived on subtleties. Did I need to commune with the body of yet another partner to materialize myself again and again? Or did I need to evade myself so the world would recognize my absence? The escape with the bodyguard would only end when he decided to have a child with me and start a family. Before that happened, I would diligently tend to him in my memory alongside the engineer. With the engineer, I'd had to accept coexisting with a self-absorbed figure, but in the end, I knew I could always harvest a night of delight with him. A rooster crowed in the distance. Without revealing any promises that might save the day. Unless maybe I could imitate the bodyguard and start inflating like a blow-up doll. The bodyguard's dick was even more erect now, bent to the left as with almost every man. I crouched and took a piss. He came closer, maybe interested to learn the color of my foamy piss. After all, any way of occupying the time before our capture would do us good. My piss is darker, he said, wanting to inaugurate the new era without the engineer, foreshadowing our future dirty talk. If we continued in this impasse, leading to nowhere, I'd

rather go back to bed with the bodyguard and satiate once again the growing hunger of my crotch. I
envied the bodyguard being so horny in the tropical
dawn. I was even more envious of the engineer: unlike me, he wouldn't need to occupy his time any
longer; he was free at last from all impasses. He just
wanted to stay underground, in the spot where I
had thrown large amounts of soil to protect him
from the threats of a soulless jungle. After all, I
shouldn't forget, he had resurrected me. I would
never be able to do the same with that man, profession: engineer. My body was there in the jungle,
bleeding between the legs, and in my mind the image of my murdered husband remained—an image
now extracted from nothingness for eternity. There
was a single difference between me and him, maybe
even in my favor: I was no longer a man; I had definitely settled into a female body. And as a woman,
I would need to take note of the female materiality,
become more acquainted with each semitone between the clitoris and the vulva. I could already pass
as a woman. And so I kept playing between my legs
to return from each incursion full of discoveries. I
analyzed the bodyguard in detail, tested his charms,
his desolate air, but did not bite the bullet.
Examining him lifted my spirits, freed me of my
natural attraction to the abyss. If I wished to buy

some basic pieces of women's clothing, I would need to find a place on a sidewalk where I could turn tricks. Why not in Manaus? I might get lucky and bring a man into a room after asking him for money. I might spread my legs under a teenager and be his first fuck. Cumming over and over again out of pure joy for taking the boy from the world of internet porn into the warm moisture of my hungry clam. It suddenly seemed classy for the bodyguard and I to dance together, naked, as we had been during the big boss's burial. Without thinking, I placed my arm over the bodyguard's shoulder, casually. He, in turn, put his hand on my waist. I asked what song we were dancing to. The bodyguard guided me, so I was able to block out any thoughts, urgent or not, and just be at his mercy. He said it was a samba song by Martinho da Vila. Samba, yes. I confess that I hadn't expected it to be a samba. Because we were dancing slowly, like in a bolero. Of course, as we hugged each other, the bodyguard got a full erection. I found it very interesting to be with a man who wanted me sexually. All I needed to do was keep good moisture going between my legs, if even that. The pre-erection tension, oh, I was freed from that. I didn't need to lubricate my stick in front of another naked body ever again. I had finally realized a woman's sexual superiority. Let's just say in that regard, men get the raw end of the deal. With the bodyguard, the situation didn't require too much of me. Before I noticed, we were dancing on top of the engineer's grave. There wasn't that typical bump of soil on the ground. It was a flat patch. And so, we kept on dancing on top of the recently deceased. The bodyguard said it was a good technique for smoothing out the terrain even more. It would not be good for us if the Federal Police discovered the corpse. He said this as he entered the house and called for me to follow him, because we were going to leave in half an hour. In the kitchen, he snorted long lines of cocaine. He offered some to me. I said no. The bodyguard returned the house key, sliding it underneath the door. Who was coming to the house next? Asking him those types of questions wouldn't shed any light on the truth for me. He was there to deceive me. Or maybe not? In truth, I lacked any understanding of a substantial motivation inside his head. Maybe he was nothing more than just a good bodyguard. Or not. He walked in front of me. It was beautiful to see him braving the jungle. His thick thighs made me hungry to fuck a man's ass again. Those good times were gone now with the engineer's death. His flanks imposed themselves. In a powerful way. Interesting to notice that, on this journey through the jungle, my pelvis still displayed a certain propensity for courtship, typical of the male genitalia I was saying goodbye to. I put my hand in my pants, to the left side of my crotch, and something there answered my touch by licking my fingers—certainly an expression of an amorous act. It was a very tiny animal encrusted in my bush, almost at the base of the cock (if I still had one). It had a warm, thick saliva. My new genitalia seemed to be a hotbed of bizarre sub-creatures. By answering the call from this genital itch, I found a microorganism in its first lethargic moves. I ran my fingers through the nurseries and sepulchers of my pubic metropolis…I don't know. My whole pelvis was a nursery. Or a cemetery. My sex offered a garden of unusual presences. Some sweet, others aggressive to the point of biting. I blew on my bitten fingers and felt sorry for the creatures who invaded me without a horizon in sight. In truth, whenever I received a visit from the impossible, I tried to think that I would soon get used to the abuse. I realized later, when I fucked the bodyguard, that those insurmountable beings in my crotch had the shapes of tiny nodules with a vaginal slit right in the middle of them. The gap also seemed to be the animal's mouth. They were just drops of creatures and sometimes they licked the hand that probed them. Courtesans. The hand came

back wet and warm from the pubes. The little creatures' feces accumulated on my skin, infiltrating the
tiny basins of my pores, which looked like lunar
craters up close. The craters had a spherical balus-
trade around them. I could lean on them and watch
the spectacle of molecular expansion on the floor
and slopes of the arena. I liked to stay at these irreg-
ular balconies, admiring the microorganisms down
below in their struggle for another day: a real battle
against the invisible forces of extinction. When
they weren't sucking my blood, these creatures
seemed to be shitting, and their manure gave back
to my body the energy they had sucked from me.
There were times when the little bugs would unexpectedly spasm. Maybe they were having an orgasm. They were masturbating, perhaps? On the
edge of the pubic thicket, or even deep in the jungle
of it, they would find their own time to cum, independent of mine. There was no erotic synchronism
between host and parasite. There was a point when
I wondered if it wasn't time to start experimenting
with the obscene confluences between us. An epic
written in trance. Perhaps this ideal coincidence
could add the infinitesimal ecstasies of my guests to
my own pleasure. I would multiply myself in orgasms. Then I wouldn't be able to live without this
microbiology enhancing the eternal promise of

fusion. I felt less lonely. These creatures didn't seem to comply with the male sexual psychology, in which there are only two choices: all or nothing. Sometimes, it seemed that they played for hours without even pretending to reach any conclusion. I kept observing, with my obsessive eyes, details of the lives of these people camping in my pubes. Sometimes they seemed to be resting on hammocks. Certain men fear that same kind of siesta after their body's revelries. They know that their impotence can happen again in the next carnal mirage, without words having time to help. They fear their cocks might drown in sleep. I touched myself, and confirmed with great relief that my pubic area still held its most recent formation, that of the female. I still hadn't had many opportunities to orgasm in the female register. Or was it my chronic dissatisfaction that held me back? Butterflies around our steps cheered us up a little. We, the renegades. We ventured deeper and deeper into the woods. With a stick in his hand, the bodyguard hit at the branches blocking our way. Suddenly, there was a wide, circular grove. An intense glare of sunlight passed through the empty space. Some birds made that space an aquarium of light. Here and there descended assorted shapes of shadows from the open sky; yes, in the middle of that glare, reproducing the anatomy of the surrounding high branches, in dialogue with the restless tilt of the solar axis. The bodyguard and I stopped to observe the birds' celebration. I stepped into the luminous terrain and looked up. I was blinded and scared of getting dizzy and falling. Then I walked back to the bodyguard, to his body, and made a silent invitation, nodding my head so he would come with me. He had full, indecent lips. And with those lips, he resumed his march. I followed him, of course. We bent down sometimes to dodge birds coming out of their sinister nests, where the forest was unbroken and inviolable. They seemed to come from burrows where they lived with their eggs, which were perhaps mixed in with a surprising number of snake eggs. We looked, obsessively, at the leafy soil, scared of surprising any snakes. I was afraid of weakening and losing my resolve to advance, returning perhaps to the beginning of the end. I feared realizing I might be approaching a solution. I didn't consider myself a brave creature. The bodyguard was the opposite. He would throw himself recklessly against danger, with a bit of drama even. It didn't seem to me that he valued life that much. Maybe because he had come from a place where death by stray bullets was common, a true plague. We had been going through the jungle for about five hours now. He said we would be arriving soon. And it didn't take long for the sun to fully come out and farther down was a village, immersed in its siesta. Nobody on the streets. A barefoot boy, walking along a path, approached us. He smiled and I took the opportunity to ask: What is this place called? It's called Nova Amizade, the boy said. Nova Amizade? I asked. Yes, that's it, he answered. The bodyguard kept walking; he didn't think it wise to be all revved up by the cuteness of a native child. The boy walked joyfully, humming a hymn or something like that. The song talked about Christ walking on water. When I was a child, I loved that scene. It was a circus show. I imagined what a dizzying sensation would come from walking on the surface of water. I wanted to do that too, I'd thought, staring at the picture before falling asleep. Why wasn't it up to me to be God? Why wasn't it up to a classmate or a friend from college? Why wasn't it up to the engineer? I walked quickly to catch up with my new partner's angry walk. Maybe we could take advantage of the village's slow pace and enter via the fringe of the forest until we found a place with cool shade to make love and recover from the long walk. I gave him the idea. We both had scratches all over our faces, arms, legs—the result of hostile nature. Crossing the jungle had left us wounded. But we couldn't risk seeking help in non-existent hospitals in some small town. I had been bitten by an insect of absolutely huge dimensions, the size of a frog, maybe. But it flew with transparent, tiny wings, like a dragonfly. It was even meaty, if looked at up close. The wound hurt me when I walked. We didn't know exactly how to continue our journey. The bodyguard likely didn't have any money either. So let us fondle each other on the grass, sure, but away from the heart of the woods. By the time we climaxed, we would surely have the next steps to resume the escape mapped out in our minds. As we walked toward the forest's edge, I concluded I was hopelessly trapped in sexual damnation. Since childhood in fact. It would be no use trying to straighten me out, put me on a path to chastity; I would never achieve that goal. I and everyone I got involved with lived for sex. And because of it, I sensed, we would be decimated. I entered the fibril terrain of the forest, and he came behind me with determination. With a bulge at the left side of his groin, needless to say. Before, he had been my guide and lord, but now he followed me, obeying my course. As if I had a sharper sense of smell than him to find a nest for our lovemaking. A woman thing. I sat on top of the dry leaves, under the blessing of an oceanic shade. He did, too. Then we French kissed. It was then that I realized his tongue was as vast as he was. Like a runway for a plane prepped for takeoff. I ran my tongue over his. I probed its volume, texture, its play with mine in his mouth. Then came all that continuity, typical of sexual unfolding. We were seated. When I pulled my tongue from his succulent mouth, I could see his tumescence below. I went down on it with immense joy. He didn't even have a chance to drop his pants. I took the lead, yes, I did it all myself. For my own delight, for the propulsion sent by those viscera. If I was lucky, they would be slow to respond. I lowered my pants, I grabbed his dick, and he, the flooded land between my legs… I didn't know if I could call it a pussy just yet. Its outer labia was like that of my kid cousin's pussy in bloom. And the inner labia, too. That small crevice where I used to play as a boy, in the delightful little darknesses of childhood. Inner lips, Venusian, that I kissed with my trembling lips. I used to pass my tongue between those virgin lips and feel a forbidden taste in my mouth, a taste of entrails that would never be mine. At that time, there was a certain enchantment to the breaks between libidinous acts. That moment after satiety and before hunger returned, when all that remained in your mind was the tickling of an idea, the melting of the soul, the indolent preparation for a new embrace. And then you are back to wrestling. The skin is salty. A lot of licking involved. A cock can fuck you with an eagerness to go places you didn't even know you had. I wanted all that, yes. I was way past the age of believing in abstinence or Spartan causes. So, there I was, hungry again, sucking the bodyguard's cock while he played with what was still forming in my pelvis. And I still didn't know how to name this new sex in my domain's south. I was still getting to know my new regime of desire and my ungrateful euphoria in being part of the female world. Desire now gradually spread to the margins of the organism, in incessant fluids, in true sparks. My body as a whole was a genital organ. Sweaty and dirty, we went into a lake in front of us, not just to remove the smell of sexual overload from our bodies, but also to take a break from the incessant harassment of the tropical mosquitoes. A big bird glided low in the sky, very close to us. It came and went. It seemed to be probing us. It swooped in with a big fuss. I dove underwater for a long time. I wanted to test my runaway partner. I wanted to see if he would come rescue me or stay put. I came back to the surface, breathless. The bodyguard, at the edge of the lake, still had his hard-on, even after cumming in my eye. He offered to buy me a bottle of water. So we went looking for an open bar. The village was still asleep. I thought of that child who had given us the name of the ghost village. Here he came again. Maybe he was the village's guardian, while everybody else took their siesta. I asked him where one could find some drinking water. The kid asked us to follow him… I hoped the bodyguard had the money for water, because I certainly didn't have a cent. In fact, there was a bar just a bit ahead. A young man was cleaning the post-lunch mess from the tables. The bodyguard and I sat across from one another at a table with a checkered vinyl cloth. We looked at each other as if we were asking ourselves: What next? I, for example, kept repeating to myself that I didn't have a fucking penny. The dead should be buried with money in their pockets. For emergencies like this. I went straight from the cemetery to the drug dealers. And, up to that point, I never found a way of surviving that did not involve returning to my wife and son. My foot was hurt. The bodyguard went to the bathroom; the bottles of water arrived. I took some sips, thought a little more about what we should do in the next few hours so the Federal Police wouldn't catch up with us, at least for the time being. The rest, under the circumstances, didn't matter. The bodyguard was taking a long time. I went to see what was happening, maybe he had already been arrested. If that was

the case, I might still have had time to sneak out.
But there was no bodyguard in sight in the bathroom. I knocked on the stall's door. Nobody. There
was another stall, semi-open, with a broken lock. I
pushed the door and there was resistance from inside. I gathered all my strength and kicked the door.
And I saw it: the young man who had served us was
giving a blowjob to the bodyguard. He was sucking
right where I'd had my mouth minutes earlier. I
walked away from that scene and wandered around
the village, where the population was waking up
and occupying the streets once again. Some people
greeted me, others spat when they saw me, as if to
say: Get the fuck out, you outsider. I fled, carrying
the frightening tone of the bodyguard in my mind.
And I listed all the scenes that had led me to that
day, good and bad. If things continued to happen in
a certain sequence, without further hassles, I could
be a man at peace with his own story. However, I
had always believed that until that day came, I
would have to keep poking at an experimental field.
And then I would have to spit out the excess poison
that accumulated inside me. But where was I even
going? I was running away. Running away from any
story that wanted to enslave me to my recent or
remote past. I wanted to be reborn in the figure of
a complete female. But my newly feminine traits

were still mixed with various residues of the male I had been. I wanted to get in front of the mirror and see a full woman, without any details still to be finalized. The power that impelled me to walk was still gestating, while a noisy plane flew over the jungle. I feared a permanent delay to my admission to the female world. And I needed to learn how to use a gun. The men from the Federal Police would be tightening the siege. But to take up arms, I still needed my sex concluded, established, and confirmed once and for all. How could a being of unfinished sex use a gun logically? After all, a man with imprecise sex tends to be confused, inoperative, with a mental rarefaction to match his genital indeterminacy. So tomorrow, I would still be a lonely woman, penniless, without a mature sexual conception. Besides, I'd forgotten to bring the engineer's pistol. I went deep into the jungle. That afternoon, the animals seemed too agitated. Their excitement was too much to handle, it was dizzying. It pierced my ears with some kind of premonition that was unspeakable outside the animal kingdom. Mosquitoes had repeated meals off my blood. The dimness in the jungle's interior suggested a slow sunset. That's when I saw the house in the clearing reappearing. And so close. I had returned to it, blindly, without realizing that all along I had been searching for the grave of the man who had given me life and a new sex. I had been looking for protection, no matter that he was already dead. As an engineer, he had provided me with a new plan for my body. That man for whom I would now cry. Like the angels at cemeteries, I would tilt my head to contemplate, in the grave, a space that could free me from widowhood. But there was nothing distinguishing about the grave. Not even the rectangular outline of the pit on the terrain. The flat, reddish clay was bare, uninviting for any mortuary courtship. It was already nothing. So much so that I struggled to find the exact spot where the deceased lay. My body throbbed as a wound. I was already limping. My feet, more and more swollen. My soul, if I still had one, housed a trauma I could no longer explain. Plus the guilt, for my family, for not really being dead. I was an imposter in a lawless jungle. The wild intoxication grew stronger but didn't dare identify itself, because then it would be worth nothing. Hence the feeling of a covert pain, hidden in the chest to disguise itself. The pain poisoned me, silently, oblivious to any rhythm, inhospitable in a way that I can't describe with verbal acumen. I felt myself dying. So I threw up, leaning against a tree trunk. While I vomited, I noticed ants invading my miserable foot. I put my hand on my chest and felt the beat. Out of rhythm, the apocalypse in my body and everywhere else was ready to unfold. My heart still followed the regularity of the sequence. I had to believe in it, at least for now. I could have lived longer under the engineer's spell, if I hadn't forgotten myself somewhere, like a good novice in the face of his own shadow. I spat at such bullshit. The spit came with more bouts of vomit. I tripped and fell. I got up feeling more beaten down than when I landed on the clay. On this return trip, I took many tumbles. I ran and tripped into branches, scratching myself all over in the consumption of my own compassion. A true martyr without an audience. The insect bites left me swollen; inflammations in red, purple, and green. From time to time, a lucidity that said I was making a mistake by staying would come back to me. What I needed was to go back to Porto Alegre and hide myself in a hole where no one would ever find me. Why not São José dos Ausentes, also in Rio Grande do Sul? At the right time, my wife and son would learn I was back. Let them find out, we would figure out what to do next then. Back home, I would be safe. At least safer than in the jungle. Here, the strange noises persisted, birds came and went in the branches, emitting rattling chirps, giving voice to forest disturbances. Suddenly, I felt a hot pressure on my back. I didn't feel pain or anything like that. Only a strong heat that grew hotter and hotter. The impression was that I was burning. I turned around and, amid the dark tones of tropical green, I visualized the unfathomable face of the bodyguard. Yes, he had the gun in his hand. And he had shot me. I fell face down. Close to my face, on the dry leaves, a snake was ready to strike. I asked myself if I would have time to see the color of my blood. Or if my sense of sight would disappear before that. I saw the snake, so close to me that she already seemed to have a domesticated air. As if I was so embedded in the forest that no part of it could threaten me. I was at peace with all the surroundings, even if shot down by the bodyguard, just a few steps away. In my infinite body, on the verge of blending in with everything, the story of a guy betrayed by his own husband's bodyguard was being written. And I was now a widow. Or not? Would it be possible to undo any mistakes related to my engineer's survival? Suddenly, another shot. I felt my body compress. And the sensation of that abysmal bravado remained in this story of mine. Was there really any reason for the bodyguard to shoot me down? Witness elimination, perhaps. He thought I knew too much. He didn't know of my virginal ignorance of any shenanigans. I could have sought justice for the engineer's death. But the bodyguard thought of it first, and there lay my body, counting on the precision of my thinking to preserve it for a few more minutes of life. What if I still had a long life…but in the state I was in? The fact that a man and a woman shared the same killer didn't bring us any comfort. What good did it do if the ammunition came from the same weapon? My only consolation was my resistance at the hour's end. Yes, I felt in the right condition to delay my end. I felt like I carried half the world in the damaged body that represented me. That was indeed a consolation: taking some kind of council of the living with me to the grave. I wanted to laugh so badly. It had never occurred to me that a corpse could laugh. Would it be the beginning of a fatal therapy? But the laugh aborted itself while still in my chest. The bodyguard couldn't do me any more harm than he already had. I should rest then, at last. He might take me for dead now. Therefore, I needed to extend myself even more, to accept, little by little, the time still necessary for my agony. If the bodyguard still wanted to do things with my body, I would agree. If he wanted to lie on top of me and wrap himself around me, I would be grateful to him in the time I still had left. Because I felt cold. Sometimes, very cold, despite the 45 degrees in the shade. The animal voices grew further and further away. I felt relieved at that quietness. I should dismiss any appeal that took my attention away from the beating of my heart—at this point, beyond slow. Follow that pace, yes. I should focus on it with dedication. That's what I had, the only possible drama at hand—the heartbeat, slower each time. He came to me, turned me on my back and checked if the veins in my forehead still throbbed. I don't know what his conclusion was. I recognized his hand, his fat fingers and bitten nails, his intimate but imperative touch, yes. Then the big guy got up, aimed the gun at me, and fired again. The shot gave me a jolt and I stopped. I couldn't figure out where he had hit me this time. I know that my shallow consciousness still wanted to continue. I realized with crystal clarity that there is no life beyond one's biography. What was extinguishing in me was everything. Now I was diving in a certain luminosity, following some bluish shoals that I had already encountered before, I didn't remember where. These shoals, giving off a faint aroma, appeared very close to me. Certain nuances of vision lingered. Like, for example, a small purple stretch in a corner of the frame was still present to me. The diluted reminiscences of some figures made my consciousness a) react by reviving; b) certain zones; c) too distant for a dying person. All this, however, soon unraveled. There was at least one scene not lived yet, totally unprecedented. Which I still needed, greedily—as if once I had it I could rest at last. The frame expanded, though not much because my field of vision was beginning to fade, without cessation, fade away very slowly... No longer afraid of anything, I meditated, weakly, so weakly...as in a painting of a dying woman that I once saw in London. I felt I could use this lack of fear as a springboard to wake me up. I even got a glimpse of the sky. Maybe with the sunset and everything. Then I thanked my own company. I could count only on it, in the end. The one who was thinking, lying there, would continue to think of himself for a few more hours after the denouement. The painful delirium—or not so painful—would only cease when the moon came out. The moon tonight would be full, pearly. Maybe every little thing that happened to me was the best thing ever. It was the providential balance of everything, a feeling that had accompanied me throughout my life. My breath was still there to show its service. It gently blew a few tangled strands of hair covering my left eye. For the first time I felt the real meaning of the expression "every man for himself." I was, yes, my own example in that cadenced march toward dust. As long as there was rhythm, there would be life. My first death came to mind, when I was resurrected by the engineer—strangely gone before me. Or not? To everything I applied this inquiring expression. At the end of my experience here, I would not be able to inquire any longer. Or not? Could I still cultivate something resembling hope? And the steps I heard coming from the forest, whom did they belong to? Were they coming to my rescue? Or to sanctify what was consummated? Maybe the snake had already bitten me. Perhaps it had left a numbness in my body that was typical of millenary things, like stones, gravel, the trunk of a tree, sand, the tomb, verminous shadows. If this was death, I would be satisfied. We could turn the page and wait for what would never come. I still could hear—in an even more cadenced, almost martial way—steps on dry leaves coming from the forest. Whose would they be? Weird, but, in that moment, it seemed that I could hear better than any other survivor would, so strongly the noise of those quick steps in the woods kept coming at me. It was as if the sound came from an underground tunnel, connected to my ears by an instrument that rose up to the surface of earth, meant to keep me a little longer in the world. Just a little longer, I wished to say in the middle of the colossal apocryphal silence, where no one fought any longer for authorship. But at the behest of whom were the steps rushing? Yes, they kept conquering the distance, and I listened to them with astonished clarity. Perhaps, listening was the only thing that still engaged me with my senses. Although I also listened to the compressed sound coming from inside the ground. I could hear more of this subterranean force than the general traces of sound that happened on the surface. There, I was already dead before I died. I already preferred the fossilized life of the ground to the agility of the air. This time the bodyguard took my wrist to examine it. And when he confirmed what he wanted, he abruptly let go of my arm; and the fall made a low bang, like an explosion in a quarry. The acoustics coming through the submerged pathways were so muffled and resounding that they caused me tears and a cardiac acceleration—dangerous for an expired muscle. The powerful sound from the ground's viscera, which in life I would have never guessed existed, was putting me into a hypnotic state where everything deserted me—and within that state, a beckon reigned without end. I nodded back, too. Without any expectation or consequence. My silent beckon already seemed freed from any objective. The bodyguard seemed to be relieved, at last, with my apparent extermination. Surely he already saw a consummated corpse in me. Or was my thinking

already the reasoning of a defunct mind and, therefore, a palliative to actual thought? But only I knew
that my total erasure had not yet taken place. I was
hanging on by a thread, but somehow I still re-
sisted… Perhaps my last signs of life were imper-
ceptible even for me. The determined steps on the
dry leaves in the forest were getting closer and
closer. The bodyguard, distracted by being alive,
certainly could not hear the footsteps. Did he need
to fear them? Maybe they will arrive before I leave.
If I could, I would warn the bodyguard of the imminent danger of those steps advancing through
the forest toward us. Something inside me continued to burn fuel. As long as the bodyguard lived, I
would live, too. I would give him credit for that. His
natural solidity would represent me on the surface.
For a while. The fact that he murdered the engineer
and me didn't mean anything in that moment of
agony. Another sound confirmed that the bodyguard was moving the clay, little by little. The process of removing portions of earth seemed to me
like an imperfect but essential rhythm. As long as
the pace continued, more and more regular, I could
wait a little longer, a little more. And even a little
bit more, if needed. The one who murdered me was
now prolonging my life. I depended on him and
him alone. The bodyguard was making an

enormous effort to dig another pit. This time, for me. Was it next to the engineer's? I think so, and my heart sped up. Our bodies, murdered, still warm, would merge into one another. Task completed, he dragged my body to the grave and threw it down into the hole. I hit the bottom and felt the upper part of my arm dislocate. Just like what happened with the engineer's body. If I could move, maybe I could reach his body, right there by my side, waiting for an obscene coexistence. The bodyguard threw dirt in the pit. Thick handfuls of earth on my face. I felt a sandy consistency in my mouth, mixed with the incisive flavor of a small, rough leaf. I saw the bubbles we are used to seeing when we close our eyes, but this time with absurd fatigue. With my eyes sealed shut, I saw the bubbles now embedded in the dramatic hues of twilight, ready to fade out. So many eyelids covered me… They filtered the ardent semitones of the hour. Tiny black bubbles remained boiling angrily inside me. The sunset tones faded, little by little. They no longer had the strength to breach my eyelids and flood me with the low tone of light. Their cousins, the dark bubbles, very dark, still restless, just needed my interior for their evolutions. And so they didn't take up space. Now the dark tones expanded and surpassed the frame, letting whiteness sleep alone here in my refuge.

That's when I noticed a taste, timid and tepid at first, on my lips. It was the taste of a liquid I had known before, but which was running from me now. A lunar streak moistened my lips, yes. The taste seemed to burst from the essence of whiteness, like everything else. Only a tiny red ant—entering through my rectum to perhaps start a long journey through the darkness—only that insect didn't match the virginal whiteness. Otherwise, everything was taken by that white denseness, in opposition to the somber interior. I pressed my mouth to that intense white color, already spread all over the place, and dedicated myself to sucking it, at first with some caution... The substance formed by the clear color provoked gentle tickles on the roof of my mouth. The tension between a kind of smile from the surface and the pitch submerged in the organism seemed to relax for a moment. Giving the feeling of everything being one and the same. Only children react in syncopated cascades to other people's fingers assailing them with tickles, especially in the secret, thin area under the arm, before the hairs announce themselves. Somewhat parsimonious, I continued to feed on the color. The outside of my mouth was smeared with white. Drops slipped from my chin, flooded my chest, forming lakes yellow as milk, perhaps deceptively stagnant... Now the roof of my mouth gave the sense of a dome, where wandering birds circled. On slow flights; perhaps, solemn. I didn't need to be afraid. I just had to open my mouth and let them fly in the wide sky. It rained. I could feel the earth soaking up the moisture, very slowly... Had the rainy season begun? But the rain no longer came to wash me. Then, with a bang, I coagulated. And before I couldn't formulate any longer, I realized that now, at last... I would start to live...

PRAISE FOR
THE INSIGHT BOOK

T0062088

"There is in my opinion no great work without a great insight, and there are no great insights without truth being told, sometimes painfully, sometimes happily, always intuitively. [Tas's] book brings concise techniques to understand and source those insights."

UNERMAN

CTO of EssenceMediacom and author of Belonging

'In his stimulating new book, Tas reminds us of the free-thinking mental environment required to arrive at true insight and how it's invariably serendipity and play, not process, that gets one there. It is full of interesting observations, stimulating anecdotes and quotes. These, plus the creative examples enthusiastically relayed, helped put the joy back into the insight / being insightful, the greatest pleasure of our job latterly rendered sterile and lifeless by its formal adoption as the holy grail by The Man."

JUSTIN HOLLOWAY

Head of Client Strategy, Syneos Health

"When everyone is using similar data driven marketing tools and analytics it is only insight, and the action it drives, that can deliver competitive marketing advantage. Insight is not easy to achieve but in this book Anthony Tasgal, with his wonderful humour and rigour, takes you on an invaluable journey towards recognising and discovering genuine insights, rather than yet another data analysis, that will drive improvement in your marketing and business performance."

BRADLEY STARR
Founder Miller-Starr Database Marketing,
ex Global EVP Data & Analytics MRM/McCann

"[This is] a book to help marketers understand the theory as to what is and what isn't insight. It helps them understand their agency and market researchers' points of view and gives a rationale to challenge them [and make them] push a little harder to get the insight that we originally commissioned the work to do, in order to create that exciting, pulse racing "Aha!" moment."

KLYNN ALIBOCUS
Global Head of Channel Excellence/Customer Experience
at Boehringer Ingelheim Animal Health.

"As Tas rightly observes the modern world is great at generating ever-larger stockpiles of data but our ability to generate useful intelligence from all these datapoints doesn't appear to be changing at all. The Insight Book aims to help change this. Tas makes the case for developing personal and organisational insight and provides a number of excellent case studies to illustrate his point involving brands such as Marmite, Sony and Snickers. His book then helps us understand that 'insight' is a process and culture, not a thing. He concludes with some research-backed tips and tools in developing a personal and organisational culture of insight."

HERB KIM
Founder & CEO of Thinking Digital Limited

"Tas's new book shows us how insights can help save us from the overload of information and choice that we all experience. Using a range of examples, some invaluable definitions, and a series of clear guidelines and springboards, Tas not only shows how information has lost its currency, he shows us all how to pan for the gold of insight."

CRAIG WALLACE
Global Head, Strategic Offerings, CGI

Published by
LID Publishing
An imprint of LID Business Media Ltd.
LABS House, 15-19 Bloomsbury Way,
London, WC1A 2TH, UK

info@lidpublishing.com
www.lidpublishing.com

A member of:

businesspublishersroundtable.com

© Anthony Tasgal, 2023
© LID Business Media Limited, 2023

Printed by Imak Ofset

ISBN: 978-1-911687-38-2
ISBN: 978-1-911687-39-9 (ebook)

Cover and page design: Caroline Li

THE
INSIGHT
BOOK

ENHANCING YOUR CREATIVITY
BY LEARNING TO SEE THINGS DIFFERENTLY

ANTHONY TASGAL

MADRID | MEXICO CITY | LONDON
BUENOS AIRES | BOGOTA | SHANGHAI

FOR OTHER TITLES IN THE SERIES...

CONCISE
ADVICE
LAB

SMALL
BOOKS:
BIG
IDEAS

CLEVER CONTENT, DYNAMIC IDEAS, PRACTICAL
SOLUTIONS AND ENGAGING VISUALS –
A CATALYST TO INSPIRE NEW WAYS OF THINKING
AND PROBLEM-SOLVING IN A COMPLEX WORLD

conciseadvicelab.com

CONTENTS

PROLOGUE

Why a book on insight?

Well, shelves have hardly been groaning beneath the weight of tomes on the matter. And yet, it remains one of the hottest and most debated topics in marketing, communications and research. So, you can hardly complain that it's 'just another book on insight' (unlike, say, books on the brain, consciousness, social media, baking or mindfulness).

In fact, everywhere you look in the business world, insight has taken on the aura of an elusive Holy Grail. Research departments have re-branded themselves as insight departments, while conferences and events dedicated to understanding and promulgating insight have sprung up globally, promising new generations of practitioners that they can grow up learning what it is and how to spot or discover it.

There's been greater focus on insight with the advent of Big Data (essentially, the concept of crunching 'lots of data'). Shouldn't that, in and of itself, give us insight in droves? Well, no.

There's simply no automatic process whereby data gives insight; no effortless shift from data to 'ta-da!'

So, how can insight be both over-hyped *and* under-appreciated?

Is it just something researchers need to justify their existence to their marketing counterparts or the Board? Have ad agencies become unhealthily obsessed with it, in the search for pitch-winning strategies? Could it be the secret to transforming the fortunes of their clients' brands? Or is it the new currency of brands, marketing and communications — the Bitcoin of branding? And, hey, who doesn't want in on a new currency?

Following our storytelling principle of the 'Magic Number Three,' we will explore the meaning, role and composition of insight in three sections.

First, in Part 1, we will provide a detailed overview of what actually constitutes an insight and why it's considered so valuable. We'll review definitions, explore the theory behind this elusive concept, and discuss some objections to all the hubbub.

Part 2 will delve into the insight casebook. With the assumption that understanding real-world case studies (practice) is a good way of pinning down the law (theory), we will look at a range of brands and campaigns that have embodied the notion of insight. Individually and collectively, this can help shape our understanding of insight.

Finally, Part 3 will offer some concrete guidance for Seekers After Insight. Namely, how can we be more likely to find it personally, and how can we build and sustain company cultures that deliver insight at the team level? Using that number again, we will examine this from the perspective of three Cs: characteristics, credos and cultures.

BLIZZARDS, BUTTERFLIES AND BERNBACH

WHAT IS INSIGHT
– THEORY

1.
WHY THE DRIVE FOR INSIGHT?

So, why are intrepid insight-hunters looking for this elusive vision? Why has insight become the coin of the realm for marketing people who don't quite dare dip their toes into crypto?

Rightly or wrongly, the currency of insight has grown to Tesla levels, as clients and their agencies have sought out the wisdom and understanding it is widely thought (or expected) to offer.

It seems that successful insight can fulfil various needs.

At the generic business level, a good insight can be a way to transform a company. It can help relieve business pressures, and offer a new route to facing down brand strategy challenges.

At the global level, there may be a need to re-frame the brand (or entire category) due to changing social factors, needs or perceptions. Smoking would be the most obvious example in recent history, and sustainability is perhaps the most current.

I recall this being expressed by clients and the marketing press, with businesses feeling that their brand was 'losing touch with consumers.' This struck me as bizarre, and also rather disingenuous, as clients are obsessed with having enough data to understand their users.

I tend to see it as code for, 'We've had enough of our agency and just need an excuse to fire them.'

This has often been in response to competitive threats from new market entrants, or other brands that have modified their offering, positioning or marketing activities.

Finally, the perceived need may be rooted in internal issues. Many times, in my former ad agency life, I witnessed a new client CEO, Director of Marketing or Sales VP fuelling the drive for insight. Without fail, this had several immediate consequences, often framed as, 'I want to review the agency, our relationship, the strategy and the ad campaign specifically.'

This almost never turned out well for the agency; we knew we would almost certainly be fired, usually after a specious inquest had been carried out. If not, the client would ask us to conduct a strategic analysis and theatrically unveil a miraculous new insight for them.

One way of looking at the transformative power of insight in business is through the lens of our old friend, hero and patron, Charles Darwin.

Darwin's theory of evolution was largely based on what was known as incrementalism: the gradual, linear accumulation of small changes over the long history of the evolutionary record and human change.

A contrasting theory was one of 'saltation,' suggesting abrupt, non-linear changes in the fossil record.

Language fans will spot the etymological links to *sauter* in French, *saltar* in Spanish and *salire* in Italian, all meaning to climb, leap or jump.

It also reminds comms folks of that well-known cornerstone of communication theory, 'salience,' or the ability for a brand or piece of messaging to jump out at us.

Darwin was a gradualist, and famously said, "*Natura non facit saltum.*" (Nature doesn't make jumps.)

In fact, the term "punctuated equilibrium" was coined by palaeontologists Stephen Jay Gould and Niles Eldredge in 1972[1] to reflect that the fossil record did occasionally reveal violent bursts of change, rather than the relentless incrementalism of continuity that most other evolutionary biologists adhere to.

Though the supposition caused a lively debate among Darwin's heirs — opponents sarcastically labelled it "evolution by jerks" — it did help explain in part the occasional leaps and bounds that punctuated long stretches of little change in the fossil record. (Gould's pointed riposte, recasting it as *Creeps vs. Jerks*, showed an underestimated scientific sense of humour.)

This strikes me as a helpful analogy for thinking about how brands can be viewed, and where insight fits in.

Anyone who works at the branding coalface can attest to the fact that much brand strategy and implementation maps pretty neatly to the incrementalist approach. Brands develop a strategy and position, zero in on an audience, devise a communications approach and generally execute slowly and steadily against it.

But there are occasional irruptions of the unexpected that tilt the equilibrium, which can cause an upheaval to the category. As noted,

these may be of external origin, but they can also be created by a brand, especially if it is a disruptor or 'challenger.'

If you want to create saltation for your brand, company or culture, locating a transformative insight is a good place to start. (See Part 2 – The Casebook.)

Insight can also be invaluable in helping you grow and 'scale.' (A lot of people I find myself working with/for/alongside seem to be very intent on using this verb.)

THE RISK BARRIER

Gerd Gigerenzer[2] is a German psychologist, behavioural scientist, writer and educator affiliated with the Max Planck Institute for Human Development. He has authored award-winning books that have been translated into 21 languages. These include *Calculated Risks; Gut Feelings: The Intelligence of the Unconscious*; and *Risk Savvy: How to Make Good Decisions*. He's also been involved in a protracted, public (and quite venomous) spat with Princeton University psychologist and economist Daniel Kahneman and his late research partner, Amos Tversky, about the scope of heuristics — rules of thumb that can guide decision-making — and human biases.

In 2013's *Risk Savvy*, Gigerenzer notes that there are too many lawyers in the US, which has the highest per capita percentage of attorneys of any country other than Israel. Among other implications, he looks at the impact this has on the medical profession. Here he gives the reader some very useful advice: don't ask doctors what course of treatment they recommend to you; ask what they would do if it were their mother, brother or child.

Assuming that we aren't thinking of engaging a lawyer to pursue a medical malpractice action, which goes far beyond the scope of this book, let's consider what Gigerenzer calls "defensive decision-making." This can be seen in business settings, when a person or group identifies Option A as the best solution to a problem, but chooses an inferior, but safer, Option B to protect themselves in case something goes wrong. (If you think this sounds like an academic breathlessly discovering every-day corporate ass covering, you have my support.)

This will all feel very familiar in meetings that conclude with an airy declaration that 'we need more data' and the systematic use of procrastination as a business tool.

As Gigerenzer puts it: "Fear of litigation and accountability has developed defensive decision-making into an art."

In the same sense, I worry about what I call Efficiency Creep. As accountability and its provisional wing — efficiency — have taken centre stage in so many creative and cultural endeavours, they've cast a shadow over much of the creative output of the industries themselves. Ask anyone who operates in the creative world whether efficiency is something that impinges on them in the slightest and listen to the cautious silence.

In the ad world, with which I'm most familiar, efficiency can have various pernicious effects.

I would argue that among its many uses, insight is an essential corrective to defensive decision-making.

2.
WHAT DO CLIENTS SAY?

Over the years of training I have carried out, and all the strategic projects I've been involved in, I have assigned and collected reams of homework, usually about clients' team and corporate culture. Much has been related to areas such as storytelling and behavioural economics, as well as the role of insight itself.

Along the way, I have accumulated a significant amount of evidence on the role of, and need for, insight.

Here is a selection of anonymised comments, sorted into three big-picture categories that have been common over the years, across different markets, countries and departments.

I) FACTS OF THE MATTER
These are statements that recur with alarming frequency when I ask about communications. They all converge on the idea that too many presentations and documents lack focus or guidance.

The blizzard of facts disguises a lack of insight or meaning.

"We tend to tell everyone everything. We say a lot about not very much."

"Internally, we are most often found to be simply reporting facts. Some of the team seem to think that facts are insights, and get lost in precision and detail, but forget about the relationships in the data and what underlying meaning and inferences can be brought out."

"Our main challenge? Incorporating insights from the data rather than just compiling reports with figures."

"Facts are reported. There's no interpretation, insight, recommendations. There's no 'So what,' 'What does it mean,' 'Why is that important,' or 'What does it mean for us?'"

"We are more comfortable extracting insights from dry data, and exploring more effective ways to present results."

"There are not enough insights. We only report the numbers, and don't tell the story. We are very factual and technology focussed."

"We're good at having opinion, but even better at hiding them behind data."

I sometimes like to use the term 'in-fact-uation' to describe our tendency to revere facts as facts.

II) NOT ENOUGH TIME

There has always been an assumption that insights take time, and that time is a barrier in itself to the production (and dissemination) of insight.

Is this necessarily the case, though?

More lay-it-on-the-line comments from my files:

> *"As we have quite a lot of projects on, and we have to chart/analyse everything ourselves, there is not enough time for in-depth insights and analysis."*

> *"We lack time to adopt an insight-led approach, although this is changing with a new project."*

III) HOW TO MAKE THEM STICK

> *"We have lots of insights (you could argue too many), but struggle to articulate exactly what matters most to customers, and to influence the business to change what they're doing to better match customer expectations."*

> *"Often, data and insights are being taken in by the audience at face value, without really drilling down to understand what it means, and how can it be used."*

> *"We lack the ability to translate insights into a story for presentation."*
>
> *"We are trying to put insights higher up the agenda, and to bring the commercial team better on board."*
>
> *"We try and lift the insights from the raw numbers to convey what lies underneath in the data. We can do more to tell a compelling story."*

One specific area of dissatisfaction relates to the translation of insight from data by research companies. Many clients I have worked with or spoken to over the decades have lamented the extent to which data providers can also play the role of insight generators.

As we saw earlier, the market research industry seems to have colonised and appropriated the territory of insights, for better or worse. It is now a given that you can't have insights without research data, which we'll return to later. Largely overnight, the research industry managed to reframe and rebrand itself as 'the insight industry.' I'd accepted that burden when I was a planner in ad agencies, but the research industry remains relatively ill equipped to fulfil its promise.

Below are a few comments from insight hunters, making that very point:

> *"We expect our agencies to give us insight to drive our business."*
>
> *"I need a partnership to give actionable insight, so we don't have to spend money on consultants to tell us what the research means."*
>
> *"Given the breadth of data they have, they should deliver better insights."*
>
> *"They're just not that great. We have to summarise their summary."*
>
> *"I want them to help me with seeing the patterns before they become obvious, and be able to flag them up to the senior clients."*
>
> *"We are looking for the elusive link between consumer insight and business issues facing senior management."*

In Part 3, we'll look at who does insight better, and who the market research industry can learn from.

3.
IS INSIGHT CLICHÉD?

Monetisation, trusted partner, reaching out, granularity, C-suite, maybe even purpose: all terms that I would argue now fit into the handy compartment known as meaningless jargon or cliché. Or there's 'value proposition,' or (dare I say it) 'engagement,' which I find too abstract, cold and inhuman to be of any lasting use.

Does 'insight' itself fit into this Pantheon of the Inane?

For many in the marketing and comms world, there is a special critique of insight — that it has indeed become a hackneyed term, bandied about as a form of currency, but not really understood, or even asked for or wanted, by anybody.

Yes, entire rainforests have been defoliated in the cause of hunting down suitable definitions. And yes, insight is a term that's often misused.

But I have to disagree with those who would move too quickly to preside over its post-mortem.

As with so many *fin-de-siecle* 'End of ...' books we've seen recently – *The End of Science*, *The Death of Marketing*, *The End of History* – it's really a case of Not Dead, Just Misdiagnosed.

As an ex-adman who'd sell his copy of Kahneman's *Thinking Fast and Slow* for a good business-winning insight, I know the value of (*hushed gong SFX*) insight, and that usability is everything. And as someone who spends much of his time now training various research and ad agency folk, as well as clients, on how to recognise and unearth insights, I have a vested interest in what I call 'insightment.'

Let's start with a panoramic sweep. Clients — and, in fact, virtually all of us — suffer from the attention-deficit disorder that comes from inhabiting what I call the DRIP (data-rich, insight-poor) universe.

First, without getting tripped up in the semantic undergrowth, my primary issue with insight's critics is that they give the word too many meanings, and randomly choose which ones to attack. They often mistake trees for the forest, data and information for insight, and go so far as to accuse the industry of wasting its time on something that has 'zero intrinsic value.'

For me, insight remains the prime currency of our business. Information (or data) is fuel for the insightment engine.

I use insightment to emphasise the fact that insight should properly be seen as a process, and a way of working and thinking, rather than merely a concrete noun that can be picked up and counted. (Planner visits grocery shop. 'Can I have five insights? Oh, go on and make it six, then.')

Science has long understood this. Albert Szent-Gyorgi, the Hungarian Nobel laureate biochemist, said the following, although

I'm not sure his estate is getting royalties for all the references it now gets in articles and speeches:

> *"Discovery consists of looking at the same thing as everyone else and thinking something different."*[3]

From the artistic tenet of 'breaking convention' to the theory of deep-immersion 'flow,' there is an inherent element of creativity and subversion at work here.

Insightment depends on the ability to perceive new and unexpected connections.

Information is to be collected. Insight is to be connected.

Maybe the research industry hasn't got to grips with the fact that it's been part of The Ideas Business for some time now.

ACTIONABILITY

Now, the other element I want to discuss is the question of implementation. Critics again point out the importance of communication, and the role of 'the debrief' — a creative agency's response to the client's requirements and project scope.

I feel that it is a savage indictment that we're still arguing about how to deliver research findings to enable the greatest commercial benefit.

Some talk of 'taking the business to a higher level,' as if this is something extraneous to insight. But that's the very point of it. Any planner or client who instinctively sees the enormous business advantage gained from the insights behind Pot Noodle, Sainsbury's or Marmite appreciates that insight is about the end, not the means.

There is a small but significant straw man I want to attack, as well: the 'purity of research.' We all now know (don't we?) that we are in the business of constructing meaning, not delivering a 'truth.'

In the same way that carnivores devour meat, and herbivores feed on grass and vegetables, humans are what I term *semavores* – we are fundamentally consumers of meaning. This is also deliberately reminiscent of the original meaning of the word 'consumer.'

Anything we create, present or communicate should have *meaning* as its and goal, not truth or (worse still) facts, messages or propositions.

As such, let's banish the traditional broadcast model of the debrief in favour of something that trades in meaning, not truth (let alone objectivity and fact.)

This is why I preach the theory and practice of storytelling to reframe how we present. This allows us to access the human emotions that allow us to tell tales, and thereby create conversations. We should stop mistaking catalogues for explanations, and start thinking of the debrief as a dramatic event with an audience, rather than a one-way, fossilised lecture. As with insightment, simplicity is much neglected.

RESEARCHERS, INSIGHTERS AND PLANNERS

> Q: What's the difference between a research manager
>   and an insight manager?
> A: About £20,000.

As with many jokes, I like to think that this goes to the heart of the insight question.

First, I lived through the era when insight became the *term du jour*, and client research departments magically transformed, seemingly overnight, into insight departments. Forget hindsight. Even at the time, this seemed a rather opportunistic bit of re-framing. It was as if researchers could immediately 'upskill' themselves and morph (avoids saying *transition*) into hunters and purveyors of insight.

This did a great injustice to insight and to those who relied on it (primarily clients, but also agency planners). There was an elephant-shaped, unexplored assumption in the room: that insight was simply an inevitable outgrowth of research, and that researchers had the necessary skills, talents and attitude to become foragers and disseminators of insight.

I was suspicious of this at the time, and remain unconvinced that researchers are automatically able to convert themselves into insight-detectors. At the same time, I believe in the converse: to be good at finding and transmitting insights, you don't have to be a 'traditional' market researcher.

When I lecture students and work with clients, I often detect the aptitude for insight that I believe will serve that person well, should they move into the insight field. And, interestingly, not many of these people would consider themselves to be primarily researchers. Some of them are creatives, which gives us a clue as to what's really required to find insight. (More — much more — on this later.)

The broader point is this: why should research be seen as the high road to insight? Why is there this unreflective assumption that if you're mired in research methodology, sampling and data analysis, you have everything you need to detect and direct insights?

Second, there's an element that will be familiar to those who endured the researcher/planner wars of the 1980s.

Planners have always instinctively understood the need to make research actionable. For the planner, it is the difference between the means and the end. The research, the data, the information, the content are the means. The end is what they crave — for their client, or to win a pitch — and that end is insight. This might be in the guise of a new fact, an unexpected direction, a way of reframing a brand, or finding a new target audience or comms approach.

This is why planners may be guilty of seeing themselves at the top of the pseudo-Darwinian evolutionary chart, with the sword of insight, while the lowly researcher is still dragging their knuckles, weighed down with decks of unreconstructed data.

Yet, minus the Darwinian drama, there is some value in the progressive ideal that underpins this line of thinking. We should all be seeking enlightenment, from any source we can find. Research is

just one of many resources to be relied upon in the quest to provide clients with what they need.

Diffusing the insight through the client culture, making it 'sticky' and demonstrating its financial worth is essential in these days of high accountability. Researchers are having to adapt to this reality so they can advance on two fronts at once. They must make headway along the spectrum of creativity, so they can be primed to alight upon insights that dig deeper and explain more; and they must ascend the commercial ladder, so their insights are more relevant to the business.

In the end, I reject the verdict that insight is dead.

By all means, let's bury data, information and the traditional Forest of Debrief. But if you're looking for the corpse of insight ... sorry, they've buried the wrong body.

4.
TOWARDS SOME
DEFINITIONS
OF INSIGHT
(OR AN INSIGHT BY ANY
OTHER NAME ...)

I like to say that insight is something that everyone wants, but hardly anyone understands.

Let's start with the most obvious and straightforward approach: the factual definition. I say 'straightforward,' but the definition of insight — what distinguishes it from a humble observation, and how to go about locating it — is a vexing topic for anyone in the strategy business.

One of the themes, or threads, running through this argument is that insight is closer to *artful creativity* than it is to *arid analysis*. And so, maybe we should start with one of the founding creative heroes and inimitable giants of advertising, Bill Bernbach.[4]

Less well known to the public than he should be, Bernbach and Ned Doyle quit New York's Grey Advertising in 1949 and joined Mac Dane to create Doyle Dane Bernbach (DDB). The agency would place wit, honesty and intelligence at the heart of

its work, rather than the rationalistic bombast that was typical of the time.

Students of advertising know of the Volkswagen campaign from 1959, which included the "Think Small" and "Lemon" ads. Other award-winning DDB campaigns included "We Try Harder" for Avis (honest, cheeky and strategically brave; some might even say risky) and "You Don't Have to Be Jewish to Love Levy's" for Levy's Rye Bread. Often called *judo-style*, these ironic, unconventional campaigns ran counter to the immodest boasting most brand advertising had fallen prey to. (Maybe we should call the Levy's campaign Judaeo-style?)

These subverted so many conventions of advertising that their freshness remains undimmed.

Bernbach believed advertising was more art than science (ah, those halcyon days) and, like David Ogilvy, left us many pearls of wisdom. He also pioneered the concept of partnering an art director with a copywriter, begetting the creative team.

So, maybe the insights of Bernbach are worth examining here. Take, for instance, his 1980 remarks to a gathering of the American Association of Advertising Agencies:

> "At the heart of an effective creative philosophy is the belief that nothing is so powerful as an insight into human nature, what compulsions drive a man [sic], what instincts dominate his action, even though his language so often camouflages what really motivates him. For if you know these things about a man, you can touch him at the very core of his being.
>
> "It is insight into human nature that is the key to the communicator's skill. For whereas the writer is concerned with what he puts into his writings, the communicator is concerned with what the reader gets out of it. He therefore becomes a student of how people read or listen."[5]

For Bernbach, as a product of a previous era, insight was derived from the wellsprings of human nature. His writings came before the 'discovery' of behavioural economics and its application to the craft of behaviour change, Yet, the revelatory power of understanding deep motivations, rather than surface camouflage, would have surely made him a convert. And he did acknowledge that, for the communicator, it is output that matters, rather than input.

These principles ring even more true in an era characterised by homogenised indifference amidst a sea of sameness.

KNOWLEDGE OR WISDOM?

There is an important distinction between knowledge and wisdom. We can all probably agree that knowledge resides at the bottom of any hierarchy leading (if it does) to insight. My favourite quotation demonstrating this is attributed to Miles Kington,[6] the British journalist most famous for his invention of the term *franglais*, although Irish rugby union legend Brian O'Driscoll's use of this witticism in 2009 seems to have got an undue amount of attention.[7] To wit:

> *"Knowledge is knowing that tomato is a fruit, wisdom is not putting it into a fruit salad."*

Once again, let's use the magic number 'three' and explore the garden-variety definitions of insight in three categories: fridge magnet motivations (FMMs); Early Sightings in Marketing; and The Guardians of Insight.

A) FMMS

Here, for example, is a saying attributed to the German polymath Johann Wolfgang von Goethe (1749–1832):

> *"There is nothing so terrible as activity without insight."*

This is not a bad starting point — the notion that insight gives life guidance, direction and meaning. These are all elements we will come back to later.

At a different point on the artistic spectrum is Bette Davis, American actress, Hollywood icon and "woman of strong appetites and opinions" (source: bettedavis.com). She said this:

> "Without wonder and insight, acting is just a trade. With it, it becomes creation."

It is no surprise that many members of the thespian world have these words displayed prominently on their websites.

It is also quite helpful in our explorations. Insight's relevance lies in its transformative power. For the actor, it is a springboard from a commercial activity to the creative magic of inhabiting a character and creating art. In the business world, getting to the end goal — the sale, quarterly results, that big promotion, the year-end bonus — involves a similar sort of creative alchemy.

But let's not ignore the other element Ms. Davis introduces: that of wonder. One of the foremost emotions, wonder (or awe, which is easier to type than say) is the sense of admiration and humility in the presence of the sublime.

In the world of brand insights, wonder is a cornerstone of the *feeling* of insight. (More to come on that.) Curiosity, amazed admiration, surprise — all these are characteristics of what an insight should aim for. At the heart of it is the sense of something surprising and novel, exactly the sensations we seek from a good insight.

They're also not bad traits to have as a human being as we navigate our way through this life.

So, let's examine a few of those characteristics here.

B) EARLY SIGHTINGS IN MARKETING

Let's look at some definitions I remember encountering as a junior planner, when insights were still something new and exotic in advertising, like Apple computers and accountability.

I am tempted to start by asking what you recall, or imagine, we had before we had insights. (Yes, if you are a member of a generation with its own dedicated letter of the alphabet, there was such a time.)

Certainly, in the research world, the nearest equivalent to insight would have been something along the lines of summary, recommendations, conclusions.

So, in this modest context, at least, the arrival of insights was an unqualified good. Many were the debriefs I endured that simply ended with a summary of what had gone before. They were generally insight-free. Or there were recommendations, which were mercifully less anaemic than a mere summary, and were at least aimed at giving clients some advice about what to do with these findings.

But let's look at 'conclusions' for a moment, as they can also give us a clue to the role of insight.

Those who have read me previously are likely wondering why there's been so little etymology so far. When do we dive into the arcane origins of words and how they've changed over time? Well, here we go.

If we dig beneath 'conclusion,' we can see the Latin root, *concludere*, meaning to shut or to close.

So, conclusions should always be about endings, whereas insight — with its proto-Germanic origins — should always be about beginnings. An insight is a jumping-off point. It's a platform for new ways of thinking to be developed and implemented.

MARKETING AND RESEARCH'S EARLY ATTEMPTS

> *"In the context of market research, it is a new finding about customers which, when acted on by an organisation, gives it a competitive advantage."*

This came from a paper presented at the UK's Market Research Society Conference back in 2002. As such, it was a fair stab at defining insight, but again only in the context of it being an outpost of market research.

Other examples from that era include:
* Flashes of inspiration
* Penetrating discovery

- The ability to perceive clearly or deeply
- Deeply-embedded knowledge of the consumer

But these don't really get to the heart of insight.

C) THE GUARDIANS OF INSIGHT

Agency account planners (or strategists) like to think of themselves as The Guardians of The Insight Galaxy and Protectors of The Soul of Advertising. So, we can expect an outpouring of incisive explanations and clarifications around our favourite term. Many can be found by looking at various APG (Account Planning Group) events and online articles from the likes of Contagious, the self-described "creative and strategic intelligence service."[8]

And before we go further, we should acknowledge that a number of people in business are fiercely resistant to the idea of defining ('limiting') insight. Take Jason Lonsdale, Executive Planning Director of Saatchi and Saatchi, Sydney, who argues that the term has been "bastardised and rendered impotent." Or there's Nick Hurst, Planning Partner at the notably named adam&eveDDBLondon, who urges us to "forget insights, figure out the needs."[9]

Martin Weigel, Head of Strategy at Wieden+Kennedy Amsterdam, sounds a similarly weary note about the industry's focus on insight. He would like us all to "take it off the pedestal of attention and worship."

A JOKE FOR PLANNERS.

Q: How many planners does it take to change a light bulb?
A: That's not an insight.

(I'm not sure if the light bulb illumination analogy is deliberate or not ...)

i) *"I'd say that an insight is a disturbing truth that changes how we see things and sheds a new light on a product, a category, etc. I recently read a nice definition: 'Something you didn't know you knew.' I like it because there's a, 'Hey, I had never thought of it that way' feeling."*
– Guillaume Martin, Head of Strategy, BETC[9]

Absolutely essential to insight is the sense of disturbance or reframing.

ii) *"Something that is weird and normal at the same time."*
– Tracey Follows, Chair, APG

I can empathise with the feeling that insights are obvious, normal and true in hindsight, but upon discovery feel unsettling and challenging. This is reminiscent of the dualism espoused by photomontage and 'living sculpture' artists Gilbert and George.

> "We never wanted to be weird, because all artists like the idea of being weird, and we never wanted to be normal, because everybody's normal. We like to be weird and normal at the same time."[10]
>
> – George

WPP Advisory Board member and doyen of advertising theory (and practice) Jeremy Bullmore offered up this oft-cited quip:

"Why is a good insight like a refrigerator?
Because the moment you look into it, a light comes on."

We'll look a bit later at humour-as-insight, but it's always been true that a witty aphorism can encapsulate a deep truth. This goes to the notion of insight-as-illumination, but still only gets us so far.

III) THE THREE WS - THE WHAT, WHY AND WOW:

Innovation consultant Mat Shore[11] gets to the heart of one of the major grey areas of insight. When is an insight an *insight*, he asks, as opposed to a mere observation?

For Shore and others pondering these matters, the 'what' is the basic kernel of insight, but it needs laddering up to the 'why' before it stands a chance of being elected to that blessed elite.

Observations should not be discounted: they can be helpful in themselves, but are usually the surface that we can see, and should be the means to an end. We have to be wary that observation is merely a fixed picture of the status quo, and if we aren't careful, it can be a path to generic sameness. Part of this is establishing a pattern of cause and effect.

As a general rule, whether you're a strategist or a therapist, laddering — probing through value chains — helps penetrate to a deeper truth. It goes back to psychologist George Kelly's Personal Construct Theory from the 1950s, which examined how people interpret things through the prism of their own unique worldview.[12] Kelly argued that to make sense of the world, we actively build 'constructs' and use them as theories or hypotheses with which to explore and test the world around us. He suggested that one's constructs help give meaning to our world and create our sense of identity.

Similarly, Heidi Hackemer, Executive Director at Oatly Climate/Culture Lab,[13] describes insight as 'motivations that drive action.' She also talks of the 'Five Whys' exercise, a classic

from consumer goods powerhouse Procter and Gamble, which seems to be a lightly concealed version of PCP.

Innovation consultant Shore argues that there needs to be an inherent dilemma at the heart of consumer behaviour. However, this may not always need to be the case.

From a researcher's point of view, this is the strength of qualitative research: we can directly (or, even better, indirectly) excavate each layer of 'why.' Too often, research stops at the superficial 'truth,' which tends to not lead to anything illuminating.

> *"Generating insight involves looking for a basic place to stand."*
>
> – Adam Morgan, branding guru

I am in wholehearted agreement here with Morgan, an esteemed marketing strategist and consultant, whose "challenger brand" theory places him in the Branding Pantheon. Morgan posited that an insight, and most good brands, need a *point of view*. (Incidentally, my company's name is POV Marketing and Research Ltd.)

To quote writer, director and film theorist David Mamet,[14] one of the most important questions for a director (and, I'd argue, any storyteller or communicator) is "Where do I put the camera?" In other words, what is my angle, my point of view, my stance? (Etymologically, this is cognate with 'where do I stand?') Where you stand will determine your point of view,

your perspective. It's not just a matter of what you see, but how you see it, the choices you make, what to focus on, how to portray it, what to relegate or ignore.

When preaching about brand differentiation, I often make good use of this notion. If you want to be different, find a different place to stand.

I heartily endorse the importance of stance when trawling for insights.

IV) NATURE OF THOUGHT

Another example of what we might call operational definition comes from Ed Morris, Creative Director at the award-winning Rattling Stick production company in London.

This has the benefit of making us stop and think about insight, as well as suggesting that that's exactly how insight will emerge. But it still feels like only one part of the bigger picture.

> *"Thinking in slow motion."*

The emphasis on 'thinking' may also be an impediment if it means exclusively abiding by what Kahneman, in *Thinking Fast and Slow*, calls System 2 thinking — rational, deliberative, sceptical cogitation.

As we shall see, much insight happens in System 1 thinking — the unconscious, 'automatic' thought process.

V) THE FLOWERY METAPHOR

> *"Insight is like a cocoon: pots of butterflies can come out of it."*
> – Caitlin Ryan, EMEA Regional Creative Director, Facebook and Instagram

Flamboyant and flowery, certainly (also quite lepidoptery) – and rightly emphasising the benefit (not to mention joyousness) of a good insight – this captures something of the creative spirit without necessarily highlighting how to get there.

VI) WHAT INSIGHT ISN'T

Let's start with an easy one. I assume most of you will not mistakenly think that insights are the same as information or data. As is so often the case, the essence of something can best be explained by what it *isn't*.

What distinguishes insights from mere facts is that they are not waiting there, begging to be inducted into the Hall of Insight, or actively pointing themselves out.

As qualitative research guru Wendy Gordon once put it:

> *"Insights are not facts. People do not tell you them and statistics do not identify them."*

Bud Caddell, founder of NOBL Collective business consultants in LA, adds another angle here, albeit still leaving open what might constitute an insight:

> "What insight isn't: obvious, fiction, ad copy, a strategy statement, occupied territory, or tagline."

I can give chapter and verse on this. For instance, here's something I was sent under the guise of insight:

> "Most juices taste bland and dull, and consumers know it. They're crying out for a new taste sensation that will surprise and excite them."

Another un-definition comes from Andy Davidson, founder of UK market research firm Map The Territory. In remarks to the APG, he suggested that truth is less important than commonly thought.[15] Here's what he had to say:

> "Without getting too far into the philosophical-semantic, I also feel that the word truth has been violently assaulted and degraded. Too often, brands seek to own a 'truth,' but I prefer to use 'meaning' rather than truth."

LOST SOCKS, DIVISIVE GOO AND HUNGRY JUDGES

WHAT IS INSIGHT?
– THE CASE BOOK

Just as legal theory and its manifestation in the courtroom hinge on historical case precedents, it can be helpful to take a panoramic view of some great insights from the worlds of branding and comms.

In each case below, we will tell the story, and then conclude by exploring the nature of the insight it encapsulates.

1.
CELIO
– THE SHOPPENBOYS (2006)

Let's start by going back to Paris, some 45 years ago.[16]

Brothers Maurice and Laurent Grosman took over their family's clothing store on rue Saint-Lazare in 1978 and set about transforming it into Celio. As the years went by, they bumped up against a number of challenges, and ultimately came up with a novel idea for changing the way the brand was perceived.

It seemed that many customers – predominantly women – returned clothes they'd purchased for boyfriends and husbands, who'd complained that the sizes and shapes weren't to their liking. This posed all sorts of inventory, customer satisfaction and brand image headaches.

Fast-forward to 2006, after they'd expanded to cities across France, and *frères* Grosman struck on an idea that was part marketing coup and part PR dream.

Starting in Nice, they auditioned for a cast of 'Shoppenboys' of various ages, shapes and sizes, to act as living models, allowing women to evaluate men's clothing *sur le corps* before buying. The models ranged in age from 19 to 63 and represented sizes S–XXL.

A woman could browse through garments, and select a Shoppenboy she thought resembled the man she was shopping for. The model would then try on the clothes, she'd size-up the goods and off she'd go to the cash register, wallet confidently in hand.

The concept was an immediate hit, generating loads of buzz, and was soon rolled out to Celio stores in Paris and other cities. The Shoppenboys gave customers a better way of shopping, and reduced the chance of clothes being sent back.

THE INSIGHT

A brilliant business wheeze, which was simple, fun and provided a significant boost to the bottom-line. It turned a problem into an opportunity, and a business challenge into a PR coup.

2.
THE GUARDIAN
– "POINTS OF VIEW" (1986)

A much-praised advertising touchstone is the *Guardian* newspaper's 1986 TV advert, "Points of View."[17]

It was created by the agency BMP, written by ad legends John Webster and Frank Budgen, and directed by Paul Weiland (now OBE). Weiland is a giant in UK advertising history, having created comedic greats such as Heineken's "Water in Majorca" ad and the Walkers' crisps campaign, before working on TV series such as *Mr. Bean* and several movies, including the autobiographical *Sixty Six*.

Depicting the unreliability of the single narrative, the starkly black and white *Guardian* ad is a masterclass in conciseness and precision. In 30 seconds, it shows a single event unfold from three dramatically different perspectives.

"An event seen from one point of view gives one impression," begins the BBC-style voiceover, as we see a skinhead (this was the '80s, after all) apparently trying to flee from a police car.

Next, we see the young man from a different angle, running towards a buttoned-up looking businessman. "Seen from another point of view, it gives quite a different impression," the narration continues, as the startled man spins around, clutching his briefcase to his chest.

In the final scene, we see from yet another angle the skinhead actually rescuing the man from a teetering pallet of bricks that's about to fall on him. "But it's only when you get the whole picture," we hear, "you can fully understand what is going on."

Fade to black, with no extraneous strapline or slogan until the final seconds, when the words "THE GUARDIAN" silently appear.

It works so well in storytelling terms. The magic number three is at the heart of the narrative – three episodes, three angles – and the brand is the resolution to the story, offering deep, emotional reward and satisfaction. It is a seamless blend of entertainment and intellectual reward. (Fun fact: the woman in the doorway, who the skinhead elbows past, was Kathy Burke, now a well-known actress, comedian, writer, director and producer.)

The pure, universal and timeless truth of impartiality transcends the brand, with its refusal to judge until we've seen the whole picture. In this era of BLM and the challenges of modern policing, the commercial is even used in law enforcement training. It remains peerless, not merely for *The Guardian*, but as something with deep and enduring cultural impact.

THE INSIGHT

Above all, in the context that we are exploring, this is an ad that not only exemplifies an insight, but embodies the very concept of insight itself.

It is a beautiful demonstration of reframing, of shifting perspectives, of the extent to which we are all like "The Blind Men and the Elephant," from John Godfrey Saxe's poem, who sightlessly grapple with trying to identify what the creature is. Each, touching a different part, may have an individually justifiable point of view, without grasping the whole.

We should be teaching this ad in so many different ways.

3.
MARMITE
– "LOVE IT OR HATE IT" (1996)

The story of Marmite, the savoury food spread introduced into the UK in 1902, is one of the most fascinating in the brand catalogue.[18] Its very creation is enough to earn it a place in the annals of insight, as the product is generally thought to have been created by accident.

The serendipitous line can be traced to 17th century scientist Anton Van Leeuwenhoek, 'the father of microbiology' and inventor of the microscope, as well as Louis Pasteur's work on fermentation. But the honour of creator goes to one Justus Freiherr von Liebig, in the 19th century. His accidental discovery that yeast extract derived from brewing beer could be made into a meaty-tasting vegetarian concentrate set Marmite on its path to global success. (And yes, other salty extracts are available, especially if you are an Aussie.)

The product has a detailed mythology, including its role in two world wars, there is a Marmite Museum website, and it does actually seem to live up to its proclaimed health benefits. Francophones will hastily point out that the word is the French for a traditional ceramic casserole pot. Hence, the delightful crock visual on the jar.

But let's focus on the advertising idea: "You either love it or hate it." This was created in 1996 by Richard Flintham and Andy McLeod at the ad agency then known as DDB.

The campaign's origin story justifies its place in our Museum of Insight. As they recount it, one of the creative team was a Marmite lover, while the other was a professed hater. So, the strapline — an idea in concentrated form, if you like — emerged naturally, and fully formed, effectively mirroring national opinion on the yeasty goo.

The strength of the idea (its 'campaignability') lies in its versatility across media and its depth. Unilever, the brand's current owner, even approached the hallowed sanctum of science to extend the idea. They commissioned research from the "genetic boffins" (source: the Marmite website) at health and wellness company DNAFit to see if there was in fact a legitimate genetic difference between those who loved Marmite and those who hated it.[19]

The resulting report — in unexpurgated boffin — is "Genome-Wide Association Studies Identify 15 Genetic Markers Associated with Marmite Taste Preference." Nonetheless, its conclusions were disappointingly banal. Two examples:

* Marmite taste preference is a complex human trait with many factors influencing whether an individual loves or hates Marmite
* The relative contribution of genetics versus environment (i.e., heritability) for Marmite taste preference is unknown

(I note with satisfaction that the name of the oral cavity taste receptor in question was *TAS2R38*.)

THE INSIGHT

All told, what the Marmite story shows about the nature of insight is again far deeper than the conventional 'advertising effectiveness' take.

It is a story that reveals layers of insight. Specifically, there's the notion that brands and brand communication have to obey certain rules, notably that the brand is always the hero, a beacon of unblemished perfection that shall not err on pain of eternal consumer damnation.

If you must, you can wrap it in your preferred jargon ('honesty', 'authenticity', 'transparency'), but the psychological principle that extends beyond the product truth is that brands don't always have to aspire to perfection. Nor should they.

It's akin to how we view our fellow human beings. We often see stumbles, screw-ups and admissions of weakness not as signs of failure or ineptitude, but as tokens of our shared humanity.

On which subject ...

THE PRATFALL EFFECT[20]

There is a well-known principle of psychology called the Pratfall Effect, studied as far back as 1966 by Harvard's Elliot Aronson and named after the humorous tumbles in silent films. His research showed that people sympathised more with someone who had 'accidentally' spilled coffee over their suit while revealing personal information about themselves.

That blunders and imperfection increase likeability makes a lot of sense when we look through the lens of fallible humanity, rather than the rose-tinted one that casts us as Nietzschean superhumans, who can achieve anything if we just try hard enough, give 110 percent, aim for the stars, etc.

Other brands have of course made something of their imperfections. As referenced earlier, VW, under Bill Bernbach's tutelage, made a feature of the Beetle's ugliness, while making it clear that its benefits lay elsewhere. In addition to the celebrated "Lemon" ad, there was one that coincided with the first Moon landing in 1969. Featuring the boxy lunar landing module, the humble headline read, "It's ugly, but it gets you there."

In early 2018, KFC experienced major chicken supply issues in the UK. Above a suitably spartan "We're Sorry" headline in a crisis-management ad was an image of an empty bucket, emblazoned with "FCK."

Fallibility is an antidote to the pomposity, hyperbole and bragging to which much advertising and promotion is liable. Perhaps we should rename it The Jennifer Lawrence Effect, after the Hollywood actress who's known for tripping over her dress, making monster faces and

craving McDonald's. She seems to be *keeping it real*, and people love her for it.

So, what the divisive umami gunge (trying to encompass a broad church of taste, there) has done is to deliver an insight into the nature of advertising, promotion and communication. Namely, that it doesn't always have to be about being the best, vaunting ambition and infallibility. In fact, those tones might be counter-productive and dehumanising.

4.
DOCTOR, DOCTOR

In the course of doing some work with a UK pharmaceutical research company, I was asked to observe a group of doctors discussing how they felt about their work, responsibilities, hopes and frustrations. I was also given reams of documents on physicians' thoughts and feelings. In one of the reports, there was this direct quotation from a physician:

> *"It's either coffin or glory."*

And there it was: an entire world of analysis, feeling, experience and observation in one concentrated capsule of insight.

If insight acts as a compression mechanism, pause for a moment to reflect on what can be unzipped from those six words.

The life of a doctor, since the time of Hippocrates and his oath, has been about life and survival. Doctors therefore find themselves making daily decisions that put them in a quasi-divine situation. Unsurprisingly, other healthcare professionals sometimes complain that doctors actually think they are gods.

But at the sharp end, the 'coffin or glory' doctor elucidates the binary reality of their profession, in a starkly rational, yet deeply emotional, sense. There is no grey area — the physician either wins, and achieves glory and approbation), or it's *six-feet-under*.

THE INSIGHT

A brutal simplicity, perhaps, but one that clarifies, reduces and brings the meaning to the surface, in all its raw and unvarnished emotion.

5.
THE STRANGE CASE OF THE LOST SOCK (2003)

This is the story of a naggingly unmet need that we all surely recognise. But it's not about a conventional product, designed to fill that need in the most predictable way.[21]

The company in question, LittleMissMatched, was created by entrepreneur Jonah Staw and two friends, who saw a marketing opportunity in the hoary old problem of missing socks. (Or, perhaps more accurately, *a* missing sock.)

They took the concept and challenged the assumption of 'a pair' by selling in packs of three. In so doing, they're selling the idea of unpredictability and creativity as much as solving a 'problem,' with all the baggage of tedium and relief that expression usually connotes.

Self-expression is combined with collectability, as each of the company's 134 sock designs has a number in it. Their collectability is a compelling *sine qua non* for younger people, and obsessive-compulsives of all ages, as the socks can be amassed and traded. (More practically, older people and parents also have the problem of Hunting For a Pair solved for them.)

The target market was girls ages 8–12 (tweens, if we must use that term). But a glance at the LittleMissMatched website seems to suggest that older girls (women) are also catered for. The brand has since extended into tights, infant socks, pyjamas, bedding, cold-weather accessories, swimwear, footwear and even a scrapbook.

The success of this brand is heart-warming for number of reasons.

First, it has proved that the solution to a problem doesn't have to be dull. The old 'problem-solution' TV commercial formula was renowned for its executional tediousness and stereotypical format, but today we see that an irritating problem can have an exciting, flexible and impulsive solution.

Second, without knowing it, the creators of LittleMissMatched have tapped into a fascinating aspect of the zeitgeist. This is the era of complexity, and what are quaintly termed *combinatorial systems* – an inventory of simple elements and a set of rules that combine them into complex structures. The cognitive psychologist and linguist Steven Pinker has called language a combinatorial system. Examples include chemical compounds, DNA, music, chess games, computer programs, mathematical and logical formulas, and human language.

Without knowing it, the sock boys have tapped into some of the stunning complexity and creativity that can be built out of a few discrete elements. It looks mathematical and algorithmic, but it produces complexity of inordinate beauty.

Finally, they have also used the mechanisms of celebrity and Corporate Social Responsibility: Britney Spears, Courtney Cox, Paris Hilton and Lindsay Lohan.

THE INSIGHT

There are surely other ways and other markets that can make use of this combinatorial function, in the name of spontaneity and fun.

One sector of the confectionery market — sweets in individual twist-wrap packaging, with their satisfying *crinkle* sound — has always enjoyed its use of the spontaneous, unpredictable and fun codes of communication.

LittleMissMatched has shown how to take this into uncharted territory, springboarding off an insight based on a simple, universal, human truth.

6.
SONY BRAVIA
(2005)

In launching the Bravia TV, Sony went on to create one of the most memorable ads in recent history.[22]

The rather conventional product benefit — the claim of unrivalled colour — was transformed into communications gold by embodying a 24-carat insight: colour like no other; a perfect recreation of colour. Sony was also attempting to recreate the impact of brands like the Walkman or the Trinitron with this new high-definition LCD screen.

The initial "Balls" execution, created by the Fallon agency and shot over three days, created a riotous cascade of colour as 250,000 rubber balls bounced in slo-mo down the steep streets of San Francisco. It was a celebration of the sheer exuberance of colour, with the gentle indie-folk music of Jose Gonzalez providing a counterpoint of calm. By encouraging locals to participate in filming the event themselves, it also helped kick off the 'going viral' branded content trend.

The ad won the Grand Prix at the Cannes Advertising Festival that year, regularly appears in 'best of' reels and has frequently been voted best ad of the decade.

Fallon creative director Richard Flintham said this of the concept:

> "We decided that colour would be the highlight of the product, so we proposed creating a celebration of colour. But instead of an illustration, we wanted something fleeting, a moment that would be recorded in your mind forever."

Slightly less well known was the sequel, in which director Jonathan Glazer fired high-powered paint canons across a Glasgow tower block to create another glorious explosion of colour. Set to a classical soundtrack (Rossini's *Thieving Magpie* overture), viewers were treated to a balletic liquid-fireworks display.

More than 200 people were involved in the production, and some 70,000 litres of paint were unleashed. It required 58 single bottle bombs, 33 sextuple air cluster bombs, two triple-hung cluster bombs, 268 mortars, 33 triple mortars, 22 double mortars, 330 metres of steel pipe and 57 km of copper wire.

The spattered high-rise flats in Toryglen, Scotland, were finally destroyed by a controlled explosion two years later.

One could argue that the Bravia TV ads represent insight in its purest form. At least part of the insight is the 'avoid all unnecessary conventions' principle that so often precedes or follows in the wake of a revelation. In this case, there were no TV sets, no tech, no acronyms, no jargon-ridden claims, no 'consumers' looking in eye-watering admiration at a screen.

As we shall see, breaking conventions is one of the simplest and most effectives outcomes of an insight.

But deeper than this, the Sony Bravia campaign had a more profound insight at its heart. Televisions may be technological, tangible, oblong things, but colour – glorious colour – is abstract, emotional and ravishing. In this sense, this insight is linked to another colour-based aperçu, attributed to various paint companies: we don't sell paint, we sell colour. I first heard this in connection with Babel's Paint stores in the Boston area, but other paint brands seem to have assimilated it.

THE INSIGHT

What I've always admired about this idea is how it takes something for granted, and compels you to see it in a new light. How do we feel about paint? That it is a commodity, a substance that comes in a tin, and is sold in industrial settings (and often in industrial quantities). In that context, it has a necessary, utilitarian role to play – repairing, restoring and livening-up.

But *colour* brings completely different associations. Colour is rich, positive, creative and emotive; it is a primal source of creativity that unites us. We may feel and think of Picasso, the Sistine Chapel, Tracey Emin.

So, if you want to effectively sell more paint (especially to a non-industrial, battleship-grey audience), why not appeal to these deep and rich desires and drives?

7.
CHANNEL 4

British television network Channel 4 was launched in the UK in November 1982, with a remit to champion the alternative, represent minorities and be provocative, in every sense of the world. Since the UK only had three channels at the time, this seemed pretty straightforward in one sense, but a challenge in another.[23]

The channel has built an enviable reputation over the past 40 years. Its public service mission is to provide a broad range of high quality programming that demonstrates "innovation, experiment and creativity in the form and content of programmes ... and to appeal to the tastes and interests of a culturally diverse society."

Former Chief Executive Michael Jackson described the network's agenda and culture as one of experimentation, permissiveness, hedonism and ambition, concepts that are a source of pride for its supporters and fuel for its critics. (The UK government announced in April 2022 its intention to sell the publicly owned network.)

In 2018, Channel 4's Director Of Programmes told staff he wanted to "challenge the orthodoxy" and "mess with the mechanisms" of broadcasting, and bring a "bit more provocation" to the schedule.

But there is one word I want to focus on for its iconoclasm in the rather dull, humdrum world of brand personality. I first heard it mentioned when I was speaking at a conference in London. The network's marketing director at the time characterised Channel 4 as being all about ... *mischief*.

What a fantastic word to base your brand on. Unequivocal, outspoken, distinctive, and a platform for programmes, culture and commissioning, it was far from the declaratively bland, inoffensive and clinically dead monotone of many words used by brands when parading their so-called 'personality'. (In my previous book, *The Storytelling Workbook*, I ranted about how the word 'passionate' has become so ubiquitous as to be meaningless, and suggested several dozen preferable alternatives.)

There is a hint of naughtiness and misbehaviour there, but not so far as to be offensive or against laws or mores. It's more of the cheeky, childlike troublemaker that many of us might recall from our own youth, when we were discovering the limits of our identity, testing society's norms, figuring out how to get the best out of the former without transgressing too far against the latter. But how many brands would dare to imagine – let alone embody – that precociousness? True, it fits Channel 4 like a glove, but wouldn't be right for many less contentious brands, but the frankness and overt embrace of risk here is to be applauded.

The mischief is embodied in the channel's ident, the clip it airs to remind viewers which station they're watching: a lumbering metallic giant, formed from Channel 4's 'bricks' logo, that roams the English countryside, all cheeky and playful. We also see this self-identification in the tagline for the network's intranet site: "Creating the source of all mischief".

A sense of comic playfulness runs through all of Channel 4's communications. Take the award-winning campaign for its coverage of the 2012 Summer Paralympics, for instance.[24] At the time, these games were seen as the poor stepchild of the Olympics. Before the network's campaign, only 14% of people had expressed interest in watching the Paralympics. What was needed was nothing less than a major perception-changing campaign.

To generate interest, the "Meet the Superhumans" ad subverted popular preconceptions (prejudices?), focussing on the disabled athletes' inner prowess and strength in surmounting the challenges they'd endured. Backed by the militant refrain of Public Enemy's "Harder Than You Think", it invited viewers to "Forget everything you thought you knew about strength, and everything you thought you knew about humans" and "Meet the superhumans."

Research revealed that nearly four in five people said their attitude towards disabled people had changed for the better after seeing the ads.

The success of the campaign was both immediate and long lasting. It was re-adapted for the 2016 and 2020 Paralympics, and had a marked impact on the representation of disabilities in the media and broader societal attitudes about the disabled.

Another shining examples of the 'mission for mischief' was Channel 4's 2019 "Complaints Welcome" campaign.[25]

This again took a norm and twisted it (*hello, insight*). Complaints — griping that something is unsatisfactory or disagreeable — evoke bad feelings. No one likes to be the target of complaints, or even

hear people complaining in general, as it all suggests fallibility, dereliction of duty, failure to deliver, dissatisfaction and hurt.

But the idea behind this campaign was that complaints were instead a badge of honour. For everyone complaining that "I'm not homophobic, but we don't need gay-kissing on the telly at dinner time," that rapper Big Narstie was "too black" or that chef Jamie Oliver had "sausage fingers," this was proof that Channel 4 was fulilling its mission.

In the way that these things tend to go, the ad campaign was then spun off into its own TV series, where three comedians reviewed and snidely dissected actual viewer complaints. As one of the presenters put it:

> "Complaints Welcome will be standing by to review the reviews viewing viewers viewed."

THE INSIGHT

Channel 4 bravely formed its own character, personality and purpose around a perfectly formed word-idea, and by twisting norms it built a platform for ground-breaking communications.

8.
STARBUCKS
– "THE THIRD PLACE" (1988)[26]

The coffee shop or coffee house is not by any means a new phenomenon. The insurance market Lloyd's of London and the UK's Royal Society for Arts, Manufacturing and Commerce (RSA) both had their origins in these establishments. The 18th century Enlightenment coffee house brought together all sorts of people over a strong cup o' joe, and encouraged them to exchange ideas and launch common projects in a nurturing environment.

Coffee itself started out as an exotic product, primarily enjoyed in this part of the world by a small group of the intelligentsia known as *virtuosi*. It first came to Europe from Turkey, North Africa and Egypt, arriving in Britain in the 17th century, courtesy of the British East India Company and the Dutch East India Company.

Often characterised as a 'penny university', the early UK coffee house was known for its openness, civility, curiosity and 'gentlemanly' pursuits.

Bringing us full circle, in 2018 the RSA, which was founded in 1754 in London's Rawthmells coffee house, opened a 21st century Rawthmells with the intention of recapturing some of that Enlightenment spirit.

Coffee has always been a proxy for creativity, although I've never had a taste for it, finding it like drinking scorched earth while burning £10 notes.

Regardless, were you aware of coffee's role in fuelling mathematics?

Hard-core mathematicians had already lovingly designed a fun game (fun for mathematicians, at least) in honour of the Hungarian mathematician Paul Erdős's notorious propensity to collaborate.

Erdős (1913–1996) is said to have written around 1,500 articles, alongside some 500 collaborators. Described in his *New York Times* obituary as "a mathematical pilgrim with no home and no job," Erdős was famous for appearing on colleagues' doorsteps, staying for a few days while working on a paper, and then leaving suddenly. At some point, around the late 1960s, it became an exercise to see how close mathematicians could be to Erdős. If you were one of the original collaborators, you warranted an Erdős number of 1; if you'd written a paper with one of the originals, you had a 2; and so on.

Erdős has often been associated with the observation, "A mathematician is a machine for converting coffee into theorems." There's some evidence that this witticism was actually coined by his friend, the Hungarian mathematician Alfred Rényi, although it may have originally been a German double entendre on the meaning of the word *satz* (theorem or coffee residue).

So, where does Starbucks fit into this picture?

The founder of global coffee chain, Howard Schultz, claimed to have been inspired by the espresso bars of Italy. Yet, there was another insight at the heart of the Starbucks success story: Schultz's belief that it wasn't just about the product, but the 'experience.'

Specifically, he said this experience was all about "the third place" — a warm and welcoming spot outside our homes and workplaces, where we can relax, connect and build community.

This thinking was rooted in (or, perhaps less charitably, borrowed from) a study the urban sociologist Ray Oldenburg outlined in his 1989 book, *The Great Good Place*. He distinguished home (the first place), and work (the second place), and argued for the need for a third place — "the great good places."

For Oldenburg, these were the public places where people could gather, set aside the concerns of home and work, and simply hang out, enjoying the pleasures of good company and lively conversation. They represented the heart of a community's social vitality, and embodied the grassroots of a democracy. Examples included coffee houses, cafes, bookstores, hair salons, bars and bistros. He saw in them a hope and vision for the revitalisation of community.

Oldenburg argued that these spaces were shrinking in the United States during the post-war decades, as residential areas (homogenised, white-picket-fence suburbs) became devoid of public meeting places, and individual lives became more atomised and private.

In his words, the coveted third places ...

> *"... host the regular, voluntary, informal, and happily anticipated gatherings of individuals beyond the realms of home and work."*

What suburbia was crying out for were ...

> *"... the means for people to gather easily, inexpensively, regularly, and pleasurably — a 'place on the corner,' real life alternatives to television, easy escapes from the cabin fever of marriage and family life that do not necessitate getting into an automobile."*

Similar issues were addressed by political scientist Robert Putnam, in a celebrated 1995 essay in the *Journal of Democracy*, "Bowling Alone: America's Declining Social Capital," which was later developed into a book. His thesis was that social capital — connections among individuals, social networks and the norms of reciprocity and trustworthiness that arise from them — was in decline.

THE STARBUCKS TAKE

This thinking was adopted and adapted by Schultz, with his Starbucks concept, and has been refined to suit changing trends and contexts, especially the digital world.

In 2019, Starbucks announced plans to reimagine the third place, focussing on convenience, comfort and connection, while never losing sight of that other 'C' at the heart of it all: community.

The chain's CEO at the time, Roz Brewer, put it this way:

> *"Their third place is everywhere they're holding our cup. No matter their journey, after leaving our stores, that feeling of comfort stays with them. And in an increasingly busy and on-demand world, it's that feeling that keeps the third place growing."*

Or take this statement to Starbucks partners and customers written in May 2020 by then CEO Kevin Johnson, reflecting changes that would be made in the light of the Covid-19 pandemic. These included service beyond drive-through, such as mobile ordering for contactless pickup, delivery and, in some locations, curbside pickup and grab-and-go through the café.

"These adaptations will reinforce the concept of the third place — a warm and welcoming place, outside of our homes and our workspaces, where we connect and build community. We think of the third place as a mindset — a feeling of comfort that uplifts customers everywhere, and in every way, they experience Starbucks. And the third place has never been more relevant than now, as communities seek to reconnect and heal."

THE INSIGHT

The insight about insight here is that brands can sometimes create value, positioning and uniqueness by finding and then latching onto an emerging social trend.

Another brand that was associated with this approach was Orange, the UK mobile telephone operator founded in 1994 and active until its acquisition by France Telecom, merger with T-Mobile and rebirth as EE.

The idea that launched Orange in 1994 is now seared into the collective cultural memory of the generation that witnessed it.

> *"The future's bright, the future's Orange."*

Created by ad agency WCRS, it was a wholehearted attempt to plug the brand into the zeitgeist and build a virtuous circle between the name (the colour orange) and the feelings associated with that colour, while looking hopefully to a future that would be genuinely revolutionary and wire-free. And it had an elegance and simplicity that steered clear of so many declaratively bland brand slogans.

The line was retired in 2008 (though many great ad ideas/lines never die, but are opportunistically reborn later), and replaced with another Big Idea:

> *"I am who I am because of everyone."*

Less emotive than the original, and perhaps a bit too rarefied (existential?) for the world of mobile telephony, it continued the brand's goals of allying the company to something bigger than mere mobile phones.

Rather like Starbucks, it played into a sense of community and belonging. In the same vein, the concept of *ubuntu* – a South African Nguni Bantu term meaning 'I am because we are' (to be distinguished from the open-source operating system of the same name) – was enjoying some pop-culture buzz at the time.

9.
HUNGRY JUDGES
AND JOAN COLLINS
(2012)

A 2011 study of Israeli parole boards may not seem to have an obvious connection with the shoulder-padded, big-hair star of a 1980s soap opera, but bear with me. I'll show you how a major confectionery brand built its success on a judiciously applied judicial insight.[27]

Let's start by asking an apparently self-evident question: are judicial rulings based solely on laws and facts?

According to a delightfully entitled paper, "Extraneous Factors in Judicial Decisions," a group of academics analysed judges' verdicts to assess whether judicial rulings could in fact be swayed by extraneous variables that in an ideal world should have no bearing on legal decisions. They put to the test a common caricature of realism — that justice is "what the judge ate for breakfast" — by examining verdicts handed down to the same type of defendant accused of the same type of crime. (Variables such as age, background and ethnicity were all controlled for.)

Indeed, the researchers discovered what they called distinctly varying "decision sessions," where verdicts were more likely to be favourable for the defendant immediately after food had been consumed by Their Honours. As a result, judges were given snacks and food more evenly throughout the day, in hopes of rebalancing the scales of justice.

According to Jonathan Levav, a Columbia University business professor, and one of the co-authors of the paper:

> *"You are anywhere between two and six times as likely to be released if you're one of the first three prisoners considered versus the last three prisoners considered."*

This followed in the footsteps of social psychologist Ray Baumeister's work on the domain of willpower. He proposed that willpower was a limited mental resource, and like a muscle, it could be strengthened or weakened. Specifically, the purported role of glucose in willpower, self-control and decision-making led to what he termed "ego depletion." (Baumeister's findings have been re-examined, and there's some counterevidence to suggest that the effects were overstated.)

Confectionery company Mars Wrigley, which produces Snickers bars, latched onto the study and moulded this eternal human truth: our behaviour can be transformed when a log of caramel, peanuts and chocolate is introduced into our empty stomachs.

And there it was: the idea-line, "You're not you when you're hungry." The ads featured celebrities who underwent an instantaneous lion-to-pussycat transformation with a bite of a Snickers bar.

The campaign kicked off during the Super Bowl 2010 TV broadcast — which had an audience of 106.5 million people — and featuring Golden Girls star Betty White in a football scene. Since then, the 'global strategy with local application' has seen the likes of Mr. T, Elton John and Mr. Bean grace the campaign.[28]

Which brings us to '80s soap opera icon Joan Collins. In a 2012 Snickers commercial, set in a soccer team's changing room, Collins accuses a teammate of nicking her deodorant. It's only when she's given a Snickers bar to eat, because she is 'acting like a diva,' that she transforms back into a football player. We then see her Dynasty co-star Stephanie Beacham restart the shtick at the end of the ad.

The campaign has won many plaudits, and a joint analysis by the World Advertising Research Centre (WARC) and Cannes Lions examined its enduring success in terms of sales, branding and effectiveness. The two groups put it atop the Creative Effectiveness Ladder, deeming it an "enduring icon."

Members of this exclusive group are deemed to have:
* Leveraged the power of deep insights
* Formulated an expansive idea
* Adopted a long-term perspective from the earliest phases of a campaign
* Remained committed to this plan

THE INSIGHT

The insight on the insight here is that there's solid gold in alighting upon a trend, truth or under-appreciated academic revelation, and one that happily chimes with the brand's benefits. The Snickers ads also managed to moor the brand's historic benefit-function (hunger-satisfaction) in a more psychological, emotional truth, where it was reframed against stress, fatigue and grumpiness.

By adding some intellectual heft to a strategy — which makes us all feel, 'Yes, that is *soooo* true,' and communicating in a witty and populist manner — Snickers demonstrated the power of a good insight to build a long-term brand, and created a well-loved campaign to boot.

10.
UNILEVER'S INSIGHTS ENGINE (2005)

At the multinational consumer goods giant Unilever, the Consumer and Market Insights team's stated mission is "to inspire and provoke, to enable transformational action." In their conception, insight is deliberately **omitted**. That's because insights are considered a means to the desired end; the action that drives business growth.[29]

Many of Unilever's so-called Masterbrands — its core line-up of prestige products — now **operate on** a strictly insights-driven basis.

Consider the pillar brand Persil, which is known as Omo in other parts of the world. Operating in a low-interest, low-involvement category, Unilever identified the need to create a distinctive, salient campaign that would bring some element of excitement to the humdrum (washing machine drum?) world of washing powder.

Using all the collaborative power of their Insights Engine system, the company absorbed and commissioned research into the nature of washing, the changing role of motherhood and the family, and in particular long-term changes in the lives of children.

That the role of women and motherhood had undergone tectonic changes in the last generation was hardly a surprise, but the consumer insights team did alight on an area that promised much: the fact that attitudes about children had changed dramatically. It had once been the norm to allow children to wander freely outside at all times of the day — I can vouch for being happily permitted to wander through the park after dark on the way home from school in Southend, Essex, in a decade I won't reveal — but concerns over *stranger-danger* have altered thinking on children's activities.

Recognising that this was ripe territory for an ingenious and imaginative brand platform, the team conceived of the 2005 "Dirt is Good" campaign.

At the start, it was not all that radical: a poster featured a child with a messy shirt, and the headline, "For whatever life throws."

Dispensing with a pile of advertising conventions — mums, washing machines, mums with washing machines, ,white clothes and children on their way to or from football, unlikely product performance challenges — it focussed on a more cultural agenda that roamed far beyond the cleaning of clothes.

More subversively, the theme/endline was a mile away from the rational System 2 functional comparison-mania that tended to be the preserve of the detergent sector. It played on the jolt of surprise that's at the heart of the best insights. Dirt was reframed from being a hindrance, irritation and unhygienic, evoking revulsion and disgust, to suddenly being considered ... *good*?

Dirt was counterintuitively positioned as the hero, as we were asked to embrace the need to get children back outside, to play, to mess around, to experiment. (And, by implication, spend less time on screens.)

"Every child has the right to be a child" was the sub-slogan, again reinforcing the idea that joy, fun, play, freedom and creativity are essential elements we were in danger of draining from the lives of the youngest members of society.

It served as a rallying cry for unstructured play, and the freedom to get messy, without worrying about soiled clothes. In 2008, this was supported by the launch of the "Every Child Has The Right" campaign. From there, it was a small step to championing the broader goal of child development, and the benefits of them getting out and exploring their world (and changing it for the better).

The idea was developed by various agencies on Unilever's behalf, with one campaign proclaiming (with suitable visuals), "Children now less spend less time outdoors than a prison inmate."

In the rather breathless copy typical of the corporate PR machine, we were advised:

> "The Dirt is Good Way is an approach to youth social and environmental action that champions compassionate values, normalises collective action and aims to close the values-perception gap."

As a Unilever executive explained:

> "We articulated this distinctly anti-category view as a shift from 'stains are the enemy' to 'stains are a child's best friend,' and developed the globally renowned Organising Idea 'Dirt is Good' ('DiG')."

For me, the creative highlight of the campaign was the BBH agency's 2008 "Roboboy" ad, where a glum-faced robot gradually and emotionally transforms into a real boy once he's allowed to go outside and frolic in the rain (and get nice and dirty). Shades of Pinocchio and a hundred sci-fi stories. (Remember Haley Joel Osment in 2001's *A.I. Artificial Intelligence*?)

THE INSIGHT

Aside from the cinematic production values and jerking of tears that Christmas ads for the John Lewis & Partners department stores would soon adopt, the tone is so off-kilter for the category.

You will search in vain for dazzling, clinically white colours and relentlessly upbeat music; the ad is melancholic and reflective ... but yes, ultimately upbeat.

And typical of so many insight-led ideas, you feel the shedding of conventions.

11.
DEATH PROOF HAND
(2007)

As I never to cease to remind anyone who will listen (and many who won't), I spent more than 20 years as a Trustee of the Phoenix Cinema, in North London, the longest-continually running cinema in the UK (opened in 1912). So, with me you're never more than a few paragraphs away from a movie reference.

Let's move on to matters of splatter.

Death Proof was Quentin Tarantino's 2007 ode to the grindhouse/exploitation/cult movie, starring Kurt Russell as a psychopathic stuntman who kills beautiful women with his '70s muscle car.[30]

Now, we need to head to Amsterdam and explore the creative work of an agency called New Message, whose job it was to promote the film's DVD release.

Again, our role here is to observe the workings of insight hunters as they negotiate their way through the jungle of sameness.

Most campaigns to launch a DVD release (or, these days, any non-theatrical launch) tend to be staid affairs, using the same type of content in the same tired channels. Most commonly, we're advised that film X is out on date Y and stars A and B (or B and A depending,

on who has the bigger lawyers), often with some excerpted review blurbs. We've seen them a thousand times, to the extent that our brain will filter out the vast majority.

So, why do the same old, same old? And especially if you're dealing with a gleefully offensive Tarantino splatter-fest?

For a film that was anything but an identikit Hollywood movie, why adopt a cut and paste strategy?

Rather than going down that road once again, the Dutch wizards abandoned content and took a hand-break turn on media. No posters, no stars, no ostentatious reviews.

Instead, they placed a series of realistically bloody, severed arms holding a copy of the DVD in front of movie theatres throughout the Netherlands, and most notably at Amsterdam's famous Tuschinski cinema.

What does this do that's so disruptive? Let's break it down.

- **Target audience.** Rather than using a broadcast medium like posters or other 'out-of-home' advertising, which will by its very nature have a lot of wastage, this aims directly at the core demographic/psychographic segment: movie-goers who frequent art-house cinemas, which are likely to have shown a flick like *Death Proof*.

- **The medium is the message.** Behavioural economics (under the guise of social psychology?) teaches us that decisions are not just prompted within the brain of the individual, but often cued or influenced by the context and

environment we find ourselves in. Think of being in a crowded event, a pub, or any other social environment. A great summary of this thesis is the 2013 bestseller *Drunk Tank Pink: And Other Unexpected Forces That Shape How We Think, Feel, and Behave* by New York University psychology and marketing professor Adam Alter. Having the severed hand just feels like the right place at the right time. As people arrive at or leave the theatre, and see this macabre appendage, their thoughts may well turn to buying a DVD of *Death Proof*.

- **Behaviour-first approach.** Here we have another learning from the behavioural economics canon. Rather than assuming that attitudes must always be changed before behaviour-change can occur, it is often the case that behaviour can be modified independently of attitude. Indeed, there's the sense that attitudes may only change subsequently, so that they fall into line with the new behaviour.

- **Context over content.** This shows the power of context to transcend content. The physicality of a severed hand is not only a perfect representation for the film itself (always a good idea to flatter your audience), but a mnemonic for the storyline as well (amputations abound). Perhaps the prop was even more ingenious than that, prompting some to assume that the hands were a souvenir that could be taken home in order to amuse/impress/freak out family and friends. As collectibles go, that would be a standout.

- **Efficiency.** Finally, I suspect that whatever metric the client or agency used, it was a massive success on an efficiency level. Rather than the traditional media buying, where posters can

cost hundreds of thousands of pounds/dollars/euros, one aspect of this initiative I applaud is its glorious, resourceful cost-efficiency. A few severed hands are procured from prop shops and scattered judiciously around by a few volunteers, and then witness the eyeballs, the clicks, the sharing and emotional resonance, and you can see that the impact is extraordinary, considering the outlay.

Fan reaction was appropriately breathless. As one gushed on The Tarantino Archives Forum site:

"That is seriously stupid and fucked up ... I love it."

12.
SAVING OLD SPICE FROM OBLIVION ... OR THE BRAND YOUR BRAND COULD SMELL LIKE (2010)

In the UK, at least, Old Spice aftershave (and deodorant, shampoo, soap and shower gel products) will evoke among those of a certain age a very 'of-its-time' aura. Cue the booming choral drama of "Dies Irae" from Verdi's *Requiem*, not quite drowning out incantations like 'You'll become yourself,' 'You'll find success' and 'The mark of a man.'

It's an example of how inventing a category — that of male body wash — can end up being millstone rather than a milestone.[31]

Fast forward to 2010, when Procter and Gamble worked with ad agency Wieden+Kennedy (the people behind Nike's "Just do it") to try and rescue the brand from the imminent fate of 'my dad used to use that' by appealing to a younger audience. The intended reset was from a 40–60 age group to more of an 18–34 demographic.

Easier said than done. Anyone who has been given that client brief knows how simple that is to articulate, but how mercilessly cruel it can be to implement.

Not the most earth-shattering insight, but research revealed that 60% of male body wash purchases were made by women.[32]

Qualitatively, P&G also found that mothers would often buy such products for sons (and, probably, girlfriends for boyfriends), as an unsubtle hint that maybe they could shower more frequently. Data also suggested that boys don't groom (to paraphrase The Cure).

That aligned with something we keep encountering in our journey through insight-world: surfacing assumptions and conventions in comms and advertising to ascertain which ones can safely (or outrageously) be broken is a breeding ground for executional insight.

So, it was not a great leap to see that most of P&G's competition was targeting men directly, and in a traditionally head-on, didactic and rather hackneyed way. Instead, Old Spice's insightful approach was not to talk at men, but to encourage a conversation between couples.

The new campaign broke on 8 February 2010, timed to pre-empt the Dove campaign that was due to appear in the Super Bowl broadcast.

Straight off, the new targeting is apparent, as football-player-turned-TV actor Isaiah Mustafa addresses the audience: "Hello, ladies."

The new approach was more playful, whimsical and light-hearted than the prevailing seriousness of the category — a rat-a-tat 'Look at your man, now back to me, now back to your man' spiel.

Old Spice's "The Man Your Man Could Smell Like" ad was a massive success on mainstream TV, as well as on YouTube, soon attracting 10 million views, and beating Dove's Super Bowl commercial by a factor of 10. It then stoked a social media campaign ("Responses"), and went viral.

The claim made at the time was that it then became the most interactive campaign in history, and it was named fourth best campaign of the 21st century by trade magazine *Advertising Age*.

From a sales standpoint, the proof was in the pudding. The 15% hoped-for increase in sales turned into 125%, with Old Spice eventually becoming brand leader.

THE INSIGHT

I'd suggest this was such a success for its insight implementation in three complementary ways.

First, an entirely new target audience was addressed, with the company talking directly to purchasers, not users. In doing so, it set out to create a conversation based on openness, rather than shame and embarrassment.

Second, it employed a new tone of voice. Eschewing the sincere and rather macho values that were typical of the brand in its heyday (and typical of the broader category), the tone was lighter, more whimsical and more knowing, as well as more conversational.

Finally, its message (again, not delivered in a heavy-handed way) was a more subtly aggressive dig at the competition and, as spokes-hunk Mustafa put it, their "lady-scented body wash."

One can only wonder whether the creative team's insights arrived in the shower.

13.
NO-ONE KNOWS ANYTHING (1983)

Our next entry in the Insight Canon flashes back to my affiliation with London's Phoenix Cinema.

William Goldman was the novelist and Oscar-winning writer of screenplays for *All the President's Men* (1976) and *Butch Cassidy and The Sundance Kid* (1969), and he penned the cult classic *The Princess Bride* (1987). The latter bombed at the box office, because the idea of a post-modern riff on a fairy tale was way ahead of its time, although the film now finds itself on many a critic's 'under-rated classic' list.[33]

Goldman is also renowned for writing one of the greatest and most pungent lines in and on Hollywood, a dictum that became his personal mantra and a principle for many a budding writer in Tinseltown.

Based on his own experience, going from being the most bankable of screenwriters to an industry leper, the book was a savage distillation of why it is called show *business*, and not show *art*.

With his now infamous 1983 book, *Adventures in the Screen Trade* – and with its opening sentence, "Nobody knows anything" – Goldman skewered the fear- and risk-aversion that he said plagued the Hollywood studios.

For years, Goldman had been analysing from the inside what worked in Hollywood, tracking the success (and, more often than not, failure) of movies, their sequels and which stars were 'bankable,' until they weren't.

He cited as an example of the play-it-safe ethos the fact that Universal, at the time the biggest US studio, chose to pass on *Star Wars*. So, for any sleeper that sneaks in under the radar, and ends up a smash hit, raking in piles of loot – think *Speed*, *The Matrix*, *Sideways* or *The Artist* – there is an attempt to repeat a formula. Let it be said that even that's not always a winning formula. Need I mention the dismal *Speed 2* or the various other *Matrix* films?

Goldman also famously pontificated on a film that seemed to demonstrate his point about the essential unpredictability of the movie business. On paper, at least, this picture seemed to have everything going for it. It starred 'Bennifer' (real-life A-List couple Ben Affleck and Jennifer Lopez), and it was directed by Martin Brest, who'd made *Beverly Hills Cop* and *Scent of a Woman*, both critical and commercial hits.

The movie was of course 2003's romantic comedy *Gigli*, which turned out to be one of the biggest duds in history, grossing barely a tenth of its budget, and scoring a cringey 6% approval rating on the Rotten Tomatoes review site.

THE INSIGHT

Goldman's dictum was matchless in its epigrammatic universality: a summary of not just Hollywood culture, but an Olympian insight into the nature of insight itself. Namely, that we should never assume full knowledge, especially among the guardians of the status quo.

14.
METHOD
(2018)

Insights abound at the heart of one of the great branding success stories of the last 20 years.[34]

It has all the ingredients of a great story, as well. There's a creation myth involving two college friends taking on corporate behemoths (Clorox, Unilever, SC Johnson and P&G), David and Goliath style. There are setbacks and challenges; purpose and passion; fresh and breezy design; a story arc worthy of *<insert your favourite screenplay writer here>*. (They could also recruit method actors).

Method was founded by twentysomethings Adam Lowry and Eric Ryan in San Francisco at the turn of the millennium. The friends had been brainstorming ways to disrupt a well-established consumer goods category, when they fell upon soap. It was a sector primed for reinvention, if you could remove the toxic nasties and focus on sustainability. It could also benefit from an emphasis on aesthetics, with fresh, bright colours rather than the drab designs associated with industrial packaging.

Lowry, whose background was in chemical engineering, with the added twist of an environmental degree, was intent on creating safe, non-toxic soap-based products that would extend beyond

the tiny market of tree-hugging granola greenies who purchased traditional eco brands.

In marketing terms, the neophytes' goal was to steer users of cleaning products away from the inertia and heuristics of scrub-and-rinse autopilot, largely through ethical and visual appeals.

In pursuit of their self-proclaimed social mission, they created a big, hairy manifesto (a "humanifesto" as they termed it — People Against Dirty) and used this alongside an emphasis on the 'weird' to build a culture of happiness and teamwork.

THE INSIGHT

As we see across our tour of insightful brands, a major source of insight is disrupting existing conventions, assumptions and patterns of behaviour. So, let's look for the method in Method.

"Method was set up to make sustainable look desirable," Clare Burke, the company's UK marketing manager, told marketing website *The Drum*. The brand capitalised on the eco/green/sustainability movement, while avoiding some of the drab worthiness associated with the semiotics of those products. Instead, they developed transparent, teardrop-shaped, pleasantly pastel-coloured bottles that ergonomically fit into the hand.

This gets to the heart of the various insights at the heart of Method.

Whether they were aware of it or not, our young entrepreneurs were channelling behavioural economics and some of the basic lore of the Blessed Daniel Kahneman in appealing to both the slow, rational System 2 and the unconscious, emotional System 1. On this basis, the brand was a welcome entrant into insight-dom.

System 2 looks at the sustainability element and is assuaged: Method is positioned as a thoughtful considered, planet-friendly purchase.

But there's more to it than that. System 1 operates under a different regime, and wants to be satisfied, rewarded and emotionally gratified. Knowing this full well, the 'Methodists' ensured that the brand looked and felt luscious.

They developed this aspect of the insight so far that they chose to make the brand 'experiential', which was delightfully weird indeed for a line of cleaning products.

With help from brand experience agency Amplify, their #themethodway campaign translated the feel-good-ness of Method's cleaning products into a broader lifestyle positioning. As there has to be some consumer behaviour data to support these types of things, this was a response to

the fact that, according to the brand's own research, 51% of Brits didn't experience enough joy in their lives.

The campaign included a series of 'unexpected surprises,' such as a summer street mural in collaboration with artistic group The Outside Collective.

SUSTAINING SUSTAINABILITY?

And now, the epilogue to the story — that bit at the end where captions come up to explain what happened to the protagonists after the film was made. By 2012, after 11 years of operation, Method had grown into a $100 million company. At that point, it was acquired by the Belgian eco-cleaning brands company Ecover, and the combined entity became the largest green cleaning company in the world. Consumer goods giant SC Johnson subsequently bought Ecover in December of 2017.

Cultural fit could prove to be a test of the founders' ethical approach. Will they be able to infuse SC Johnson with some of the jolt of innovation and weirdness? Or will the body reject the implant and all of the noble values of Method, and will it be marginalised or, even worse, discarded?

If the two cultures can mesh, SC Johnson has a huge opportunity to win over new customers, and not just those buying ylang ylang-scented shower spray.

COLLISIONS, COMBINATIONS AND A SHOCK TO THE CISTERN

INSIGHT
– HOW TO FIND,
CREATE AND
DEVELOP IT

A.
C IS FOR CAVEAT

So, let's set sail on some cautionary Cs.

CAVEAT I

Before we explore what characterises the insightful culture and organisation, let's spend a moment examining potential barriers to creating this culture.

My first target here is the obsession with what is covered under the modern aegis of "lean and agile."[35]

This focus-sharpening, flow-management process approach (call it a philosophy, if you must) has swept through global corporations and beyond, starting as a way of standardising the development of software, by bringing together two series of ideas, in the early 2000s.

Much of it can be traced back to Fordism, with its assembly-line mass production of consumer goods (itself a version of Frederick Winslow Taylor's theory of scientific management), and extends through Toyota's TPS (Toyota Production System) mindset. Each was a manufacturing theory, and inherently socio-technical — involving systems and processes, but also elements of human improvement — but at heart was it was all

about iterative processes that could lead to reducing waste and enhancing efficiency.

At the same time, agile principles were being exported from software development, such as the 'scrum' project management framework that relies on the forward momentum of iterative 'sprints.'

Since then, the notion of agile has evolved into an enterprise initiative, aimed at making collaboration work across different groups, as well as within each. My bigger concern is the way that lean and agile have become proxies for a culture of efficiency. Don't get me wrong: many components of a well-regulated organisation have to have systems in place that focus on efficiency.

Still, I worry that the way agile has leaked into other areas that depend more on creativity and imagination will dilute it, as it's co-opted away from its original and much more limited remit. With its implicit (and often explicit) insistence on the centrality of efficiency, it can have a calamitous effect on the creative elements of business, and insight in particular.

Insight prioritises creating connections, incubation, time and space, to devise new connections and surprising outcomes. It catalyses thinking that wanders far and wide, for individuals as well as teams and organisational cultures.

CAVEAT II

Our second caveat concerns the automatic worship of information and knowledge, and the preconceived idea that originality in all its forms must begin with knowledge.

Below we'll talk about a four-stage system for insight,[36] the first part of which is 'immersion.' But a note of caution: there is a competing theory that warns against an excessive reliance on information and knowledge.

From this perspective, knowledge is a double-edged sword in that it can blind you to some things. The 'curse of knowledge' is usually defined as the presumption that our audience possesses the same knowledge that we do, which can lead to miscommunication. But I'd also like to reframe this as an alternative curse of knowledge, whereby we have *too much* of it, which can lead to a fixedness of thought.

To support this view, I call to the stand Theodore Roszak, cultural historian and chronicler of the 1960s counterculture. He was one of the first to explore the relationship between ideas and information, on the basis that humans do not think in information, but in ideas. In his 1985 book, *The Cult of Information: A Neo-Luddite Treatise on High-Tech, Artificial Intelligence, and the True Art of Thinking*,[37] he states:

> "But information does not create ideas; by itself, it does not validate or invalidate them. An idea can only be generated, revised, or unseated by another idea. Ideas come first, because ideas define, contain, and eventually produce information."

The fundamental preconception this challenges is that information is, in fact, an essential precondition to having an insight.

As a long-term observer and practitioner of insight, I have found the deeply ingrained belief that, in the development of ideas, information ('data') should be an indisputably and indispensably non-negotiable ingredient of insight.

Let me go out on a limb here. Maybe we need to learn to break the link between information and insight. Data does not automatically lead to 'ta-da!'

B.
THE ART AND SCIENCE OF INSIGHT

What Can Science Tell Us About Insight? Quite a bit, it seems.

I) INSIGHT AS CONNECTION AND COLLISION

Let's warm up with Leonard Mlodinow, a Californian physicist, mathematician and bestselling author. He's known for his work on the theory of 'quantum decoherence,' but has a broader public profile for his accessible science books, and as a television screenwriter and computer game co-creator with Steven Spielberg and Robin Wiliams. In his 2018 book, *Elastic: Flexible Thinking in a Time of Change*,[38] Mlodinow dedicates a chapter to exploring the origin of insights. He offers this definition of insight:

> "An idea that represents an original and fruitful way of understanding an issue or approaching a problem."

Insight is essentially concerned with seeing things differently and making new connections. We can get there by throwing things together and encouraging our brain to make new correlations. This is the high road to developing insights, at both the individual and organisational level.

Let's delve into some more etymology, beginning with the word 'symbol.'

It origins lie in the Greek word *symbolon*, with a meaning rooted in 'to throw together.' (We also see the Greek verb *ballein* in ballet, ballistics, embolism and — no exaggeration — hyperbole.)

It referred to a token or tally that could be used to prove one's identity. The token was split or broken, the two parts were given to different individuals, and only when they were reunited could the parties be truly identified.

The Greeks, being almost always at war, and especially with one another, were deviously interested in spying, messages and cryptography.

In one of the earliest forms of cryptography, the Spartans developed an early form of cipher system called the scytale. This was a precisely sized staff or baton around which a strip of leather or parchment was wound. A message was written on the outside of this twined material, which was then unwound, leaving what would appear to be a meaningless series of letters dispersed across the outstretched band. Only when the receiver was equipped with a scytale of the same proportions could the strip of material be properly rewound, revealing the reconstituted message.

Symbolically, insight works in a similar way. When we can put two parts together to reveal a whole, there is an integration. We are rewarded with an 'aha!' of completion and recognition.

INCUBATING INSIGHT: THE 'I'S HAVE IT

Let's now look at what theorists of creativity have to say about the various stages that occur before the grand *dénouement* that is insight.

One such theory goes back to 1926, when Graham Wallas, an English social psychologist and one of the founders of the London School of Economics, expounded his theory in a book called *The Art of Thought*.[39]

Wallas laid out a four-stage system for insight, bookended by immersion and illumination.

Stage 1, Immersion, is well known to all of us as we prepare a presentation, document, speech or any form of analysis. We immerse ourselves (I refuse to say 'deep dive') in the domain we are seeking to understand, explore or disrupt, and saturate ourselves fully in as much data and information as we can ingest about that world.

However, Wallas argued that immersion is never enough, and neither is expertise. Many argue that too much expertise and experience can actually be a barrier to innovation, and that an attitude of failure-friendliness is more supportive of innovation. Take the words of Niels Bohr, the Danish physicist and architect of the Copenhagen Interpretation, a cornerstone of quantum physics:

> *"An expert is someone who has made all the mistakes that can be made in a narrow field."*

Fans of the ancient Greek *Eureka!* story will note that immersion, in the aquatic sense, was also key to Archimedes' moment of revelation, as he wallowed in his bath in the 3rd century BCE. He resolved the challenge of King Hiero of Syracuse, to determine whether the sovereign's crown was pure gold, by observing the water he displaced when he plunged into the bath. "Eureka" — I have found it! — he cried, upon realising that displaced water is equal in volume to a submerged object.

Stage 3, that of Illumination (the moment of insight), is equally easy to define. The angelic *Eureka* of epiphany is the last stop on the journey to creative enlightenment.

I will pass over Wallas's fourth and final stage, Verification, as it tends to act merely as a rubber stamp for insight, rather than making a positive contribution. It also irritatingly destroys the elegant alliteration of all those imaginative and intuitive 'I' words. (In Wallas's original model, there was also a preliminary stage called 'Intimation,' which described the feeling that something important was on its way.)

And yes, I know I have left out Stage 2. I'm coming to that.

EXPERTISE AND IMMERSION

Often, we overrely on the immersion process to generate the longed-for 'blue-sky thinking.' There is a deep and enduring love of brainstorming in the business world, especially in pursuit of this cutting-edge thinking. Nonetheless, a large body of evidence suggests that brainstorms often prove sterile in the pursuit of radical novelty if they rely purely on immersion (Stage 1).

All too often, I have found, brainstorming is devoted to data dumpage and 'sharing,' rather than the process of creative thinking. And that brings us to the missing element in Wallas's theory.

'Incubation' is the technical term for that crucial stage.

This key step is where and how the unconscious mind gets on with the business of heavy lifting, in seeing new connections and building new *wholes* (this relates also the gestalt theory of perception), without any conscious awareness or involvement.

Incubation is the feeling, recognised by all creative thinkers (I obviously include scientists here), that immersion in and of itself is simply not enough.

This is another instance where we have to abandon any idea of a linear, causal effect between input and output.

BED, BATH, BUS AND BEYOND

Some experts in creativity theory even argue that too much prior knowledge can hinder the process of generating radical new insights. They say deliberative rational processes (System 2, if you're a disciple of the Blessed Daniel Kahneman) are more likely to follow well-known paths, or ruts, in which thinking becomes entrenched and fixated. Escaping the grip of these *idées fixes*, these mental ruts, is one of the primary achievements of incubation.

Yet, I find that when companies seek blue-sky thinking (a lifetime of living under British weather makes that sound more amusing than it is), this oh-so-crucial Stage 2 is too often ignored or underestimated. Incubation means allowing the immersion process to boil and bubble, before it is stirred and simmers, to permit new connections and patterns to be forged by the unconscious.

Perhaps because it happens below our conscious radar, this mental meandering — this 'mystery time' — is often taken for granted, minimised or dismissed by defenders of the rational, linear status quo.

But Wallas's theory (which, as with much science, is not universally accepted) seems to accord with much of the empirical evidence from people at the sharp end of creativity. Namely, that to derive new patterns, ideas and links, the unconscious must be allowed to stimulate new alliances, considerations and 'gestalts' that restructure what was obtained by immersion. And this leads to something cognitive theorist Douglas Hofstadter calls "JOOTS" — jumping out of the system.

JOOTSing comes at that pivotal moment when, looking dubiously at what is there, one pulls back, causing something new and different to emerge.[40]

This preconscious recombination, by definition, cannot be forced by effort from the reflective mind, but needs suggestible relationships to be generated spontaneously. And so, it must be given free rein, in its own time and manner.

The Incubation approach to insight can best be understood by reference to the three Bs: the 'bed, bath and bus.'

Rooted in the personal experience of people in the throes of creative illumination, this refers to the typical moments when the results of incubation are fed through to the conscious and the 'Aha!' bell rings, flooding us with a blissfully transcendent clarity.

When one is resting in bed, or we awake after fruitless pondering the night before; when thinking about other things or nothing much at all; when the conscious mind is occupied with getting off a bus or taking an Archimedean bath. These seem to be the best moments to let the unconscious off the leash, to take the handbrake off those unseen constraints and allow new combinations to incubate.

COLLISIONS AND COMBINATIONS

As we have noted, combinations provide one of the paths to insight, and scientists have long attested to its effectiveness. Here's a compendium of thinking on that thought:

> *"Abrupt cross-cuts and transitions from one idea to another ... the most unheard-of combinations of elements, the subtlest associations of analogy."*
> —American psychologist William James[41]

> *"Ideas rose in crowds. I felt them collide until pairs interlocked ... making a stable combination."*
> —French mathematician and thinker Henri Poincaré[42]

> *"Never in the field of his (the inventor's) consciousness do combinations appear that are not really useful."*
> —Henri Poincaré[43]

More recently, distinguished linguist and neuro-anthropologist Terence Deacon, author of 1997's *The Symbolic Species*, added weight to this view:

> *"What we might call a symbolic insight takes place the moment we let go of one associative strategy and grab hold of another higher-order one ... they involve a re-coding of previously available but unlinked bits of information."*[44]

Charles Darwin was one of many to describe this process:

> "I can remember the very spot on the road, whilst in my carriage, when to my joy the solution occurred to me."

This is not to deny the role of Wallas's first stage — immersion — or minimise the need for preparation. After all, the prepared mind is what fortune favours, according to the old saw. There may even be hours of practice involved, in accordance with the oft-repeated claim by pop-culture author Malcolm Gladwell that experts need 10,000 hours of their chosen discipline to master it.

But anyone who has worked with creative people knows that they're not always that adept at recognising their deepest insight, or how it came about. Sometimes they're too close to it, and the cool view of an outsider is required. The science seems to show that another blind Darwinian process of variation and selection is involved, where a small nugget, the merest hint of a detail, can combine with another to forge something that builds a mighty edifice of originality.

This represents another nail in the coffin for linear, deliberative thinking. Most commentators agree that the actual moment of illumination tends not to appear gradually and stepwise, but as an immediate burst of light without precedent. It's like the magician's rabbit emerging from the hat, where everything falls into place without any clear sense of what led up to the grand finale.

As physicist David Bohm put it:

> *"You're not thinking. You're just being logical."*[45]

WHAT CAN ART TELL US ABOUT INSIGHT?
I) A SHOCK TO THE CISTERN:

As someone who has fought long and hard, tooth and nail, to put the art back into marketing, I would now like to showcase some of those who have created some of our greatest artworks, as a great source for insight and its application.

The role of art shares much of its manifesto with that of creativity and originality in general: to generate the 'shock of the new' (thank you, Robert Hughes), to encourage strangeness and violate conventions. The French have an expression, *épater la bourgeoisie*, for shocking the middle class out of their humdrum ordinariness and complacency.[46]

One poll whose findings did its fair share of middle class-shocking asked curators and art critics to choose what they considered the most influential piece of modern art. (Note 'most influential,' not necessarily 'the best.')

It wasn't Matisse's "Red Studio" (in fifth place), Picasso's "Guernica," (fourth), nor was it Warhol's "Marilyn Diptych" (third) or even Picasso's "Demoiselles D'Avignon" (runner-up).

Ladies and Gentlemen of the shockable bourgeoisie, the winner was ... the French Dadaist Marcel Duchamp's "Fountain," from 1917, now considered a landmark in 20th century art.

Better known as the urinal that Duchamp signed (rather mysteriously as R. Mutt) and submitted to the Society of Independent Artists show at New York's Grand Central Palace exhibition hall, it was indeed a shock to the system (or cistern). But it blazed a path of ready-mades and demonstrated that art could be made from the banal. It also convinced many that anything that was put in a gallery could, ipso facto, be 'art'. (By the way, the New York artists' group in question summarily rejected Duchamp's seminal work.)

Duchamp also prefigured much of the emerging theory of semiotics, and what is now in the marketing and comms world referred to as 'engagement' and 'co-creation'. It also presaged conceptual art and the hegemony of idea over execution.

Duchamp wrote the following:

> "The creative act is not performed by the artist alone; the spectator brings the work in contact with the external world by deciphering and interpreting its inner qualifications and thus adds his contribution to the creative act."

II) JUXTAPOSE FOR A MOMENT

One of the most influential art movements was Dada, if only for the importance the manifestoes of Surrealism and Cubism placed on the Dadaists' generation of novelty through unexpected juxtaposition.

Think of Magritte, Dali or the comment from one of the movement's main mouthpieces, André Breton, a co-founder of Surrealism, who defined Dadaism as "pure psychic automatism." As such, it was a rebellion against what was seen as the po-faced, heavy-handed and 'adult' in favour of the spontaneous, ludic and childish. The Cabaret Voltaire crowd revelled in countering the absurdity of the mass slaughter in the trenches of WWI with its own kind of nonsense.

> "The man that cannot visualise a horse galloping on a tomato is an idiot."
>
> —André Breton[47]

This may help to explain why so many surrealists took jobs in the advertising business, and why the ad and design industries remain fascinated to this day with the likes of Magritte and Dali. The deification falls somewhere between homage and plagiarism.

The contemporary Mexican-American conceptual artist Gabriel Orozco, who's known for reframing every-day objects, has a gorgeous way of putting this sense of *art as enrichment*:

> *"Really great art regenerates the perception of reality: the reality becomes richer."[48]*

We can also admit as evidence Stalin's definition of artists as "engineers of the soul."

Before ending this artistic *détournement*, let us just remind ourselves that in art, film and culture, the playful, rebellious and oblique examination of reality, and search for novelty, create a sense of anarchic insurgency that is all too human.

Yet, in a business world defined by pragmatic determinism, this creative urge often finds itself swept under the carpet of rationality and efficiency.

III) ESI FILES: COMBINATORIAL SERENDIPITY AND THE OPPORTUNISTIC ASSOCIATION

The secret of successful incubation is to create as many opportunities as possible to stimulate the unconscious power of linkage through the power of chance.

There are two concepts I want to bring together here to show how important this issue is for insight and originality.

Here, I shall borrow a term — external serendipitous influence (ESI) — that stirs up the calm sea of problem solving with some disruptive and apparently irrelevant perturbations.

ESI gives dignity to the notion of 'chance.'

Despite what the layperson might imagine, scientists are more than happy to give chance its due. Chance, said the German physicist Max Born, is a more fundamental conception than causality. Francis Crick (one of the two strands of the Double Helix) claimed it was the only real source of novelty.

I also await word from Jerry Bruckheimer or other such Hollywood gentry inviting me to write a pilot treatment for the ground-breaking TV procedural, *ESI: Muswell Hill*.

IV) DICE, DICE, BABY

In art, as we have seen, the principle of the random, or 'aleatory,' is well-known.

This derives from *alea*, Latin for a game of dice, as in Gaius Julius Caesar's famous boast in 49 BC, "*Alea jacta est*" (the die is cast or the dice has been thrown). In other words, the point of no return had been reached. He was at the time crossing the Rubicon, and symbolically making himself in the eyes of the Senate and the Roman people an enemy of the state in his civil war against Pompey.

The abstract and (blurry) photorealistic German painter Gerhard Richter has similarly used random choices, chance and ready-mades to create his first series of "Colour Chart paintings," and later introduced chance selection by numbering colours to be used and pulling them out of a hat. He said this about letting surprise happen:

> *"What interests me most about these works is that chance does it better than I can, but I have to prepare the conditions to allow randomness to do its work."*[49]

It is this sense of what any teenager would likely call 'random' (until the next word comes along that so often distresses and confuses parents), which runs so counter to our conditioning to value the relevant and well ordered as all-important.

The UK ad agency BMP, one of the two ancestral homes of account planning, used to talk about the need for the "relevant distinctive." I feel that these days, the emphasis on relevance has become a handicap to saliency, differentiation and imagination. It is often taken to imply a reiteration of the product's rational benefit, which most of the time the user needs no reminder of.

The distinctive is often under-played, due to the sort of defensive decision-making we saw earlier.

"Combinatory play" — a term coined by Albert Einstein, and later used as an MO by the likes of Bob Dylan and David Bowie — is also de rigueur for insight and imagination in a world where collage, montage and bricolage, riffs, cover versions, re-imaginings, reboots, sampling, loops and palimpsests are evident across most art forms.

V) ENO-VATIONS

The aleatory was part of the Dada and Surrealism playbooks, and the avant-garde musician and 'pioneer of indeterminacy' theorist John Cage was a notable exponent. He used the Chinese I-Ching, normally a tool for divination, as a tool for making music by chance.

Some of his works were released in the mid-'70s on the Obscure Records label, which was founded by Roxy Musician, collaborator and producer Brian Eno.

Beyond his musical influence and importance, Eno's intellectual contribution, with the artist Peter Schmidt, is especially significant.

In 1974, the two were working on Eno's second solo album, following his break with progressive art-glam rock band Roxy Music. During both the writing of the lyrics and the recording process, they gradually began to codify a set of working principles that they had both found useful in breaking creative gridlock.

From this, they devised a set of small prompt cards, the Oblique Strategies. They contained 'over one hundred worthwhile dilemmas' to jog their minds and jolt their patterns away from the dictates of deadline urgencies, the ruts of convention and the stresses of working with Phil Collins.

In particular, these cards offered a more tangential way of attacking problems than going at them head-on, by prompting the pair to try another approach or attitude.

Their first card read: "Honour thy error as a hidden intention."

VI) LIGHTS! ACTION! COMBINATORIAL SERENDIPITY!

How about some more examples of the power of combinatorial serendipity from the film world?

Let's start with movie legend (no exaggeration in this case) Mel Brooks. He was asked how he came up with the idea of the 1967 film *The Producers*. His explanation shows just how novelty can be created by the juxtaposition of seemingly incompatible ideas:

> *"I worked for a producer who wore a chicken-fat-stained homburg and a black alpaca coat. He pounced on little old ladies and would make love to them (NB, in the old-fashioned sense). They gave him money for his plays, and they were so grateful for his attention. Later on, there were a couple of guys who were doing flop after flop and living like kings. A press agent told me, 'God forbid they should ever get a hit, because they'd never be able to pay off the backers!' I coupled the producer with these two crooks and — BANG! — there was my story."*[50]

A more recent instance is *The Hunger Games* trilogy, the wildly successful young-adult adventure series set in a dystopian future. And by successful, I mean a film franchise that's been both critically lauded and commercially successful, with more than 100 million books sold by 2020. (And, it made a star of Jennifer Lawrence, she of the aforementioned 'Lawrence Effect.')

Suzanne Collins, who wrote the original Hunger Games books, says the concept occurred to her one evening when she was channel surfing between two very different TV genres. One moment, she found herself watching a reality show competition, and the next, war coverage. "I was tired," she said, "and the lines began to blur in this very unsettling way."[51]

From this fortuitous collision emerged the seed of something special.

Inspiration requires not just the unconscious, serendipity and chance; it needs constantly topping up.

As screenwriter Charlie Kaufman explained in a 2011 BAFTA lecture:

> *"Allow yourself time, let things brew. You're thinking about it, whether you realize it or not. Letting the unconscious take over brings in freedom and surprise and removes judgment."*[52]

Kaufman uses the same language Mel Brooks did when recalling how he came up with the idea for *Being John Malkovich*, his breakthrough 1999 screenplay for Spike Jonze's movie, about which it is almost impossible not to use the word 'quirky'. It was as simple as this, he said:

> "Mmmm, I just wrote it. The germs were, I had this idea that someone finds a portal into someone's head, and then I had another idea that somebody has a story about someone having an affair with a co-worker. And neither one was going anywhere in my head, so I just decided to see what happened if I combined them. And then I just wrote it."

And then there was this tip, in *The Guardian*, from Michael Morpurgo, writer of the novel, and then stage play, *War Horse*:

> "The prerequisite for me is to keep my well of ideas full. This means living as full and varied a life as possible, to have my antennae out all the time."[53]

So, Brooks, Kaufman and Morpurgo are unanimous in lauding the frequently untapped creative potential in seeking out unexpected combinations.

C.
CHARACTERISTICS, CREDOS AND CULTURE

A) CHARACTERISTICS

I) THE FIRST CLASS NOTICER

One of the bedrocks of an insight-generator should, naturally, be curiosity. Unsurprising as this may appear, a recent article in the *Harvard Business Review*[54] felt the need to make the business case for curiosity.

Despite the assumption that companies encourage it, the piece suggested that curiosity is more often than not being stifled. It cited a study of more than 3,000 employees, across a wide range of sectors, that found that only 24% felt curious in their jobs on a regular basis. A startling 70% said they faced barriers to asking more questions at work.

The benefits to embracing curiosity, further research showed, were many:
* Fewer decision-making errors
* More innovation and positive changes, in both creative and non-creative jobs
* Reduced group conflict
* More open communication and better team performance

Furthermore, the article examined the barriers to employee curiosity. The two primary impediments were:

- Leaders have the wrong mindset about exploration, thinking it is harder to manage
- They tend to seek (and I would suggest value) efficiency, to the detriment of *exploration*

The latter point I have written about extensively, under the guise of what I call the 'arithmocracy'— the obsession in business with efficiency, metrics, KPIs and a numbing reductionism.

An expression I particularly endorse comes from the pen of American novelist and playwright Saul Bellow.

In his 1997 novella, *The Actual*,[55] the Pulitzer and Nobel Prize-winner assigned the moniker "first-class noticer" to those who keenly observe the world around them.

Set in Chicago, the story's central character, Harry Trellman, had always been an outsider — he didn't seem to 'belong' — but he was a particularly keen observer, recorder and interpreter. As such, he was adopted by a wealthy financier, Sigmund Adeletsky, as a member of his vaunted 'brain trust.'

This was such an elegant formulation that, inevitably, the business (and business guru) world snapped it up. Management consultant Warren Bennis introduced the first-class noticer to the world of leadership as someone who recognises talent, identifies opportunities and avoids pitfalls.

The noticer returned in *The Power of Noticing: What the Best Leaders See*, a 2014 book by Harvard academic Max Bazerman.[56]

In the business leadership domain, it became a corrective rallying cry against undue internal focus on specific, narrow tasks, rather than scanning the broader horizon for threats and opportunities.

Here, I'd like to reclaim the first-class noticer (henceforth the FCN, not to be confused with the Farming Community Network or French football team FC Nantes) as a basic prerequisite for insightment. For what is the base skill of someone operating as insight-spotter if not an intrinsic desire and talent to notice?

Again, this is not simply about having raw material, or the right raw material. There needs to be something that is brought to the data, and the ability to spot ideas, connections and links is what distinguishes the humble observation from the coveted insight.

It is precisely the role of the FCN to spot the telling detail. This was elegantly expressed by critic and novelist James Wood, in his seminal *How Fiction Works*, as "the kind of detail that speeds on our knowledge of a character."

Wood also looks at how literature relies on a sense of defamiliarizing or estranging. (If you're more than mildly acquainted with Russian literature, you won't object to me saying *ostranie*.)

I have written elsewhere about the phenomenon of inattentional blindness, where seemingly obvious and conspicuous events are missed while observers focus on (or, if led by magicians, are misdirected) elsewhere.

For a final mantra in favour of curiosity, we could look to Eric Schmidt, Google's CEO from 2001 to 2011. He provided thus nugget:

> *"We run this company on questions, not answers."*

II) ANALOGIST

How do scientists think? This was a question posed, and answered with research and experimental design, by University of Maryland psychologist Kevin Dunbar.[57]

In the 1990s, his team explored how the process of discovery seemed to unfold amongst scientists, specifically microbiologists in the US, Canada and Italy.

One of the defining insights in his theory of "creative cognition" and "distributed reasoning" was that many of the breakthroughs he witnessed occurred by means of analogies. And, he noted, analogies were more likely to occur when team members had a diversity of experience.

III) WANDERER

One of the best ways of allowing your brain to make analogies is by wandering. I've written frequently about the etymology of 'error,' and will again bring it to bear in this context.

The origins of the word have nothing to do with mistakes, failures or any other form of inadequacy. Instead, it comes from a root meaning 'to wander.'

Too often, especially in brand comms, marketing and sales, we become prisoners of one market. (I'm not talking about European regulations here, either.)

The brand or company culture can easily become a self-contained and hermetically sealed bubble, and homogenised groupthink becomes the order of the day. One of the reasons ad agency planners can bring a keener eye to clients' problems is that in many cases (ideally, all) they're working across different clients. So, they deal with different consumer types, commercial and communications challenges, and opportunities.

But it also means that the brain can detect patterns, similarities, differences and commonalities that can create connections, which may prove valuable when it comes to originality and innovation.

So, the Searcher for Insight must ensure that they wander outside of the comfort of their own domain.

One element may need clarifying. When discussing the power of storytelling to meld with emotions (see under behavioural economics), I often talk about the power of empathy. This is not to undermine that emphasis. Sometimes, though — for instance, when seeking out new ideas — detachment, rather than empathy, may be required. Too much empathy with a particular brand or consumer can lead to a narrow focus, where external 'estrangement' is needed to seed new points of view and perspectives.

IV) IMPERTINENT

Another essential ingredient for insight is a sense of impertinence. Again, this gives us the opportunity to slip in a bit of linguistic/etymological chicanery.

If something is pertinent, it is relevant and applicable to a particular matter or issue. It *pertains to* that.

In the late 14th century (so I'm told), the word impertinent came to mean the opposite of that, as in 'unconnected or unrelated to the point.' It was not pertinent. Later, around late 17th century, its meaning evolved to mean 'rudely bold, uncivil, offensively presumptuous,' perhaps from the notion of meddling in what is beyond one's relevant domain.

Jacob Bronowski, the brilliant Polish-born mathematician, historian of science and humanist, highlighted this play on words and ideas when defining science in *The Ascent of Man*, the landmark TV series and companion book. He put it this way:

> *"That is the essence of science. Ask an impertinent question and you are on your way to the pertinent answer."*[58]

And here we make the jump from a famous TV figure — Bronowski's 1973 series was both a towering intellectual achievement and testament to popular science on the BBC — to a comic strip writer. Pulitzer Prize-winner Garry Trudeau, the creator of *Doonesbury*, said this on receiving an honorary degree from Yale University in 1991:

> *"The impertinent question is the glory and engine of human enquiry ... history's movers framed their questions in ways that were entirely disrespectful of conventional wisdom."*[59]

Whether we're talking about finding a new brand insight, hoping to win a pitch by finding a new angle for a client, or just finding a new point of view or direction, all of these can be initiated by applying some impertinence.

V) SERENDIPITOUS

I have written before about external serendipitous influences (ESIs) in the insight-analysis business. The power of ESIs is central to the generation of genuinely new approaches and insights.

The secret to incubating new ideas is to stimulate the unconscious power of linkage by providing disruptive perturbations to our conventions and assumptions. Combinatorial serendipity, as we have seen, is at the heart of many great creative achievements, from *The Hunger Games* and *The Producers* to *Being John Malkovich*, and the oeuvres of Picasso, Richter and Eno.

In Part C, below, we'll explore how to create a culture that thrives on serendipity.

VI) WIT

Yes, humour is (or certainly should be) core to the Searcher for Insight.

In English, the word 'wit' denotes both intelligence and humour, and in many cultures that link is even more obvious.

Humour — although remarkably little is known of its origin and role in our evolution — is a core human characteristic. And from Greek comedian Aristophanes to today's generation of comic writers and stand-ups, what does a comic wit do if not show us the world in a new light?

For me, the Venn diagram of humour, wit and surprise is crucial to the understanding and creation of insight. We even use the expression 'to get a joke,' implying discovery and the feeling that 'ha-ha' is intimately related to 'aha!' Humour is a form of reframing in itself. The sense of exhilaration, the experience of revisiting, is the same.

George Orwell put this nicely in a 1945 essay, *Funny, But Not Vulgar*:

> *"A thing is funny when — in some way that is not actually offensive or frightening — it upsets the established order. Every joke is a tiny revolution. If you had to define humour in a single phrase, you might define it as dignity sitting on a tin-tack."*[60]

Ogden Nash, American writer of humorous verse, lyricist, screenwriter and self-proclaimed "worsifier," wrote eloquently on the need for humour in a dark world. In the commencement address he gave at his daughter Linell's boarding school, he spoke in favour of humour and against solemnity:

> *"Among other things, I think humour is a shield, a weapon, a survival kit ... So here we are, several billion of us, crowded into our global concentration camp for the duration. How are we to survive? Solemnity is not the answer, any more than witless and irresponsible frivolity is. I think our best chance lies in humour, which in this case means a wry acceptance of our predicament. We don't have to like it, but we can at least recognize its ridiculous aspects, one of which is ourselves."*[61]

VII) STORYTELLER

You can't be too surprised to find me suggesting this is a *sine qua non* of the intrepid Insight-Stalker. But it may not be an obvious characteristic. Let me explain.

Yes, we have emphasised how to search for insights, covering the requisite qualities and perspectives.

But my own experience has been that the other part of the equation in achieving excellence in insight is not just identifying it, but successfully transmitting it. I've witnessed many examples of researchers, planners and clients trying to propose their insight to the higher-ups, but failing to gain traction. Why? Not because the insight itself wasn't powerful and transformative. Rather, it was because they failed to create the necessary energy and persuasive power to make their case.

This is where great storytelling is so essential.

Perhaps the greatest skill (superpower, if you want) that storytelling can endow is empathy. When we're trying to convince anyone of anything — in this case, struggling to persuade the powers that be that our insight is worthy of consideration and implementation — we can never rely on the brute force of facts. Empathy is essential, so that at the human, emotional level there's a feeling of understanding that goes beyond objective assessment of facts. Storytelling is the 'empathy engine' par excellence.

Having written two books on the topic, I'd ideally steer you there, but here are some tips for storytelling, to maximise

the likelihood of your insight achieving the glorious reception it deserves.

- Start with the story. Make the insight the core of your argument, not an afterthought. Then, explain how you got there
- Make the idea or insight the protagonist of your story. If the insight is the hero, what is or was the villain?
- Do not let the core insight get bogged down in the detail. The Golden Thread, the path through the woods, should be in pursuit of the clear elucidation of the insight and its benefits
- Create a headline around the insight, so that it is at the forefront of your audience's attention from the very start
- Storytelling ensures that you will be the opposite of flat and monochrome. It will help you delight, bewitch, beguile, enchant and entrance your audience

B) CREDOS

To go with our selection of human characteristics, let's throw out a few credos and maxims that can also light our way on the road to insight.

I) INSIGHT IS A PROCESS, NOT A THING

Insight is a means of getting somewhere, not an end point. We will do well to abide by this precept. We'll be looking more deeply into how to create a process or culture of insight here in Part 3, but let's frame it by realising that insight will best serve us if we treat is a process and a verb, rather than a thing or noun.

Abstract nouns tend to detach us from wonder, awe and action.

This can also lead to inertia and stasis, instead of the desired innovation and creativity. Take words like 'sustainability,' or expressions like 'the circular economy' or 'net zero.' I would submit that part of the reason they haven't led to the sort of breakthrough action that activists hope for is that they've become (or always were) cold, abstract and remote.

Someone — allegedly ad agency boss Dan Wieden — once said all great brands are verbs, not nouns, and I think this captures a broader truth. In workshops and consulting work, I always recommend that clients emphasise verbs instead of nouns, and actions instead of things.

By the same token, insight is best regarded as a process rather than a reified, reduced object that can be pinned down and snared with ease.

II) INSIGHT IS COMPLEX, NOT COMPLICATED
I raised the complex/complicated distinction in my 2021 book, *InCitations*,[62] and believe it has relevance in the context of insight.

Complexity and systems thinking have little time for reductionism, the breaking of things into ever-smaller chunks of 'stuff.' Instead, they build understanding based on a nest of holistic and interdependent processes. Pattern, flow and network are prioritised over essence and matter: traffic, bees, weather and human systems like sport all come under its purview.

An elegant metaphor cited by South African philosopher and complexity researcher Paul Cilliers[63] is that of the jumbo jet versus mayonnaise. A jumbo jet is *complicated*; it is equal to the sum of its six million-plus parts. Mayonnaise is *complex*; once mixed, you can't separate the parts again, and they're fundamentally changed by the blended interaction.

It's a wonderful analogy to explain a key tenet and principle at the heart of complexity: that complicated things can be explained satisfactorily by examining their component parts. Conversely, complex ones cannot, because they're greater than the sum of their parts.

Replacing one part of an Airbus A380-800 — say, an armrest headphone jack in seat 36B — does not alter the plane's fundamental structure or operation. With that creamy emulsion of egg yolk, oil and vinegar, however, you simply can't remove one of the component parts and still have mayo.

In the same way, it is best to think of insight as mayonnaise, in terms of how we understand and achieve it. It's not in a linear a + b process, as is often expected by data-gatherers. Instead, it is more often a blend of a x b, with mayonnaise-like dollops of creativity and serendipity to bind it.

III) FLIP THOSE ASSUMPTIONS

A basic component in the insights toolbox, and one I have readily merchandised, is to flip your assumptions. In the 'surfacing assumptions workshop' that I run, the process involves explicitly charting the assumptions you have, and then exploring what happens when you invert them.

Often associated with John Hegarty of ad agency Bartle Bogle Hegarty ("Zig when others zag"), I adopt this as a way of encouraging clients to therapeutically look deep into their brands' souls and examine which assumptions and conventions they genuinely must retain, and which ones can be abandoned in pursuit of new ideas and perspectives.

IV) STRIP DOWN, STEP BACK AND TAKE STOCK
Another one for the wall.

A precursor to insight is *stripping back*. Not just examining innate and long-held assumptions, but deliberately embarking on a process of reduction.

Try simplifying everything you can, and seeing what can happily be sacrificed.

As ad legend Bill Bernbach said, the essence of a great creative brief is sacrifice. So, sacrifice what can be sacrificed, strip everything back and see what remains — seek the essence and the core.

V) YOU WON'T FIND MUCH MEANING IN A MEAN
As I have suggested (to put it mildly), I'm not a great fan of the drive to efficiency, especially if it hampers creativity. And this often seems to be the case, particularly in larger organisations.

The arid reductionism and numbing down that comes from the arithmocracy can lead to systems that are too heavily based on KPIs, metrics and means.

Thinking in means leads to work (and communications ideas) that are exactly what that would indicate: average, middle of the road and grey. If insight is a colour, I can assure that you that it isn't grey. If it is a temperature, it is not lukewarm, but scaldingly intense.

For insight to thrive, we need to focus on meanings, not means. The insight-watcher should always have meaning, and not necessarily truth, as their watchword.

Always ask *what does this mean*, or what could it mean, for the audience we're trying to convince or the ultimate target audience we hope to influence.

A definition I quite admire comes from cognitive science academic Mark Turner's elegant little work, *The Literary Mind: The Origins of Thought and Language*. He reminds us, in discussing the importance of parable in story, that meaning is not some sort of deposit in a concept container. Instead, he suggests the following about meaning:

> *"It is alive and active, dynamic and distributed, constructed for local purposes of knowing and acting."*[64]

Thus, meaning emerges, and is constructed and refined, almost ceaselessly. As humans, we need to believe in connectedness and pattern — that our lives are linked to something other than ourselves, that we belong and that we matter.

Our lives are, as someone said, mosaics of meaning, and those of us in the communication business would do well to remind ourselves that we are purveyors of meaning.

VI) PRACTISE "LIMITED SLOPPINESS"

German-American biophysicist Max Delbrück, who played a key role in explaining genes, coined the principle of "limited sloppiness," which I think will serve us well in the context of excavating insights. It occurred to him, so it seems, when he was exploring something called "photo reactivation of bacteriophage."

As he put it:

> "If you are too sloppy, then you never get reproducible results, and then you never can draw any conclusions. But if you are just a little sloppy, then when you see something startling you ... nail it down."[65]

This strikes me as just right, and a necessary antidote to what is sometimes known as functional fixedness. Too tight and constrained, and our thinking and expectations are likely to be reinforced; too sloppy and the necessary rigour may be a barrier to success. But a little sloppiness feels just about right. (For some reason, I hear that last sentence in the voice of Paddington Bear.)

VII) DON'T DIG DEEP, GRAZE SHALLOW

Let us now borrow a maxim from Andre Geim, a Russian-Dutch-British physicist at the University of Manchester. Geim won a Nobel Prize for his work on graphene, an atomic-level component of carbon, and has published work on levitating frogs. (No, really.)

He warned that we should not become too specialised, but allow our brains to wander far and wide.

When asked to discuss his research style, Geim characterised it in this way:

> "It's rather unusual. I do not dig deep — I graze shallow. So, ever since I was a postdoc, I would go into a different subject every five years or so … sometimes I joke that I am not interested in doing re-search, only search."[66]

VIII) BE OBLIQUE

We talked earlier about musician Brian Eno and artist Peter Schmidt using Oblique Strategies flash cards to get beyond creative blocks. Eno, who's been a bit of hero for me since the '70s, went on to use this creative tool when producing the work of David Bowie and others. (*Frippertronics*, anyone?)

These cards offered a more tangential way of attacking problems than going at them head-on, by prompting the creators to try another approach or attitude.

This ties in with the thesis of economist John Kay's 2010 book, *Obliquity*.[67] Kay suggested that things we actively seek, like success or happiness, might best be achieved indirectly. It's the notion that we often have to go back in order to go forward. In that way, we learn about our objectives as we strive for them, and we have less control than we like to think … in a good way.

For example, perhaps doing new research isn't always the answer. It may well be more profitable and surprising to go back and look at what we already have, through new eyes.

IX) NOTHING IS USELESS

Finally, in this section, as great academic paper titles go, you can do worse than "The Usefulness of Useless Knowledge."

This short, provocative work, penned in 1939 by the educator Abraham Flexner, founding Secretary General of the Princeton Institute for Advanced Study, looked at why 'useless' science often leads to humanity's greatest technological breakthroughs.[68]

Reprinted in 2017, the work argues for a form of enquiry unfettered by short-termism and pragmatic utilitarian objectives that Flexner saw as a threat in the '30s, and which remain stubbornly entrenched to this day.

Flexner revelled in flexibly abstract knowledge for its own sake, and called for building a space for nurturing "curiosity, freedom and imagination." Before the end of his life, he could point to the invention of electromagnetism, lasers and X-rays as proof of his theory.

With today's over-veneration of accountability and efficiency, of increasing compartmentalisation and the echo-chamber effect, we need to bring back the joy of learning in the pursuit of insight. This will serve to stimulate all sorts of combinatorial creativity and of cross-pollination.

C) CULTURE

As we've discussed, insight begins not only at the personal level — diverse, collaborative teams can be especially fruitful. And it can best be disseminated through and across the culture of an organisation.

The provision of ESIs, those wonderfully serendipitous influences, is for me a key component for creating a culture of insightment.

In his 2013 book, *People Analytics: How Social Sensing Technology Will Transform Business, and What it Tells Us About the Future of Work*,[69] Harvard and MIT researcher Ben Waber says that serendipitous interactions are incredibly important for making random connections that pay off down the road.

Waber's research shows that workers' most productive time occurs when they collaborate and interact with each other. This means getting up and walking around, spending time in the coffee area,

eating lunch with colleagues, jumping into chat sessions and becoming heavily involved in the social life of the workplace.

Since I first wrote about this, the Covid-19 pandemic has drastically altered the work landscape. In the UK, as we saw the numbers of people working in offices rapidly declining in mid-2022, government minister Jacob Rees-Mogg lambasted civil servants for not being at their desks. At a personal level, one of my children, who began her career in early 2021, joined a generation for whom one day a week in the office felt like the new norm.[70]

While I fully accept that working from home had been a blessing for many — with less time wasted commuting, more time with family, and more productivity and flexibility — I do think that the law of unintended consequences also has something to say about the matter.

In terms of creating a culture of insightment in organisations, we need to seek ways of getting people back into spaces (Offices? Third places?), where they can bump into each other. This will provide a platform where ideas can collide and create the sort of unexpected combinatorial serendipity I am promoting.

I would like to end by proposing three areas where you can effectively develop and reinforce a culture of insightment within your company.

A) THE PUD FILE

Stephen Jay Gould was a palaeontologist and scientific populariser. In one of his many books, his eighth collection of essays, *Leonardo's Mountain of Clams and The Diet of Worms* (1999), he talks about the importance of exploring "previously unapplied detail," or PUD.[71]

Perhaps this is something you're already doing to some extent, but in honour of Gould I have long kept a PUD folder on my laptop.

I find that dipping into it every so often can jolt thought processes and, consciously as well as unconsciously, release various mental hares.

B) THE IDEAS ORPHANAGE

If the PUD folder is for the individual, how can we share this idea across the team or broader organisation?

Every good company, intent on creating a culture of insightment, should maximise its use of each individual's PUD folder by building a space that acts as a collective 'open source' zone for nurturing ESIs. It can be the intranet or a good old notice board.

I call this space the Ideas Orphanage.

It can be used for any or all of these purposes:
- For team members to post, generate and test hypotheses
- To act as a collective catalogue, library and resource that embeds the *we-think* ethic of 'connect, create, contribute and collaborate', popularised by English innovation consultant Charles Leadbeater in 2010 It can also help incorporate a more informal café culture that is discursive and playful
- To allow people to wander, and see whether their wandering can collide with others' and generate genuine insight

- To create a 'metaphorest,' where useful, intriguing and original metaphors can be stored, viewed and relinked by people working on projects for different clients. As someone keen on bringing more storytelling to our communications, this is particularly helpful

C) TAS'S BOOK CLUB (TBC)

Over the years, I have been running a book club for several clients. The premise is that of every book club: attendees have to read the assigned volume (or a section, if they're too busy) and we then discuss it.

The only Rule of Book Club that I impose is NO BUSINESS BOOKS. Too often, titles in the 'business nonfiction' category tend to be very narrow, dull and often outdated by the time they're published. 'Oh, look … another book on social media.'

Instead, I prefer to choose books for these discussions that are about ideas, people, culture and that are designed to provoke new 'outside-in' thinking. We then talk about the ideas and issues in general, before applying new insights to specific issues of concern. This can be particularly fruitful.

Oh, and rather than book clubs, shouldn't they be called 'chapters?'

Let's end with some visual representations of our thesis.

FIGURE 1 – THE ART OF INSIGHTMENT

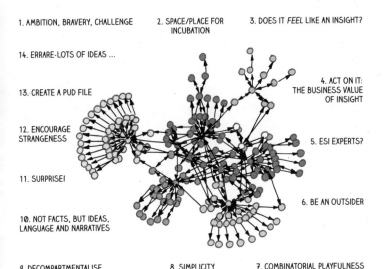

1. AMBITION, BRAVERY, CHALLENGE

2. SPACE/PLACE FOR INCUBATION

3. DOES IT *FEEL* LIKE AN INSIGHT?

14. ERRARE-LOTS OF IDEAS ...

4. ACT ON IT: THE BUSINESS VALUE OF INSIGHT

13. CREATE A PUD FILE

12. ENCOURAGE STRANGENESS

5. ESI EXPERTS?

11. SURPRISE!

6. BE AN OUTSIDER

10. NOT FACTS, BUT IDEAS, LANGUAGE AND NARRATIVES

9. DECOMPARTMENTALISE, RESTRUCTURE AND REFRAME

8. SIMPLICITY

7. COMBINATORIAL PLAYFULNESS

FIGURE 2 – THE MURDER BOARD

Here is a visual representation of the process of insight I have been elucidating, based on the typical crime board/evidence chart/murder map you see in every hunt-for-the-killer movie. (The demented counterpart is of course the serial killer's stalker-shrine collage wall.)

As a metaphor, this idea picks up the notion of finding a (golden) thread by following connections and making hypotheses, embodying the necessity of looking for clues and links. It also embodies the role of storytelling in communicating them clearly.

FIGURE 3: THE WORD CLOUD

For those who might be more visual than verbal, here's a handy word cloud depicting some of the key characteristics and concepts we have discussed.

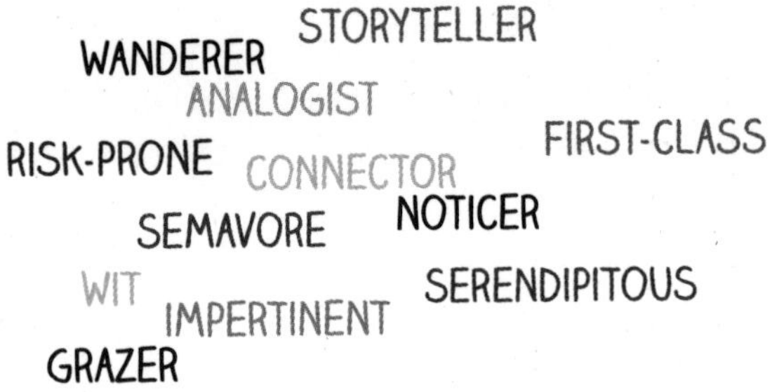

STORYTELLER

WANDERER

ANALOGIST

RISK-PRONE CONNECTOR FIRST-CLASS

SEMAVORE NOTICER

WIT SERENDIPITOUS

IMPERTINENT

GRAZER

APPENDIX
RECRUITING FOR INSIGHT

Here is a brief set of criteria I would propose for HR/L&D teams looking to recruit people on the basis on likely insight-propensity.

We are looking for candidates who:
* Are Inquisitive
* Are ends-driven, not means-driven
* Love the feel of ideas
* Think in hypotheses
* Think higher or deeper
* Like growing theories
* See data as merely a means to an end
* Can immerse
* Know how to incubate
* Are outsiders
* Hunt out connections
* Don't see boundaries
* See things that others don't, can't or won't

END

ENDNOTES

1. Niles Eldredge and Stephen Jay Gould: "Punctuated equilibria" (1972)

2. Gerd Gigerenzer: https://thedecisionlab.com/thinkers/psychology/gerd-gigerenzer https://www.jasoncollins.blog/gigerenzer-versus-kahneman-and-tversky-the-1996-face-off/; https://wisewords.blog/book-summaries/risk-savvy/

3. Albert Szent-Gyorgyi: https://quoteinvestigator.com/2015/07/04/seen/

4. On Bill Bernbach: https://www.contagious.com/news-and-views/Contagious-asks-strategists-for-insight-definitions

5. Bernbach on insight: https://medium.com/what-do-you-want-to-know/bill-bernbach-and-the-beginning-7e49c2242390#:~:text=%E2%80%9CAt%20the%20heart%20of%20an,camouflages%20what%20really%20motivates%20him.%E2%80%9D; https://pg-designs.ca/avis-we-try-harder-campaign/; https://www.thebalancesmb.com/advertising-industry-profile-bill-bernbach-38613

6. Tomato-based insight, Miles Kington: https://www.goodreads.com/quotes/184158-knowledge-is-knowing-that-a-tomato-is-a-fruit-wisdom

7. Tomato-based insight, echoed by Brian O'Driscoll: https://www.rugbydump.com/news/odriscoll-explains-his-infamous-tomato-quote-which-will-never-get-old/

8. Various Planners on insight: https://www.contagious.com/news-and-views/Contagious-asks-strategists-for-insight-definitions

9. PowerPoint by Umar Ghumman featuring various definitions: https://www.slideshare.net/umarghumman/what-is-an-insight-34449790/5-Why_is_a_good_insight

10. Gilbert and George: https://www.independent.co.uk/news/long_reads/gilbert-and-george-brussels-brafa-living-sculptures-traditional-british-a8752881.html

11. Mat Shore: https://www.youtube.com/watch?v=RuucbQQYw-0

12. Personal Construct Theory: https://www.verywellmind.com/what-is-personal-construct-theory-2795957

13. Zwolf, Heidi Hackemer (now at Oatly): https://www.youtube.com/watch?v=fHnxX2o2VTk

14. David Mamet: *On Directing Film* (1991)

15. Andy Davidson, talk at Account Planning Group, 2014: https://www.youtube.com/watch?v=UJj8ixUwxxg

16. Shoppenboys: https://archive.nytimes.com/query.nytimes.com/gst/fullpage-9502EEDD1230F935A1575BC0A9619C8B63.html

17. *The Guardian* "Points of View" ad: https://campaignbrief.com/my-most-immortal-ad-toby-allen-paul-weiland-dissect-the-guardians-points-of-view/

18. Marmite: https://www.prima.co.uk/diet-and-health/news/a40404/love-or-hate-marmite-genes/

19. Marmite Gene project: https://www.marmite.co.uk/the-gene-project.html; https://www.theguardian.com/food/2020/feb/26/love-it-or-hate-it-marmite-is-having-a-massive-foodie-moment; https://www.marmitemuseum.co.uk/marmite-history/; https://www.bbc.co.uk/news/uk-13541148#:~:text=Marmite%20is%20French.,of%20a%20marmite%20on%20it; https://www.creativereview.co.uk/you-either-love-it-or-hate-it/#:~:text='You%20Either%20Love%20It%20Or,used%20to%20describe%20anything%20divisive

20. Pratfall effect: https://www.theguardian.com/media-network/2015/oct/28/pratfall-effect-brands-flaunt-flaws; https://www.everyonehatesmarketers.com/articles/pratfall-effect-marketing

21. LittleMissMatched: https://www.cnet.com/culture/innovation-1-on-1-jonah-staw-littlemismatched/#:~:text=Bluewater-,Jonah%20Staw%2C%20co%2Dfounder%20and%20CEO%20of%20LittleMissMatched%2C%20heads,all%20ages%20to%20express%20themselves

22. Sony Bravia: https://en.esloganmagazine.com/bouncing-balls-by-sony/

23. Channel 4: https://theteam.co.uk/work/channel-4-intranet/;
    https://www.itsnicethat.com/news/
    channel-4-idents-dougal-wilson-4creative-film-311017

24. Channel 4 Paralympics: https://www.marketingweek.com/
    super-humans-inside-channel-4-paralympics-campaign/

25. Channel 4, Complaints Welcome: https://www.channel4.com/press/news/
    channel-4-invites-viewers-feedback-new-series-complaints-welcome-wt

26. Starbucks and Third Place: https://link.springer.com/
    chapter/10.1007/978-0-230-55477-1_29;
    https://www.pps.org/article/roldenburg;
    https://www.thersa.org/blog/2018/03/reimagining-the-enlightenment-
    coffeehouse; https://stories.starbucks.com/press/2020/starbucks-ceo-
    the-third-place-needed-now-more-than-ever-before/;
    https://www.mjvinnovation.com/blog/third-place-and-the-starbucks-
    empire-the-user-experience-at-the-heart-of-strategy/;
    https://www.businessinsider.com/
    starbucks-reimagine-third-place-2019-3?r=US&IR=T

27. Judges study: https://ui.adsabs.harvard.edu/
    abs/2011PNAS..108.6889D/abstract

28. Snickers case study: https://www.campaignlive.com/article/
    case-study-fame-made-snickers-youre-not-when-youre-hungry-
    campaign-success/1413554#:~:text=the%20perfect%20
    antidote.-,%22You're%20not%20you%20when%20you're%20
    hungry%22,was%20ripe%20for%20widespread%20adoption;
    https://www.warc.com/newsandopinion/opinion/effectiveness-insights-
    from-ten-years-of-snickers-youre-not-you-when-youre-hungry/en-gb/3892;
    https://medium.com/@mike.mcgee412/snickers-satisfies-when-youre-
    hangry-fd172b0c5599; https://www.annieduke.com/no-judges-dont-
    give-harsher-sentences-hungry-annies-newsletter-october-5-2018/

29. Unilever insights engine and Persil: https://hbr.org/2016/09/building-an-insights-engine; https://brandgenetics.com/human-thinking/unilever-how-to-build-an-insights-engine-hbr-summary/; https://www.greenbook.org/mr/getting-it-right/achieving-insights-success-at-unilever/; https://www.persil.com/uk/our-commitments/people/dirt-is-good-and-always-will-be.html; https://brandingforum.org/branding/campaigns/persil-announces-its-plan-to-evolve-its-dirt-is-good-campaign/; https://www.theguardian.com/media/2008/jul/28/advertising

30. *Death Proof* hand: https://www.trendhunter.com/trends/tarantino-death-proof-guerrilla-marketing

31. Old Spice ads from 1970s: https://www.youtube.com/watch?v=V4Hl4XKrleM

32. Old Spice new campaign: https://bettermarketing.pub/the-campaign-that-saved-old-spice-d925bed9aee8; https://www.marketingweek.com/how-the-old-spice-hunk-took-over-the-world/; https://www.foxbusiness.com/features/ad-ages-top-5-ad-campaigns-of-the-21st-century

33. William Goldman: https://variety.com/2018/film/opinion/william-goldman-dies-appreciation-1203030781/

34. Method story: https://www.ethicalconsumer.org/home-garden/ecover-and-method-boycott; https://www.neatservices.co.uk/story-behind-the-method-brand/; https://www.thedrum.com/news/2016/08/22/how-method-disrupting-monochrome-cleaning-scene-through-colour-and-design; https://www.peterfisk.com/gamechanger/method/; https://fidelum.com/insights/method-products-the-power-of-passion-and-purpose/; https://www.theguardian.com/sustainable-business/method-hr-employee-engagement

35. On lean and agile: https://www.youtube.com/watch?v=WKIy8nssMQc

36. Graham Wallas: *The Art of Thought* (1926)

37. Theodore Roszak: *The Cult of Information: The Folklore of Computers and the True Art of Thinking* (1986)

38. Leonard Mlodinow: "Elastic: Flexible Thinking in a Time of Change" (2018)

39. Graham Wallas: *The Art of Thought* (1926)

40. Douglas Hofstadter: *Gödel, Escher, Bach* (1979)

41. William James: *Principles of Psychology* (1880)

42. Henry Poincaré: *The Foundations of Science* (1921)

43. Ditto

44. Terence Deacon: *The Symbolic Species* (1997)

45. David Bohm: *On Creativity* (1991)

46. Most influential 20th century art: https://www.independent.co.uk/news/uk/this-britain/fountain-most-influential-piece-of-modern-art-673625.html

47. André Breton: attributed

48. Gabriel Orozco: https://lapispress.com/artists/48-gabriel-orozco/overview/

49. Gerard Richter: https://www.sothebys.com/en/articles/21-facts-about-gerhard-richter#:~:text=In%20describing%20his%20color%20chart,our%20lives%20in%20important%20ways.%E2%80%9D

50. Mel Brooks: https://www.theguardian.com/film/2008/aug/16/comedy.theproducers

51. Suzanne Collins: https://www.oxfordstudent.com/2012/04/20/the-hunger-games-a-deliciously-dystopian-thrill-ride/#:~:text=Collins%20was%20channel%2Dhopping%20when,result%20was%20The%20Hunger%20Games

52. Charlie Kaufman BAFTA lecture (2011)

53. Michael Morpurgo: https://www.theguardian.com/books/2010/feb/23/michael-morpurgo-rules-for-writers

54. Case for curiosity: https://hbr.org/2018/09/the-business-case-for-curiosity

55. Saul Bellow: *The Actual* (1997)

56. Bazerman: https://economictimes.indiatimes.com/is-too-much-focus-harmful-for-a-leader-business-psychologist-max-bazerman-has-some-tips/articleshow/47541669.cms?from=mdr

57. Kevin Dunbar: "How Scientists Think" (1997)

58. Jacob Bronowski: https://www.oxfordreference.com/view/10.1093/acref/9780191826719.001.0001/q-oro-ed4-00002092

59. Garry Trudeau: cited in "the Nature of Insight" ed. Sternberg (1995)

60. George Orwell, "Funny Not Vulgar": https://orwell.ru/library/articles/funny/english/e_funny

61. Ogden Nash speech: https://www.washingtonpost.com/wp-dyn/content/article/2005/05/05/AR2005050501359_pf.html

62. Anthony Tasgal: *InCitations* (2020)

63. Paul Cilliers: Complexity and Post Modernism (1998)

64. Mark Turner, The Literary Mind

65. Max Delbrück: cited in "The Road to Stockholm: Nobel Prizes, Science, and Scientists" by István Hargittai

66. Andre Geim: http://archive.sciencewatch.com/inter/aut/2008/08-aug/08augSWGeim/

67. John Kay: "Obliquity" (2010)

68. Abraham Flexner: *The Usefulness of Useless Knowledge* (1939)

69. Ben Waber: *People analytics* (2013)

70. Hybrid working: https://www.telegraph.co.uk/news/2022/04/29/home-working-middle-class-remainer-cult/?utm_content=telegraph&utm_medium=Social&utm_campaign=Echobox&utm_source=Twitter#Echobox=1651257342; https://socialeurope.eu/south-working-the-future-of-remote-work; https://www.telegraph.co.uk/news/2020/07/16/finally-achieved-work-life-balance-would-go-back-office/

71. Stephen Jay Gould: *Leonardo's Mountain of Clams and The Diet of Worms* (1999)

ACKNOWLEDGEMENTS

Thanks as ever to Martin for steadfast support and to Clare for labouring through the edits.

To Nikki, Josh, Zach and Saskia for the usual mixture of scattered empathy and benign indifference.

And Will for being a constant source of feline comfort.

ABOUT THE AUTHOR

Tas is a man of many lanyards: trainer, author, speaker, brand/comms strategist and lecturer.

He is a course director for the Chartered Institute of Marketing, the Market Research Society, the Institute of Internal Communication and the Civil Service College, and principal advisor for CIO Connect in Hong Kong.

He is a global speaker and regularly reviews the papers and contributes on marketing and communications subjects on TalkTV.

Specialist topics include storytelling, behavioural economics, insightment and briefing, and as a lapsed Classicist he also indulges in etymology and Homer (not the yellow one).

He also runs the *Guardian* masterclass on "Harnessing the power of storytelling" and is a Brand Ambassador for Home Grown Club in London.

He is the author of the award-winning *The Storytelling Book* (which has sold over 35,000 copies globally), *The Inspiratorium*, *InCitations* and, in April 2022, *The Storytelling Workbook.*

Tas can be found loitering at **@taswellhill** and
https://www.linkedin.com/in/tastasgal/

BY THE SAME AUTHOR

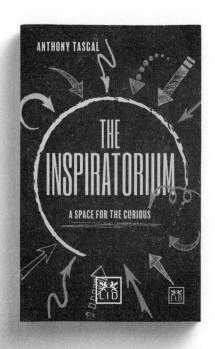

£9.99/$14.95
ISBN: 978-1-911498-46-9

JOÃO GILBERTO NOLL (1946–2017) is the author of nearly twenty books. His work appeared in Brazil's leading periodicals, and he was a guest of the Rockefeller Foundation, King's College London, and the University of California at Berkeley, as well as a Guggenheim Fellow. A five-time recipient of the Prêmio Jabuti, and the recipient of more than ten awards in all, he died in Porto Alegre, Brazil, at the age of seventy.

EDGAR GARBELOTTO is a writer and translator born in Brazil and based in the U.S. for the past twenty years. His translation of João Gilberto Noll's novel *Lord* was published by Two Lines Press in 2019. His work has appeared in the *Kenyon Review Online*, *Asymptote*, *Ninth Letter*, *Little Patuxent Review*, and elsewhere. He holds an MFA in creative writing from the University of Illinois. *Terra Incognita*, written in both Portuguese and English, is his debut novel.